BEST NEW AMERICAN VOICES 2004

BEST NEW AMERICAN VOICES 2004

GUEST EDITOR
John Casey

SERIES EDITORS
John Kulka and Natalie Danford

A Harvest Original • Harcourt, Inc.
Orlando Austin New York San Diego Toronto London

"What Is Visible" appeared in different form in the *Atlantic Monthly.*
"The Platform" appeared in different form in the *Threepenny Review.*
"This Is Not Skin" appeared in different form in *Ontario Review.*
"The Garden" appeared in different form in *Ploughshares.*
"The Quickening" appeared in different form in the *Massachusetts Review.*
"Michiganders, 1979" appeared in different form in *Quarterly West.*
"Dancing Lessons" appeared in different form in the *Atlantic Monthly.*

www.HarcourtBooks.com

Library of Congress Cataloging-in-Publication Data available upon request.
ISBN 0-15-600722-3   ISSN 1536-7908

Text set in Adobe Garamond
Designed by Lori McThomas Buley

Printed in the United States of America
First edition

ACEGIKJHFDB

In memory of Amanda Davis,
whose work appeared in *Best New American Voices 2001*

CONTENTS

PREFACE

Any history of American literary culture in the twentieth century must include an account of the flowering of writing workshops after the Second World War. For established writers, writing programs have provided both a chance to mentor the next generation of writers as well as a steady income. For that next generation, they present the opportunity to learn firsthand, in a classroom setting. In his book *Writing in General and the Short Story in Particular,* Rust Hills, former fiction editor at *Esquire,* observed, "If one but stands back a bit and looks, one sees that it is no longer the book publishers and magazines, but rather the colleges and universities, that support the entire structure of the American literary establishment—and, moreover, essentially determine the nature and shape of that structure."

The Best New American Voices series is a nod of acknowledgment in the direction of the workshop. Here the editors present work by some of the best emerging short-story writers—writers who just happen to be honing their craft in graduate writing programs like Iowa and Hopkins, in fellowship programs such as Stegner (Stanford), in workshops sponsored by arts organizations like the Banff Centre for the Arts, and in workshops held at summer writing conferences like Sewanee, Bread Loaf, and Wesleyan. We also solicit story nominations from a handful of justly famous community workshops like the 92nd

Street Y and The Loft, as well as the PEN Prison Writing Committee. Many of these writing programs have long and distinguished traditions. Consider that the following writers all passed through the Iowa program: Flannery O'Connor, Wallace Stegner, John Gardner, Gail Godwin, Andre Dubus, and T. C. Boyle, to name just a few. And the Stanford program has produced its own credible national literature with alumni such as Robert Stone, Raymond Carver, Evan S. Connell, Tillie Olsen, Larry McMurtry, Ernest J. Gaines, Ron Hansen, Ken Kesey, Scott Turow, Thomas McGuane, Alice Hoffman, Allan Gurganus, Wendell Berry, Harriet Doerr, Al Young, Michael Cunningham, Blanche Boyd, N. Scott Momaday, Vikram Seth, Dennis McFarland, and Stephanie Vaughn.

Each year we ask directors of writing programs in the United States and Canada to nominate the best stories workshopped during the current academic year for consideration in the Best New American Voices competition. We do not accept unsolicited submissions. We then pare down many hundreds of nominations to a group of finalists, which are passed on to a distinguished guest editor. From these finalists the guest editor chooses the winning stories to be included in the anthology. Tobias Wolff, Charles Baxter, and Joyce Carol Oates have all served as guest editors in past years.

Many of the authors of stories published in previous volumes have become familiar names: David Benioff (*The 25th Hour*); William Gay (*Provinces of Night* and *I Hate to See That Evening Sun Go Down*); Ana Menendez (*In Cuba I Was a German Shepherd*); Timothy Westmoreland (*Good as Any*); Adam Johnson (*Emporium*); John Murray (*A Few Short Notes on Tropical Butterflies*); the late Amanda Davis (*Circling the Drain* and *Wonder When You'll Miss Me*); and Maile Meloy (*Half in Love* and *Liars and Saints*). Still more have forthcoming books. We applaud all their successes.

For *Best New American Voices 2004,* guest editor John Casey has chosen seventeen stories. And we fully expect that more than a few of the names in the table of contents in this, the fourth volume in the Series, will also soon be as recognizable as those of some of our past winners. But all of the writers in this volume keep good company with one another. All of the stories included here display genuine feeling, verve, and technical accomplishment. It is always difficult to offer general observations about a group of writers with different concerns and writing styles: therefore we will let the stories speak for themselves.

We would like to extend thanks to John Casey for his careful reading of the manuscripts, for his enthusiasm for this project, for his thoughtful editorial suggestions, and for his commitment to the teaching of writing. To the many writers, directors, teachers, and panel judges who help to make the Series a continuing success we again extend sincere thanks and congratulations. To name just a few others: We thank our editor Andrea Schulz for her many efforts on behalf of the Series; André Bernard at Harcourt, Inc., for his support; Lisa Lucas in the Harcourt contracts department for attention to details; Gayle Feallock, deputy managing editor at Harcourt, for her insight and assistance; and our families and friends for their emotional support.

—*John Kulka and Natalie Danford*

INTRODUCTION

John Casey

If you were going to visit a foreign country because you were thinking of living there, what would you read to prepare yourself? A
guidebook? You'd know the monuments and museums and where to
eat. A week's worth of the local newspaper? After the international
echoes you'd be treated to politics, crimes, accidents, and sports—
the four-bar public wind chime that only jangles when there's a big
gust. If you're more ambitious, you might try a history book. Good
long-term plan. But to find out what life is like now, what the people
say and do and what's behind what they say and do, I would recommend stories. Not just those great stories the citizens had to read in
school (though that's part of the invisible scenery, as looming as the
great buildings), but stories that have just come out.

This anthology of American stories, if left by chance in the net
pouch on the seat back of an airplane leaving Tokyo or Warsaw and
bound for Seattle or New York, would offer a traveler news he wouldn't
find in a newspaper. Although it wouldn't help the traveler with cur-
rency exchange, finding a place to stay, or other immediate problems
of orientation, it would give essential human bearings. Some wishes
and actions would be familiar, some surprising. Some might make
the traveler suppose that yes, we are all alike; others would be help-
fully unsettling.

I'm dreaming up this traveler partly because a childhood fantasy of mine was to be a tour guide for a foreigner without mentioning anything that could be found in a guidebook or on a postcard. I wanted to point out a half-dozen details that, when linked up, would give a sense of how we really arrange our lives. Riding the N-4 bus to school, I'd pick out bits of dress, speech, or manner I hoped would begin a story. To spy on the ordinary is a good first step. I was fascinated by World War II movies in which the American POW escapes, only to be caught because he cuts his meat and then shifts the fork to his right hand to eat it. A neat Sherlock-Holmes thrill. What I didn't know enough to do was to find the details that would be keys to something more important, the details that would release the energy of a whole person rather than a twist of fate. The seventeen writers in *Best New American Voices 2004* aren't kids on a bus. They've been around the block. They do have the same childlike urge to decipher the world, but they also have the skill and range of experience to find the details that bring a life into sharp focus at a crucial point.

One of the things that distinguishes the short story from a poem or a novel is that the short story, while artful in its conception, is better off artless in its final form. The writer has to pick a character and a situation that apparently take off on their own. If the writer is skillful and/or lucky, the story will imply much more than itself. Take "This Is Not Skin" by Nathan Roberts. A man and a woman are on a road trip from Portland, Oregon to St. Louis, Missouri. Each of them, in one way or another, is at odds with the straight world. The arresting thing about the story isn't their sexual choices. Those have been made. The story lets them turn the full range of their personalities on each other. They dazzle each other, alarm each other, enrage each other. When they rebound back into themselves, they are not who they were. The extra dimension, the one that comes without words, is the negative space of the straight world, the geography through which they travel.

"So Much the Better" is a hockey story without a hockey game, a love story without a love scene, a sex story without a sex scene. So much the better. White space, on the ice and in a hospital room, serves as the set. What the characters (the injured hockey player, his wife, and two teammates) say and do has as much energy and interest as a play-off game.

Some of these stories are abundantly narrated—"Bunnymoon," "Healer," "Dancing Lessons," "The Garden," "Blue Night, Clover Lake," "Five-Minute Hearts," and the surprisingly comic "Irregularities." But there is discipline in their full-voice narration. Each author has put her main character downstage center, so the character is simultaneously telling the story as she is being changed by it. Each telling, no matter how apparently tumbling, is taut with detail. This is particularly true of "What Is Visible," the one story in this volume based on historical fact. The core is simple: a blind and deaf girl is desperately in love with the founder of the institution in which she is immured. She reads and signs by touch. This restricted communication makes a close chamber of her mind, a chamber in which we wait with her in the dark silence—until we discover how large and echoing it is. To say that this story would make a beautiful opera is not a criticism, but an appreciation of how the story builds in ascending layers of full and pure emotion. Each outburst feels like an aria, lingers as if it had been sung instead of thought.

At the other end of the spectrum is "Michiganders, 1979," so deliberately muted and verbally unresonant that it feels like a grainy black-and-white 8 mm film clip. But that is how it makes its point: the details of a by-the-book investigation finally open a space for the officer's pent-up emotion.

"The Quickening," "Transcription," and "Nightfloat" are work stories with more light and air and immediate clarity. Each describes a work process, interesting in itself, which creates a buildup of energy that seems to summon a moment of grace. In "Transcription," the story that describes the most oppressive job, a simple slight kindness feels like a star burst.

"The Platform" and "Vinegar" are fueled by anger. "The Platform" carefully leads up to it and fully earns it. "Vinegar" leads off with it at full pitch, and none of the sweet pampering of an idyllic vacation (that supposed balm of a middle-class marriage) can lessen it. In fact it can't help but aggravate it. It takes the emotional equivalent of vinegar stinging raw skin even to begin to deal with it.

These seventeen writers are at the beginnings of their careers, but they are not beginners. These stories are masterworks in the ancient sense of the term, meaning they are the works that apprentice artists submit to the masters to be admitted to the guild. In the case of this anthology the standard is even more rigorous. The faculties of writing programs and summer writing conferences nominate one or two stories. (The authors are often people who have come to writing after some time in another career, but in any case have served as long an apprenticeship as the surgeon who operates on your gall bladder.) These selections amount to a bale and a half of pretty good work. They're winnowed to a bushel by the series editors and winnowed again by the guest editor. The standard is artistic excellence. It is not accidental that this book is one a traveler might read to know who we are.

BEST NEW AMERICAN VOICES 2004

MISHA ANGRIST

Sewanee Writers' Conference

So Much the Better

In headaches and in worry
Vaguely life leaks away
And Time will have his fancy
To-morrow or to-day...
—*W. H. Auden*

Half the game is mental.
The other half is being mental.
—*Jim McKenny (NHL defenseman, 1965–1979)*

The Zamboni had to go around Joey Cooper, the man thinking about omelets. He was on his back, unable to feel his extremities or much of anything other than the plastic nub of mouthguard against his teeth and a few flakes of ice on one cheek. But he never lost consciousness, something he would take a small measure of pride in after the fact. Through the clouds in his skull he heard the whir of the Zamboni and, in addition to thinking about the prospect of never making omelets again, he regretted that Al, the Zamboni driver/ scoreboard operator, would have to deviate from his methodical approach to the creation of new ice. The trainers—who always seemed to be fat guys in tennis shoes with charcoal mustaches and hair parted down the middle—scrambled from their respective benches as the new team physician made his way down from the stands. Soon there was a throng around Joey, checking his vital signs and asking him who the president was.

Omelets were Joey's dish insofar as he had one. They were a gift of sorts from his semi-estranged wife. "The way I figure it, penis ownership does not exempt someone from cooking," she had said last off-season when they were still "working on it." And he had relented. While he was growing up, his mother had always cooked for him and his sister. At college he had eaten in the cafeteria. On the road with the team there were per diems and restaurants. And for the last few years before the breakup, his wife had prepared food on weekends and fed Joey and the kids leftovers during the week. Sensing her husband's reticence to get involved in food prep, Mary had assured him that he could learn to make one-course meals.

During Lesson One she had tucked her hair behind her ears and stood adjacent to him at the stove. She prompted him to pour the egg mixture into the pan just as the butter was foaming and beginning to turn golden. Joey did this and soon found himself drawn into the process, basking in the sounds of the tiny explosions of fat. Mary seized the spatula and oven mitt from him and began manipulating the skillet with deft circular motions. .

"You can't skate while you're looking at the puck, Joe. Once you pour the stuff in, you've gotta lift the base, tilt the pan, and let the uncooked part run underneath. If you wait too long you have to abort."

Under her tutelage he became quite proficient and rarely had to settle for scrambled eggs. He even took chances with the fillings.

"Please, Dad, not green olives again," Ben said without looking up from his Game Boy. "They're gross."

Tonight was to have been a rare postseparation omelet night.

"Al Gore. Now ask me who the Prime Minister of Canada is," he answered softly. "I'm sorry."

They ignored him. Maybe they didn't hear him. Maybe he didn't actually speak. Or maybe they were uncomfortable because they thought he was apologizing for not picking up his man in the defensive wedge system that Coach insisted on playing even though, as Joey tried to point out on many occasions, the Hammerheads had a ton of goal scorers and the fans wanted to see run-and-gun, not dump-and-chase. Dumping the puck ain't hockey, Joey maintained. He had even written this on the chalkboard in the locker room.

"Why'd you do that?" Mary asked.

For a moment he thought she was referring to his most recent thing with a girl in Youngstown. How could she know about that? He pictured a bare midriff and enormous doe eyes watery from pollen; the girl had pressed a twenty into his hand and asked him to buy allergy medicine the next time he went to Canada. "You need a prescription for it here," she had said. "They take American money, don't they?"

He said to Mary, "What makes you think it was me who wrote that?"

"Duh. Um, well, your handwriting for one. And the fact that no one else on the team would do it."

He told her that dump-and-chase was why hockey was in trouble. "People don't mind the fisticuffs. They like it—I understand that part. But they want to see goals."

Now he drifted back to the ice; he imagined a fluky bounce on the mushy, non-Zambonied surface where he lay leading to trouble—the team was only up by one with one period to play. Mary used to tell him that he worried too much, apologized too much.

"Well. I'm sorry," he had said to her.

The new physician clucked his tongue and put his ear to Joey's mouth.

"I'm breathing, goddammit," Joey huffed in a whisper, inhaling the doctor's cologne, a syrupy alcoholish mix that burned his nostrils. "Where's Doc Fleming?"

"Your team has a new healthcare provider. We're cheaper."

"Nice to meet you, Cheaper. Now please get me the fuck off the ice and stitch me up or whatever it is you gotta do."

"Shut up." Another cluck. "Stitch you up? That's funny. Hockey players are funny." He motioned for the paramedics.

Joey looked skyward and caught sight of the Prize Blimp, his determination to play suddenly displaced by gratitude that he now had what felt like unlimited time to gaze up at it. He wanted to point, to raise his glove, but he could not. He knew that for many, the four-foot Prize Blimp was more entertaining than Mid-Atlantic League hockey could ever be. On some nights—say, when the crowd was thin or the team was dead tired from playing its third game in three days—he would take an extra moment when he skated off between periods to scan the airspace above the rink and see where it was. The Prize Blimp dropped coupons, mostly two-for-one at a pizza joint, free car wash with fill-up, that sort of thing. Al's son Hal pulled a lever on the radio controller and a clamp released them. Joey squinted past Doctor Cluck's comb-over to see the clamp open and half a dozen tiny rectangles of yellow paper flutter like geese in formation, down to the second deck where a smattering of kids in baggy jeans, backward baseball caps, and hockey jerseys hopped over seats and extended their arms upward to catch the coupons. He took perverse comfort in knowing that those kids were oblivious to his condition, to the redirection of the Zamboni, to everything but the flutter. *You must focus* Coach liked to say.

Which was exactly what Joey had been doing when he tripped over Plenkov and went sprawling into the boards headfirst. Joey was out of position and he knew it. He was trying to be cute (surely this was in Coach's mind), thinking he could make a headman pass to Melnichuk streaking up the other side. Coach will say I probably got what I deserved, Joey imagined.

Coach was his father-in-law.

In the ambulance he felt a strange vibration in his body, a prickly pulse resonating just below the surface of his skin. He ignored it, only nodded and smiled at the EMT, a scrawny guy with glasses and a steel wool beard who wanted to talk about other fabled minor league hockey injuries. "You're gonna be fine. Remember that guy from Muskegon had the same thing happen? Flew straight into the boards—ka-*pow*! He was back in the lineup in days." He squinted at the irregular green blip representing Joey's heart. "Weeks anyway."

Joey thought of a speaker the team had brought in at the beginning of the season. Bam Andrews was a one-time winger who'd bounced around the IHL and spent parts of two seasons with the Blackhawks. He was known mainly for a longstanding record that his teams' media guides called attention to every year: Most Career Penalty Minutes Without Scoring A Goal. Now he was a money manager in Chicago; his topic was "Life After Hockey." Joey supposed that the unspoken message was that if a goon like Bam could make it as a civilian, then there was hope for the least prepared among them.

"I use the same grit and determination in the market that I used to use on the ice," Bam told them. In one scarred hand he held a stack of index cards. His reading glasses sat atop a warped boxer's nose; once in a while his head would jerk in a violent tic and cause the glasses to go askew.

Frankie Corrigan, reeking of Stolichnaya he had bought from some Russian players coming through Duty-Free, and said to be bitter about a late-season demotion from the Islanders the previous spring, raised his hand. "So, like, if you disagree with your accountant or your broker, do you haul off and sucker punch him the same way you did Keith Ellis in '84?"

The two men had to be separated.

The fact of the matter was that Joey had already pondered Life After Hockey, although he did so less often these days. When they still lived together, he and Mary had talked about starting a summer camp. Mary would administrate, keep the books, hire and fire, make things presentable; Joey would be the gung-ho-rah-rah-horseback-riding-songs-in-the-dining-hall-s'mores-at-the-campfire-rollerhockey guy. His son and daughter would remind him of this on occasion, still hopeful that the familial shards could somehow be gathered up and pasted back together.

By the time he arrived at the hospital he could move his limbs; he felt strangely normal, as though nothing had happened. He was sent for X rays and an MRI. It was only when the nurse taped electrodes to his chest for the second EKG that he sensed the vibration again. He grabbed her wrist and then let it go. He hoped he had been gentle enough so as not to convey the panic inside him.

"It feels like electricity," he said.

"These don't *do* anything," she said as she attached the last two to the skin below his nipples. "They just measure your heartbeat."

"No, no. It's not that. When you touch my hair. It's electric. *It feels electric.*"

She was midforties, thin with short auburn hair and a minimum of makeup; her gravelly voice was pleasant but no-nonsense, almost like Mary's voice. He squinted at her nametag but couldn't make it out. Her quizzical look dissolved into a smile. "Are you hitting on me, Mr. Cooper? Now hold still." She took the measurements with what he thought was a provocative touch and advised him to get some sleep.

This is Mary LaPierre the machine said with a slight emphasis on her maiden name. Joey imagined her screening her calls or else writhing in ecstasy astride her boyfriend and imploring him to be quiet because Ben and Jessie were asleep down the hall. His insides tightened. The resident said she suspected a bruised spine but that she'd have to wait for the attending to make a definitive diagnosis. Joey took the sedative the new nurse offered and nodded off. It was not a good sleep. The electric vibration had abated but still he thrashed around, unable to get comfortable, constrained by the tether of the IV.

He tried the phone again. The nurse had made him want to hear Mary's voice in all of its soothing resonance. When Joey signed the Altoona deal, she had gotten a public radio job in town.

"They said my voice is mellifluous."

"Is that good?" he said.

He preferred heavy metal to news and classical, but he liked listening to her as he got up, stretched, and got ready for practice; he could hear her striving to sound reassuring. "Take a little extra time," she would urge on bad weather days. "No one will blame you if you're late." Eventually they fired her; she was never given a reason, but by her desk at home she kept a framed memo from the station manager chiding her for her "lack of professionalism" during a fund drive.

Joey said, "Look, it's none of my business, but maybe offering phone sex for $250 pledges wasn't the way to go. It's a small town."

"They oughtta lighten up a bit. That station met its goal because of me."

Now she was "head cheerleader on this sinking goddamn ship," words she'd spoken to the local sports columnist who once implied she'd gotten her job in the team's marketing department because she was Coach's daughter. "I like my job," she told the guy after a game delayed for hours by a power outage, "but if this is the best nepotism can do for me, then that's pretty sad, eh?"

Hammerhead attendance was still fairly high, thanks in large part to her tireless coordination of player and mascot appearances, ticket giveaways, TV and radio ads, and community relations.

Joey was fully awake now, his skin strangely sensitive and irritated by the rough starch of the hospital linens. His mind revisited a short trip he and Mary had taken years before when they still lived in Ohio, before the kids were born. It was late spring and he had been promoted to the IHL just in time for his new team to get knocked out of the playoffs. One Saturday morning she roused him from bed and told him they needed to go somewhere.

"I'm always going somewhere," Joey said. "Can't we stay home?"

"That's exactly the point," she said. She was already pulling on tights and sliding her arms through the black bra she knew he liked. "Wear a shirt with a collar."

She led him through the rain to the rail platform.

As they boarded the mystery train, Joey had made up his mind that he would let it go, that whatever this was about was okay with him. A few guys in the league carried their aggression with them all the time—they brawled, smacked women around, kicked their dogs, and god knows what else. Joey didn't approve, but he could almost understand it—they were all programmed for violence, like pit bulls or soldiers. But that was meant to stay on the ice, the occasional bar fight notwithstanding. When they were not wearing skates, most guys were civilized, gentle even. Some would actually get pushed around, as if all the skills learned in juniors, all the aggressive shooting and shouting, the pep talks about discipline and quick decision-making, the constant warnings never to back down, all of that drained out of their bodies when the game ended. Instead, they gave up their autonomy willingly, gladly. Parents. Agents. Wives. It was easier that way.

Their destination was the Cleveland airport. Where are we going? Joey asked on the main concourse. Do we have plane tickets? We're here, Mary said. They interlocked fingers and stopped in every shop. At the Tie Rack, Mary found a tie adorned with multicolored sticks and pucks.

"I can't wear that," Joey said.

"Oh, I disagree," she said. "The shirt was for a reason."

Joey raised the collar, put the tie around his thick neck and fumbled his way toward a Windsor knot. They finished up at Cinnabon.

"They never taste quite as good they smell." Mary bit into a cinnamon roll slathered in a sugary white paste. She was deadly thin, could eat anything and did. Joey wanted a danish, too, but couldn't bring himself to say it out loud—it would have meant admitting that the season was over, that his nutritional regimen could be abandoned for the next three months. He looked at the sticks on the tie and noticed a curve in the blades.

"Borderline legal," he said to Mary.

She smiled and crumpled her napkin. "I might have to get something else to eat. Why are you looking at me like that?"

"So you mean to tell me," he began.

"Yes," she said. She enclosed his hands in hers across the Formica. "Look at all of these people carting heavy bags around, running to catch planes, angry because their flights have been canceled, their luggage has been lost, they had to wait in line at security, they miss their kids, they've been wearing the same clothes for two days."

"And we should be grateful that we don't have to deal with that."

"Exactamundo. We can just be here as spectators and relax. Think how stressful it'll be when we have kids and you're in the NHL. Both of which will happen soon."

"Uh-huh. You're a royal nut job."

"And you can't win a face-off without cheating."

"I'm sorry," he said.

"Stop it," she said. "And no apologizing for apologizing."

He watched a haggard flight attendant on wobbly heels—eye shadow streaking toward her temples—struggle to roll a large black bag down the concourse. Mary held up the hand she'd been stroking and bit Joey's knuckle, hard. He was still sorting out the intoxicating message of lust and pain when she stood to buy another pastry.

In the morning there was a gentle knock on the door to the hospital room; Joey saw the handle turn slowly and fluorescent light spill in from the hallway. "Mary," he croaked. But it wasn't her.

"Hi," Plenkov said with a rare tentativeness.

"Alexei." Joey clicked off the TV and hummed the bed up to a sitting position.

"What is your condition?" Plenkov stood at attention at the foot of the bed, his bushy brows converging in concern.

Joey no longer had to fight to conceal his pleasure at his friend's East European solemnity. "The MRI didn't show squat. I hate that goddamn tube. Anyway, Doc says no lasting neurological damage, whatever that means."

"I do not understand."

"My spine is bruised, but I'll be fine. I still feel a little electric tingle. Doc says that's common. But I'll be back next week for Delaware."

"Really?"

"Write it down."

"That is fantastic news." Plenkov submerged a hand in the gym bag he'd brought, pulled out a box of drugstore chocolates and placed them on the side table with a delicacy that made Joey tremble and want to laugh.

"I don't need these," he said.

"Well. Okay then." Plenkov picked up the box and started for the door.

"Get your ass back here, *tovarishch*."

His visitor turned, the mischievous light in his eyes fading quickly. "I am terrible sorry for what happened, Coop."

"I was out of position."

"I should pay attention more."

Plenkov was a big guy, a classic bruising defenseman. In their time together with the Hammerheads the two men had gravitated toward one another; each saw himself as the broken, cynical veteran taking up some draft pick's roster spot.

"Shouldn't you be at practice?"

Plenkov rolled his eyes. "Coach says I can come for a *feezit*." He exulted in exaggerating his own accent.

"He's all heart that guy."

"No. He is neutral zone crap."

"*T'yem lootchsheh*," Joey said. The Russian phrase "so much the better" was one he'd heard years ago—at a junior clinic a Russian as-sistant coach used it while diagramming a breakout play. Joey liked it and began saying it indiscriminately, much to Plenkov's displeasure.

"You do not use appropriate way," he told Joey again and again.

Plenkov began to pry at the box of chocolates with his thumb. A bone in his wrist stuck out too far and needed the attention of an or-thopedist. Joey looked at his friend's relief map of a face. He had a cut under his eye from a high stick and an assortment of other marks from where pucks, sticks, and fists had opened miniature fissures.

He was among the last defectors—a Red Army kid who had made contact with some NHL scouts at a tournament in Prague in the late eighties. Drafted for his toughness, he had had six solid years in post-Gretzky Edmonton and post-Cup Montreal. "I am always arriving late to everywhere," he liked to say.

"Neutral zone what?" Joey said, trying to keep a straight face. "How dare you insult Coach."

"Vahk you," Plenkov laughed.

Plenkov knew how to curse and insult in English from his years in the US and Canada, so much so that he was now in a position to teach others; he and Joey had teamed up to offer a new kid from the Czech Republic, Jan Hrbek, help with some of the vernacular. Joey had given him an index card entitled "The Essentials Of The English Language." Included on the card were such choice phrases as "Get the fuck off from my truck, Peckerhead," "You leave me no choice but to bust open a can of whupass on you," and "Empty-net goals are for chicken-choking losers."

Plenkov translated as best he could, gesticulating broadly with those big hands and searching for comparable idioms in Russian and Czech. Jan looked at the Russian with a serious frown, jotted a few stray marks on the card and noted everything in a little spiral notebook.

As Plenkov was leaving Joey's hospital room, Joey watched his friend accidentally clip Mary in the head with the door as she was entering. She was startled more than anything; Alexei looked down at her with concern.

"Keep your elbows up, Mare," said Joey from the bed.

"Alex, hi. You're going to kill the whole family, you crazy Cossack," Mary said.

Plenkov's eyes narrowed, unsure as to how best to respond to Joey's almost ex-wife.

"I am so sorry," he said. He backed down the hall with his hands raised.

"My God, it's an apology festival with you two. Listen," she called after him. "We've gotta talk about the autograph gig at the mall." Plenkov was a popular attraction in northwestern Pennsylvania, as aspiring young hockey roughnecks liked to query him about assorted ass-kickings he'd administered over the years. Plenkov would flash a broken smile and tell the kids they were better off learning how to pass and score goals.

Joey was stuck on Mary's reference to them as a family. It hadn't felt like a family to him for a long time. He had Allergy Girl and the others while she had Pete the lawyer. At times he wondered what the kids thought of Pete. Joey would bring up his name around them and try to read their body language but he could never tell. They were diplomats, his children.

"Where exactly *are* the kids?" he said to Mary.

"They'll be here soon. How are you feeling?"

Joey broke the news to himself. "They're with your dad at the hotel."

Coach liked to put the team up at the Hampton Inn or the Ramada one night a month, usually the night before a home series. *Treat it like a road game. Avoid the distractions.* Except he couldn't resist his grandchildren.

Mary stifled a smile and picked up Joey's chart.

Joey swallowed and tasted antiseptic hospital Jell-O. "Aw, Mare. Goddammit."

" 'Joseph A. Cooper.' That's all it says. How come doctors can't write legibly?" She flipped the pages on the clipboard and raised her eyes to him. "Listen, Joseph A. You're already out of the lineup, you cost the team the game—how much deeper in the doghouse can you get? The kids bring him pleasure at least. And they love room service."

"He's gotta go to practice."

"Duh. He'll find the kids a ride. MacAllister can run practice. It ain't the Stanley Cup finals. Your team's going belly-up anyways." It was the sound of someone picking a scab.

"Nice of you to stop by to cheer me up. Have you worked 'belly-up' into the new marketing campaign? A beached shark maybe?"

He took her in anew. The winsome look, the plucked eyebrows, the purple dress, the cinched belt. The leather briefcase emblazoned with the smirking hammerhead, its snout sculpted into a hockey stick. Her hybrid persona of the sexy cartoon exterior and the gruff, I-can-hang-with-the-boys demeanor was enchanting when they'd met in 1986; he was surprised it still tugged at him with such force now.

He imagined reinhabiting the frame of her daily life. She was not like the women he'd known before and since: Hooters refugees with big hair and boob jobs, Canadian white trash or Euros with naive visions of chartered airplanes and nice restaurants. She was a Torontonian, a coach's daughter who understood Saskatoon bus trips and gashes on the head that don't heal until summer, if at all. When Joey started cheating, she did nothing, said nothing; only ground her teeth at night until she had to see the team dentist and get fitted for an appliance. One night, as Joey was walking a bit too amorously with a new girl through the lobby of the St. Catharines Best Western, he thought he saw Coach through the window, hovering at the taxi stand, waving the wire contraption at him.

When I coach, I tell them: Thinking is the worst thing a hockey player can do. Off the ice, though, you better fucking think. He had warned her about Joey, about athletes in general. *Narcissism plus isolation gets you more narcissism.* Mary used to laugh a strange forced laugh as she told Joey about these platitudes, these equations, each repeated as though it were written in some coaching book somewhere. Joey would shrug and swallow, unable to participate in her bitter mirth.

He half hoped Coach would reduce his ice time for these transgressions, punish him somehow. But he never did.

Hockey's hockey.

"I talked to Abrams about Tampa Bay," Joey said to her. "I think I've got a shot at a two-way deal: two twenty-five when I'm up."

"And when you're down?" She sat on the bed and smoothed the raised stitching on the hospital bedspread with a burgundy fingernail.

"Thirty. Thirty-five."

"You get fifteen percent of your base while you're in the minors? And this was your *agent*? Does he understand that his commission on nothing is still nothing?"

"You'll get your check."

"It's not *my* check. Ben and Jessie will always be fifty percent yours, Joe. I know you got bonked on the head, but did we have this conversation or not? Jesus. Even if this team doesn't fold, odds are sooner or later you're gonna get hurt again. It'd be nice to have a little money put away for when your career's over."

"Can we talk about this later? How's Ben's math?"

"This *is* later. I got him a tutor. He's Fraction Boy. Okay, Joe. Hope you feel better. Road trip next week—you'll need to perform for your honeys, eh?"

"Mare."

But she was in the doorway, Hammerhead bag hish-hishing against the purple fabric as she walked.

Nurse Janet—blotchy, plump, with a matronly bun and a smoker's wheeze—said his kids were sorry they'd missed him. She implored him to eat more. The night before she had asked him for an autograph, blushing and saying that her husband had gone to a few

Hammerheads games and would occasionally drive to Pittsburgh to see the Penguins play.

He bit once into the rubbery cornbread and grimaced. As soon as Janet left, he plucked the IV drip from his arm with a wince, found scrubs and a white coat in the closet, stuffed his uniform and still-dirty pads into a pillowcase, and waited for a sufficient distraction to develop at the nurses' station, which happened soon enough. A father and a son—both bloodied, bandaged, and drunk—were being admitted to the floor, exchanging loud recriminations from their respective gurneys.

"Who the fuck taught you to drive?"

"You did, asswipe. I mean *Dad.*"

Joey's own dad was a gaunt man with a grave jowl who had played in the Pacific League for a while. He was deliberate in all things: the way he carried himself, the way he skated, the way he unrolled a newspaper. Even on the rare occasions when he fought you could see him studying his opponent while he kept his fists raised. When Joey was eleven, his father had presented him with a sharpening stone in a frayed leather case. *I never want to see you with dull blades. Understand?* In their hockey-crazed house where Mom would put on goalie pads from time to time Joey knew this gift was not to be taken lightly—it was as sacred as a prayer shawl. He watched the father and son get rolled in opposite directions of the ward, still hurling invective. Joey silently thanked his own dad for not taking the angry gurney route.

He tried to appear inconspicuous as he moved down the hall, but feared his flickering current would betray him. He felt weak and sore—not the good midseason endorphin sore, but rather the flat, empty ache of not playing all summer and then trying to hang with the rookies in speed-skating drills on the first day of training camp.

His knees buckled slightly as he scampered down the hospital stairwell and dug a cell phone out of his bag.

In the cab the driver asked Joey what kind of doctor he was.

"Uh, a proctologist," Joey said. "Actually, I'm not really a doctor. I'm an orderly. God knows I could use a doctor for any number of things. Or at least a good oral surgeon." His bridgework—courtesy of a puck to the mouth at practice in 1993—was beginning to rattle around a bit too freely when he talked and ate. He steadied it with his finger; Jamie in Akron liked for him to take it out so she could run her tongue along his gums.

"What's so funny?" he said to Lloyd the security guard at the arena.

Lloyd was a rotund man with plaintive eyes and a conspiratorial smile who had, on occasion, been known to remove several disorderly patrons from the venue all at once by wedging his nightstick through their belt loops and yanking them out the door. Between peals of congested laughter he posed a question similar to that of the cab driver. "Where's your stethoscope, *Doc*?"

At the rink, a few guys milled around the locker room. Most were already out on the ramp, waiting for the pregame skate to start. Joey's arrival sparked a flurry of relief and confusion. "Joey's here! Wasn't he paralyzed? Can he even talk?" He smiled to himself at his teammates' subtext: You're a tough motherfucker, Joe, even by hockey standards.

As he began the lengthy and complicated ritual of suiting up— jock and cup, shin pads, hockey socks, tape, pants, skates, shoulder pads, elbow pads, sweater, mouth guard, helmet, gloves—he was filled with a sense of well-being similar to the one he used to feel with Mary when they were at university, where he'd first played for Coach LaPierre. After practice, Joey would shower and go to her apartment.

They'd drink gin and tonics from coffee mugs and watch the sun fade behind the soccer stadium. The booze would settle in Joey's chest and he knew that this would be as good as he would feel all day. Soon he would give in to the impulse to say something sentimental or clumsy.

"Is that your best cross-ice pass?" Mary would coo with a loving sneer as she began to remove his clothes.

In the morning Joey would often be subdued by a hangover and terrific soreness in his back, thighs, ankles, and shooting hand.

Now, though, was much closer to the peak moment. The faint throb at the base of his spine and the metallic dry mouth from the painkillers had diminished, swamped by the adrenaline prospect of striding onto the ice.

A skinny kid with a bad complexion came over. The new equipment guy. "Coach wants to see you if you can make it to his office."

Joey thought about ignoring him, pretending that his injury somehow prevented him from understanding anything anyone said. Instead he replied in a quiet voice. "Okay. Thanks." The electric field was beginning to percolate throughout his chest again. Better to avoid Coach altogether.

As he laced his skates, teammates came by and tapped him on the shoulder with their sticks in the time-honored hockey way: at once affectionate, macho, and girded by superstition. A few asked how he was and wondered how the lines would be reshuffled in order to accommodate his return.

He waited in the queue that had formed at the entrance to the ice. When the public address announcer—Al's other son, Hank—introduced *"youuuuuuuuurr Altoona Hammerheads,"* Joey started up the ramp, using his stick for balance and trying to look as natural as possible in skates that suddenly dug into the bottoms of his feet.

"Why?" barked Plenkov in his ear. "Delaware is *next* game."

"You mean I'm early?" said Joey. *"T'yem lootchsheh."* He took in the thickening crowd and felt the buzz in his torso intensify—sharp tactile sparks poking at his insides. He placed a glove on Plenkov, a gesture of reassurance that soon became necessary as a crazy vertigo overtook him. Why was everyone skating so fast before the game even started? He squinted at the press box but could not see Mary.

As his chest cavity continued to dance with activity, he lost one skate edge and then the other. Plenkov scooped an arm around his waist and did his best to guide him toward the bench. Joey could hear children shrieking, Coach ranting in a voice cracked with agitation *(Why are you here why are you here why are you here?)* and yelling at Plenkov, who waved him off with his free hand. Jan Hrbek dropped his stick and skated over to support Joey's other side, making sure he had a firm grasp before looking at Coach straight on and spewing accented vitriol. *Vahk you vahk you. Heez your son-een-law.* And after a pause: *Peckerhead.*

Joey wanted to tell Jan to relax. Coach was concerned and had every right to be upset. Joey scanned for landmarks, hoping this might steady him somehow. He saw the Prize Blimp held fast above the Zamboni at the end of the ramp. Sharkie, the gray mascot adorned with dozens of felt teeth. Two Pee Wee teams clutching their tiny sticks, fidgeting with their phosphorescent Gatorade, waiting to square off between periods.

And now Mary, a darting purple blur, negotiating her way down the steep steps leading to the bench, skidding onto the ice in heels. Would she even make it to him? Could she cradle him in her arms and let him hear the mellifluous voice do AM-style "traffic and weather together" once more before he blacked out? Would she find her way back to the hospital so they could map out a life of one-match clubs, care packages, canteens, and sleep outs?

His vision and balance soon became impalpable, not to be trusted.

His mind was awash in images of omelets, the asymmetrical part in Jessie's hair, and the tattered bandage of black tape at the end of his stick. Don't touch me, he wanted to say to Plenkov. I am electric. Skate away. Away now. I am porcupine. You'll get zapped.

He seized upon his teammates' anger at Coach. The sublime resolve in his wife's motion. The liquidy warmth climbing up from inside his jolted nervous system, a sensation that had not been stirred since Juniors, since his father had committed endless frozen morning hours to lacing up skates with him on the edge of a tiny pond in a tiny corner of Ontario. Father and son had clacked their sticks, leaned in over an imaginary face-off circle, and watched each other through the mist of their mingled breath. Now the same hazy fever rose again. He could not help but know that, soon enough, it would dampen the voltage, dull his quills, firm the palette of eggs in the skillet, soften the ice beneath him.

SHANTHI SEKARAN

Johns Hopkins University

STALIN

The streets of Madras disappeared the day Kaveri's brother was born. Torrential rains forced women to walk down Mount Road with their saris hitched over their knees. The local chapter of the Communist Party of India had to cancel its pro-atheist rally. Bicycle rickshaws were roped to the stone pillars of houses and storefronts, where they floated, pointless and empty. In a bungalow just off of the main road, a midwife splashed across the sitting room to order a servant to find fresh towels, as sheets of water continued to slide in beneath the door.

The mother who lay on a cot in the bedroom had been carrying the washing down from the roof when the first drizzles began. Kaveri had watched as her Amma halted at the top of the stairs and grasped the banister, suddenly seized by pain. The washing basket slipped from her hands and sent a scatter of plaid dhotis and floral saris down the stairs, where they still lay in bright confusion. When Kaveri ran to find her father, he knew without asking that it was time to call the midwife. The contractions carried on through the afternoon, and the sheet that covered Amma grew damp with her sweat and heavy with the room's humidity.

Out on the stone porch, Kaveri Chethan sat on her father's lap, listening to a story and tugging at one of her braids. Through the open front door she could hear her mother's anguish. Appa held her small hand in his and spoke softly, his voice calm despite the wails that drifted from the bedroom. He told her about a man who had raided the Hindu temples of a town nearby, emptied them of deities and priests, and filled every room with wonderful books and paintings. He had done it so that the people of his town could live without barriers between them, so that everybody could be the same, just the same. Appa stopped suddenly, and they heard a throaty yell erupt from the bedroom.

Kaveri's Amma gripped the sides of her cot and sent a gush of water spilling to the floor, where it streamed into the puddles of rain that had already collected. Riding the wave of his mother's fluid, the boy baby inched crimson-covered into the midwife's waiting hands. The old woman tugged gently at his little shoulders, her fingers nearly slipping, and pulled him into the room. Holding him up to the light, she slipped a finger in his mouth, then laughed when he started to cry.

The boy dried a rosy beige once the birth film was wiped away. When he was placed in his father's hands, his eyes closed in tidy slits and he raised his two fists to the ceiling. It showed he would be strong, the midwife said—a soldier.

The rains retreated that night, and Minoo the servant swept the puddles out the door with a straw broom. By morning, the leftover moisture had dried up and vanished.

———

The next afternoon, Kaveri brought a tray with two cups of coffee into the sitting room. She walked slowly and placed one foot directly in front of the other. Minoo had filled the cups to the brim, and the milky liquid rippled and threatened to spill with each step Kaveri took. She breathed in the clouds of chicory that steamed upward.

"Nandri, Ma," Appa thanked her as he took a cup from the unsteady tray. He would tell her later always to serve guests first, but he hadn't the heart to do it just then. The elderly man, as usual, said nothing to her, and barely paused midsentence to take his cup. "Our daughters are our treasures, Comrade Chethan," he said, "but it is our sons who will truly advance the cause. If the Brahmin males are the spokesmen of their caste, then it is the atheist men only who can approach them. For this your son is a blessing." The old man was there a lot lately, Kaveri noticed. He would sip coffee in the front room and speak in a steady baritone, though he never said a word to Kaveri. Appa would listen to him for hours, and occasionally ask a question.

Kaveri stepped out onto the porch, still holding the tea tray. The air outside was growing crisper as the evening settled in. When she burrowed into her corner of the wicker bench by the door, she could still hear the men's voices. But they faded quickly when she turned her attention to the expanse of street that stretched between the foyer's squat pillars. The vegetable seller started down her block, as he did every day, balancing on his head a shallow basket piled high with produce. "Okra!" he shouted. "Okra, potatoesspinachgarlicokrapotatoes." All Kaveri could see was okra. She wondered why men who sold things always made their voices so shrill and ugly, as if they were shouting through their noses. She wondered if they spoke the same way at home. He scooted past her quickly, walking with precise and rapid steps down the block and around the corner.

Across the street, Prema Aunty squatted on her porch. Kaveri would visit with her sometimes, but Amma let her go only when Appa was at work. Her neighbor didn't look up at her; she was too busy drawing *kolam* on the smooth tiles. The Divali festival was coming soon, and the other families on her street had been preparing for days. Prema Aunty dipped her finger in a bowl of white paste, and used it to dab dots around a larger design. Amma used to draw *kolam,* she remembered, but they had since stopped doing such things.

Prema Aunty's *kolam* reminded her of her own artwork, and she hopped down from her seat to examine it. The bench's wicker would press imprints onto her skin, especially when she flipped the skirt of her frock over the back of the seat and let the grooves sink directly into her flesh. Moving away from the door, where Appa couldn't see her, she lifted her skirt and twisted back to peer at the engravings on the backs of her thighs. She fingered the crisscrossed lines and grinned.

It was then that an object in the back corner of the porch caught Kaveri's eye. It sat tucked against a pillar, almost camouflaged by the gray brown shadows. Squatting on her haunches to examine it, she found that it was a bird. Its body was a soft brown, except for the light gray of its chest and the streaks of iridescent blue and green that marked its wings. Kaveri decided it was male, since boys wore brown and blue.

He lay on his side with his eyes open, but didn't move. She reached out to stroke him, expecting him to fly away, but he lay still and let her move her finger down his chest. She paused when she felt a faint pulse. Then she noticed that his chest ballooned and sank, almost unnoticeably, beneath her touch. "You're still alive," she informed him. "You should fly away." Scooping him into her palm, she held him out before her. He was lighter than she'd expected. "Go!" She ordered, and tossed the body into the air, expecting it to take flight and disappear. The bird stayed limp, and fell back into her palms without a sound. Kaveri thought that perhaps he needed a rest. He might have even been sick. She tucked him back in his corner where it was dark and quiet.

She wondered then what her brother was doing. Nobody would let her touch him the day before, but she thought that perhaps today he'd be able to play. First, though, she would have to hide the bird— if she left him on the porch, Minoo would surely sweep him away. She carried him to the sapling that grew beside the porch, and covered him with a light blanket of twigs and leaves. Then she picked up the serving tray, slipped through the front room where the old man was still talking, and entered the bedroom.

Amma slept facing the window, snoring softly, her head resting on the bend of an elbow. Her long braid spilled over the side of the coir cot. Between her and her parents' beds a loop of thick cloth hung from the ceiling. Kaveri walked to the sling and peeked through its opening. Her brother was awake, naked, and he looked back at her stoically. He was long, she thought, for a baby. Already his feet poked softly out of the cloth cradle. They riveted her, these dumplings with toes, and she bent down to study them more closely. They weren't dry with white mounds of hard skin like Appa's, nor stained dark like her own. They were as pillowy and smooth as the rest of him. She wanted to touch his soles, but she wasn't supposed to bother him.

With her index finger she reached out and stroked the thin skin of his arch. The toes stretched and curled in response. Then she poked at the slightly thicker cushion of his heel. She tickled him there with her nail, hoping to make him laugh. He made a sound that was neither a laugh nor a whine, but a single clear syllable that said he knew she was there.

Kaveri was sure she could pick him up if she tried. All she had to do was get an arm around his waist and hoist him onto her hip, like she had seen the women on her street do. She placed her tea tray on the floor. When she reached into the sling, she found her arms weren't long enough to get to his waist. So, with a hand around each ankle, she pulled him toward her. He edged forward slightly, but the rough cloth kept him in place. Still, he was close enough now, and she reached through with both hands to cup his waist. She braced herself, held her breath, and pulled him up. She almost had him, when his head flopped backward. Then he started to kick at her and delivered a sound wallop to her forearm. His fists rose to his ears, and he began to cry in a choked wail. Kaveri let go, and sent him falling back into the folds of the sling. When she stepped back she kicked the metal tray and sent it clattering across the stone floor. Hearing the commotion, Amma sat up and twisted around to see. "Kaveri!" Her voice was raspy with sleep, but shrill. "What are you doing there?"

"Sorry, Amma." She said it in English, as Appa had taught her. The baby's cries grew louder, more desperate. Amma clicked her tongue and hoisted herself to her feet. She bent gingerly to scoop the baby into her arms and rock him. Kaveri picked up the tray to take to the kitchen, but stopped in the doorway and turned to look. Her mother seemed far away when she held the baby. The sunlight had resurfaced, and it beamed now through the window, turning Amma into a shadow with wild wisps of hair that rose from her scalp like a halo.

Kaveri wasn't punished that night for trying to hold the baby without asking. But at dinner, as they sat over mounds of rice, Amma told Appa about the incident, and they both laughed. Kaveri didn't like to be laughed at, so she stopped eating and picked at the threads of the banana leaf on which her food was piled. She was silent for the rest of dinner, until a thought occurred to her. "Appa," she asked, "what is the baby called?" That was still to be decided, Appa said. Comrade Mohan was coming over the next day to help them choose.

Amma wanted to name him Anand, happiness. They would see, Appa said, they would have to wait and see. When her parents rose from the table, Kaveri stuck her hand into the brass vessel and scooped up a fistful of rice. She put it in her pocket for her bird.

The next morning, when she came home from her weekly grammar class, the old man was already sipping coffee in the sitting room. Amma looked less tired today, and she smiled as she held the baby to her chest. The room's low light made her skin look dusky, and her eyes glowed whiter than usual. Without a word to her parents or their guest, Kaveri set her satchel down and went to sit beside her brother. When Amma clicked her tongue and asked her to say hello to Comrade Mohan, she looked up solemnly and said "hello" in English. The man nodded, and she saw his whiskers rise slightly, but he said nothing. So she turned her attention back to the baby, and started counting the creases on his face. He lowered his eyelids at her suspiciously.

"I have given some thought to the matter of the boy's name," the old man began. Kaveri sprang to her knees on the divan, interested at last in what he had to say. "It seems to me your boy has strength, both in spirit and in body. For this reason, I would like you to give him a name that I would not recommend to many other people. He shall be named after a great leader, a man of the people, who leads us still today. I have chosen for him: Stalin, man of steel." Amma gasped, and turned to Appa, who looked back at her and beamed.

The argument started as soon as the old man left. Kaveri could hear her parents from the front porch. Amma refused refused refused, she said, to give her son the name of a living man, let alone a politician, let alone a politician who was not even Indian. And it was inauspicious to name a child after such a prominent man. Appa's voice grew stern as he scolded Amma. It was the Hindus who cared so much about auspicious names and times and dates and stars. In his family, he said, there would be no such superstitious nonsense. Appa went on to argue that Stalin was not a politician, but a leader. "Yes," he said, "there is a difference." More than this, it didn't matter if the name was Indian or Russian or English, because Stalin was a man of the world. It would be an honor for their son to have such a name, and Comrade Mohan's wishes should be respected. The argument continued until both of them were yelling. Kaveri had never heard them shout at each other, and she wanted no more of it.

She stepped down from the porch and walked to the sapling, where the leaves and twigs sat just as she had left them the day before. When she stooped down and cleared the debris, she found that the bird was slightly damp—he had probably grown cold during the night. He was awake, she decided, as his black eyes were open and watching. She placed a finger on his chest, and a tiny beat answered back. She turned him round, and the streaks of color on his wings caught the sunlight and glimmered.

She reached into her pocket now and brought out the rice she had been saving. Using her fingernail to pry open his beak, she crammed a few mottled grains into the bird's mouth. "Eat," she coaxed. His beak didn't move. He would eat the rice later, she decided. He was just storing it for now.

It occurred to her then that if her bird could get cold, he could also get wet. If it rained again that night, he might even be washed away. She tucked the small lump into the folds of her skirt and walked back into the house. Neither Appa nor Amma noticed her, as they were still talking. She was glad, at least, that they had stopped yelling.

In the bedroom, Kaveri opened a low drawer of the wardrobe. There she found neat stacks of Appa's handkerchiefs. She chose a blue one to match the bird's stripe. Carefully, she wrapped the small body into the folds of the kerchief, and rolled it into a cylinder that she hid in the dark space below her bed.

It was then that she heard a small noise from the sling, and she found her brother sucking on his hand. Stalin, she thought. The name sounded good enough, though she was hoping her parents would name him Krishna, like the sweet baby god Prema Aunty had told her about, who never got into trouble for stealing the fresh butter from his neighbors' homes, because who could get angry with God? She suggested the name to Appa once, but he only made a strange sound and said nothing more about it.

Later that evening, Amma sat Kaveri down and taught her to hold the baby. She showed her how to support his head, and how to make sure his lower back didn't sag. Finally she placed the baby in his sister's lap. Kaveri held him hesitantly and kept him balanced squarely on her thighs, inches away from her torso. They had decided to name him Stalin Anand, Amma told her. Stalin Anand looked at Kaveri thoughtfully for a few moments, before breaking into the wail to which she had grown accustomed. "It's okay," Amma said. "Hold him a little longer and he'll get used to you." So Kaveri watched her brother cry, and noted how quickly his face turned red. She couldn't recall her own face ever turning red, but she was probably too dark. "I'll need you to help Appa on Sunday, when he takes Anand to the town center."

"What for?" Kaveri asked. She couldn't imagine what business a baby would have in the busy streets of town.

"Well, Comrade Mohan—you remember the man who was here?" Kaveri nodded. Amma and Appa were always asking her if she remembered such obvious things. "Comrade Mohan asked Appa to bring him to a gathering in the center of town. I can't go, I'm still a bit tired, but I want you to go with Appa to help him with Anand." Amma paused and cupped her hand around Kaveri's. "This is your job, ma. Make sure Appa comes *straight* back home as soon as he can. The baby will need feeding, and I don't want you three staying around and doing unnecessary things." Kaveri looked at her brother and wondered how she could be expected to take care of him. Abruptly, he stopped crying and stared back, as the red melted away from his face.

That night she checked to see if her bird had eaten. His beak was empty, so she placed a few more grains by his side. Before she tucked him back in his corner, she stroked his chest and felt his faint thump-thump.

That Sunday, Amma pulled Kaveri out of bed early. She bathed her daughter herself, massaging coconut oil into her hair and weaving it into two slick braids. Then she came at her with white hands and rubbed a thin dusting of talcum powder over her face as Kaveri pursed her lips and squeezed her eyes shut. Amma brought out her new skirt and blouse, made from violet cotton and trimmed with dark blue silk. After Kaveri drank a cup of warm milk, Amma watched her wash her mouth, and then took her into the bedroom, where she lined the girl's eyes with thick black lines of *kohl.* She looked her daughter over and smiled. When she left the room to check on the baby, Kaveri ducked under the bed and felt for her bundle. The bird sat where she'd left him. He had been eating his rice, but he was still too weak to move on his own. She tucked him into the pocket that Amma had sewn into her skirt.

When she walked out onto the porch, Appa was waiting for her. Stalin hung close to his chest in a sling. She took Appa's outstretched hand and led him off the porch and through the front gate. Wearing her new skirt and blouse, walking down the road with just her brother and father, she felt extraordinary. When she waved to Prema Aunty, who watched from across the street, she knew she must have looked tall and graceful.

They hailed a bicycle rickshaw at the corner and rode it to the central square on Mount Road, where tailor shops and tea stalls looked onto the carved façade of a temple. Today, the view of the temple was partially blocked by a high platform. One of the people on stage was the old man who had given Stalin his name. Kaveri was surprised by the number of people who were in the square; she had never before seen such a gathering. Scores of men, and a few women, stood facing the stage. Poles with ropes strung between them reined in the crowd. Some spectators carried red flags with yellow symbols in the corners. She had seen the symbol on a small book that Appa read sometimes; it was a star, next to a crescent moon with a sort of handle.

Comrade Mohan was speaking when they arrived. His voice was loud enough to carry to the back of the crowd. When he saw Kaveri and her father, he motioned for them to join him on the platform. It was for this, she knew, that Amma had taken so much time dressing her that morning. Holding Appa's hand, she climbed the five steps to the stage. They stood a few feet behind Comrade Mohan and listened to him speak. He went on for a long time, and she began to wonder why she and Appa were even up there.

"In this temple behind us, the Hindus are performing their *pujas*. They bathe their stone statues in milk, while on this very road people are starving and begging for the few *paisas* we can afford to give them!

"Our enemies will try to tell us that the Communist cause is atheistic and godless. My friends, we are atheists, but godless we are not." With a flourish, he stepped back and turned to Appa, who placed Stalin in his arms, and pushed Kaveri a few feet forward. "*This* is our God!" the old man said, turning the baby's face to the audience. "*We* give our milk to our children. And we worship a future free from the yoke of Brahminical tyranny! For the Hindu temple is nothing but a house of theft and sin!" Kaveri stopped listening to the man. Stalin had started to cry fiercely, angry at this stranger's touch. The old man grew suddenly uncomfortable with the baby and looked for Appa to take him back.

Just as Appa scooped him back into his arms, a loud crash sounded at the opposite side of the stage. A fight had erupted between some spectators and a few men who had moved in from the edge of the group. Kaveri watched the men lunge at each other, their movements growing broader and wilder with each swing. The crowd began to bob and sway, falling erratically into itself. Some men were winding their way toward the brawl, looking to join in. Others were trying to get away. People began to push, and Kaveri saw one man turn around and shove his neighbor away from him. Her heart began to beat faster and she looked at Comrade Mohan, who was still speaking. The neighbor shoved back, and the crowd moved forward. Within seconds, men and women stood flattened against each other, suddenly unable to find their space. Several were climbing onto the stage, trying to escape the crush. Kaveri felt their footsteps booming through the platform's wood and stepped back, reaching for Appa. The crush was moving in on them, and she couldn't see how they would get out.

Appa looked about wildly and rushed toward the platform steps. "Kaveri!" He shouted to her over the noise. "Come with me!" She descended first, and watched him step carefully down the stairs, clasping Stalin to his chest. He was halfway down when a man in a khaki shirt ran off the stage and pushed him to the side. Kaveri watched as Appa fell into the crowd and disappeared.

"Appa!" She tried to shove her way to where he must have fallen, but a foot knocked her to the ground. A woman screamed. "Appa!" She found herself caught between adult legs, reaching for the edge of the crowd. She squirmed among knees, straining for breathable air.

When she emerged, she was at the back of the platform, a few feet away from the temple. Her knees burned and the dust pricked her eyes. She yelled for Appa again, but her voice bounced off the buzzing swarm and faded. She looked for him, but couldn't see above the heads. Men in brown uniforms holding clubs descended on the crowd, and Kaveri ran between the stone pillars and into the temple. Several people were filing through the temple's vestibule. Their clothes were smudged with dirt, and one woman held her elbow and wept. Appa wasn't among them, but perhaps he would be inside.

She noticed the rows of shoes spread before the temple doors and removed her own slippers. Beneath her soles the stone was cool and smooth. There were no lights in here, except for the flames of a few small oil lamps, and Kaveri's eyes had to adjust to the dark. She craned her neck to look out to the street, hoping to spot Appa from where she stood. She could hear nothing from inside the temple, and all she could see were policemen shoving men away from the crowd.

Looking up, she saw a giant stone cow that towered above her on a platform. It rested flat on its belly, with its arms and legs tucked under. A collar of beads was carved around the cow's neck, and Kaveri wondered why an animal would wear jewelry.

From farther inside the temple, she heard the steady clanging of a bell. She walked through a second door, into the main hall, where the air grew warmer and stuck to her nostrils when she tried to breathe. At the far end of this large room, a group of people gathered in front of an even smaller door. Kaveri walked toward them and watched from the back of the crowd. The young boy next to her stood, like his father, with his palms pressed together, and leaned in to peer through an archway into a tiny room. On either side of the archway hung strands of palm-sized oil lamps, each lit with a single flame. Inside the small room two men stood with their backs to the group, shirtless and wearing plain white dhotis. They chanted, making sounds that meant nothing to Kaveri. Their voices echoed loud and nasal through the room. Between them stood a statue that was no taller than Kaveri herself. But for a small loincloth, his black stone body was bare, and it glistened wet in the sanctum's dim light. He clutched a spear in one hand, and the other hand he held at chest level, palm facing out. Like the rest of his body, his eyes were carved from black rock. They stared vacantly, without eyeballs. Below a long slender nose was carved a small smile. A gold-plated arch stood behind him, and on each side of him rose a tall peacock feather—shiny green and blue with an eye at the center. She thought of her own bird then, and felt for him in her pocket. The cloth bundle was still there, and when she squeezed him, he felt soft, a little like a tomato. The bell began to clang again.

"Om Muruga!" The people around her shouted. They bellowed it again, and then once more. By the time Kaveri thought to join them, they stopped and fell back into silence. She brought her hand out of her pocket and clasped her palms together.

Once she had asked Prema Aunty what people did at temples. Prema Aunty answered that they went to ask God for protection or help, and sometimes money. It seemed unlikely, Kaveri had said, that God would give something away just because she asked for it. Prema Aunty had answered that that was what God did. But sometimes people left gifts behind, like sweets or money.

The group began singing then, and the shorter of the two priests waved an oil lamp in front of the idol. Kaveri closed her eyes and asked for Appa to find her. She remembered how Stalin squirmed and cried when the old man held him, and how surprised Appa had looked falling into the crowd. He might even be hurt, she thought, like the woman she'd seen earlier. She scrunched her eyes even more tightly then, and kept them closed a long time, until she felt weightless and the room's heat throbbed in yellow circles behind her lids.

When she opened them again, the tall priest was walking along the perimeter of the group, holding out a brass plate. The boy standing next to her looked up at his father, who handed him a five-rupee note. When the priest approached them, the boy placed the note on the plate, but Kaveri had nothing to give. Then she remembered her bird, and brought the bundle from her pocket. The priest, seeing she had something to give, bent toward her with the plate. When he straightened up and moved down the line, a roll of blue cloth sat atop the nest of rupee notes. The short priest followed close behind, and he dropped a spoonful of milk into Kaveri's cupped palm. It was warm and sweet and a little rancid, but she was thirsty, and those few drops made her feel better.

The *puja* was over, it seemed, so Kaveri followed the group as it oozed out of the sanctum's heat. In comparison, the air in the main hall felt fresh. Appa and Stalin might even be in the temple by now, she thought, perhaps looking for her in a different room. She started toward another gathering in the far corner of the hall, when a rough hand snatched the back of her collar.

"*Dey!*" A gruff whisper cut the thick air. "What do you think you're doing?" She twisted around to find the short priest standing behind her. He let go of her blouse and grabbed her by the arm. "What's the meaning of this?" He held out Kaveri's offering. The blue cloth was unfurled, and on it rested the body of her bird. His feathers had gone gray, and a fly clung to his eyeball. The priest made a loud spitting sound and Kaveri jumped. "What are you trying to do," he rasped, "putting such a filthy thing in God's plate? *Chih!*" He gripped her arm more tightly and, almost lifting her off the ground, pulled her through the main hall, through the tall doors, past the giant cow, and into the open air. Once there, he spit on the ground and threw down the bundle. The bird's body rolled off Appa's handkerchief and into the dust. "Pick that up," he ordered. "Filthy girl... pick that up and take it away." The priest kicked at the dust and sent a cloud to settle on the dead bird. Then he turned and walked back into the temple, disappearing into the shadows.

Kaveri squatted down to examine the bird. Her body still trembled with alarm, and she wanted Appa. The street was quiet now, and she could hear the fly that buzzed around the bird's head. She had brought a pinch of rice in her pocket, and now placed a few grains by his beak, just in case. But nothing happened. He looked dry to her, emptied of life. She reached out to stroke his soft chest, but the feathers had grown coarse. Just then a flash of red caught her eye, and she looked up at the empty platform in the distance. The crowd had dispersed, the policemen were gone. Perhaps Appa had gone also. A red flag with a yellow handled moon flopped over the side of the stage, its edge trailing into the dust.

"Kaveri!" Appa's voice startled her, and she swung around to look for him. He was running toward her, holding Stalin in the sling against his chest. When he reached her, he kneeled down and Kaveri fell into his grasp. He wrapped his free arm around her. She was impossibly tired, suddenly, and began to cry. She wept hoarse sobs into Appa's ear, nearly yelling at times. She had been so good until then, she thought. She hadn't cried since the day last month when she fell off Prema Aunty's roof. Before long, Stalin joined her, his wails sounding just beneath her own. When Appa let go, she noticed a streak of blood along his hairline, and a pink patch on his arm where the skin had been scraped away. She peeked into the sling to examine Stalin. He looked untouched, but for the tear stains on his cheeks. He stopped crying and blinked at her.

Appa folded her hand into his. "Come," he said. "I shouldn't have brought you here, should I? Let's get home." Kaveri nodded, and bent down to wrap up her bird and take him along. "*Chih!*" Appa said, when he saw what she was doing. "Don't touch that thing, ma.

It's dirty-dirty." He squeezed her hand and hauled her up. Kaveri wanted to protest; she wanted to keep her bird, but she was tired. She let Appa pull her away. He walked slowly, and she could see that he was limping. Perhaps Amma would make him better. She wiped a film of sweat from her upper lip; her palm still smelled of sour milk.

RENÉ L. TODD

University of Virginia

VINEGAR

Audrey knew it was a mistake when the Halaka Maui welcome girl glided toward them at the airport gate.

"Aloha, Mr. and Mrs. Connell." The girl looked only a few years younger than Audrey, but she was dressed like a souvenir doll, with black blue hair swaying behind her shoulders and a red-flowered sarong. Audrey bowed her head for the lei, watching Ben to see whether he, too, knew it was a mistake, and whether he would fix it.

The girl reached a lei toward Ben's head, but he caught it in his fingers. "This is lovely." He smiled and gestured broadly to indicate the girl, the leis, and, apparently, the airport. It was part of Ben's charm, this fatherly graciousness, his dark hair just tinseled with silver. "But I told the concierge not to send anyone. We're getting a car."

The girl took a step back. She nearly bowed. "Our mistake," she said politely, and Audrey echoed it in her head—yes, your mistake— as she watched the sweep of the girl's dark hair. Go someplace warm,

Dr. Rivkin had suggested. The Luv Doctor, they called him, to show how ironic and casual they were about going to a couples counselor. Someplace you can relax, he had said, so smug with his Motherwell prints and aquarium and his little Zen sand garden. Someplace, Audrey added now to herself, swarming with beautiful dark-haired women. And there it was again, that name, swooping through Audrey's brain. Julia Ogawa. Audrey touched the ends of her short, blond hair, glancing at Ben, as if he must have heard the name chime between them, pinging off their separate skins.

"Do you need help with your luggage?" the girl asked. Audrey pictured the girl heaving bags from the luggage carousel, her hair disheveled and sarong askew. "Our driver could help you," the girl said, and Audrey realized that the girl was really offering his help, not her own.

"We'll take care of it," Audrey said.

The welcome girl stepped back for them to pass. "Hang loose," she called after them, waving her closed hand, pinky and thumb extended.

Audrey wondered if this was something she needed to learn. "They won't bill us for that, will they?" she asked Ben as they threaded through the airport. "She said it was their mistake." A mistake, Ben had said that dazzling night when her anger burned bright points between them, when the name—Julia, Julia Ogawa—was an invocation that hurled china to the floor, that shattered lamps and mirrors.

Ben draped his arm over her shoulders. "Don't worry about it," he said. "This is a vacation."

Audrey shifted her beach bag to her other shoulder, irritated that Ben hadn't simply clasped her from the other side. His arm lay heavy on her neck.

She shrugged out from beneath him. "Don't tell me what to worry about," she said as she walked quickly ahead.

She brushed past a couple in faded beach clothes, deeply tanned, walking hand in hand toward the gate. They looked at her curiously; their eyes flicked behind to Ben and back again. She felt a mean pleasure at making a scene. Ben hated to fight in public; he hated the way people stared, wondering if she was his wife or his daughter. She wanted him to be angry, to shake her and tell her to stop acting like a child, but she knew that he would not. He would see this as another minute exaction of the cost of Julia. He would think there was that much less of her anger to be borne later.

Audrey walked ahead of Ben into the room, touching the yellow and white quilt, the cool pebble-skinned oranges in the fruit basket. Ben tipped the bellman—an angelic sort of bellman in a white mandarin shirt and trousers—who prattled on about tennis and luaus, about the Haleakala volcano. A couple had gone snorkeling yesterday and spotted three sea turtles. You just have to dive deep for them, the bellman was saying.

Audrey opened the glass door to the deck, kicking off her sandals to walk on the smooth, hard wood. "Will that be all?" she heard behind her. The bellman's voice sounded distant, muted by the sound of the sea. Audrey stretched her arms along the rail, looking out at blue sky meeting sea, rippling white ribbons of waves. She felt her forehead, the skin at her throat, expand to mirror the distance of sand and ocean. Maybe the Luv Doctor had been right after all.

"Honey?" Ben called.

She answered by going inside. The room was dark after the sunlight.

Ben lolled on the bed, filling it with his arms and legs. "Isn't this great?"

He was asking for credit, praise for finding the resort and buying the trip as penance. She went into the bathroom and ran her hands along the cool marble countertop. There was always a phone in these resort bathrooms, for grown-ups so important they needed to take calls at any moment. Ben was that important, but she wasn't. She turned on the tap.

"I bet we could get in eighteen holes if we left now." His voice nearly drowned in rushing water.

"Nine." She crinkled open the paper wrappings of soap smelling of orange and cinnamon. She worked the soap between her hands, gliding it into foam, and then rinsed her hands and face. Now she smelled of orange and cinnamon. She turned off the tap. "We won't finish eighteen before dinner." She slipped the other soaps—long, smooth oblongs in white paper—into her pocket. When the maid came to turn down beds, she might replace them, and Audrey could have those, too.

"If we're only going to play nine we should wait." He lay on the bed with his arms above his head. The undersides of his arms were pale and white. "Get the twilight rate."

"We're on vacation." She climbed onto the bed and fit herself in the space next to him, breathing his sweaty, travel smell. "So what if we pay full rate?"

"If we pay full rate, we should play eighteen."

She pressed into his chest. His breath was loud in her ear; she couldn't hear the ocean anymore. "I don't think people should play golf in Hawaii. I think you're supposed to snorkel or climb a volcano or something." Her head raised and lowered as he breathed.

He toyed with a strand of her hair, pulling just slightly. "Good thing we brought the clubs, then."

"I read it somewhere." Audrey lay back on the pillow so she could hear the ocean again. "They replace the local vegetation with all that grass. It's bad for the environment."

"Right." His hand went still. "But it wasn't bad for the environment when we played at Pebble Beach. Or Vegas. Grass was pretty green out there in the desert."

Audrey closed her eyes. If they were at home, she might have been swimming laps—sneaking out from work to trace a thick black line through calm artificial blue. Hardly anyone swam at her gym, and some days she floated slowly up the lanes, watching the San Francisco fog roll over the glass atrium, reaching for the glaze of blue sky. Once, a small red plane crossed just over her, and it felt like a sign, somehow, a secret.

Ben didn't understand that some things never come back. Ben had simply opened his arms to catch the bright things that had been his parents' and were now his—the summers in Tahoe, his grandfather's still-gleaming martini set. Audrey might never come to this place again. A bar of soap, a remembered scent of orange and cinnamon, might be all she had left to show from this trip, from their year of marriage.

One night before they were married, she had whispered to him as they made love, had described a fantasy that they would ask another woman to join them. She had touched her breasts the way she would touch that woman's, had told him of all that she would do and touch while he watched. She lay against his chest afterward—legs entangled, the bleach smell of semen rising from the sheets—proud of her own daring.

"I actually did it with two girls once," he had said. Almost contemplatively, as if it were something he had forgotten.

A stone dropped in her throat, sank slowly through the thick liquids that had just filled her. "Anyone I know?" She kept her voice even and soft. It had been scarcely imaginable to her—those pictures, that dream.

She felt a small heaving as Ben shrugged beneath her. "It was the seventies," he said. Audrey had spent the seventies in sneakers and braces. She pulled the sheet higher; her thighs felt slimy and cold.

"But they weren't as good as you, Baby" he said. She had let him kiss her then, so they wouldn't have to speak.

"My wife is an excellent swimmer," Ben told the man at the beach store. He tried on another snorkel mask. It was too tight, pulling at the skin around Ben's eyes, shiny and white, and smoothing away his usual creases. The new Ben looked eerily blank and malleable, a clay model not yet stamped with Ben-ness. This pale, unlined Ben could be anyone, could be someone who did not love Audrey.

"His mask doesn't fit," Audrey said to the man. The sign had said STEVE'S SURF STORE, so this must be Steve. He was about Audrey's age, a beach bum who had extended adolescence into his twenties. Audrey watched the pale line of skin rimming his drawstring shorts.

"I guess your husband has a big head." Steve grinned at her. PR banter, she knew, but it helped to solidify something in her chest. She laughed, and looked doubtfully at her mask. The plastic mouth-piece was scarred from past teeth. The black air tube looked as if it had been hacked off some car's fuel line.

"We clean 'em." Steve rooted around in a bin of masks to find an-other for Ben. "It's really hygienic."

She smiled brightly at Steve and Ben. "Don't worry," she said. "It won't be the first time I've put my mouth where someone else's has been." She watched Ben out of the corner of her eye as she stretched her smile around the plastic mouthpiece.

Ben ignored her. "She swims all the time," he told Steve, as if she weren't there. "She swims for miles and miles."

Audrey watched him through her mask; now he looked dark and vaguely rippled behind the plastic. Ben had never seen her swim. At nights he complained that her hair smelled of chlorine. She whooshed her breath into the tube and out, and tasted something stale and dusty.

Steve unfolded maps for Ben, tracing beaches and reefs. "Ulua," he said. Audrey echoed the word to herself, feeling its guttural drop in her throat. "Some mornings I go there first thing," Steve said, "and just sweep around that peninsula there."

Audrey felt a rising warmth for people who would spend their mornings this way. She pictured Steve balanced on the edge of a bed gray with morning, pulling on still-damp swim trunks. She breathed through her tube as Steve spoke of tides, of coral ridged with poison. Don't touch anything down there, he was saying. Don't climb on the coral. You could destroy whole ecosystems. This could have been her life, she thought. A world so basic it ran with the tides, worried about coral.

"There's no lifeguards, you know." Steve caught their masks and fins into a string bag. He pushed the receipt across the counter for Ben's signature.

"No worries." Ben stuffed the receipt in his shirt pocket. Ben had adopted a new, casual island-speak, as if he were a different person here, a parallel-universe Ben. Audrey met Steve's eyes, then looked away. Ben took Audrey's elbow, guiding her gently ahead of him toward the door.

Steve waved the little pinky and thumb sign. "Hang loose," he called after them.

"Hang loose." Ben waved back over his shoulder. He held the door so that Audrey could pass through ahead of him to the parking lot. She stood waiting in the glare of asphalt and windshields until he unlocked the car.

Audrey raised her hand against the afternoon sun, trying to blink away the black splotches she saw dotting the sand and sea. Her sunglasses were in the car with the towels and wallets. She followed Ben across the beach, clutching fins and mask to chest. They passed a lone and very tan woman gleaming like an oil slick. Audrey watched Ben's eyes travel over the woman, and for a moment she saw the woman's dark hair unfurl like a matador's cape. Julia Ogawa. It was the name of a dancer, or a soap opera star.

Audrey dropped her fins in the water, thinking she would step into them; they floated in two different directions, big blue clown feet. Ben laughed, waving his fins as she chased her own. She plopped down, sitting in the middle of the surf to tug on the fins, furious now with the ripple of blue horizon, with the powder-puff clouds and round, hiccuping laughs of children. She struggled to stand up in her fins, sand washing away beneath her feet.

Ben sloshed toward her, offering his hand. She pushed his arm away, digging her fists into the sand for leverage. He rolled his eyes and held his hand out as before.

She took it, heaving up on the strength of his arm. For a moment, they seemed to be themselves, the air swinging easily between them. She felt the briefcase calluses ridging his fingers, the softness of his palm.

Ben handed her his fins, balancing on one foot, then the other, to take each one from her and put it on. "Don't expect to see fish all at once." He pulled on his mask.

"I know." She fit the rubber seals of the mask onto her face, stretching her lips rubbery over the mouthpiece. She blew air once through the tube—a slight whistle, like air over a bottle—and pushed away from him into the water, taking small breaststrokes until she could barely touch her toes to the sand. She dove.

Fish. Fish everywhere. Sleek shimmers of red and blue neons. Angelfish the size of her palm, yellow and black in bumblebee stripes. A school of black fish swam in front of her, each cordoned with white lines, as if wearing little Chanel suits. She reached to touch them, but, without seeming to alter their course, they glided out of reach.

"Oh my god," she said, forgetting her mouthpiece. In the water her voice made a high-pitched squeal, like a porpoise.

She bobbed up, looking for Ben. He was still standing, watching her. He waved, the little Hawaiian wave with his pinky and thumb extended. "Hang tight," he called before taking in his mouthpiece, and she laughed, because he didn't realize he had gotten it wrong. Hang tight, hang loose. She laughed into her mouthpiece and dove again.

The horizon gone, only blue and the quivering lines of sunlight rippling shapes onto the sea floor. Bright ribbon flashes of fish. Ben swam up, a mass of white limbs behind his plastic windshield, hollering through his tube—so loud and garbled she knew he intended it to be a joke. He pointed to fish again and again, waving in excitement.

They swam together, following the reef, chasing one bright fish, then another. She felt Ben's hand, once, on her arm. He pointed to a school of black angel fish tagged with purple and gold. Audrey pointed, too, to show him that she had seen. It was like being inside an aquarium, as if she and Ben had been plunked down inside the saltwater tank—with its careful filters and temperature controls—in Dr. Rivkin's office. They would swim there among the fish, staring at the angry couples in the waiting room, the ones holding hands but secretly, silently, digging in fingernails. The couples would be amazed, she thought, to see her and Ben swimming among all those bright colors. The Luv Doctor would wonder where they had gone.

Audrey floated, bobbing on the surface, letting the larger waves jostle and carry her. The only world here was this thick layering of blue into blue, the whooshing sound of her own breath, the counter-tempo of her heartbeat. She and Ben swam close, tracing the porous reef rock. The fish would see them as another school, she thought, two alien sea creatures. The sun felt warm on her back, the water cool and soft as talc. The sea floor sank farther and farther beneath them until she grew vertiginous, then reached her arms to steady herself. They had swum so far, she realized; they must have been in the water for hours.

Ben tapped the back of his wrist. Time to go in. Audrey shook her head. Her muscles felt loose and scraped clean, tired after the long swim. But the shore would be filled with beautiful dark-haired women, with the chorus of Julia, Julia Ogawa. Audrey took a breath and dove deep, feeling water draw heavily into her tube. She headed toward the murkier depths where shades of blue blurred to a sort of mist, wondering what a sea turtle would look like—just a shape, a pattern in the sand. It would be an accomplishment to find one, a story. She pictured herself with Ben at the hotel luau, suddenly tan and strong-looking, her leg sinewy above her sandal. Ben watching, admiring as she told attractive strangers how she had found the turtle, how she had searched for it in the depths, alert to its slightest motion. She swam out farther and dove again.

The water was cooler beneath the surface. She missed the steady rhythm of her own breath; now her chest grew tight, seeming to expand below the water as she dove again and again. She swam beneath the surface, startling a school of puffer fish. They were ugly fish, spotted yellow and gray, with waxy, bulbous eyes. One swam straight toward her—he seemed angry with her, rebuking her. She wondered if fish were capable of anger, of any emotion at all. Its gaping mouth opened, then closed; its gray scales darkened into hollows when its jaw stretched. He looked like Dr. Rivkin, she decided, with his schlubby round face floating above his sweater and corduroys. For a moment, she wanted to laugh and show Ben. The Luv Doctor, so smug and ecological in his Doc Martens. Infidelity is not insurmountable, the doctor had said, sounding so pleased with his little wordplay. Audrey had looked around, thinking that he must have it printed on some needlepoint pillow, until she realized that both Ben and Dr. Rivkin were watching her. Waiting, she realized, for her to begin the surmounting.

Audrey pushed up through the surface, yanking out her mouthpiece to gulp air, straight and sharp into her lungs. She felt a seasick lurch as she looked to the horizon, blue water into gray sky. Where was the shore? She spun around, dog-paddling. That must be the shore, but so far away, flecks of pale pinks and yellows and tiny quivering lines of beach people. The reef was dark and small; they were long past it. Bile slip-slid up her throat, prickling heat along her breastbone.

She turned, searching for Ben. Squinting, she saw the thin black reed of his snorkel to her right, the blurry mound beneath the waves. A wave slapped cold and brackish into her mouth. Ben didn't yet know how far they were from shore. People make mistakes, Ben had said on Dr. Rivkin's sofa. How much do I have to be punished for it? He had stretched his hands wide apart, indicating some mass of punishment, while angelfish swam decorously behind Dr. Rivkin's head.

Audrey leaned back into the water, stroking toward the shore. Ben would be scarcely visible from the beach, she thought, just a speck in the miles and miles of ocean. She reached back and pulled, one stroke closer to shore. How long would it be before he realized she was gone? she wondered.

A wave rolled beneath her, then reached Ben, and splashed over the top of his tube. He bobbed upright, sputtering and slapping the tube from his mouth. He grinned when he saw her, waving his little Hawaiian sign. Hang tight.

Audrey pulled upright and swam toward him. It was what she had meant to do all along. "We're too far," she shouted. She tilted her head toward the shore. His eyes followed. His mouth was already open to breathe; she could not tell if there was panic or fear behind his mask, but he had seen. She bit on her tube and pushed into the sea. She pulled her strokes tight, her cupped hands close to her belly, and kicked hard. Her breath in her ears grew faster, louder.

She turned her head, looking for Ben. He was strong, but he was no swimmer—his stroke was sloppy and inefficient. How could you expect to live in the world if you didn't swim a few laps? "Ben!" She treaded water, waiting for Ben to draw close, her arms heavy and tight now that she was no longer stroking forward. He swatted his tube out to gasp in air, coughing up slime strings of phlegm. She turned her head.

"I've got to rest," Ben panted.

"Rest?" Her voice high. The word was an entry point for fury, a knife slit filled suddenly, flooding, with anger. "You can't rest." A waste of energy even to ask for something so impossible, like calling for champagne or room service, waiting for one of those angelic bell-men to appear in his white mandarin collar and wide-legged trousers, bringing them rest on a silver tray. Ben could slide him a few small bills, palm to palm, and flourish the tray toward her as if it were something he had done or accomplished.

She bit on the tube and pushed into the sea. She pulled her arms in and in and in, climbing the rope that would lead her to shore. Ben was behind her now, a pale speck on the darkening green sheen of a wave. Her body pushed through the water fast and clean. This was what she had wanted all the time: to swim away, to push and pull and tear and kick until a whole ocean lay between them.

Dark pains shot through her arms, her legs, but the seafloor was now climbing to meet her. A thick column of reef rose through the surface, leaving only a narrow crevice. Her body grew heavy at the thought of swimming around, those wasted strokes. She grabbed the rock, pushing her body sideways and through to the surface.

Her skin stung as waves surged her again and again into the rock. She felt the soft mosslike growth along the coral, the rubbery spines of sea succulents—her hands, her legs, were scraping them off and into the sea, but she didn't care. She could wait here a moment, on the rock, until it was covered by high tide. The shore was closer; people looked real and substantial, as they closed umbrellas and shook sand off towels and beach chairs, to go home.

The sun was behind her now, and the sea turning dark. She hadn't really believed that she could leave Ben, that he could be left. She looked toward the shore, felt the rock holding her up, and wondered if she could bring herself to let it go.

Audrey. She heard her name as if she dreamed it, woven in with the waves and the roar of water swirling in her ears. Audrey. He was calling her. She couldn't see him, but splashes sounded close, his voice rising into panic. He must have swum wide around; he was on the other side of the rock where he couldn't see her. She grasped again at the rock, clinging against the slap of the waves. Audrey. His voice thin, drowning in the sound of the waves. This was what she had wanted—for Ben to taste the fear of being alone, of being abandoned. The fear she tasted all the time.

Then she heard nothing. She pushed off from the rock, back into the waves, her mouthpiece bobbling against her neck. She rounded the rock to see him rise, gasping and blowing water from his tube, in time to see him flip and dive again. He was searching for her. She dove after him, trying to catch up, amazed that he could swim— now, after all this—so fast and deep.

She caught his leg. He turned—slowly, as if swimming in syrup. His arms, pale and bloated, reached for her. She thought for a second that he would embrace her, happy to have found her. Instead he was shaking her, hands and fingers digging and squeezing into her arms, wrenching her back and forth beneath the water. She screamed, losing her breath, and still he shook her, holding her under. She curled up, trying to shield herself, trying to get away.

Her knees hit his chest and she pushed. She kicked toward the surface, scissoring hard until she burst through, sucking in air, noisily filling her lungs.

Ben rose beside her, breaching like a whale. He slapped out his mouthpiece. "Don't you fucking disappear like that." He gasped in air, his eyes raging behind his mask. "What was I fucking—?" He swiped at his mouth, breathing hard. "What was I fucking supposed to do?" His arms slapped sloppily as he treaded water. She felt a cold, hard space open up in her head, a feeling she recognized like a fist. She had made him angry; she had caused him pain. He looked beaten, an old boxer slumping around the ring, barely able to throw a punch.

She pushed back into the water, but swam slowly, staying close to Ben. The beach had to be close now. She signaled to Ben and he dove with her low along the reef, where they weren't fighting the waves. She pulled herself forward on one crag, then another. Behind her, Ben did the same. We are destroying whole ecosystems, she thought.

The bottom drew close. She stood now, feeling the sand pull at her feet, dragging herself through the shallows. Ben struggled beside her. He yanked off his mask, flinging it to the sand. His face was pale and slack, marked with red imprints from his mask, and his eyes were mobile and unsure. He gulped in air, wiping his eyes with the backs of his hands. He nodded at Audrey once, between heaving breaths, as if to acknowledge something she had said.

She could hear people now, could see them big as life. A woman in a beach chair glanced up at them behind sunglasses, then turned the page of her book. A boy in red trunks ran past them, hollering, into the water. Audrey wanted to stop the boy, to catch him while his skin was still dry and sun-warm, to warn him, somehow, or prepare him. Before she could speak, he was bobbing, shrieking gleefully, among the waves.

Ben lay sprawled on the bed, unmoving from where he had flung himself, one arm across his eyes. Audrey watched him through the shower door, as the water beaded and trickled down the glass between them. She pressed her palm against its cool, smooth surface, leaning on the wall as the shower rained needle-stings into her sunburn and scrapes.

Her limbs were dull and slow as a sleeping child's. She reached for the oval of soap, rubbing it between her palms. She was amazed, somehow, by its lather and the rising, now familiar, smell of orange and cinnamon. Someone—perhaps the bellman in his cool white linen clothes—had put this soap here for her. She soaped her belly and ran her hands over her shoulders. She traced the cuts and gashes on her arms and legs—long, thin slashes, some trailing into tiny dotted lines, each lipped red and swollen. The ecosystems had fought back.

She opened the shower door, groping for the phone. It seemed a silly luxury, to phone from the shower, but it was there and she could. Scrapes and burns, she explained to a distant, polite voice. The shower spattered loud behind her. Coral. Sun. Do you have hydrogen peroxide? she asked. I'll send you something better, the voice assured her, and Audrey looked at the phone gratefully, stroking it drunkenly before she hung up.

She wrapped herself in a thick terry robe to answer the door. The angelic bellman balanced a jar of white vinegar on a tray with a glass canister of cotton pads. He looked solicitously alarmed when he saw her. She touched her face, pressing the tender spot of a bruise on her cheek. She pressed a five-dollar bill into his palm, their hands meeting briefly.

"You can have the shower now," she whispered to Ben when the bellman had left. She untied her robe, dropping it to the floor before pulling back the sheets to climb in next to him. The fan twirled above them, turning a breeze soft with sugar and blossoms. Ben lay unmoving, eyes closed. He smelled of sea brine and sweat, like old beach towels.

She tipped vinegar cool onto the cotton, raising it toward her face. Ben's chest and arms were crisscrossed with scratches. She reached the cotton to his shoulder, feeling the muscle clench beneath his cold skin. She tried the next dab on her arm, whistling her breath in as vinegar sliced into the cut. She swabbed them both, painting the ridged cuts on his arm, her leg, until the sharp vinegar smell rose from both of them.

"Did you ever color Easter eggs?" she asked.

He stirred slowly, as if waking. He caught her hand as she swabbed a cut on his chest and lifted it to his face, so the vinegary cotton was beneath his nose. "Yes," he said. He expelled a short breath, almost a laugh. "Exactly."

He kept his hand on hers until she moved to rub his neck and shoulders, stroking the prickling hairs on his arms just turning to gray. Ben's breath slowed, his eyes still closed, and she wondered if he had fallen asleep. She closed the bottle and lay beside him, the back of her hand resting lightly against his. She lay listening to the waves, a dull roar that might have been anything—a distant highway or a plane. She lay listening for the moment they would begin to speak, softly, of the depths they had swum, of the fish that swirled bright around them, of the way they had drifted so far.

KIMBERLY ELKINS
Florida State University

WHAT IS VISIBLE

> *I was so fortunate as to hear of the child [Laura Bridgman], and immediately hastened to Hanover to see her... The parents were easily induced to consent to her coming to Boston, and [soon] they brought her to the Institution.*
> —Dr. Samuel Gridley Howe, quoted in Charles Dickens, *American Notes*, 1842

Miss Wight says that Julia will be here any minute, and that I must dress to see her. Julia has returned from New York today a month early, the cook told Miss Wight, *and without Doctor*. I wish that I could have a cameo of Doctor's head to wear as a brooch on the lace collar of my black day dress above my silver cross. And then at night, alone in my bed, I would push the pin of the brooch right through the skin in the hollow of my neck so that his dear face would stay with me the whole night long and I could run my fingers over his raised likeness and never sleep. My companion, Miss Wight, who lives with me here at the Institute, says they do not make cameos of men, but I don't understand why not. Everyone says that Doctor is the handsomest man in Boston—who would not want him as an ornament? I would carve the cameo myself if I could procure the ivory and a good, small knife with the money I've saved from sales of my piecework on Exhibition Days (oh, look: handkerchiefs embroidered by Laura Bridgman, the deaf, mute, blind girl), and then I might not suffer as unbearably when he's away—six months this time!

I know his features as well as my own: the strong, wide brow and bushy eyebrows; the long prow of his nose between the deep-set eyes; the bristly fur of mustache half covering his upper lip, and the plump lower lip that I have traced with my finger a thousand times but never met with mine. And his beard, Doctor's beard—I would spend an hour curling each hair with my blade all the way up to the prominent ridge of his cheekbones. Before I work the thick masses of curls for his hair, I might please him with my learning of phrenology—his decade-old passion—by rendering expertly each bump on his skull. Ah, there it is: the well-developed veneration bump right at the top between firmness and benevolence, evidencing the faculties of his divine creative spirit and his quest for the sublime. I round the twin bumps of ideality at his temples that display the disposition toward perfection, toward beauty and refinement in all things, and then notch the bulge of individuality between his eyebrows that sets them so far apart and him so far apart from lesser men. And the affection bump situated on the upper back of his head, so prodigious that the famous phrenologist, Dr. Fowler, cautioned him at thirty-five that he must find an appropriate object on which to indulge its vast benefits—dare I carve that affection with my little knife?

If I had been twenty as I am now, I think Doctor might have chosen me instead of Julia. Dr. Gallaudet and Mr. Clerc at the Hartford

Asylum for the Deaf both married students, and they were just silly, deaf girls—nothing like me, the star pupil of Dr. Samuel Gridley Howe, my own dear Doctor, of the world-famous Perkins Institute for the Blind. I was taught to read and write with Doctor's miraculous raised-letter books, visited by thousands, including Mr. Charles Darwin, and given an entire chapter in Mr. Dickens's *American Notes*. Mr. Dickens says that I am the second wonder of North America; apparently, only the roar of Niagara Falls is more impressive than what I have achieved in dark silence. But I was only thirteen when Doctor's affection bump forced him to choose an object, and look who he chose: Julia Ward, known for being in possession of all five senses and then some, and as the author of "The Battle Hymn of the Republic," an anthem that I understand from Miss Wight and others might be a fitting accompaniment for their married life! And anyone who has eyes to see confirms that Julia has not lost the weight from her last child, and that the fabled blond locks are now tricked out with gray. Gossip flies into my hands as easily as it does into the ears of others, and lands buzzing on my palm like flies.

Miss Wight shakes my arm. "Hurry," she spells into my palm. "Julia is waiting for you."

I would like to make her wait, but I am too anxious for news of Doctor. I tap my way exactly thirty-eight lady's steps down the corridor, then a sharp right, and twelve more through the foyer to the public room. My movements are very precise. I enter the room slowly, my head held so high that my bun almost slides down the back of my head, and am about to take the twenty-eight steps from the door to my visiting chair when the air directly in front of me is suddenly and violently disturbed. Julia has rushed me; she hugs me against her bosom. Though she has three children of her own, I think she fancies herself some sort of mother to me—does she not realize how I have blossomed and flourished so long and so far without my own mother, with only Doctor to meet my needs? And Miss Wight, a little, I suppose. I pull away from Julia quickly, holding her hand in mine, but at a full arm's length. Thank God she is no longer staying here at Perkins often, now that she is off waging campaigns with the suffragists and the abolitionists. I gather my skirts and settle into my chair by the hearth, angling it just so to catch the last of the November afternoon's warmth on my back.

"How was your journey?" I spell into her hand, but before she can switch hands with me, I push on. "How is Doctor? When does he arrive?"

Julia writes a few words about her trip into my hand with her stubby fingers, not half the length of mine. Her fingers feel thicker than on last visit, and it is curious to me that her palms always sport light calluses; even Miss Wight, a lady of much lesser station, has no calluses. Julia spells as slowly as my uneducated visitors from the country, and it is clear she should stick to writing songs because a book would take her twenty years at this slug's pace.

And then finally, in answer to my question: "Doctor Howe will be arriving a week from tomorrow."

"Only a week, not a month?" I quiz her palm, thrilled that I might touch him so soon but anxious that I have so little time to prepare.

Yes, a week tomorrow, she assures me, and now she is scratching on about her projects. I am Doctor's pet, and so she must have her own: repressed women and slaves. I feel a simultaneous affinity and disgust for both.

"Laura, you should speak out on these important humanist topics on Exhibition Days; you have a grand platform from which to share your views. You can write on your chalkboard for the crowds who come to see you, and influence people from all over the world."

"On Exhibition Days," I scribble as fast as I can, knowing she can't keep up and will only understand the half of it, "Doctor likes for me to demonstrate my knowledge of geography,—SAUSAGE—reading comprehension—FINGERS—, and to show my penmanship, needlework, and ability to recognize people by their hands."

"But, L," she spells now, using only an L for "Laura" because either she is lazy or mistakenly believes that I must hold her in affection (only Doctor and Miss Wight do I *allow* to diminute me that way), "surely you care that women and Negroes should be free."

"I AM NOT FREE," I write, pushing down so hard that my nails press into her palm. "I am not free to even BE a woman like you."

"Of course you are a woman," Julia's fingers press equally hard and slide on the valleys of my palm, which has begun to sweat. This almost never happens; I use a dusting of powder to keep my hands fresh and dry, and take pride in my coolness to the touch. No, it is Julia's hands that are wet and polluting mine! I pull my hands away and wipe them slowly and deliberately on the folds of my skirt.

"You are all black to me," I write. "Everything is dark to me, and everyone is the same. I think it is the same for God." I wish I were brave enough to rip off the fillet that covers my eyes, to force Julia to see what I cannot.

Julia is excited, the tips of her fingers nearly dripping. "You could write that next week for the visitors," she spells. "Exactly that."

"Ask your husband," I telegraph back, and her hand waits, and then falls away. I wonder about the bumps on her head, if Doctor finds them all pleasing. I reach up suddenly toward where I think the top of her head will be, but instead my fingers catch her on the ear, and I hold it for a second, bending the soft, pliable rim up and down, marveling that through this sweet little maze she is able to hear, to let in the whole world, and most of all, the multitude of Doctor's sounds, his laughs and sighs. I know how to laugh, too—I laugh a lot—it is apparently the one thing I learned to do well as a baby before the scarlet fever robbed me of four of my five senses. And Doctor says my laughter is a beautiful sound, like angels' beating wings, but as I hold Julia's ear, I make one of my other sounds, the ugly ones I am not supposed to make, that Mr. Dickens wrote "are painful to hear." It is the sound I have felt from Pozzo, the Institution's dog, thrumming in the cords of his neck. I push my index finger hard into Julia's ear. I push it in again and again, and her hands are on my shoulders and on my elbow and so are Miss Wight's, and I could do it harder still, but I take my finger out of her ear and allow them to push me back into my chair. I feel the vibration in the floor as the guest chair is moved away from me, out of reach. I slow my breathing and extend both my arms into the air in front of me, my palms facing up in supplication.

I know I have been bad and that Miss Wight has gone to get the gloves, but I am sure Julia is still in the room, waiting. Yes, she takes my hands in hers, trembling, and I let her hold them before I tap on her knuckles to let me spell. I have slapped my teachers many times but never, ever, Doctor or Julia. I have slapped even poor, dear Miss Wight twice this year and I have grown accustomed, probably too accustomed, to asking for forgiveness from both the persons I have hurt and from God. My friends always forgive me, and so, too, I am certain, does God, but He absolves me only on the occasions when I am truly sorry. This is not yet one of those occasions.

"I am sorry if I hurt you," I write. "I pray I did not hurt your ear."

"A little," she spells back, "but I am fine. I didn't mean to upset you." Julia is taking this extremely well; I suppose that suffragists and abolitionists also get their dander up from time to time.

"I only wanted to feel for the bumps on your head," I tell her, and there is a pause before she answers.

"I do not much believe in the science of phrenology, as my husband does," she writes.

I am shocked; to my knowledge, no one has disagreed with Doctor on this, though I myself have had some doubts.

"If we are born with these bumps that govern our character, then how are we to grow and change?" She fills my hand with this, then waits.

I take a long time to gather my thoughts, unsure if I want to share them with Julia. "I think maybe," I pause and qualify myself further, this time careful to form each letter slowly and precisely so she will understand me fully, "maybe it is possible that phrenology interferes with the idea of free will."

"Yes, yes," Julia writes so emphatically and in letters so large that she traces the stem of the first Y on my wrist.

"Did Doctor give you a phrenological examination before you were married?" I ask her.

"Before we were even pledged," she writes back. Her fingertips bounce lightly up and down on my palm and I know she is laughing. "Dr. Combe said that my self-esteem was far too elevated. That was the bump of 'destructiveness' you were going for just above my ear, but don't worry, it was not destroyed."

I laugh, too, but then Miss Wight tugs on my arm and all I have time to spell is "Don't tell Doctor" without even a "please" before Miss Wight is pulling the gloves on my hands. Of course I have to be punished for what I did to Julia, but still she kisses me long on the cheek before she goes and I grab at her skirt. Just a touch, if only of her scratchy serge, before the glove isolates that hand.

"Tonight and all tomorrow," Miss Wight taps through the thick cotton of the glove. Everyone knows, even the little blind girls when they come sidling up and reach for my hands, that I am not allowed conversation when I am wearing the gloves. Though my punishment is deserved, it is worse than the solitary confinement cells in which they punish criminals, because not only am I cut off from all human

contact, I also lose all but the roughest impressions of the world itself. Touch, my one intact sense, and now it is thickened and furred
almost to nullity by the gloves, an item which on other young ladies
my age would mean they're going out for a stroll. No one can com-
prehend the multitude of pleasures I receive from my fingertips, the
hours I can spend stroking Pozzo's wiry, tangled fur, careening my
fingers down the long whip of his tail, rubbing the softness of his
firm belly. And the ladies' clothes! their silks and satins, even the
roughness of the out-of-towner's cotton broadcloths; the deep crush
of velvet collars and the short, nappy rub of their felt hats. And I am
never more stirred than when I find the sharp quill of a plume on a
hat and can run my fingers up and down the feather.

Miss Wight taps me on the shoulder, and I know I'm being sent
to bed early as further punishment. She takes my arm in hers and
walks me down the hallway to my room, but she writes nothing to
me tonight, not a word, and I know it's useless to ask her to spell out
Doctor's last letter again into my palm; of course, I have largely
memorized all his letters, anyway (*L—Yet another phrenologists' conference today—I ought to have my head examined!* and *The Parisians
feed their dogs at table,* but most of all: *Dear L, I miss you so.*).

I'm left alone to change into my nightgown, and it is the rule that
I cannot remove the gloves even for bed. For my worst punishment,
four years ago, I had to wear the gloves in bed every night for a
month, because someone—I am still not sure who, Miss Wight, or
to my greatest horror, maybe Julia, who was staying here because the
Institution was short of help for a few weeks—caught me in the act
of self-exploration. It wasn't the first time, and it certainly wasn't the
last, no matter how many times they've gloved me. I was on my
stomach (Tessy, one of the blind girls, let me in on that trick) since
of course I can't hear anyone coming, and if I am mightily preoccu-
pied—both hands down, as they were that night—then I won't feel

even the slight vibrations of movement from the wooden floor creaking. A sudden smack on my upper arm, and I pushed down my nightgown and turned over, my hands up, waiting for the intruder to write upon them. Instead, a fist came down on my forehead and "NO" was rapped across my brow by hard knuckles. I pulled the blankets up under my chin, and a minute later, a cold, dripping washcloth was flung at my face. Every night for the next month, the thick cotton gloves were left on top of my nightgown, and taken away again the next morning after I'd changed into my day dress. I made sure that the gloves were spotless, unspoiled each morning, but it was a struggle.

Though Doctor had delayed my religious education until I was sixteen because he was away often in Europe and did not want me tainted by the doctrines of Calvinism (he is an ardent Unitarian and does not go in much for the actual words of the Holy Bible), I begged him to raise the Bible for me, and after months of labor by the Institution's publishers for the blind, I was given the Bible entire, except for Revelation, which he has still refused to let me read. I have devoured that great book (I am a very fast reader), and have never found anything that I believe speaks against my explorations of my body. The spilling of seed is written against, but I don't see how that applies to me. And even if it does (Tessy is the only one who has ever explained the relations between men and women to me, and her effusive ramblings might have left me ill-informed, so I could be wrong on this point), I still contend that the unique condition which my Maker has forced upon me for His own unintelligible reasons might also grant me an exception—a special pardon, if you will—when it comes to touching. The sensitive, peaking nipples of my breasts, and that whole silken netherworld are God's gifts to me. My universe is manifest only through touching, and I refuse to be a stranger to it.

———

So if Doctor can't ever see his way clear of Julia and the trouble she causes him, then he must at least find me a suitable young man, soft-skinned and well-spelled, from among his vast acquaintance. Miss Wight has been promised to the Unitarian minister who has been visiting me; she will leave me soon for this man with deeply ridged fingernails. I am fair to pleasing, I think, dark-haired and pale; my features regular, only my nose a little long. "Petite," I have had spelled into my palm many times by visitors, and Mama says I am like a little bird. Who might not love a little bird, I am hopeful, even if it is locked in a dark and silent cage?

But I must remember to eat, to eat more; I vow to chew and swallow all three meals every day to fatten myself for Doctor. My bones poke through my skin, and I think it is much nicer to touch the soft plump pillows of Miss Wight's hands than to feel my birdy bones. It is so hard to eat, though, when I taste almost nothing; the fever that took my eyes and ears took even the senses of taste and smell. I move my jaws and grind my teeth and pass my tongue over the lumps of whatever it is that slides from the forks and spoons, but it seems a meaningless exercise. I would much rather dip my fingers into the warm pond of the soup and plumb its depths for legumes; rend the slick skin from the chicken and peel away the sheaves of muscle until I reach the hardness of the bone; tear the bread into a hundred tiny pieces and roll them into buttered balls I juggle over my plate; squish through the pliant mounds of the potatoes; ravage the soft pulp of the baked aubergines; and burrow both fists into pie I will never know the sweetness of. Soak the whole feast in milk. The only delights of food for me are in its destruction, and it so disappoints me that I can no longer indulge my play now, not at my age and not at my station in life as the world's most famous woman, second only to Queen Victoria (second only to *Julia!*), and certainly not with Doctor coming next week.

Yes, yes, he will see me fatter, and I will fatten my affection bump, too. I tried once before to elevate its standing at the top of my head by beating on it several nights with the ends of my knitting needles, but that increased it hardly at all. Now I have a whole week, and this time I will not shy from employing the best tools at my disposal: the heels of my Sunday lace-up dress boots. I slide from my bed and crawl along the floor to my closet, and there it is: one boot for my affection. Doctor arranged for Julia, after all, to undergo a thorough phrenological examination by the famed Dr. Combe before they were pledged, and so I will make certain that even to Doctor's less-trained eye, the enormity of my capacity for love will be impossible to miss. He hasn't seen me for almost six months, so I think he will not perceive my faculties as greatly changed, but only rendered more pronounced by his acute perception on the matter.

I take one boot with me to bed and pull up the blankets, leaving only the top of my head uncovered. I hit myself hard on the spot I have studied from the raised charts he has given me. Harder, harder, and it hurts, yes, it hurts, but it will be worth it. While I do not believe that my character, especially my ability to love faithfully and well, is sealed within the physiognomy of my skull, Doctor does, and so I rally my cause—Love! Love!—with each shuddering vibration through my temples and down my jaw. I move the heel of the boot closer to the front of my head and strike at the positions of benevolence and veneration, because I know that these are the qualities that impress Doctor most and these are his own largest visible faculties.

Today, today, Doctor arrives today, and I am ready! I have eaten all my meals this week, even asking for seconds on several occasions, much to the surprise and delight of Miss Wight and of the cook. I feel very cheerful and plump, no little bird, but a downy hen. I have been careful, ever so careful, to wear my cotton bonnet with the tie strings all week so that no one might observe the heightening of my bumps. I have used the excuse of helping to clean and scrub the premises for Doctor's arrival, because I always wear my bonnet when I clean so that no strands of my long hair might escape from my bun and be dirtied. Miss Wight was pleased because I am a very good cleaner and she likes to see me clean. I cannot see the dirt, of course, but if you sit me down in an area and give me some good rags and a bucket of soapy water, I will scrub and scrub until you tell me it is spotless. This quality will also prove me a good wife; the only bad thing is wearing the heavy cleaning gloves, but they are necessary to protect the softness of my hands, which Doctor will soon be touching, again and again.

I run the duster over the top of my armoire and let the feathers stroke the heads of my Laura dolls, all sixteen of them, the twelve-inch likenesses of me that were sold—with their eyes poked out and little green grosgrain ribbons tied over the eyeholes—across the country, and even in England, in the days when Doctor's educational exhibitions drew standing-room crowds. As I tickle the tiny molded toes of my Lauras, it occurs to me that if I am to have a *real* life— the *realest* life—then I must no longer allow myself to quicken with these constant reminders of my fame, and besides, I am too old to play with dolls, to hold mock teas for all my sixteen selves. The little girls who cuddled me are all grown up, and most of them probably have their own babies to play with now, as I intend to. Carefully, I take the dolls down from the armoire, and place them in a heap on the bed beside me. One at a time, I rock each Laura to sleep, humming a tuneless lullaby I'm sure would make a real baby cry, and before I push the dolls into the dark beneath my bed, I untie the ribbon from the sightless eyes of each porcelain head. I braid the ribbons into a thick, soft plait, and then fold it beneath my pillow because green will bring me luck.

Green is the color I remember with the most pleasure: green from the grass outside our house in New Hampshire. Blue still spills from that square of sky visible over the bed where I lay ill for almost a year. Mama says my eyes were bright blue before they shrunk behind my lids. Red I have a strong and disagreeable sense of, from when they bled me with leeches. And black, black I know the longest and best because it is my constant companion. These are the only colors I can recall or imagine with any clarity. It is yearning alone that shimmers in my darkness, and the shades of my deepest desires cannot be described, just as I am certain that the color that is God is not known to any man.

I pat the hands of my clock's glassless face over the armoire—it's almost time! The bonnet comes off and I check the bumps. They are raised and sore, the veneration one, especially; I hope they are not red. I've woken every morning with a headache from the boot's work, but the pain is nothing compared to gaining my share of life's affections. I arrange my hair in a low bun on the back of my head so that the bumps are shown to their best advantage. I have even taken the additional charge of plucking a few hairs from the tops of each of them, so that they might be seen more clearly. I change into my best Sunday dress, my only silk one—a rose pink *robe l'anglaise* that Miss Wight says gives me color—and lace up the dress boots that have nearly knocked me senseless. I slip the green fillet over my eyes and go to meet Doctor, as nervous as I have ever been.

I know that Doctor is not here yet; I can always tell when he is in a room—the air warms and condenses almost imperceptibly and its weight tilts me gently in his direction, as if I were borne aloft on the high end of a seesaw, but losing balance, sliding slowly toward him on the ground. I sit in my chair by the hearth, pinching at my cheeks to redden them, and wave away Miss Wight's attempts at conversation. I am almost faint with worry when suddenly the air shimmies with heat and I feel the floorboards tense and then shift heavily—Doctor at last! But he doesn't come near to me for a good ten minutes, probably talking with Miss Wight, and I force myself to wait patiently for him like a lady. I used to run whimpering to him like a puppy whenever he came in, but I have learned to wait, no matter how painful. Finally, the chair beside me is pulled out, and his hand takes mine.

"L," he writes, "you're looking very well."

I am shaking—he must notice—but I write the next line of our customary greeting. "Thank you, Doctor. And you?" It is our little joke, our routine, and now he lifts my hand to his face so that I may feel myself how well he is looking.

"Oh, yes," I write as I limn the familiar perfections of his profile, "you look very well." I round the tip of his nose just as he snorts out a laugh, and my fingers catch his delight. "How was your trip?"

He fills my hand with his travels even as he mouths them, allowing my fingers to float in front of his lips so that I can feel the different forces and velocities of the puffs of air as he exhales the names of places I will never touch: New York, London, and then in a warm fluff of breath, "Paris." "Paris," he says again—he knows the exquisite pleasure that the rushing air of any P gives me—and in my excitement, I rub my fingers against his lips. They are soft, but slightly dry; chapped, maybe from riding in the wind. I am pulling open the lower lip with two fingers when he grasps my wrist firmly and pushes my hand down into my lap. I am too bold today; I have never tried to open Doctor's mouth before. I can tell from the movement of his arm holding mine that he is leaning back and away from me.

"L," he writes, "what has happened to your head?"

"Nothing," I reply. "It is fine, as always."

"It looks like a woodpecker got loose on it. Maybe you have banged it on the bedframe."

That is what he sees—an *accident*? I cannot write a thing. My hand is limp under his heavy one and I don't even let my fingers stray across the beloved hairs on his knuckles.

"Dear L," he writes, as if composing a letter to me, as if we were still corresponding from a long distance apart, though I am trembling right here in his hands, "I have made a special trip back here just to speak with you."

And not to see your beloved wife? I want to write.

"After I returned from Europe, I took a train from New York to New Hampshire to see your family." There is a stiffening in his fingers, as if he's finding it difficult to write, and I worry that he might have contracted the rheumatism. Mama has it and she can scarcely bend her fingers to converse with me.

"Mama and Papa are well?" I ask.

"Of course," he spells. "They miss you very much, and we all think..." His fingers stop, only the heat of them hovering above my palm, and then he etches the words into my soul, firmly and furiously. "We all think it best if you go back to New Hampshire to live with them now."

My fingers panic; they scrabble all over his palm, paw at his arm; I am squeezing his hands, reaching for his face. Doctor pulls away until I stop moving and sit perfectly still, my hands shaking, but folded in my lap. What happened? Did Julia tell him I questioned phrenology, or that I hurt her ear? Did Miss Wight tell him? After an eternity, he reaches for my hand again and spells into it very slowly.

"Your education is finished here, L. We have nothing else to teach you."

I write as deliberately as he does, though usually we are both so quick with each other that no one else could possibly keep up. "Do you not see that I am ready, Doctor, that I am fit for finer things?"

"Do you mean a convent?" he writes, and I realize that he does not see me at all. I shake my head violently "no" and wipe at the wetness soaking through my fillet.

He pats my hand. "Good. I think you have too much temper for a convent."

His fingers strike again in the hollow of my palm, but I am thinking about my favorite Bible passage, Mark 7:32–34: "And they bring unto Jesus one that was deaf, and had an impediment in his speech; and they beseech him to put his hand upon him. And he took him aside from the multitude, and put his fingers into his ears, and he spit and touched his tongue; And looking up to heaven, he sighed, and saith unto him, 'Eph-phatha,' that is, Be opened."

Every night before I go to sleep, I put my fingers in my ears; I spit and touch my tongue and, looking up to heaven, I sigh and write the ancient word upon my hand. I spell it across my forehead; I open my thighs and write the letters down that slope, against that place, the only place, that is as dark and silent as the cave inside my head.

I pull my hands away from Doctor and stand up. "Eph-phatha," I write across the width of Doctor's forehead, between the temples of his ideality, and I laugh because I have finally spelled a word he does not know. I run to the door—it is far fewer steps than twenty-eight when I am running—and down the hallway to my room.

I want to write this all out, but I am denied the pleasure—or pain—of ever being able to read my own words. Doctor will be able to read them, others will be able to read them, but I will not. So I write this out into the air, in a grand and looping cursive, and what is invisible to man will be visible to God.

PEYTON MARSHALL

University of Iowa

BUNNYMOON

I stood in my filthy overalls and boots serving deviled eggs to a drunk woman who had lost her rabbit.

"My dear," the woman said. She knelt on the floor and peeked under the dust ruffle of the couch. "A lady should take care with her appearance." A small flowered hat with a veil was pinned to her hair. "I'm talking about hygiene," she said. "That's what I'm talking about."

"I don't work here," I said. "I live here, or my parents do."

"Well, good, then you can get me a flashlight." The hat bobbed as she crawled along the length of the couch. "Pooks," she called. "Pooks!"

I looked for the flashlight in the kitchen pantry, but it was missing from its hook. Through the window I saw my mother and several other ladies standing around a makeshift wire pen in the backyard. Rabbit cages were stacked on the picnic table. Christmas lights circled the fence and in the heat of late afternoon they gave off a pink glow. The ladies were drinking punch and introducing rabbits to each other. It was serious business. They called themselves the House Rabbit Society.

I leaned on the kitchen counter and poked at the plate of deviled eggs. I purposely hadn't changed out of my overalls. I wanted to grab my mother by the shoulders and shake her but this was the next best thing: dressing for the job we were ignoring. I had come home to clean out Jared Woodson's place. He was my godfather and had been dead three months. His house had been on the market almost as long, and recently had been sold. Nobody had been inside since the funeral, not even his widow, Marelda. There was still flatware in the dishwasher, outgoing mail beside the door. As a child I spent a lot of time with the Woodsons. They had a daughter, Sarah, who died when I was six. I don't remember her.

"Pooks!" The woman in the living room was giving off little bursts of sound like a steam train. "Pooks," she cried.

"I'll be back in minute." I hurried down the hallway, past my father's office. Handel's *Water Music* played through the closed door. My father taught American history at the local community college and refused to have anything to do with rabbit matching. He called it the worst kind of optimism.

"Mom." I pushed through the crowd in the backyard and tugged on her elbow. She was wearing a T-shirt dress she had appliqued with rhinestones that shimmered as she moved. "Some lady lost her rabbit and needs a flashlight."

Mom squeezed my arm and pulled me close. "Look," she said. "It's happening." In the pen was an albino rabbit the size of a large throw pillow. It was Ralph-the-Unmatchable and he was grooming the back of a small doe.

"Not a good idea," I whispered. Ralph was a biter and a bully. Many times I'd had to carry him back to his cage in the garage, pinning him to my chest while his hind legs kicked in fear.

"They have love at first sight," Mom said. "Just like us."

There was a smattering of applause as the doe's owner pushed forward with a single cage. Ralph would be going home with her. It would be a bunnymoon to see if their affection lasted through the weekend. Usually, the friendlier rabbits were adopted quickly and Mom was left with an assortment of ornery and eccentric bunnies that fought and sulked and didn't get along with anyone. We had eight in the garage. She considered them her specialty.

"I looked for the flashlight in the pantry but it's not there," I said. "Any ideas?"

"Leave out some lettuce, silly." Mom tapped me on the end of the nose. "We don't chase what we can bribe."

"Nice."

"Just see how calm he is," she said. Ralph and the doe looked like two furry pom-poms in the cage. "Peace for the problem child." She refilled her glass with punch and walked away. My mother was small, almost child-sized, but she made up for it with what she called zip. Her body could move as fast as her mind, which gave her the sudden and precise movements of anger. There was no middle ground; it was stop and go. Sometimes she could not contain her own energy and would walk into a chair or a wall, then turn suddenly and knock over a lamp. As a child, I learned not to get too close.

Beyond the fence our yard extended for several acres. The property had once been part of a farm; the remains of a small apple orchard were visible on the side of the next hill. The trees were evenly spaced and mostly dead, branches bare and twisted as roots. They looked like trees planted upside down. My father had cut a few and sold the lumber but quit when he wrenched his back. He said there was a new understanding; he let the trees stand and they let him walk. A breeze traveled down the hill, ruffling the long grass as it approached. I felt suddenly dizzy, and the many voices became a mumble of sound. Ladies in their flower-print dresses looked like upholstered chairs wandering through the yard. I wanted to spend the summer in Eugene but Mom had called to say they needed me here. It would have been selfish to stay away.

A bug lantern hung beside the back door, humming. Invisible pests vaporized in a spark of green light and a small sound like a bedsheet tearing. Marelda Woodson stood underneath it and my mother rose on tiptoe to whisper something in her ear. My mother spoke with her hands darting in different directions as if casting a spell and the rhinestones on her dress sparkled. Marelda nodded, her face pleasant but shuttered. She was a large woman who wore rings on all her fingers and kept candy in her pockets. She was shy. She covered her mouth when she laughed, and usually after speaking she would wave her hand in the air to brush away her words. She moved in with my parents after Jared's funeral and took over my old room. It was still intact, the same posters, the same furniture, but it had a new smell to it: lavender and dust and something sour. Last night, as I lay on the sleeper couch, I heard her moving above me, making all the sounds I used to make.

Jared died mowing the lawn. Marelda found him lying in the grass, staring at the sky. The mower had traveled on without him, stopped by the fence, where it caught at an angle and tore a hole in the earth. It was an old mower, made before safety releases. After the funeral I stood in the backyard and examined the swath cut into the grass. It looked like someone had tried to burrow under the fence.

The hat-lady was not in the living room and I did a quick check of the first floor but couldn't find her. I ate a deviled egg that went down like a salty piece of rubber, then put the rest in the refrigerator. Handel had progressed to the more triumphant movements of the *Water Music*. My father called them the splashy parts. I knocked on his study door.

"Is it over?" He looked up from his desk. Paper had accumulated in stacks, forming a horseshoe around him.

"They're still at it," I said. "Ralph found a friend though."

"Not a pot of boiling water?"

I shook my head. "You haven't seen a lost rabbit recently?"

"Not recently." He took off his glasses and rubbed his forehead. "Lord, the things your mother gets into. She wanted to move the beasts into the pantry. You know we don't even park in the garage anymore. She says the carbon monoxide damages their brains. Can you imagine?" He set his glasses down and positioned himself for a lecture. "Rabbits have no real memory," he said. "They lack the ability to imbue the present with any sort of context. Do you know what that means?"

"Bliss?"

"It means they have no hindsight. Without that there is no interpretation of suffering, no contemplation." His eyes were far away. I knew the look. I could leave the room midconversation and hear him continuing from the hall. "They are content. The present is overwriting memory until there is no brain to damage. If their nervous systems were any keener they'd all expire from anxiety and still this means nothing. One day I *will* walk into the pantry for a can of soup and find one of the little beasts..."

"Then you can eat its delicious, undamaged brain."

He stopped to look at me. "Yes, there is that."

I had learned to feed him his own sarcastic humor. When he was off in his world it seemed only something from that strange planet could get his attention. My father lived in an invisible place of yesterdays, where all the moments of history were more interesting than this one. Details did not concern him. Matching socks, clean clothes, vacations—they were too small to register. Mom bought him gray suits and blue sweaters, all neutral colors that could be haphazardly matched. He wore clip-on ties of muted stripes and plaids. Once I gave him a tie that had a pornographic picture hidden inside the folds of fabric. I liked knowing something he didn't.

My father wanted me to be a history major. I had always been careful to get good grades in subjects that were important to him, and now he believed I had a natural aptitude. It crushed him to see me "waste the talent." For the past year I had been studying English at the University of Oregon. I read everything I could. I enjoyed writing papers and arranging ideas. But recently I had become aware that my work could never be real work. I wrote papers on texts that everyone wrote about. I came to unsurprising conclusions with ordinary observations. None of my ideas contributed to a larger understanding. There was a level on which a mind could really live and then there was a level on which it could merely function.

The party went late. There were only two rabbits to match after Ralph, but it wasn't going well. Mom had eight males in the garage and I carried them out one by one. The ladies roared their disapproval whenever a bunny bit or scratched. Polo was the latest disappointment. He was white with a gray spot shaped like an alligator. As I carried him back to his cage the women clucked and shook their heads.

"Coming through," I said.

"Oh, honey, there you are." My mother was waving me over. A man in a suit stood beside her. He wore cufflinks in the shape of golf clubs, but the rest of his attire was conservative, as if he could only allow himself small extravagances. A briefcase sat wedged between two polished loafers, no pennies. "This is the nice gentleman who sold Marelda's house." Mom patted his arm. "And what a fine job he's done."

"Thank you," he said. He squinted at Polo, whose paws protruded in front of me like a pitchfork. "So, what is it, exactly, that you're doing?"

"We're having a party," my mother said.

"Of course." A small wrinkle appeared between the realtor's eyebrows. "Won't keep you then. I just wanted you to know that the doorknobs are still missing."

"Not missing," Mom said. "We have them."

The realtor picked up his briefcase. "If you don't mind, I'll just drop them off."

Mom rested a finger on her chin and tapped. "I can't recall exactly where they are," she said. "Greg put them somewhere. I'm sure he had them when we changed rugs for the summer." Mom gave me a little wink.

"Greg?" The realtor pulled a gold pen out of his pocket. "How do we get ahold of him?"

I stared fixedly at the top of Polo's head. There was no way to get ahold of Greg. He was my nonexistent boyfriend, my mother's creation, forever on his way into town, in traffic, delayed, circling in a perpetual holding pattern. Mom dropped his name in front of men she considered "suitable bachelors." She said competition made a woman's stock go up. I felt depressed to think the most attractive thing about me could be someone else.

"Well." Mom suddenly lifted her hands in the air, almost knocking the realtor in the face. He took a step back. "We'll just call him in Seattle," she said. "Really, he's the most wonderful boy. Have you met Greg?" The realtor shook his head. "He's Gracie's young man. Very handsome. Almost a lawyer."

I took Polo to the garage and set him in his cage. He hunkered into a sullen ball. The other rabbits shifted nervously, noses like pistons. There was only one window in the garage and it was on the wall above the cages. Sunlight made a square on the floor and during the day it moved slowly in front of the rabbits, always within their sight but never touching them. I scooped fresh kibble into the food dishes and removed the trays beneath the cages. I tapped them over the garbage can, then lay fresh newspaper. Mom kept stacks of papers that collected faster than they were used. I spread open a front page. A young, clean-cut boy who could have been Greg stood behind a podium. I lay him in the tray, face up.

Greg was twenty-four and studying law in Eugene. We weren't living together and he often traveled because his mother's family still lived in Italy. I fed his cats. Greg was more believable than my real boyfriend, who smelled of coconut lotion and conducted conversations with a Brazilian parakeet, whose name he often changed. We were freshmen and lived in the same dorm. I was his sometimes girlfriend, the default when nothing else was working. I wasn't as lovely as his other girls, but felt that was something I could make up for if I knew the right way to be. I thought the real boyfriend was a secret code and if I took notes, treated him like a class, then I could learn the language and ace the exam. I laughed at his jokes, even the ones I didn't understand. I was clean and neat and keenly interested in anything he wanted to talk about. I agreed with his points of view until he told me it was boring to be right all the time.

"You're right," I said. It slipped out.

There would be no Greg if Mom knew about the real boyfriend. Her willingness to embellish Greg was a vote of confidence in me, a sign that I was still the right kind of person. The last night I spent with the real boyfriend, I awoke to him tapping my shoulder. "What?" I tried to sit up, but he wouldn't move and I had to struggle.

"Stop," I said. Sometimes he goaded me into fighting with him. I pushed at his hand. "I don't want to fight." I rolled off the edge of the bed and he followed, tapping my shoulder, palm flat as if he were dribbling a ball. I couldn't get away and he wouldn't speak. He backed me down the hall into the little dorm kitchen. People watched. In the end, I hit him on the side of the head with a Tupperware bowl. He stood on a chair and called me an uncooked piece of pasta. He said I was the onion soup that made everything in the refrigerator smell. He said I was astronaut ice cream. I didn't understand.

Through the window I saw the realtor sniff a cup of punch, then toss the contents into the bushes. "Hello," he called and opened the door. "Marelda said the knobs were in here."

"She did?"

"She said Greg put them in the hutches." The realtor raised his eyebrows and pointed to the rabbits in cages along the wall.

"No, over there." A tarp was draped around a collection of moveable wooden hutches. I peeled it back. They smelled of urine and mildew and I pretended not to notice. "We used to keep the rabbits outside in these," I said. "But stray dogs began sleeping underneath. They ate a few of Mom's finest and gave all the rest heart attacks."

"Huh."

"Well, not all." I spun several of the hutches around and started opening doors. Most of the cages were empty, but a few held assorted tools and bicycle parts. "Did Marelda say anything else? Are they in a bag, a box?"

"No," the realtor said. "Look, if this is going to be so impossible I'll just buy new ones."

"You can't. New ones aren't made with spindles." I had been using a knife to turn the door latches at Jared's house, wedging it slantwise into the exposed square of the mortised lock. "Modern hardware is too big. You'd have to redrill the doors." I stood up and pulled a cobweb out of my hair. "They're not here."

"Maybe you could call Greg."

"He's in Italy."

"You mean Seattle." The realtor developed a blush of irritation. "What is going on here? I have the buyers arriving from New Zealand on Monday!"

"Don't yell at me." I banged one of the hutch doors closed. "I'm not your client. You're as much to blame as my mother, or anyone else. The house has been on the market for months and it looks like crap. If you needed doorknobs so badly, then why didn't you take care of it in March? You're the realtor."

"I'm not *the* realtor, I'm *the fourth* realtor." His hands on his hips, he drew his coat back like wings. Bunnies shifted in their cages. They didn't know when they were safe. "I've been working for Mrs. Woodson two weeks. She won't pay for upkeep, won't write the fees into the contract. I don't mean to alarm you, but your mother and Mrs. Woodson are..." He looked at the ceiling. "Perhaps the loss of Mr. Woodson has caused a disturbance."

"Of course it has."

Outside there was a chorus of cheers. The realtor frowned. "Why are there so many rabbits everywhere?"

I sat on the porch of the Woodson house while Mom and Marelda fought over the house keys.

"It looks like this one but it's nickel." Marelda flipped through a prickly mace of keys.

I sipped my coffee and stared at the yard. The flower beds were overgrown, but I recognized several pieces of garden art. There was a squirrel, a mole, a chipmunk, all cut out of wood and painted with friendly, human expressions. They were planted in the ground like signs. Their real counterparts were not welcome. A loose shutter hung from the wall at an angle, like a saloon door. Viney tentacles twined the porch pillars, and orange poppies bloomed in the cracks in the stairs. All the time and care the Woodsons had put into their home had come to this in a matter of months; every effort was easier to undo than maintain.

Mom snatched the keys out of Marelda's hands. "Give me those, you old biscuit. I'm not standing here all day."

"It's one of the square ones." Marelda hovered, impatiently waving her hand. "Pull it toward you," she said. "Here. It's my door."

Inside, the house was just as I remembered it. A corkboard of messages hung above the telephone table in the hall. There was the same braided rug on the living room floor and yellowed doilies on the backs of overstuffed chairs. A soda bottle stood on the windowsill, rubber bands looped around its neck. They were part of Jared's collection of useful things he never used.

Marelda pulled a calendar off the corkboard and stuffed it into a trash bag. "I'll be glad when a year is gone and there are no more firsts. I hate the firsts."

"We're recycling paper, remember?" Mom crossed the room with an armful of magazines and dropped them on the carpet. "We'll start piles. Whites, mixed, and glossies." She pointed to spots on the floor.

I set my coffee on the sideboard and tugged open one of the drawers. It was filled with wooden thread bobbins, pen caps, and knife handles with the blades broken off. Strips of cardboard divided them and several neatly bowed shoelaces lay on top. Jared collected things that had become separated from their more useful halves. When I was a child he took me to yard sales to look through free boxes. That was where he found his "orphans" as he called them, all the things people didn't mind losing.

I knelt and opened the bottom drawer. It hummed with china and made the delicate rustle of a dinner party. Inside were sugar bowl lids. Some were painted, or scalloped, some antique and so fine they were translucent, but most were cheap, ordinary dime-store china.

Jared said people valued things they couldn't easily have. He called it the power of paucity. I picked up a lid with cuneiform writing and a wing painted along one side, part of a now missing bird in a now missing picture.

"Who will want these?" I asked.

"Junk is junk." My mother paused in her paper sorting to thumb an old magazine. "Yesterday's news," she said.

Marelda looked at the nest of lids in the bottom drawer. "I told him there was no point in saving things, but he said he'd change my mind or die trying." Marelda took the lid out of my hand and scraped at the paint with her nail. "He said that about everything though."

Mom spent the morning moving debris from one end of the room to the other. She had the darting swiftness of a hummingbird. Drawers were opened and contents spilled onto the floor. Marelda wandered through it slowly, looking at things, then putting them down. She whistled bars from different songs, the excerpts so short there was no discernible tune. A few times I noticed her standing in the corner playing with her rings. "Did it look this awful when I lived here?" she asked and we said no.

We decided to put pictures on one end of the couch, books-to-keep on the other, important papers in the middle, and hats and coats on the floor in front. But despite our resolve the room became a salad of items; piles fell into piles. It was as if the drawers and bookshelves had been compressing their contents—and now that it was all out in the open everything was swelling.

I sat in Jared's recliner and stacked the sugar bowl lids inside a laundry basket lined with newspaper. The shape of Jared was imprinted on the cushions, but the weight of my body was slowly distorting it. When I was younger, Jared used to take me sailing on Puget Sound. I drank sodas and let my feet dangle in the water. Salt dried to my skin and I poked jellyfish with the butt of a fishing pole. Jared talked the entire time, explaining what he was doing, showing me how to tie a boson and fold a sail. I was allowed to know his thoughts. It wasn't until I was older that we grew apart. There was less to say and our time was reduced to obligatory holiday visits and family dinners at which we were all polite, inquisitive, and cautious. I folded newspaper around several of the finer china lids, smearing my hands with ink. It seemed wrong to miss Jared now when I had not missed him before.

I was in the car with Marelda and Sarah on the day Sarah died. Marelda was making a turn when another car ran the light. Sarah and I were in the back seat. I had no memory of the accident, just a fabricated image of the metal car door swelling inward like a bubble, moving through Sarah as it strained toward me.

For a while after the accident I stayed with the Woodsons when my parents took trips or evenings out. Marelda and Jared bought me puzzles and dolls and a pair of roller skates. They came to school plays and recitals. They vacationed with us at the beach. But I was always aware of Sarah, her picture perched on the mantel, or magneted to the refrigerator. Her eyes followed me and at Christmas and birthdays I felt I was opening her presents, eating her cake, enjoying her happiness. I had her parents' love and I felt the responsibility to be as good as she would have been, to live a happy life, and prove there had been no mistake on that afternoon in the car when we chose seats.

"Maybe we should rethink this," I said. "Why don't we start in the basement and sort things in the backyard. If we make a mess on the main floor everything will be harder."

"We're not making a mess," my mother said. "Marel, are you making a mess?"

"Not me."

At the basement door I reached for the doorknob before realizing it was gone. "Shit." I rubbed my face. "Why exactly are there no doorknobs?"

"It frustrates thieves," Marelda called from the living room.

"It frustrates me." I rummaged through the silverware drawer for a knife to turn the latch. Mouse droppings dotted the countertop; on the windowsill above the sink was a gauze of spider web glowing like thin cotton in the morning light. Marelda watched from the doorway. "How did you show the house with no doorknobs?" I asked.

"I didn't show it."

"I know, but the realtor did."

"Not many people wanted to come inside."

"Why didn't you trim the lawn?" We stared at each other. Wisps of hair had come loose from her braid and stuck out like whiskers.

"Would you like a peppermint candy?" she asked.

I shook my head. "At least have a sale."

"It would kill Jared to see his things paraded through the streets."

Mom was suddenly standing beside me, parting curtains and tugging at blinds. The air lit up with reflective dust. "I don't want strangers in here poking and pawing," she said. "People get so smug when they smell a bargain."

"We're not concerned with other people right now." I tossed the knife on the counter. "You don't want to donate or sell anything. You don't want to junk it and we can't store a whole house in our basement. So what is the plan?" I felt a squeeze of panic. Marelda put things off. She was always making lists and losing them. Mom wasn't normally like that; she was irritated by untidiness. It was as if their personalities were contaminating each other. I looked at Marelda. "How can you get a place of your own if the money from your estate is tied up here? Don't you want a home?"

"You're clucking like a silly bird," Mom said, pulling aprons out of a drawer.

"Why did you have me come home if you don't want my help?"

"You didn't have to come." Mom handed an apron to Marelda, then draped a frilly calico around my neck and stood behind me to tie it. "We told you it would be a tight squeeze with the four of us in the house."

"But you asked me to come."

"Did we?"

Marelda unwrapped a peppermint candy, and the crackling cellophane sounded like the continuous rustle of a small fire. I must have looked confused because she reached out and squeezed my arm. "Of course, we're happy you're here," she said.

Sarah's photo watched from the wall. She was laughing, standing in a sandbox in a crinolined sundress. She looked perfect. I was beside her and we both had our shovels raised. It was the favorite picture, reproduced so many times the negative was gone. Now there were only copies of copies.

"It's just..." I shrugged and forced a laugh that sounded somewhere between a squeak and a hiccup. "Well. I can't believe you waited until the last minute, is all."

Mom made a show of checking her watch. "I choose to take that literally and since this is not, in fact, the last minute before the sale, your accusation is false and you would be right to disbelieve it. There," she smiled. "We both win."

The metal center beam under the sofa bed seemed to be rising. I moved my pillow and lay the wrong way on the mattress, avoiding its middle. The floorboards in Marelda's room squeaked and then there was the rumble of something being dragged. I imagined it was the chair I hung my clothes on in high school. I saw its legs scratching above me like a claw.

Unable to sleep, I went for a jog. I started in the orchards behind the house and slowly made my way up the hill. Dogs barked in the distance. Strays still roamed this area, getting into garbage and evading capture. The man next door had started shooting them with an air rifle and now the dogs stayed far from the houses. On the other side of the orchard was a newly laid road. It was the beginning of what was to be a neighborhood, but construction had halted when money ran low. Stakes with orange ribbons were driven into the ground, and bright painted dashes marked future utility lines. There were already streetlights and as I passed them my shadow appeared beneath me, then leapt ahead before dissolving again.

I turned onto the main road. There wasn't a sidewalk, so I ran in the middle of the street. Two miles north was the old pioneer cemetery. Many of the headstones were white squares set into the earth. In the moonlight it looked as if a kitchen floor had been broken apart and scattered, tile by tile, across the grass. The newer sections had mausoleums like miniature churches and midcentury graves with angels, their features blunted by rain and pollution. I slowed my pace. The heavy heads of sunflowers curved over the cemetery fence.

Sarah's headstone was a small toast-top sticking out of the ground. A carved rose bloomed beside her name. Next to it was a larger stone; the words Jared Robert Woodson were cut in a curly script. I crouched and traced my hand across the letters. Below his name was Marelda's with her birth date and a dash into empty space.

A police car turned onto a small road that ringed the cemetery; a spotlight meandered back and forth. Every year vandals knocked over headstones and spray painted monuments. Now the cemetery was off limits after dark. The car crept closer. I lay on my stomach. The grass was full of little whispery touches. The spotlight swung over my head several times, and then the white circle slipped away over the ground.

When I got home, I showered. I sat hunched at the bottom of the tub, letting the water strike my back and head. I didn't bother with shampoo. I had to brush my teeth in the bath because the sink pipes knocked and everyone was asleep. Through the fog on the mirror my face was blurred and full of shadows. I wrapped myself in a towel and shuffled into the hallway, clutching my sweaty clothes in a ball. The door to my old room was slightly open. The rug was dark with pale flowers, and the familiar pattern glowed in the moonlight.

I nudged the door open a little wider, slowly pressing so as not to make a sound. Marelda's shoes were in orderly pairs along one wall. They were all sensible, low heeled. A ribbon won at a history-a-thon was taped to the vanity mirror and had been since seventh grade. I stepped into the room and Marelda rolled in her sleep. I waited for my eyes to adjust. Marelda was on her back, arms folded across her tummy, and my mother was next to her. They were both under a single sheet and Mom's foot was pressed to Marelda's ankle. I stared at the exact point where they touched. It was a small surface area, three square inches at most. Their breathing was shallow, their bodies completely still.

Probably Mom stayed up late talking with Marelda, or else Marelda had been weeping over Jared and Mom had overheard and come in to comfort her. There were no tissues on the floor or by the side of the bed. It didn't mean anything, I thought. A green plastic cup sat on the nightstand. There was an electric alarm clock behind it, and the cup glowed with an eerie light. I thought of the Tupperware bowl and the real boyfriend's face as I hit him with it. He had been more surprised than hurt.

Someone was pounding on the front door. I rolled off the sofa bed and staggered into the hallway. The sudden brightness of the day made me squint. My mother was in the doorway talking to a woman carrying Ralph in a small cage. "He bit Alfalfa. She's having her ear sewn."

"Oh, dear!" My mother took the cage and handed it to me. Ralph's weight shifted inside. I heard my father typing in his study.

"I'm so sorry," my mother said.

"I'll be sending you the veterinary bill." The woman narrowed her eyes. The morning light shone through her hair. "You could have warned me he was extremely aggressive."

"I'm sure you're exaggerating," my mother said. "Ralph isn't capable of real harm."

"I need proof of a rabies vaccination."

"Of course he's vaccinated."

"I can't just take your word for it. I need to see a piece of paper!" The woman was inching into the foyer.

"Well, I don't have a piece of paper!" My mother rose to her tiptoes, the way she did when she was mad. "Please get ahold of yourself!"

The keyboard suddenly went silent and my father padded down the hall. He stood behind Mom, his hands resting on her shoulders. In some ways everything seemed normal. My parents were together and I was their daughter, standing in the hall wearing pajamas, watching their lives play out in front of me.

"You must put him down." The woman pulled a handkerchief out of her sleeve and dabbed her nose. "I'm insisting!"

"No," my mother said. "If Ralph has rabies then Alfalfa has it too and you'll have to do her as well."

"Are you threatening the life of my bunny?" the woman snapped.

"Everybody calm down." My father stepped between them. "I'll put the old chap out of his misery. I've been wanting to do it for years."

"Absolutely not." Mom glared at him.

My father took the cage out of my hands and held it up to his face. Ralph's eye glimmered like a dollop of strawberry jam. "What a rabble rouser you are," he said. "A regular Nathan Hale. And we all know what happened to him."

The woman backed out of the driveway too quickly and scraped her muffler. My mother said, "It serves her right."

Marelda was eating a waffle in the kitchen. She was standing in front of her chair, fork in hand. "What's happened?" she asked. "I was going to help, but I thought I might be in the way."

My father set Ralph's cage on the counter and poured a mug of coffee. I sat at the table and rubbed my face. The muscles were asleep, resting on top of my bones like warm clay. A triangle of toast sat on a plate in front of me. A single bite was missing.

"That woman," Mom said, pointing toward the door, "was in here yesterday eating my food and cooing about what a lovely time it was. A small disappointment and suddenly..." She bumped the table, making juice sway in the glass. "Nothing is good enough."

"I think you handled it very well," Marelda said. "There is no reasoning with someone in that state. Besides, she's a new member. We won't miss her."

My father rinsed his mug and set it on the dish rack. His movements were brisk and precise.

My mother frowned. "You're not doing away with my Ralph."

He said, "That woman has the wrath of righteousness about her. I wouldn't be surprised if she called the humane society and shut you down."

"They only shut down animal farms," Mom said.

"My point." Dad stuck his finger between the cage bars and petted Ralph's flank. "Rather a handsome fellow don't you think? You can't get laundry that white."

"I take good care of my animals!" Mom held on to the back of Marelda's chair.

"Yes, but you can't save them all."

"It's true." Marelda squeezed Mom's hand. "You can't let one bad apple spoil the whole operation."

"Don't worry," my father said. "It'll be quick. A knock on the head." He rapped his knuckles against Ralph's cage. "A little barbecue sauce..."

Mom walked out the back door, letting it slam. My father watched her and I imagined him waking up this morning, reaching to her side of the bed and wondering where she had gone. He put on a straw hat and tightened the string under his chin. He liked to wear hats and Mom insisted on straw in the summer. It was neutral. It went with everything.

Then it was just Marelda and me at the table. I sat on my hands to stop fidgeting, wondering how soon I could leave without being rude. "Did you sleep well?" she asked.

"Yes," I said. Now I was supposed to ask her how she slept. I looked at the toast on my plate.

The house was empty. I packed my suitcases, then took out everything and repacked. I folded away the sofa bed and tidied the room until it looked like a living room again. It was what I would have done if I had been a guest. "Always make your bed," Mom told me. "A hostess will remember." I was reverting to manners—they were a simple code, easy to decipher and use. Polite was always the right way to be.

I cleaned the kitchen, rinsed dishes, and put them in the washer. I picked burned pieces of batter off the waffle iron with a plastic spoon that wouldn't gouge. I took leftover hors d'oeuvres, deviled eggs, and almost-too-soggy cucumber sandwiches, and condensed them on smaller plates in the refrigerator. Eventually I heard typing through the study door. It was a lonely sound, full of starts and stops, the rhythm of my father's thoughts. I brought him a cup of tea and he thanked me.

"How did it go with Ralph?" I asked.

"He was a good sport."

"Dad!"

"Do you really want to know?" His reading glasses made his eyes small in his face. I shook my head. "Don't get soft like your mother," he said. "You've got to be a little bit ruthless to keep things in harmony. That's how it's always been." He made a vague gesture to the books on the shelves behind him. Most were history texts and tattered collections of boring primary sources. They were little pillars of color, pinstripes of thought, and they all had their backs to me.

My father returned to work. His hands reached for the keyboard. I tried to think of something to say, something to make him stop and look at me. Nothing came.

In the afternoon I walked through the orchard, taking the long way to the Woodsons. I crossed the new road and wandered through the unfinished neighborhood. Plastic ribbons on stakes fluttered like scarves in the breeze. A mound of dirt sat beside the hole it came out of. Many trees were marked with an orange X; I didn't know if they would be cut or saved.

The realtor was knocking on the door of the house when I arrived. "I'm sure it's open," I said.

"Just being polite." He looked rumpled. His suit jacket had many little wrinkles in the back where it had been pressed to a chair. "I brought doorknobs." He held up a bag. "Old ones with spindles."

In his other hand he held the garden woodcuts—the squirrel, mole, and chipmunk. He had them by their metal spikes as if they were lollipops. "Just cleaning," he said. The paint on the woodcuts was worse up close, cracked and chipping. It made me realize how much of their features I'd been filling in from memory.

The living room looked the same, appalling in its disarray, but now the kitchen and hallway had followed suit: everything was on the floor. "Jesus." The realtor rested his hand on top of his head as if pressing himself into the ground.

"You haven't been here recently, have you?" When he didn't respond, I continued. "I know it looks bad, but really we're making progress. It's one of those worse-before-it's-better scenarios." I tried to kick a little path for us, and he clutched the bag of doorknobs as if they were in danger. "Hello?" I called. There was a hushed noise behind the door to the garage. "They're in here." We walked through the kitchen, and I nudged cans of beans and peaches out of the way with my foot.

Mom and Marelda sat in the middle of the garage, repressing giggles as they ate a frozen cake set atop an overturned bucket.

"What's going on?" I asked and they started to laugh. The realtor put both hands on top of his head and pressed. The garage was home to two large freezers and both were open. It looked like a dog had unpacked them. Food was strewn in melting piles, and puddles of water were soaking stacks of cardboard boxes. Three frozen chickens thawed atop Jared's workbench. Above the workbench, he had nailed lids of canning jars to the ceiling and then screwed the jars in place. Each one hung like a polished cocoon, full of screws and nails and bits of hardware.

"We're eating Marel's wedding cake top," my mother said. She had a spot of frosting on her cheek.

"All these years I thought it was chocolate," said Marelda. "But I guess that was some other cake at some other party."

"Would you like some?" Mom rattled a box with plastic forks. I declined.

The realtor stood very still. Today, he had pennies in his loafers. "This is impossible," he said. "You're making this impossible. Have you completely lost touch with the reality of this operation?"

"What do you mean?" Marelda licked frosting off one of her rings.

"Either you hire somebody to haul trash tomorrow or I quit."

"Greg will be here in a week," my mother said. "And he has a truck. Can you wait a week?"

"A week? The buyers will be here in a week! Jesus!" The realtor began to pace. Mom and Marelda swiveled their heads back and forth to watch him. "This is my first commission," he said. "The buyer's agent is a family friend. How am I going to explain this?" He gestured to the mess, throwing his arm as if he was tossing a Frisbee. "It looks like I've screwed up. It looks like incompetence."

Marelda stuck her fork into the cake and left it standing. "Well, I'm sorry for your personal problems," she said.

"Marel!" My mother nudged her. "Be nice."

"I am being nice! This young man just called me a batty old broad."

"He did not," my mother said.

"Yes, I did," said the realtor.

"Well." My mother gave me a quick wink. "Greg would never be so rude to a client." She raised a fork in a mock toast and suddenly she and Marelda looked like Sarah and me in the sandbox holding our shovels. There was a force animating them. They were happy. They were irresponsibly, unapologetically happy.

"Fine," the realtor said. I heard him kicking debris as he waded through the kitchen.

Mom said. "He's really not the caliber of man Gracie's looking for."

Marelda nodded. "Much too old to have a tantrum."

"What are you doing?" I asked, and they said, eating cake.

I stood on the porch with the realtor. He loosened his tie, then tossed the doorknobs into the weeds. "I don't know what to tell you," he said. "Maybe you should hire a lawyer. Papers were signed." He reached in his wrinkled suit coat and produced a business card. I stared at the little white rectangle. Behind him, the door to the house was open. In the living room were Jared's collections that I had sorted and stacked. They would all be orphans again.

My father was missing at dinner. Mom checked his study several times saying, "He's always here. I can't believe he's not here."

I said, "He's probably at the bookstore." I took Polo out of his cage in the garage and we lay in the backyard together. I waited for him to explore, but the world made him nervous. The sky was so far overhead. The yard was limitless, the fence a distant marker.

That night I dreamed of Sarah. It was a ghostly, nonspecific dream in which I heard many voices at once. When I woke, I found myself thinking about the favorite picture, the one of us in the sandbox, shovels raised. There were several copies in our house, but I wanted Jared's copy, the one on his kitchen wall. I unpacked my suitcase and found something other than the overalls to wear. I had a vague plan to drive to Eugene but didn't have any particular friends to stay with and not a lot of savings. Nothing was coming together. I didn't recognize my family and couldn't make sense of the changes. They were perfect, existing apart from the messy realities.

The morning was warm and dew soaked my canvas sneakers as I wandered through the orchard. Halfway up the hill I noticed two deep impressions in the earth, two parallel lines as if something large had been dragged. I followed the path into the northern corner of the yard where it was too wild to mow. There was a flash of color through the trees, and I made my footsteps light as I approached.

It was my father. I recognized the blue button-down shirt and the curve of his back. He was sitting beside one of the outdoor bunny hutches. The cage was padded with dish towels; a large lettuce leaf and several carrots lay next to a water dish. There was a hole torn in the mesh and a thin tuft of white fur caught like a dandelion head in the screen. Dog prints spotted the ground; their nails had bitten deeper than their paws. My father stared off into the trees, one hand resting lightly on Ralph, who was wrapped in a towel on his lap. A small white foot stuck out from the fabric like a handle. He was dead. I wanted to move forward, but there was no way to get closer without making my presence known. For a few moments I lingered, watching the small movements of my father's breathing, a slight quivering under his shirt.

I climbed the orchard hill and sat on the stump of one of the cut trees. It was a long time before my father emerged, dragging the hutch behind him. He towed it like a rickshaw, leaning forward to counter its weight, pulling it by the two wooden arms that used to fasten the hutch to other hutches. The wheels gouged and flattened the grass, and in that moment I loved my father, not as he would be, not as a ghost or as a perfect man, but as he was: troubled, alone, and forever mine.

MICHELLE WILDGEN

Sarah Lawrence College

HEALER

A garden locked is my sister, my bride,
a garden locked, a fountain sealed.
—Song of Solomon

The exit comes up sooner than Beth anticipated. She darts across three lanes of traffic, whipping her head over her shoulder to check each lane.

Today she's told Anne Marie to expect her around noon. "Mom and Dad are here," Anne Marie replied. "And some other people are probably coming over."

Beth knows who the other people are, in general if not specifically. People from Anne Marie's church, bearing zucchini bread wrapped in napkins, casseroles, jugs of milk, and whole roast chickens. Beth and Anne Marie's parents will be there. Often the five of them—their parents, Beth, Anne Marie, and her daughter Hannah, who's now two—spend the day on the deck by the pool. Anne Marie's husband, Gary, is still working half days, spending the rest of the time taking phone calls from work at home.

All summer their parents have brought a steady stream of people to the house: ancient priests lured from retirement—whose hands tremble and who seem abashed and exhausted within an hour—people who have lived through illnesses and who carry Bibles under one arm the same way Beth's high school students carry inked-up folders. They come trooping up the driveway, plates in hand. Beth greets them politely, nodding as her father gives a thumbnail sketch of each person's religious résumé, and then she excuses herself to check on Anne Marie's garden.

She's assumed responsibility for the garden. While prayer services go on she often crouches in the dirt, pulling up stringy weeds and eating cherry tomatoes off the vine. The sharp fragrance of the stems stays on her hands for hours.

Beth parks next to a red hatchback she doesn't recognize and is halfway up the front walk when her mother comes out the front door. They hug. Cynthia, Beth's mother, is a little rounder these days, her cheeks and wrists softer. She stands back and touches Beth's face. She looks Beth over and asks, "Are you losing weight?"

"Nope," says Beth. For a long time she perked up at this, jogging into the bathroom to check the scale. Somewhere around the age of twenty-two, she realized her mother says it the way other people say *It's good to see you.*

"I think maybe you are," her mother insists in a teasing sing-song. They walk toward the house. Cynthia straightens her sweater, her rings glinting in the sunlight against the pale gray knit. "More than you can say for me."

"You look great, Mom."

She's still taller than Beth, probably still slimmer overall despite the recent weight gain, but Beth can't really tell anymore. She knows she takes after her father, but she can't categorize herself the way she can other people. She supposes a stranger would see her father as pudgy. She thinks of him as rounded, once describing him to a friend by saying, *There's not an edge on him.* His eyes are soft and brown, his nose a distinct little bulb, even his hair is curly.

Her mother shakes her head, her dark hair swishing around her shoulders. It used to be blond but then she dyed it, going darker as she got older, and now it's mink brown. "It doesn't matter," she says. "What a silly thing to talk about now."

Inside it's cool and dark, the air conditioner running full blast. The week before it was broken, the weather so hot they'd stayed in the basement all day. Anne Marie watched Beth and their father play pool while upstairs Cynthia made soup to freeze. Halfway through the afternoon a storm thundered across the fields, pelting the house with hail and darkening all the rooms.

Anne Marie is sitting at the kitchen table, a wheeled rack behind her, holding the IV. She gestures at it with the arm that's not hooked up and says to Beth, "Almost done. Are you still going to do my hair?"

Beth bends down and gives her an awkward hug, half an arm, clasping her shoulder and avoiding the IV tube. She touches Anne Marie's hair. It's grown back in about an inch all over. "I feel like I haven't seen this color in so long," she says. It's only brown, but it seems pretty, suddenly. "Are you sure you want to ditch it so soon?"

Anne Marie rolls her eyes. She tugs at the towel around her neck with the needle hand and Beth winces. She can't stand to think of the needle moving beneath Anne Marie's skin.

"Dad already went out and bought the dye," Anne Marie says. She hands Beth a box with a very blond woman on the cover.

"Where is Dad, anyway?" Beth asks. "And who's here today?" She hears her voice rise at the end, an ironic lilt on the last syllable, and turns away because she's blushing. It's hard to rid herself of skepticism. But Anne Marie lets it slide.

"He's out back with Hannah and the priests," she answers.

Beth peers out the window, but the yard is empty; she gazes at the fields beyond—sometimes the stalks quiver with foxes, hunting crows perched in the corn. In a few months, in autumn, hunters will try to poach the wild turkeys that cross the dead fields.

Cynthia checks the measurements on the fluid bag and Anne Marie asks, "Done?" Cynthia nods and takes the tape off the back of her hand.

"Honey, eat some more of that fruit," Cynthia says, nudging a full plate a few inches closer. Anne Marie picks up a peach slice and nibbles at it. It's excruciating to watch her eat—a single berry, a sliver of peach. When their mother starts toward the door to get their father, Anne Marie shifts the plate toward Beth with a nudge of the back of her wrist, and Beth takes a handful of strawberries, half a peach, and chews like mad, her head down and turned toward the window in case Cynthia glances back.

Anne Marie knows, and their parents know, too, that insisting that she eat is a useless little farce, but they do it anyway. Anne Marie only tolerates the food that they push at her, but she seems genuinely glad to see the visitors when they first arrive. But when they get going on the healing power of prayer or soymilk, reserve drops over her face and her replies become rote. Anne Marie's churchgoing has definitely intensified since she got sick, but Beth can still see in her sister the shell of practicality that doesn't allow for miracle cures, or for the kind of resistance to God's will that constant begging might imply. The flustered visitors don't seem to realize that if there were anything that could be done—magnets, wheatgrass, fiber pills—Anne Marie would have done it. So Beth listens for the moment when someone mentions crystals or pilgrimages, and when it comes Beth redirects the conversation to movies or books. This is what she can do, maybe all she can do.

It would be nice to be a believer, to be able to share a few topics with Anne Marie that aren't fraught with pitfalls. Or to truly agree when she's nodding away politely. When Beth moved out of their parents' house, her churchgoing stopped for good, but Anne Marie kept going. Beth always pictured Anne Marie as the kind of jovial liberal Christian Beth might have been if she'd believed at all, but this turned out not to be the case.

Shortly after Hannah was born, they were kneeling by the bathtub, Beth holding Hannah beneath the arms while Anne Marie rubbed shampoo in her hair. They were talking half-seriously about the future when Anne Marie said, "Well, public schools are crazy. Sex is *every*-where. They're all doing it before they're thirteen." She cupped a hand over Hannah's forehead and splashed a trickle of water over her scalp. Hannah looked startled. "At least if she goes to Catholic school I'll be able to sleep." Beth laughed, shifting to get a better grip on Hannah's slippery ribcage. She was terrified of dropping her. "Yeah, a couple rosaries a day will just eliminate the sex drive," she said. Anne Marie turned off the water and reached for a towel. As she wrapped Hannah up she said, not looking at Beth, "I know you make fun of it."

Beth would never have guessed that her sister would become so conservative. She'd been modeling herself after what she thought was Anne Marie for so long that it was a shock to find she had turned into someone else altogether. Beth was always just missing the mark. In college she drank tequila on road trips to the beach with her girl-friends and considered a tattoo, all the time convinced that Anne Marie would think it was hilarious, but when she reported back to her older sister, Anne Marie merely said, "I wish you were more careful."

Once Anne Marie was pregnant with Hannah, they no longer drank beer at noon or cocktails before dinner. Instead they set glasses of filtered water on stray breast pads they used as coasters and rubbed their dry winter hands with lanolin nipple cream. The difference is that Beth remembers her old ways—and her sister's—fondly and Anne Marie does not. "So you were wild," Beth said last week, when her sister made a disgusted face over an old photo. Beth had leaned over her shoulder and stared at the picture. It was a party in someone's yard, and Anne Marie was holding a can of beer and a cigarette, her long hair gauzy in the sunlight. "So what?" Beth asked. "Everyone who wasn't wild just wishes they were." "I was miserable," Anne Marie answered. "None of it was really any fun."

Anne Marie rubs the back of her hand where the needle was. Beth starts to say something, but then says instead, "I got another speeding ticket the other day."

Anne Marie smiles at the table and starts to get up. "Isn't that the third one this summer?" she asks. "You better pace yourself."

"I guess. Are you ready?" Beth asks. She runs the faucet in the sink, letting the warm water flow over her wrist. She tears open the box and lines up the tubes on the counter. Anne Marie makes her way over, her hands skimming along the chairs.

"Can you stand long enough?" Beth asks. Anne Marie nods. "I'll be quick," Beth promises.

Her sister smiles. "No," she says, bracing her hands on the counter and bending toward the faucet. "Be luxurious about it. And give me a neck rub while you're at it."

A year ago this time Beth shaved off her sister's hair before it could fall out. She sat Anne Marie down here in the kitchen and surrounded her with newspapers. They'd borrowed an electric razor from a church friend of Anne Marie's who worked in a salon. The friend was afraid to do the shaving, so Beth volunteered. She did it in neat strips, running her hand over the bare blue white scalp as it appeared, feeling for bristles of hair. Their parents sat at the table, watching as though it were a makeover. When they were done they shook the newspapers out in the yard, leaving clouds of blond hair in the grass, where Anne Marie said the birds could use it.

Beth has never dyed hair before, but it turns out to be a simple enough thing to do. She squirts the silvery cream onto Anne Marie's head and massages it in, keeping it away from her face. It's mesmerizing, her fingers in the silky wet hair, pushing it back and forth and saturating it with cream. "Does it burn?" she asks.

Her sister shakes her head. "Nope. Just smells."

When they were kids, about eleven and sixteen, Beth would submit to periodic makeovers in Anne Marie's room. She sat quietly for the curling iron and the mascara wand she believed would stab her in the eye, breathing Anne Marie's rhythmic, cinnamon-gum-scented breath while her sister held Beth still with a thumb on her cheekbone. Beth loved the makeovers but wouldn't admit it out of fear of seeming childish. She would tilt her head back when Anne Marie touched the underside of her chin, offer her cheek as Anne Marie applied makeup. It was the only time that Anne Marie really touched her.

Of course Beth was never going to look like her sister, makeover or not. Anne Marie used to be peroxided and wiry, forever draped in cracked old leather coats borrowed from inappropriate boyfriends. Even now, as a teacher who should know better, Beth has a soft spot for fast girls. She can't help but admire the way they always have one hip cocked, the tender inside rims of their eyelids lined fearlessly in black. Anne Marie looked like that for several years in the late eighties, starting at about fourteen. Beth has always missed the wild Anne Marie, the girl who got caught at parties in motels with a crowd several years older.

She used to sneak in and out of Beth's ground floor window late at night. Beth would wake up to the sound of the window opening, cold air blanketing the bed as a high-heeled boot came in over the sill. Anne Marie slid in, deftly ducking her head, often chatty and still a little drunk. Once inside she'd shut the window and sit cross-legged at the foot of Beth's bed, wreathed in the smell of bar food and smoke. Her hair would soften by that time of night, still rough with hairspray but flattened in limp wings on the sides of her head.

"It's definitely happening with Jay," Anne Marie said once. She pulled off her boots and dropped them to the floor with a thud. Beth winced and glanced upstairs toward their parents' room. Anne Marie rolled her eyes. "They're asleep," she said. "Don't tweak on me; I'm not in the mood."

"What's happening with Jay?" Beth whispered. She was in sixth grade; not much was happening with her.

"He's dumping that hooker he was dating, for one," Anne Marie told her. She leaned against the bedframe and tipped her head back. A tangle of gold chains glinted at the base of her throat.

"He's dating a *pros*titute?" Beth hissed. Anne Marie's head snapped up and for a moment her eyes shone, wide and startled, and then she turned it into a withering glance.

"Jesus," she said. "You think the best guy I can get is one who goes out with hookers? Thanks a lot." She swung her legs off the bed and stood up, kicking her boots out of her way but not picking them up. "You're such an idiot."

"Whatever," said Beth. "Just go." She was too surprised to say much more. It occurred to her that she had hurt her sister's feelings, and for a moment remorse flared through her. But as Anne Marie shut the door behind her, just hard enough to make a point without waking their parents, Beth thought, Well, now you know how it feels.

She'd been awful in a lot of ways, so flinty that Beth was aston-ished when Anne Marie cried at their uncle's funeral. Nevertheless

Beth found it all alluring—the attitude, the dangling gold hoops. She stole her sister's makeup and bracelets and her copy of *The Wall*, and listened to it each night until she had nightmares of people with their mouths grown shut, their eyes blocked with a curtain of skin. This was exactly the sort of thing Anne Marie would have mocked her mercilessly for, had Beth ever admitted it. Still, back then you never knew if she might suddenly be nice, and when she was, Beth felt like a protected equal, powerful yet safe. She knew better than to get too comfortable in those moments, however. Anne Marie's flashes of kindness were rare and startling, like the clap of a firecracker.

Beth rinses Anne Marie's hair. The towel draped over her sister's shoulders darkens with water. As the dye rinses away it leaves the hair almost colorless, parted by water and showing the white prickle of her scalp. Beth stares at the tiny pink folds at the backs of her sister's ears, the dark pinpoints of her piercings, a leftover hole or two in the cartilage. The knobs of her vertebrae curve down the back of her neck, wisps of wet hair stuck against her white skin. At the base of her neck is a purple dot, tattooed there months ago as a guide for radiation.

"Okay," Beth says, rubbing the towel over her head. When she takes it away Anne Marie's hair is pale and silvery. Her eyebrows seem startlingly dark, her eyes more gray than before. The sun glints on a drop of water on her cheek and Beth wipes it away with a fingertip. She's heard people say how lovely some women look with shorn hair, lovely in spite of themselves, and it's true of Anne Marie. Her cheek-bones stand out more now, her chin and jaw sweep up and back like the curve of some musical instrument.

Anne Marie grins at her. "How is it?" she asks. Her hands flutter over the damp hair, pushing it off her scalp so it'll dry in brushy clumps. "Do I look stupid?"

"Please," says Beth. "Obviously you're beautiful."

They make their way back to the table, Beth hovering slightly behind in case Anne Marie reaches for her hand.

The front door squeaks and their mother comes back in, holding Hannah on one hip, their father behind her. He's no taller than Beth is; their cheeks press evenly together as they hug. He's damp from the heat outside, his skin hot against her face, and when he pulls back Beth sees his sideburns are a little wet. A faint scent of sweat and lemons rises off his skin, as well as the smell of dirt and the peppery smell of tomato stems. His fingernails are rimmed in black; he's been showing off the garden.

"You must have been coming out here in the middle of the night to take care of that garden," he says. "It looks wonderful. The tomatoes are all over."

Behind her father are two men Beth's never seen before. One is obviously a priest; as her father moves back he comes straight to Beth with a preacher's instinct for greeting strangers, arm already extended. He's got thinning, dark hair in a hopeful little sweep across his scalp, a white short-sleeved shirt and dark pants. His glasses are oddly fashionable tortoiseshell ovals. He gives her the preacher handshake, Beth's hand in both of his.

"This is Father Kerwin," says her father. "He was at our church a few years ago. You probably remember him."

Beth shrugs and smiles apologetically. She doesn't remember. Her parents insisted they go to church every week but Beth didn't listen to the sermons, or even really notice the priests who gave them.

"I've heard a lot about you," the priest says. "You're the teacher?"

Beth nods. "Ninth-grade English."

"It's an important profession," he says.

Beth smiles again, a halfhearted grin that feels wan even to her, but it seems to delight the priest, who grins back out of sheer relief, it seems, showing big white teeth with that shadow around the gum-line that gives away caps. What kind of priest has capped teeth? Maybe he was in an accident. She's trying to be charitable. Behind them Cynthia joins Anne Marie, placing Hannah on the table to face her.

The priest turns and pulls forward the man who has been stand-ing behind him. He's in his forties, Beth guesses, deep lines in his face and heavy brows and a mustache, black hair so thick Beth wonders if it would even go in the other direction if she tried to brush it that way. But he's in a T-shirt and army-colored shorts, tough leather san-dals on his feet. His toenails are yellow, thick as claws. Beth holds out a hand and he shakes it briefly, saying something in Spanish.

"This is Juan," says Father Kerwin. "We're incredibly lucky to have him here. He's a healer, over from Peru just for a few weeks."

"Hi," says Beth. A healer is new. They have had priests but never a healer. "I'm sorry, I don't speak Spanish."

"Juan healed a woman who had actually stopped breathing," Cyn-thia says from the table. Hannah squeals. Anne Marie is tickling her. Father Kerwin nods, sees Beth's lack of expression, nods a little while longer.

Beth nods dumbly back. The healer stares straight ahead, hands at his sides. Why a T-shirt and shorts? Why not bow to tradition, or re-spect, or whatever, and wear pants and a button-down shirt?

"Did the church pay to fly you here?" she asks the healer. Her mother is about to kiss her father's cheek, but she looks up at Beth, mouth still pursed and eyebrows rippling the skin of her forehead. Beth shakes her hair out of her face and gives her mother a bland smile. The healer turns his dark eyes on her and stares at Beth. He quirks an eyebrow at her and Beth thinks, *You understand me.*

"It was organized between our parish and some missionaries in Peru," says Father Kerwin.

"Are you staying, Beth?" her father asks.

"Sure," says Beth. She hadn't counted on a healer. What she'd like to do is head out to the garden, but Beth can tell Anne Marie doesn't feel so magnanimous about her graceful exits anymore. Beth had been assuming this was for the best—she felt she contaminated the prayer services somehow, no matter how much she smiled or murmured, because Anne Marie knew Beth was not a believer. It had always seemed more respectful to leave.

But then a few days ago, when their parents and Anne Marie and Anne Marie's husband all gathered around and joined hands, Beth made her customary move toward the front door to check on the garden. She felt Anne Marie watching her, and suddenly Beth's reasoning felt flimsy and cruel. She kept walking anyway, out of embarrassment. Outside she knelt in the dirt and weeded carrots. She cut off broccoli and cauliflower and piled the heads in a bucket. She tore the last of the pea vines from their wires and threw them on the compost heap, next to which flourished a patch of tough old rhubarb no one had bothered to harvest. All the while she watched the house, its glass front door opaque with reflected sunlight.

The summer is almost over.

Beth sits down next to Anne Marie at the table. "Can I have Hannah?" she asks, and Anne Marie hands her over. Beth situates Hannah on her lap, resting her mouth on top of her head. Hannah is an unaccountable redhead in a family of brunettes. She has a space between her front teeth, deep dimples, and round blue eyes. She's a heavy, warm weight on Beth's thighs.

Beth was in her first year of teaching when Hannah was born, and she drove to meet her niece, feeling edgy, notching up the radio. Some of her friends were aunts and uncles by then, shopping endlessly for tiny hats. Beth found it all a little tiresome. She'd like her niece, of course, she'd find Hannah small and cute, but as she drove down 94 that day she had decided she should face the fact that she would not love her just yet. Yet Hannah had a way of suddenly laying her head against Beth's cheek that felt to Beth like a kiss from a man who'd never noticed her before. She had spent the visit hovering in the background, watching Anne Marie rub the bottoms of Hannah's feet with her thumbs while the baby gazed, rapt, at the light on the wall.

Anne Marie puts a hand to her head. Her hair's so short it's almost dry already. She rubs her hands over her scalp and says, "Well. Shall we?"

It's possible there's a wry lift to Anne Marie's eyebrow as she speaks, but in profile it's hard for Beth to tell. She looks at her sister but doesn't get a private glance in return. Maybe Beth imagined it. At these visits she often gets the feeling they are both humoring their parents and their stream of pray-ers and helpers. Their parents keep bringing them, person after person. Anne Marie gives them each the same cool smile, and Beth changes the subject when people mention Lourdes.

Beth may not have a god, but she refuses to take away Anne Marie's, even inside her own head. A random, faceless universe, Beth believes, is fine for everyone except her sister—let all of Anne Marie's beliefs be true. These days, Beth casts conviction like a handful of stones at whatever she wants. Who'll prove her wrong? When they were very young Anne Marie could make her believe anything—that Dick Clark was eighty years old, that somewhere in Washington a certain breed of cat had been taught to read. Beth believed her then because Anne Marie delivered those tidbits with such conviction. If Anne Marie says God's beckoning to her now, then Beth will damn near force herself to see the wispy outline of His hand. Why shouldn't Anne Marie have a god—even make a god with the force of her own desire—if that is what she wants? Maybe, Beth thinks, it makes everything, even this, nothing to fear.

Of course, that's being simple. But Beth doesn't know how it feels to be truly religious, and so she guesses, assuming as she did as a child that if she couldn't disprove a fairy tale it might well be real. When she was little she considered heaven to be more about fairies and magic than God, and consequently, she believed in it. It was too wonderful a thought to be doubted; there must be something. Beth had assumed, without defining it too sharply, that she could die, meet famous people in heaven, and learn to fly.

Even as she grew older and more skeptical, she still harbored the idea that after death you found out everything there was to know and did everything you'd ever wanted. It used to strike her at odd moments how close she was to knowing for sure. As a girl, putting away the steak knives after dinner, she'd look at the veins in her bare feet and hands and think how amazing it was that *that*, a little slice and enough time, was all you had to do to find something you couldn't possibly find here. You just had to be brave. You had to open something up.

She never tried to explain this to her family or friends. It wasn't the sort of thing anyone could really understand. It wasn't a death wish. She was just so curious. And still, every now and again, something catches her by surprise and she realizes she hasn't left her childhood beliefs and religious training as far behind as she imagined. It's never prayer or talk of God that brings up old habits. Catastrophes do. When she saw footage of a plane crash Beth felt her hand steal up to form the sign of the cross before she'd even thought of it—she'd only realized what she was doing when she felt her own fingertip on the hot skin of her forehead.

Later she had tried to decide what it had meant that her hand remembered the gesture. It occurred to her that the cross was really sign language, as intent on communicating with God as the words a congregation murmured under their breaths. She'd always done it out of politeness rather than any feeling that she was getting through to someone, and now she thought the impulse had simply reasserted itself, though it hadn't felt like anything the sign of the cross was meant to be. For Beth it was like covering your mouth with your hand in shock, a motion that served no function but to acknowledge something terrible. The more she thought about it, the more clearly her own sign of the cross seemed to have been a call, a hand on the arm of God, saying, *Look at this.* Except it hadn't felt quite that supplicating. Maybe more like grabbing God's elbow and jerking him around. Maybe more like, *Get down here. Now.*

"Are we ready?" the priest asks.

Their father and mother are across from Beth, Anne Marie is next to her. The priest and the man in the T-shirt stand together at the head of the table. Beth can't see her father behind a big pot of flowers, but she doesn't reach out to move it. She looks at Hannah's red hair instead and plants a kiss in it, breathing deeply. The only thing babies really smell of is baby shampoo, she thinks. She should just buy a bottle of her shampoo, and when she misses Hannah she can rub a little into her own arm and sniff it.

The table is silent while the healer stands, preparing himself, his hands braced against the tabletop. What does a man like this think, at a moment like this? Is he running a check on Bible verses he might be able to use? What if he's just going over his grocery list?

Hannah touches Beth's arm, laying a hand on it to steady herself as she shifts her weight, the scent of her hair drifting up. Anne Marie always smells of a certain brand of hair spray and perfume; maybe, in a few months, when she has to, Beth will fill the rooms in her apartment with her sister's hair spray, direct a shot of her sister's perfume to come in through the vents.

Her father reaches around the plant and takes Beth's hand. Why doesn't he move the pot? She keeps the other arm wrapped around Hannah. Anne Marie doesn't seem upset that Beth can't hold her hand. The healer holds onto Anne Marie. He bends down to her, his hands gripping her wrists, and Beth stares at his fingers pressing into the translucent skin of her arms. It's yellow, that skin. It crinkles like tissue paper. Anne Marie and the healer are their own circle.

The healer talks and the priest translates. No one looks at one another directly. Beth can't see her father, but her mother's eyes are closed. Anne Marie is staring up at the healer as though she can understand what he's saying. He directs a soft torrent of Spanish at her, and he doesn't look at anyone else. He doesn't wait for the priest to catch up to him as he translates, so their words overlap. Beth barely listens to the priest, whose words are all the kind she's heard before anyway. Instead she listens to the healer, to the Spanish T's and rolled R's clicking like stones in his mouth.

"Madre de dios," says the healer. *"Manos de dios."* He gives Anne Marie a little shake as he says something especially forcefully. The mother of God, Beth guesses, the hand of God. Anne Marie's shoulders tremble when the healer jostles her and Beth almost reaches over to slap his hand away. The topography of bones beneath Anne Marie's sweater is like a pile of pebbles and sticks. Below her shoulder her arm tapers along the bone. The healer's thick black hair has fallen in his face, and he bends further down, staring at Anne Marie. She doesn't pull back or flinch, and Beth knows she'd like to. Anne Marie has never liked people in her face.

Beth gives Hannah a little bounce, then rests her lips in Hannah's hair—she's so quiet, as if she knows it's just a good time to look at the pot of flowers on the table—and her father squeezes her hand. His palm is damp, and she can imagine the grainy tack of the garden, its torn leaves and vegetal sap and dirt still on his skin. He squeezes her fingers so hard, just for a moment, that her ring presses into the bone of her knuckle, and she bites her lip and doesn't move.

The priest wipes his forehead, stumbling over a word here and there. What does it matter if they can understand it? She's wondering if this guy really thinks he's doing something. The healer touches Anne Marie's face just then, running a fingertip over her brow and cheeks. Beth waits for Anne Marie to stiffen, but she doesn't. She looks straight up at him, watching his face as intently as if there were words scrolling across his forehead.

The priest stands up, unzipping a little black leather pouch and pulling out a vial of golden oil. He holds it up for all of them to see and says it's been blessed by someone, Beth doesn't catch who. The healer paints some on Anne Marie's forehead, and she closes her eyes and lifts her chin to let him do it. He finishes painting her brow with the oil and then asks her something.

"What would you like me to pray for next?" Father Kerwin translates. "Peace of mind? Your daughter?"

Beth waits for Anne Marie to look toward Hannah at the mention of her, but Anne Marie doesn't turn her head.

The priest is still looking at Anne Marie while the healer grasps her wrists. The healer says something, his voice rising at the end with the intonation of a question, and the priest translates to Anne Marie:

"A peaceful death?"

There's a quiver of silence when he says this. All their spines straighten, their chins draw back. He actually said it. For months Beth has been wondering whether Anne Marie hates them all for being unable to. They talk around it, they redirect the topic to the immediate things that comfort their parents, like the healers and the prayer circles, and Beth has wished she could grab her sister's hand and be the only one who can come right out and say Anne Marie doesn't have to fake it to please her and doesn't have to do this healing crap, that it's a burden and a farce. When she imagines this, which she does frequently now, she sees Anne Marie as a girl, turning those dark-lined eyes on her, her frosted pink mouth curving sardonically as she got ready to deliver some horrifying truth about penises or sex, to which Beth would lift her chin because she didn't want Anne Marie to laugh at her. You had to deal with things; you had to say them straight out.

But Beth couldn't do it, and she realizes she's been waiting to hear her sister say that she just needs some peace around here, a clear road to her death because it's coming soon, even if it is excruciatingly slow. It ought to hurt her to think of this, but when she hears the words floated out there it makes the muscles of her neck and back un-clench. A peaceful death.

She holds Hannah tighter, expecting Anne Marie's old fearlessness to resurface. She waits for a sign of the practical, impatient outlook so at odds with the healer and priests and prayer chains, and which demands they just accept what's put before them. So shock rises in her, physically, like a fizz through her blood, when Anne Marie says, her voice lilting as though she were admitting to something silly, "Oh—if you could ask—I'd like to be healed."

Beth loses all focus. Her eyes dart around, at the plant that hides her father, at her mother's hand clutching his, her diamonds sparkling, at the whorl of Hannah's red hair, and she comes to rest on Anne Marie and the healer—that golden skin of her sister's arms, crumpled as parchment and nearly bruised by the healer's thick fin-gers. They're looking at each other in a moment of total privacy, their eyes locked. He presses his mouth to her forehead and then pulls back, his lips gleaming faintly from the oil he painted on her skin. His mouth is a few inches from her silvery hair. The healer murmurs something to her, and the priest leans in to listen, but the healer won't repeat it. The priest casts an apologetic glance around the table. They all strain forward a little, but the healer's words to Anne Marie are too soft to hear. Even the priest, stretching hopefully toward the two of them to listen, cannot get close enough to translate.

FIVE-MINUTE HEARTS

"Ava kisses the way she walks," Matt says about his ex-wife. He speeds down the two-lane highway with no remorse, and as the afternoon light slices through passing trees, it momentarily illuminates the top of his head, creating little halos, one after the other that slip off.

Brenda remembers the way Ava walked. Those kisses must be something. She doesn't mention to Matt that incidentally Ava developed and refined that famous walk—a walk that contained expectant, miniature hip swoops, as if she thought someone might at any second grab those tiny handles and kiss her crotch—circa 1983. Fenderlocken High. Brenda was there, though she doubts Ava ever noticed her.

With the car windows wide open, Matt must be going seventy, though it's hard to tell; the broken speedometer of his '88 Volvo, "The Rocket," doesn't budge from zero. They—Matt and Brenda and Matt's four-year-old daughter, Iris—are on their way, already late, to an afternoon barbecue hosted by Ava.

Brenda and Matt met a month ago at the bookstore where Brenda works. Matt watched Brenda refuse the return of a book whose cover had a faint but noticeable coffee ring. He told her he admired a woman who stood her ground. Brenda was delighted that someone would see her that way.

On their first date, Matt mentioned that his ex-wife went to the same high school as Brenda. "Sure, I knew Ava Hobbs," Brenda said in a tone of voice that would indicate she knew Ava fairly well—and didn't quite approve of her. But she'd never spoken to Ava and could barely look at Ava's feet as they passed in the school corridor.

Matt went on to say that he was in the process of changing his life, changing it for good. Brenda was impressed by such an open declaration. She herself had been in the process of changing her life for good since she was about ten.

"My bed's too small, and I fall out of it!" Iris shouts from the backseat, where with seat belt stretched across her chest, she lurches and grabs the front seat, expelling her cheese popcorn breath in willful, ragged sighs.

Iris has two beds, one at Ava's place and one at Matt's. Brenda hasn't seen either. Brenda imagines Iris's bed at Ava's, thinks it must be covered in something with a high thread count that incorporates golden rosebuds. Her bedcover at Matt's is probably nautical-themed and hangs crookedly.

Matt scratches the inside of his right wrist, his driving wrist, the wrist that bears a navigator watch, an inscrutable timepiece, which looks like it weighs two pounds and causes his right forearm muscle to shorten under his tanned skin in a curvy, determined way. Matt told Brenda that he used to be a big drinker. He says Ava used to be a big drinker, too. Apparently they were such big drinkers they had to keep a case of Pedialyte in the fridge for hangovers. But those days are gone. Matt even has a new job. He sells a software program to California sheriffs that helps them keep track of criminals.

"Which bed, honey?" Matt says and reaches behind his seat to squeeze Iris's ankle.

Brenda turns completely around to listen to Iris's answer, unlike a real mother. She thinks of the board game *Life* that she played as a child ("Spin the wheel of fate, then drive the hilarious game path of fortune!"). Brenda recalls loading her tiny car with kids the size of rice and driving as fast as possible around a cardboard square.

Iris flops against the backseat. "My bed at school!"

Iris goes to two different daycare centers, one when she's at Matt's place, one when she's at Ava's. Ava works at a beauty supply store six days a week; Matt also works Saturdays. The only thing upon which Matt and Ava are united is to call daycare "school." Brenda has overheard them talking on Matt's cell phone. "When she gets out of school . . . today at school . . ." Iris has been in school since she was six months old.

Brenda never went to daycare, doesn't know anyone who did. It wasn't invented yet. She does remember kindergarten, and there certainly weren't beds. There was the laying of one's head on one's hands at a long wooden table, which smelled of grape juice and Cheez Whiz. And there was the listening to fingers tapping, jawbones clunking, and bang-plastered foreheads thudding all the way down the line, sounds that occur when one asks oneself "What Will I Be When I Grow Up?"—or that's what Mrs. Gosseltaff would tell you all that racket was, for she often urged her pupils to "give it some thought" while resting. But Mrs. Gosseltaff's students, each of them in that terrible, alone-forever, face-to-table position, weren't thinking at all about jobs, for they were beating out with tiny skulls and asso-

ciated hand bones, the *other* big question, the bigger big question:
Who will I love?

Who will I love?

The inside of The Rocket is now the temperature of a meat locker,
and Brenda asks Matt, who has the window controls, to put hers up.

"What?" he asks.

"People like Brenda make the air cold!" Iris shrieks, and this Matt
does seem to hear, since he immediately puts up his daughter's window.

Brenda figures she'll tough it out. "Iris, do you want to try your
coloring book?" The velveteen-covered mythological coloring book,
an item for which she paid too much, even with her employee dis-
count, has been shoved off to the side of the backseat, open to a picture of a minotaur whose right horn is covered in a fine layer of
orange popcorn dust.

"Do you like the minotaur?" Brenda asks Iris, who pulls at her
pale red eyebrows and stares at her lap. "The minotaur was half man
and half bull," says Brenda.

"Who's the fool?" demands Iris with all the conviction of a hard-
boiled D.A.

A chunk of hair blows into Brenda's mouth, hair she cut only last
week. She pulls the tangled lock out of her mouth. "Why are you
asking about a fool, Iris?"

"You said, 'half man, half fool.'" A motorcycle with a broken
muffler passes their car.

"I didn't say that, Iris!" shouts Brenda.

Matt glances at his watch, assessing his heart—its rapidity. Brenda
had never seen such a watch before she saw Matt's. She doesn't wear
a watch herself. Matt accelerates and The Rocket makes a startling,
heart-wrenching noise like a woman crying in her sleep.

"Hold onto your dental work, ladies!" yells Matt as the front end
of The Rocket visibly begins to shake.

Brenda wants to tell Matt to knock it off and slow down, but she feels she doesn't know him well enough, and now, due to her infallible politeness, they may all lose their lives. Her hair whips every which way, and she attempts to aim her head in the right direction, the direction that might make it stop, but no such luck, and it occurs to her that she doesn't even have a comb in her purse, and that when she sees Ava in as soon as fifteen minutes from now, and for the first time in eighteen years, she'll look like a total wreck.

A truck the deep black color of charred firewood is overtaking them, and it's unclear why the driver, whose face can't be seen through his window, is going so fast. And why does he need to race Matt and Brenda and Iris in their poor old Volvo—this mock-up, thrown-together example of a family such as never navigated the *Life* board—as they speed toward Ava and her amazing walk?

"Who's the fool? Who's the fool?" Iris keeps on.

The truck, upon them now, honks or more accurately bellows, like an animal about to charge.

Matt, Brenda, Iris, and their new friend, Del Stanger, are on the side of a barren shoulder just off the 170 in Van Nuys. Del, in his big black truck, witnessed them veer off the road as a multitude of tiny rocks flew up under the car, clattering like finger bones. The first thing he said to them was, "Everyone's lucky sometimes."

Iris pretends to wash the pavement with her hair.

"Get up, Iris," says Matt as he and Del Stanger assess the damage to the blown, back right tire.

"I want candy," says Iris, and she does lift her head, but not high enough to keep the end of her red ponytail from dragging in the dust.

"Stop this behavior within five, Iris," says Matt.

Del flops down on the embankment, as if he's glad to be in the dirt and puts his hands up into the wheel well. Matt, who never works on his own car, stands to the side of the passenger door with his hands on his hips. Del makes an unselfconscious kind of grunt, and Brenda notices the strong bones of his face. Long black hair escapes from a baseball cap that reads TRAIL. It's probably the brand name of some product that Del once lugged coast to coast. Brenda imagines Del driving in a remote area just before nightfall, sitting in the cab of his truck, very alone and overwhelmed by the beauties and mysteries that hourly pass his window. Truckers are unrealized poets, she thinks. Who else would sit in one place, day after day, talking to no one, watching everything, traveling the same piece of life road, forward and back?

"Thank you for trying to stop us," says Brenda. No comment from beneath the car. "And it's exceptionally nice of you to help with the tire," Brenda adds, too formal to her own ears.

Brenda and Matt stand apart from each other, both staring at the lower half of Del's body, which reveals a tan line between his jeans and T-shirt. Now Brenda has her hands on her hips, too. Cars pass, people look at the dumpy green Volvo stopped at a crazy angle. Some of them slow, none of them stop.

"I want candy," repeats Iris, and she stands up, seemingly aware that exactly five minutes have passed. Brenda fishes for a Life Saver in her purse.

"*Why* do you want candy, Iris?" asks Matt. "Give me one abstract reason."

Matt says he likes to make Iris's brain work. He's helping her create paths. He read an article about it in the parenting section of his electronic record storage professionals' magazine. This kind of thing makes Brenda's skin crawl, this overworking of matters. And in that instant Brenda knows that she and Matt aren't a fit. Immediately she feels a sort of internal sliding over the fact.

"Because I like candy," Iris answers after great deliberation.

"That's a concrete reason, honey," says Matt.

"It is?" Brenda says.

The bookstore where Brenda works was recently voted in the local hipster's weekly "The Expensive Person's Bookstore," although book prices, set by publishers, are the same as everywhere else. Brenda and her underpaid coworkers are the type who read Proust for kicks, who crack each other up with subtle jokes that encase the obscure fact, the scrap of unusable knowledge. Since the newspaper article, they've begun to make comments like: "*That's* an expensive statement." Most, like Brenda, would hope to seem smart and funny, though they're all riddled with sensitivities and quirks, the oddness of which they try to mitigate through enlargement.

Everyone teases Brenda about her lack of a watch and *great* disinterest in time, which she exaggerates for the sake of a joke, and to lessen the fact that she desperately worries about her hours and days, the fact that they are slipping by so easily and that still, true love has not been found.

"Well, the wheel rim is all right, and I thought your axle was tweaked but it's not."

Del stretches a long leg out from under the car, and rocks his head side to side. No one has ever looked so comfortable on the earth.

"So?" says Matt.

"So, you need a tire." Del offers to take Matt up the road to get one, and Matt questions Brenda and Iris's safety.

"Don't worry," says Del. "Mostly canine breeders in these parts. People here would sooner kill you over your dog than your wife."

"That's not my wife," says Matt as he checks his back pocket for his wallet.

Del looks at Brenda, seems to really look at her for the first time, and an expression crosses his face, as if he's remembered something, and again Brenda imagines that his thoughts are rich and deep, and she suddenly wishes she could know him.

"Thank you, again," she says and extends her hand.

Iris throws herself around his knees. To the Lexus-load of businessmen passing at this instant, Iris and Brenda and Del might look like a family saying good-bye to one another.

"You'll be okay with Iris?" Matt asks Brenda as he steps closer to her and clamps his arm around her, pinning her to him. Brenda knows that Matt will later give Iris some complicated lecture about how you just can't give your heart to a stranger because he shows up in your life for five minutes.

The men drive away in the black truck, and Brenda and Iris stand there, looking at each other. For once Iris is absolutely still. "Let's sit down, Iris," says Brenda, and immediately Iris does, too hard, right on the pavement. She even folds her hands, and this seems like something she was told to do in daycare, and it occurs to Brenda how stressful it is to be a child with everyone telling you what to do, what to want, trying to create trails in your head every other minute.

Iris starts to yawn, or it looks like a yawn, but it suddenly and vociferously mutates into crying, and this crying has a rhythm to it: sob hard, no breathing, then wait—sob hard, no breathing, then wait. This crying is more like questioning, though Brenda doesn't know what Iris is asking. It seems like asking.

And what would Ava do? But all Brenda can imagine is a girl walking away from her down a hallway, the cold hallway, the one outside the gym where the exit door was always propped open to blow away sweat, a girl with an arm lined with silver bracelets, a girl with a walk like no other girl on earth, the exact girl that Brenda would have been, if she could have been any other girl.

Matt had told Brenda that Ava lived in a typical California condo and Brenda pictured a Mexican-tiled entryway, a courtyard with calla lilies and freesia. She hadn't expected the single-story units all in need of paint, the smell of Pine-Sol, cigarettes, and, everywhere, burnt teriyaki chicken.

Everyone here looks like they could use a little help.

Two young men box dangerously close to a hibachi. An older man, wearing a leather vest over his bare chest, sits across a picnic table from a woman whose peach-colored hair matches her lipstick and nails. They both look a few beers in. Between them are three snack bowls, all of them empty. It's five o'clock, and the sky, a rinse water blue, is lined with stretched-thin clouds that look like so much illegible handwriting.

Looking up at Matt and Brenda, the woman says, "Sherry Taylor," vehemently, as if someone had disputed her name. "My Pete," she says, waving a long orange fingernail at the man. Pete nods at the two shirtless boxers and says "Dale," then "Pixie." Dale wears high white knee socks and long green shorts that hang low on his hips. Pixie ties a yellow bandana around his head. The two begin to circle each other.

"Family business," Sherry says without looking at Matt or Brenda.

"Fighting?" Brenda asks.

"Boxing," Sherry indignantly corrects her.

There are no other guests. This is Ava's barbecue? Where is Ava?

Matt, holding Iris's hand in his left, nervously flexes his right arm, his navigating arm. Last week he bought a two-hundred-dollar electric stimulus box to work his muscles. Brenda lay in her bed—Matt had spent the night—watching him attach all those electrodes; it took some doing. But Matt is committed.

Brenda spots Ava sitting in a lawn chair on an unprosperous patch of lawn. She smokes with one hand and holds a conch shell ashtray in the other, though she flicks her ashes onto the beat-up grass. Her back is to Matt and his troupe as they cross the lawn, and she is hunched over, as if she were watching late night TV—a way that no one would sit if they thought anyone were watching.

Iris runs toward Ava's chair and Ava, as if she feels a sudden burst of sun upon her back, turns around. But Iris stops halfway across the scrubby courtyard, fascinated by the boxers. Ava gives Brenda a "what can you expect?" look, and Brenda thinks she sees a flash of recognition in Ava's still wide, still beautiful green eyes. Brenda feels a small surge of pride at being able to look directly at her.

Then Ava smiles, and Brenda notices how yellow her teeth are. They were never like that. And somehow, Ava is so very pulled in upon herself. She stands up, and she is shorter than Brenda remembered her. "I thought you weren't coming," she says to Matt, and her words seem loose inside her mouth. Matt mentions the blown tire as he turns his body sideways to hug her. Ava starts coughing violently. They look like two people at the end of a dinner party that didn't go so well.

"I guess you remember Brenda," says Matt, looking at his navigator watch instead of either woman's face.

"You guess?" Brenda says, trying for a joke and an appearance of offhand confidence.

Ava nods and smokes, but Brenda can tell Ava has no idea what he's talking about. Matt might as well have said, "Would you agree that Brenda has a head?"

Ava fixates on the last half inch of her cigarette. Her hair, once thick and glossy, has been curled at the ends, but sections have been missed, and some lie absolutely straight between the waves. Ava runs her fingers through her locks, and Brenda notices how red and angry her nail beds are. She remembers a thing she once heard about Ava, a thing she forgot because she couldn't believe it.

Halfway through Brenda's junior year at Fenderlocken High, Ava had disappeared. A rumor circulated that she'd left to go to a fashion institute in San Francisco. Perhaps she was studying to be a designer. Of course she would be accepted at sixteen. She was Ava.

Brice Manelli told Brenda that Ava actually had gone to "sewing school," which was something completely different, a young women's halfway house that sheltered girls with drug, drinking, and behavioral problems, as well as indistinct or compound problems that no one could quite unravel. Brenda didn't believe any of this. What problems could Ava have?

Brice said, "Well, all I know is that I sat next to her in Home Ec, and she spent the whole time sticking pins and needles under her fingernails. And you know what she said when I asked her about it? She said, 'It always heals.'"

But of course Brenda hadn't believed that either.

Dale dances around Pixie, who has pulled the yellow bandana from his head and wrapped it around his upper arm like a tourniquet. They stare into each other's eyes as if mesmerized. Then Pixie springs at Dale and takes a swipe, hitting him squarely in his right rib.

"That's it," Sherry Taylor calls.

Once again, Ava starts hacking, this time before she gets a chance to cover her mouth.

From his plastic lawn chair, Matt says, "Have another cigarette, why don't you?" Ava stiffens. The air seems to quicken and gather between them. Matt starts to ask something, then stops, sighs.

"Because I'm too high-strung," Ava says, seemingly joyless at her ability to know what he would have asked.

"More like lazy." And this is where it starts. There might have been a blue flash in the air, and even Sherry and Pete shift their attention to Ava and Matt. In one of the condominiums someone puts on music, an old speed metal song, and Iris immediately starts spinning to this tune that has no discernable melody or rhythm.

"Why can't you stop smoking?" Matt says. "I just want to know," he adds, as he glances at Brenda, then folds his arms across his chest, affecting the stance of a reasonable man.

"Why do you bring a different woman to my home every month?" says Ava, gesturing toward her front stoop. It features a penicillin pink door behind a slab of cement littered with pizza flyers. She attempts to light another cigarette. "I just want to know."

Brenda walks over to the empty snack bowls. Just last week Matt told her she was the first woman he'd dated since his divorce eight months ago.

"This is about smoking," Matt says to Ava in a tone that one would use on an unruly child in church.

"This is *not* about smoking."

"Besides, you've been drinking."

"I've not been drinking."

"Well, you're on *something.*"

"I am not." Ava gestures wildly with her cigarette, as if to poke holes in the sky.

"Then why are you acting this way?"

"What way?" Ava chews at a cuticle. "What way?" she repeats.

Matt's face shows no emotion. He could be a man waiting at a stoplight.

"Oh, am I embarrassing you in front of your new friend?" Ava does a little rocking step back and forth.

"Stop it, Ava."

"Stop it yourself, you box."

"Oh, I'm a box."

"You're a box," and here Ava's voice cracks, "and you have no understanding about real people who feel real things, people who've been through a thing or two and know something about the accordion of life on down!"

Iris twirls past them.

Then simply, as if their past life together has suddenly come unzipped, Matt and Ava's entire history of disagreements tumbles out. Words flash and spin in the air: Liar, wrong, can, don't, you, fuck, mine, care, stop, always, you, why, shouldn't, try, you, said, why, didn't, help, me, you, you, you. Matt and Ava stand absolutely still. At this moment they look curiously formal and attentive and, in some small way, in love.

Iris spins faster and faster.

Ava tries for one last drag. Matt reaches for her forearm, which is pale and bears not a single silver bracelet. Someone turns up the ugly music, which seems to rip sideways on itself and sounds impossibly tangled. Iris spins so hard she falls on the ground. She does not cry. Matt, still holding on to Ava's forearm, shouts for her to drop the cigarette. Dale and Pixie stop boxing.

"I said, drop it!" With arms lifted, Matt and Ava are frozen for a moment, a statue of furious unity. Then Ava bites Matt's wrist. His navigating wrist. A vein in her forehead sticks out. Ava, the beautiful.

Matt falls down on one knee as if she'd bitten his leg. Ava stands with her hands covering her face. Brenda runs to him and puts one palm on his shoulder, but he pulls away from her. The mystery DJ has turned down the music, but not all the way, and Brenda can hear a tiny scrap of bass that urgently repeats, sounding like a fly caught against a screen. Tap, tap—tap, tap.

Sherry and Pete and their sons huddle around Matt. Sherry quite practically asks if there's blood. Considering her family business, this must be small potatoes. Pixie gives Matt his yellow bandana. Pete, with his hands on his thighs, leans into Matt, speaking quietly and directly, saying something that no one can hear. Ringside, there's always some fellow like this. Matt gives his complete and utter attention to this man with whom he's not previously exchanged two words.

Brenda sits in the lawn chair that Ava earlier vacated. Iris runs to her side, flushed from spinning. "I've got a bed here," she says matter-of-factly. Brenda tries to pull Iris onto her lap, and Iris does allow this, but once there she swings her feet sideways and sits quite straight. She might as well be taking a seat on a bus. Iris will be held, but she won't be comforted.

Ava hasn't moved from the spot where she bit Matt. She absently wipes her mouth with the back of her hand. Then without taking one look at Matt or Brenda or Iris, she goes to the picnic table, picks up the three empty snack bowls and with great finality stacks them one inside the other. She turns and heads toward her front door. The way she walks, she could be shoveling dirt.

Whatever it is that Pete said to Matt causes him to jump up and follow Ava. He still holds the bandana around his wrist, and as an afterthought he calls to Iris, who runs to him. Brenda trails after, but Matt and Iris are already behind the closed pink door before she's halfway across the lawn. She turns around and almost bumps into Pete and his sons. Pixie smiles, though Dale and Pete give her a look as if they've never seen her before. Brenda stands in the middle of the yard for a few moments, completely directionless.

Finally Sherry Taylor waves Brenda over to the picnic table. "My Pete knows what's what," she declares as Brenda joins her. Brenda nods and Sherry adds, "The first time we slept together that man spit on my face to see what I really looked like."

"That's something," Brenda answers, but what she's really listening to is a sound coming from behind the pink door. Iris is singing a nonsense song, and much of it is unclear except the part she keeps repeating about a man and a fool.

"Because in those days, I just lathered on the makeup."

"Sure," Brenda answers. Behind Sherry, Brenda sees Ava and Matt framed in Ava's kitchen window. She cranes her neck to get a better view.

"My Pete believes in the reality of passion." Sherry Taylor taps her fingernails against an empty beer can, and it is clear she expects something from Brenda.

"He must be very passionate."

Sherry Taylor giggles wickedly.

Through the kitchen window Brenda sees Matt hold up his forearm, watches Ava wrap his wrist in gauze. Then she cuts the gauze with scissors—huge scissors, the wrong scissors. Matt lets her do it anyway. The trust.

Matt disappears from the window and Brenda sees Ava standing there alone, head tilted in an old familiar way, a way that in high school had seemed proud and arrogant but now looks resigned. And she's free of something, too. Ava has quit her own beauty, the whole complex freight of it. But for a moment Brenda can still see it, almost see it, now more like a ring around her, something vaporous, something vanishing.

Matt pokes his head out the door and shouts, "Brenda, I'm calling you a taxi. Okay? Okay?" Just like that. Brenda doesn't give him an answer, and he doesn't wait for one.

Sherry Taylor looks at Brenda and gently asks, "What do you *do*, Brenda?"

For an instant, it seems to Brenda that she's inquiring into her past line of relationship errors, or perhaps what she will do in the future to avoid them.

"I work at a bookstore."

"Oh, I like bookstores. So nice and quiet." Sherry winks at her, as if she understands something further about bookstore work, something impractical or silly.

It would be closing hour now. Time for easing out the last customer of the day. Time to pick up the book left carelessly on the floor, splayed open, aisles from its proper home.

Sherry says, "The great thing about the book business is that people will always need to read. Just like my business. Just like boxing."

After Sherry Taylor leaves, Brenda sits at the picnic table, waiting for her taxi. The smells of chicken, Pine-Sol, and cigarettes have at last lifted, and now there is only cold night air to breathe. Brenda looks up at the darkening sky, at the fast clouds charging by, clouds that in moments will be in the next town, or the one after that. She thinks of Del Stanger, imagines him driving his black truck around the world, seeing beauty at every turn. Where is he now?

Then Brenda recalls something else about *Life*, a thing she hadn't thought of in years, about how everyone tried to avoid the "Flat Tire Miss Next Turn" square. Because while one's car was stuck, the rest of the players whizzed on by, collecting with the roll of the dice all sorts of things—jobs, marriage, kids. But of course, everything was random, everything could be lost, and none of it had to do with love.

MATTHEW LOVE

92nd Street Y

Nightfloat

Dr. Taran awoke at dusk to the blare of rush-hour traffic coming through the open window on the draft. The apartment was overheated; he slept without covers. Pain stretched across his forehead. His eye sockets were hollow with fatigue. Lingering on his skin, the remnant of a dream, was the touch of a cold hand.

The ceiling was perfectly flat, without a single defect. Each wall held a poster. Winter light seeped through the blinds. He could feel the other apartments in the building, stacked perfectly alongside and on top of one another, each with its occupants inside, high above the ground. There was a family of at least four Asian people living on the other side of one wall—a nurse, a man, and two children. Usually they avoided greeting Taran, though the man was sometimes effusive and eager to shake hands.

Taran boiled water for coffee while showering, and then read yesterday's paper while he ate. He sat at the table, admiring its blond wood. He got up and went to the window. In the hospital room across the street, a uniformed nurse moved in a slow pantomime, in and out of view. There was a patient in the bed. Taran leaned out to look up at the sky—a dense, seamless gray—and remembered the park. He had been there to see autumn. The trees had been a miracle of colors, a golden yellow predominant; he remembered wondering if all autumns were equally yellow or if they varied greatly.

There was no one in the elevator; the sealed car descended smoothly on its track. He closed his eyes and took a breath, preparing for the world. The door opened; waiting there was a woman in blue jeans. It took him a moment to place her—a surgeon, without her scrubs.

He stepped out into the noise. The wind made him swallow. Though the sky held some daylight, in the street it was dark. A jogger passed, red-faced. Taran entered the flow of people, wading upstream against the current toward the subway. Taller than most, he looked down into the oncoming faces for a pair of eyes to meet his own, a line of gaze over which he might transmit the feeling in his heart. No one looked up. They walked in thick halos of evening worry; for him, it was morning.

At the corner, out from the lee of the buildings, the air came in big gusts. It found the vents in his white coat and the pores in his scrubs. He savored it—wild, moving air—letting the chill inhabit his body. The paper box headline said SNOW WILL HIT. Taxis cheated into the crosswalk before the light turned. By the ambulance bay, the hospital workers waited for their vans. "Where that fellow is? We got to get back before the snow come!" a woman said loudly. "He probably spendin' our money on a streetwhore in the back of the van!" another woman said as though expecting laughter.

Inside the emergency room door, a man held his head at an angle and cupped his ear as though it were dripping.

"Ay!" he screamed. "Ay!"

"Roach in the ear," the nurse escorting him said to Taran.

"Really? A cockroach?" Taran said, his first utterance of the day. He could not hear his own accent though he knew it sounded foreign—Indian, with traces of his former tutor's Scots.

"It's the absolute worst. The roach panics and runs up against the eardrum. It's like a stampede," the nurse said, steering the man toward an exam room. "Don't scream any more, señor, we'll get it out, all right?"

The hall was lined with patients on stretchers. An unshaven old man grabbed at Taran. A woman talked to herself. Lying on their backs, most held up a hand to shield their eyes from the lights. One had a sheet over his head; the uncovered foot was a man's.

An old woman with her wig askew was parked on a stretcher right outside the nurses' station. "Excuse me," she said to Taran, "I wonder if you might help me for a minute. I don't know what I'm doing here. I don't know where I am."

"You're in the hospital," he said. "City Hospital. I don't know why you're here. Shall I see?"

"Please do."

The nurses' station was enclosed in thick glass. Phones rang. Doctors sat at the counters writing. The nurses stood in a huddle. There was an insistent rapping on the window. Taran was the only one to turn and look. It was the woman with the wig.

"Do you know what's with her?" Taran asked the resident sitting closest.

"Go see," the resident said, knowingly.

Taran went back into the hallway.

"Excuse me," the woman said to him. "Would you be so kind as to tell me where I am?"

"City Hospital, I just now told you. Don't you remember?"

"Of course I do. Well, apparently not," she admitted.

"Don't worry. Someone is taking care of you," Taran said.

"Korsakoff's syndrome?" he asked the resident.

"Bingo." The resident laughed. "She'll be knocking again in ten seconds, the old drunkard. She's got the short-term memory of an earthworm."

In the elevator, a woman stood watching the numbers move, knitting blindly from yarn in her coat pocket. An attending physician rubbed his bald spot then put his hands in his pockets. A child looked up at Taran; he nodded to her.

John Doe 4, in room 1522, was an endstage cirrhotic the police had found delirious on the sidewalk. There was no one to grant permission to let him die. He was propped up in bed, naked except for a diaper. In the pool of fluorescence cast by the overbed light, his orange skin looked green. His belly was massively swollen, the skin stretched taut. He had enlarged breasts but his arms and legs were spindly and short. It was as though he were pregnant with himself, metamorphosing into a larval ball, limbs retracting inward from the spent skeleton. Someone had shaved him and cut his hair. He mumbled unintelligibly.

Taran spoke. He told the man he would feel a needlestick, then the burning of the anesthetic, then a sensation of pressure, and then relief when the fluid began to drain. Though stuporous, the man was visibly calmed by the talking. Taran listened to his own voice, so gentle and unhurried, and thought of his uncle's horse, how its ears would soften when he talked to it as it stood still to be brushed and saddled. He percussed the man's abdomen and felt the fluid waves lapping back and forth.

He slipped the needle in. Bright yellow fluid rapidly traced the turns of the plastic tubing, draining it.

"Your liver weeps for you, these liters of yellow tears," Taran said.

An idea came to him—that the man's huge abdominal cavity, full of liquid, might function as a fish pond. "There is space enough for fish in there! The environment might suit them well, I think," he said.

Ashamed, he pushed softly on the belly to accelerate the flow.

"You're the float, right?" a resident asked Taran in the hall.

"Yes, would you like to sign out?" Taran said.

They sat in chairs at the nurses' station. The resident's eyelids began to descend, his head to nod forward. He whiplashed awake for a second and mumbled something, then succumbed and let his head fall to his chest. Softly, he began to snore.

Taran glanced out the window. Snow was falling, a rain of silent white. So fast and heavy it blurred his vision. He had seen snow once on a mountainside, but never falling. How was it possible that there was so much of it? You couldn't look at it without getting dizzy. It seemed to be crystallizing right there, the white dots swirling in out of the black sea of air just beyond the reach of the building's lights. He approached the window. Far down, on the street, the tops of the cars were white.

He stood on his toes and lifted the big window open. Fat flakes of snow blew in. He bent to pick them up, but at the touch of his fingertips they turned to water. As he had seen done in a movie, Taran gathered a mound of the powder on the outside sill and compressed and smoothed it into a ball. Cold and wet, the snow turned his hands red.

He shook the resident awake. When his eyes were open, Taran stood formally before him, bowed, and presented him the snowball on the platter of his palm.

"It's snowing?" the resident said. He took the ball and examined it. "This is excellent." The resident touched it to the back of his neck and shivered. Then he stood up and pitched it at the wall. It hit with a loud smack and stuck.

"Let's get this over with," the resident said, flipping through a stack of index cards. "Not sick. Not sick. Discharged. Webster. You remember Webster. Scumbag, drug-seeking asshole with a fake sickle cell crisis? He's on standing pain meds, and he will definitely work you for more. Do not give. Do what I do: use a big needle and draw lots of bloods. I want him off my service." He glanced up and smiled. "Jimson. AIDS. Drowning in diarrhea. He's got two IVs in and we're barely keeping up with his fluids. If his IV comes out, he'll definitely need another. Siciliano. Also AIDS. His brain is completely replaced by lymphoma. He's not DNR, but do him a favor and let him go bye-bye. Speaking of which."

The night shift had taken over. Visitors had been sent home; the nurses moved slowly. The food servers and cleaners sat and talked loudly among themselves. The clerks made phone calls. No one acknowledged Taran except for an older, very black man who drew back his mop to let Taran pass.

"Be careful the wet floor, doc."

"Thank you," Taran said.

Even in the hallway the sound from the TV was overpowering—the panicked footsteps, shallow breathing, and tense music were those of a horror movie. The other patient in the room, a demented old man in diapers, seemed effected. He cowered in his bed, toothless mouth agape with terror, eyes wide in retreat.

"Mr. Webster!" Taran shouted. "It's the doctor, I've come to see you."

There was no answer, so he parted the curtain. A small black man lay on his side with the TV hanging in front of him. He licked at a plastic cup of red Jell-O. An IV flowed into the back of his hand. There was a shrill scream—the TV flashed—then the sound of someone being clubbed.

"Mr. Webster, you asked to see me. Please, could you lower the volume so we can speak?"

The man studied Taran's nametag, then with exaggerated effort reached up and turned down the volume.

"Sorry 'bout the TV," he grunted. "Just trying to distract myself from the pain. Goddamn sickle cell killing me." He looked Taran over. "You working hard, huh, doc? Lot of suffering in this building and you probably the only one here. Got to suffer one hour minimum before you see the doctor this time of night."

"I'm sorry you've been unattended. They've only just paged me now."

Webster loosened the covers and started to turn on to his back but suddenly winced and grabbed his abdomen as though he'd been shot. Writhing and grimacing on the bed, he seemed possessed by pain. His face was contorted, and tears beaded in his eyes. He made a strange gulping noise and hugged himself, rolling from side to side.

A display, Taran thought. And then, guiltily to himself: *You are no better than the others.*

The pain seemed to go on and on. Webster's eye opened for a second—was he angry that Taran was seeing him like this?—and Taran placed a hand on his shoulder to comfort him. Finally the paroxysm passed.

"Doctor, you got to help me. I need medication."

"Mr. Webster, I'd like to help you. First I need to figure out what's causing—"

"Look, man. It's the sickle cell. It hurts the same as always, it feels the same, but it's worse now, 'cause you all aren't giving me enough medication. The first thing *is* the medication. Then you can mess around you feel the need to."

"Mr. Webster, I don't want you to suffer, but—"

"Well I am. I'm suffering. Doc, I been through this shit with you people two hundred times. 'We need to make sure it's not something else.' X ray. CAT scan. Blood test. Drink more water. Wear the oxygen. Same shit every time. You think I like asking you for medication?"

"You get this same pain with every sickle crisis?"

"Every time." He sat up and reached for one of the soda bottles on the bedside table. "Been drinking my fluids like I was told."

Again Taran felt that the man was malingering. Also daring to show him the manipulation.

"Sorry man, I gotta urinate."

Taran stepped outside the curtains. Blue TV light bathed the room. Outside the window, the snow streamed by. The old man was falling asleep, his fists clenched loosely like a baby's. Webster complained loudly with every movement—standing, urinating into the urinal, getting back into bed. On his chair was a booklet of word-find puzzles open to one titled CANADA. All the words had been circled and crossed off the list except TREES.

Taran's pager sounded twice in succession. He checked the numbers.

"I will give you an extra dose of Demerol," he called through the curtain. "You will let me know if it's sufficient."

The resident who'd offered Taran the opportunity to perform the lumbar puncture waited in the hall.

"How many have you done?" he said.

"Four successfully, two unsuccessfully."

"This will be your fifth. She's got great anatomy. Very thin. HIV-positive." He held up his gloved hands.

A pale young woman sat on the edge of the bed, her forehead shining with sweat. Taran introduced himself and offered a handshake.

"I'm sorry to arrive in the middle," he said.

"Oh god, a spinal tap," she said, almost crying. "It's okay. I'll be all right. I've got you two guys here. Tell me what to do."

Taran laid her down on her side facing the wall and helped her to hug her knees to her chest in an exaggerated fetal position. He parted her gown and, with bare hands, palpated the landmarks of her spine. The vertebrae were prominent and perfectly aligned. The interspaces—where the needle would go—were open wide. Inserted blindly, a full four inches deep, the needle would strike cerebrospinal fluid, clear and colorless as water.

Taran put on gloves. With lavish swirls of iodine, he browned the soft blond down on her lower back. Positioning the circular hole over the disinfected area, he covered her with sterile blue paper. He ballooned a wheal of lidocaine and massaged the knot of it.

"All right?"

The patient remained motionless. The resident nodded.

Taran unsheathed the needle and pierced the skin, angling up toward her umbilicus. All the other patients he'd tapped had been old, with fibrous jagged tissues that the needle seemed to snag on then tear through. But this woman was like a perfectly baked cake. The resistance was consistent, the tissues firm but yielding. Advancing smoothly, he tried to feel in his fingers what the needle felt in its tip.

The patient's eyes were closed, her face focused in concentration. Her thoughts arced backward, over her shoulder.

Don't think to me outward, out in the air, Taran thought. *Think to me downward, through your spine, I'll feel it.*

The needletip came up against something hard. But not bone.

"Dura," he said. The tough ligamentous membrane surrounding the spinal canal.

He gave the needle a firm push and felt something pop. The patient opened her eyes and mouth. Expecting to see drops of cerebrospinal fluid beading in the needle's hub, Taran removed the stylet.

But it was dry.

Thinking that he may have passed all the way through the canal, he withdrew a small distance. Again dry.

To tease the flow he reinserted the stylet. Still dry.

One more time.

"*Tcha!*" Taran swore. Something was wrong with the needle. Or her spine. He'd been misled.

"Okay now," the resident said. "Check your positioning. It looks good, right? You're in the midline, the angle's good, you haven't hit bone."

"I agree that it should be right here," Taran said. He pulled the stylet again then shoved it back in.

"It's luck to get it on the first shot," the resident said. "The skill is in the readjustment. Pull all the way out to the skin and try again."

You are a small child, Taran cursed himself.

Methodically, he rechecked the landmarks, smoothed the drape, and again envisioned the needle tunneling toward its goal. He rested his hand on the patient's hip.

Guide me, he thought to her.

Twice he felt on the verge of spearing the stream; three more times he went badly off line. And now on the sixth pass, concentration was fading from his hands. In the tight gloves, his fingertips felt blunt and his palms throbbed. She shifted her weight and the whole landscape of her back changed. He struggled to focus: *sea of blue paper; circular hole of skin; the silver needle; porcelain hands.* It looked to Taran like the vista of a dream. And now, in thinking of dreams, his own dusk dream came rushing forward. He'd felt something brush against his side and he had turned in alarm—it was the counterwoman from the corner store, her slender hand protruding stiffly from a coat sleeve. He was pleased (she called everyone sweetheart and when she took money or gave change, her fingers usually grazed his), but then the coat opened and there was no lower body—her legs and pelvis were gone, the abdomen truncated, the liver and spleen exposed. In the dream, there was nothing he could think to do.

He tried to shake away the vision and pushed the needle forward into the woman. But in his mind, he still saw the brown organs, the open stump of the abdomen.

Her spine was clenching against him now, her face beset with doubt.

"Just one more pass and I will get it."

She recoiled suddenly and cried out in pain—the needle had run aground of bone.

"Unhh. What was that?"

"Bones of your spine," Taran said. "I'm sorry." He stood and surrendered the needle to the resident.

At the end of the darkened hallway, the snow rushed past the window, falling hard. He put his forehead to the cold glass. Everything was white. The rooftops were white, the street was white, the line of parked cartops was nearly erased. Out in the air, the blur of dots swirled into clouds. Closer by, he could follow the trajectories of single flakes. Through the dark white fog down the street, the harsh stairwell lights of his own apartment building glowed soft as candles.

Ida Pelton was a ninety-two-year-old with multiple strokes who was admitted with a urinary tract infection. A tiny old woman, she sat perched in bed, white hair in a single braid. Her left arm was contracted, a withered wing she held close against her side. A piece of dirty adhesive tape hung from her cheek. Unaware of Taran's presence, she stared straight ahead.

Hemineglect, he guessed. Though technically her eyes could see him, as a consequence of the same stroke that had paralyzed her arm, her brain would ignore all stimuli from the left half of the world. He crossed to the other side of the room and she began to track him.

The nurse came in with wrist restraints, a nasogastric tube, and a pill cup. "Got to tie her, doc. She pull out the tube again."

"I am not in the mood to force a tube down her nose. Let's just leave her, shall we? She looks fine."

"Tube not in the next shift start, they say 'why you leave without it?' Get me in trouble, no sir. I document in my note I told the doctor. She have to have it anyhow, she due for cardiac meds."

"Let me have the pills. Maybe she will take them."

Taran straightened the gown on the patient's shoulders and tucked a stray lock of hair behind her ear. Out of the side of her eye, with an angry birdlike stare, she watched him. He chose the prettiest pill, a pastel blue capsule, and held it up, then placed it on his palm. With a sudden movement, she leaned forward and pecked it, her dry lips touching his skin.

The nurse laughed. "She like you, doc. Try another."

He displayed a small round yellow pill, which she readily took. But though he offered the little white hexagon on his palm and danced it about for her, she disdained it. To circumvent her aphasia, he gestured that she was to take *this* pill in *her* mouth and *swallow* it.

As though it were not there, she looked away.

"Oh god," Taran said. "Where's the tube?"

"Have to have an order for the restraint," the nurse said.

"Yes, of course you do," he said, still looking at the patient. "Just one second." He pointed to the piece of tape on her cheek. "You see this? They had the tube on the wrong side. This side, it bothers her. The other nostril, she will be indifferent to like everything else on that side. This may be the one benefit of her strokes. I think she will permit it."

"You the doctor." The nurse dumped everything on the bedside table and left.

"Thanks for your help," Taran said to himself. Then to the patient, "What do you say? Okay? Good, I'll round your other side."

The tube, a long snake of flexible plastic the caliber of a pen, was made to feed in through the nostril, curve down the back of the nasopharynx, pass through the oropharynx and esophagus, and then into the stomach. To soften the plastic, he coiled and uncoiled it. Then he lubricated the length of it with anesthetic jelly. Gently, he placed the tip in her nostril and began to advance.

"Slowly. Slowly."

Serene, she peered into the distance. The hollows of her collarbones were so deep it made her neck look unusually long. The gown had slid down, exposing one paltry breast. For balance he put his hand on the knob of her shoulder.

The tip encountered the back wall of her nose—she flared her nostrils and narrowed her eyes, but held still.

"You are doing wonderfully, Mrs. P. You are quite a good girl."

With the corner of her mouth that still moved, she smiled.

The tube safely made its downward bend through the nose. Taran readied for the next obstacle. "Have you lost your gag reflex, Mrs. P.? I hope so but I'm afraid we shall see."

He inched forward and right away she began to cluck against the plastic, blinking furiously but otherwise not moving. He fed the tube in quickly. There was a momentary resistance—which didn't feel at all correct—but he pushed past it and stuffed in the remaining length of tube. Hopeful, he pumped a syringeful of air into the tube while listening over her stomach with his stethoscope. No telltale sound of air.

"You've curled it in your mouth, haven't you?"

She held her lips cinched shut.

"We will try again."

He withdrew to the nasopharynx and tried another maneuver—pulling her head forward to alter the angle of the throat. But she strained back against the pillows and diverted it again. He tried torqueing the tube differently and then feeding it at different speeds. Each time he reached the critical point at the center of her face—the intersection of nose, mouth, foodpipe, and windpipe—she deflected it with her throat muscles.

He lifted her lip and slid his finger in between her gum and cheek. Cringing at the feel of hard toothless gum, he levered open her jaws. There behind her tongue was the coiled plastic. He pulled the coils out and she started to wrench away—so he laced his fingers through her hair at the base of her braid and gripped. With his other hand in the back of her throat directing the tube downward, he advanced. He could feel her squeezing her face against him, flexing her muscles to block. She emitted a terrible little noise. Then she exploded. Whipped her head from side to side—*No, no, no, no, no.* Hit at him—with surprising strength—with her good arm. Sputtered and struggled and spat.

"Stop!" he shouted at her.

With her murderous hen's eye, she glared at him sideways.

"Stop this now!"

He went and closed the door and then got on the bed next to her and enfolded her in a headlock, pinning her good arm between them. The hand over her face seemed to calm her, as if she were a cat. But when he forced his other hand into her mouth and the tube tip touched her glottis, she bridled against him with all her remaining spirit, her fragile skull threatening to fracture in his embrace. But he had her now and for her own supposed good he sank the tube.

The hallway was empty, the floor deserted. He sat at the nurses' station writing in the charts. Suddenly the wall clock wound through a strenuous movement, ticked audibly for several seconds, then went quiet. He looked up but avoided seeing the time.

He stood. Without knowing why he went to the window. The white streaming of the snow had stopped. Abruptly it seemed. And the world was now utterly transformed: draped with a heavy bunting of snow, the building across the street (all hard edge and block concrete before) was now curve and elegance. The fire escape was a delicate lattice of cotton. A loop of black cable dangling from the floor above was frosted with a perfect U. The snow-covered city gleamed dark pewter, the color of starlight. He stifled a shout and ran to the elevator.

As he rode down in the empty car, the impulse to run out into the snow evaporated, but he padded on through the halls. The automatic doors to the side entrance parted cleanly. He stepped up on to the snow and pitched forward, surprised at how far he sank. The cold powder pushed its way up his pant leg.

Nothing sounded. Nothing moved. The cars stood frozen in place, buried under vague, enormous mounds. Only one set of footprints and the paw prints of a dog marred the snow's surface. Holding his white coat closed, he stepped in the footprints, then veered and plowed out into the street to the pristine middle of the intersection. He turned to look down the avenue. There, gazing down upon him—as if in wait—was the cold, accusing eye of the moon, edging up over a building.

ALIX OHLIN

Wesleyan Writers Conference

TRANSCRIPTION

This is a preliminary report for a 65-year-old Caucasian man who entered complaining of shortness of breath.

Walter was coughing again. He sat up in bed, his red face hanging over his chest like a heavy bloom, coughing. He didn't try to speak or even wheeze; he dedicated himself to the fit with single-minded concentration. Carl watched the oxygen threads quiver across Walter's cheeks. The cough ran down like an engine, slowing to sputters, then ended. Carl handed his uncle a glass of water, and he drank.

"Thanks," Walter said. He pressed one of his large hands against his sunken chest, passed the glass back, and took a few breaths.

"How do you feel?"

"I feel fine," Walter said. He grabbed his handkerchief from the bedside table, hacked up some phlegm, looked at it, and put it back on the table, folded.

"Do you want something to eat?"

"No," Walter said. He looked at his watch and his features brightened. "Time for my beauty routine," he said.

Carl fetched the towel and the electric razor. Walter took off the oxygen and offered his face, eyes closed. He didn't have much facial hair but he always insisted on being shaved before a visit from his girlfriend, Marguerite. His skin was cool and pale and evenly colored, like clay or a smooth beach stone. While he shaved, Carl thought about how Walter's face had looked when Carl was a kid; it was swarthy and stubbled, deeply tanned by cigarette smoke, and it was weird to see his uncle's skin now, so papery and light, as if it were in transition to becoming some entirely different substance. The bedroom was quiet except for the mosquito buzz of the razor and the hiss and pump of the oxygen machine. Every once in a while Walter drew a labored breath. When he was done Carl dabbed Aqua Velva on his face; Walter was and always would be an Aqua Velva man. Walter ran his right hand over his cheeks and down under his chin, then frowned.

"You missed a spot," he said. He reinserted the oxygen in his nostrils and walked downstairs slowly and purposefully, carrying the oxygen line raised and behind him like a king with his robe. Adding to this effect, his wispy hair stood up and waved, crownlike, above his balding head. By the time Marguerite showed up he was installed in the living room. He sat in his favorite armchair, his thick, veiny ankles visible in the gap between his brown pants and his brown socks.

Marguerite said, "Hi, handsome."

She was wearing a flowing green pantsuit with gold buttons and she smelled like roses. She and Walter had been dating for years. They'd met in the home, and when Walter left her behind to move back into his house with Carl, Walter earned the reputation among the residents there as a heartbreaker. But Marguerite came to see him faithfully every Tuesday and Thursday. She took a taxi and they drank weak coffee that Carl made and played gin. Marguerite looked better than Walter did, in spite of being older than he was, but she was delicate, and getting a bit, as Walter put it, soft in the head.

Sometimes she'd smile at Carl and say, "Oh, dear, my mind is going. If you see it anywhere, could you tell it to come back?"

Other times she'd forget words and Carl, walking past the living room, would see her sitting on the couch with her hands up in the air like an agitated bird, saying, "I'm so stupid—what's the word I want?" Walter never knew which word she wanted.

Carl put out the coffee, went downstairs to his office, and turned on the computer. He put on the headset and listened.

General appearance: patient exhibits pedal edema. Earlier this evening patient was found by a relative who brought him in for examination.

He had started working from home a year ago, when he moved back in with Walter, in the house where he'd grown up. Walter didn't say anything to him about the first heart attack, just checked into the convalescent home and then called to announce the change of address. Carl understood that this was Walter's dignity in action: the refusal, at all costs, to be a burden. But when he went and saw the place he felt sick. The fecal smell, the dim light, the wan, shrunken people like some alien and unfortunate race, these had frightened Carl and pissed him off. He resolved to do whatever required—including quitting his job, moving back home, and taking care of Walter himself—to remove Walter from it. While he was sitting in Walter's room a man passed by the open door in a wheelchair, then back in the other direction, then again, and again. When he noticed Carl watching him the man bared his gums and laughed.

"Walter," Carl said, "we're getting out of here."

"Don't trouble yourself, son," Walter said, but he was clearly pleased.

Before he set up his own business Carl was employed by a transcription service at a hospital, and he didn't realize how much he hated going to work every day until he no longer had to do it. Everything about it—the commute, the workplace banter, the fluorescent lighting and bad coffee—had filed him down into points. Carl had no ear for gossip. He didn't tell jokes, and he was uneasy with the siegelike camaraderie of the office. He was not a people person. And now that he was away from those things he was a great deal happier.

He worked only with the voices and he turned them into reports.

Transcription was a habit that could be mastered and even internalized. When he was watching television with his uncle or shopping for groceries, he would hear people's voices and almost unconsciously transcribe them, his foot tapping as if he were working the foot pedals, as if he had reality on tape. In medieval monasteries there was a room called a scriptorium where certain monks labored all day long, transcribing the world into text, and it seemed to him there was an equivalent purity to the work he did in this bare basement room. Correct spelling and correct grammar, the unadorned finality of the perfect text: an astringency that pleased him.

Vital signs: steady and strong. Temperature 99.6 degrees, respiratory rate 20.

Carl worked for exactly one hour. It took him forever to get through reports by Dr. Sabatini, who was his least favorite of all the doctors. Here was the height of rudeness: he ate while dictating. Chomps and smacks between words, slurps and molars grinding. It was disgusting and it necessitated guesswork on the part of the transcriptionist, which Carl hated but it was either that or ask him to clarify every other word. Sabatini sounded like a jerk, too, his syllables impatient and clipped. For some reason that Carl could not specify, he also sounded bald. The suspicion couldn't be confirmed, though, since they'd never met. Carl avoided the hospital as much as possible, which was almost always. The world of technology made this miracle happen.

Most days he stayed downstairs until five, at which time he and Walter ate dinner while watching *Jeopardy!* Between the two of them they always did better than the contestants. If they could go on as one person, Walter sometimes said, pretending they were Siamese twins or with one of them hidden behind the other, well, they'd clean up. Walter was a game show fanatic. The first summer that Carl came to live with Walter, when he was eleven, there was a guy on *Tic Tac Dough* who had a summer-long winning streak, and at the time, through childish superstition, he felt that as long as that guy could keep winning, as long as Walter cheered him on, then everything would be okay. He and Walter watched every day; the tension was almost unbearable. This was years ago of course, after Carl's mother died of what Walter liked to call "the rock-and-roll lifestyle." In the stairwell there was a picture of her, Jane, from high school, smiling broadly, even crazily, as if she were drugged—a glimpse of the future, maybe—and there was a picture of Marie, too, even though she and Walter had only been married for five years before she left him for an Army man and went to live on a base in Germany. She still lived there, and every year she sent Walter a Christmas card. On the inside she crossed out the German words and wrote "Merry Christmas!" instead.

Skin: unremarkable. Head: atraumatic. Chest: there are coarse mid-inspiratory crackles heard at the right lung. Factor contributory to congestive heart failure: smoking 30 years.

At the end of the hour he went back upstairs. The television was on, sound turned up loud, and both Marguerite and Walter were dozing, their cards still spread on the table. Marguerite had gin. Carl stood behind the couch and coughed softly. Marguerite made a kind of low moan and her face sagged terribly in the second before she pulled it into her usual cheery expression. She glanced at Walter and then at Carl.

"I guess I'd better be off," she said.

"I'll call your cab."

"Thank you, dear. You're a—" she looked down and turned the loose gold rings on her fingers, then said, as if to the jewelry, "what's the word I want?"

"Blessing?" Carl said, since this was what she usually called him. Marguerite beamed.

"Just so," she said.

After he'd called he took her elbow and they began the slow careful walk out of the house and down the driveway. She leaned against him and clutched herself closely around the waist as if her entire body were a purse containing valuables. They stood at the end of the driveway, waiting. Marguerite swayed a bit in the wind.

"You know, dear," she said, "he doesn't look too good."

"Walter?"

"Dear," she said, remonstrating. "Of course Walter."

"Well, he's sick," Carl said.

"Has he been making his weekly visits?"

Carl began to tap his foot. "You know I take him, Marguerite."

"I know you do, dear." She looked at him. She took a tissue from her white handbag and dabbed a bit at her nose. "It's just, well." She sighed. "At the home we get excellent round-the-clock care."

"Walter hates the home," Carl said flatly. Marguerite took a deep breath, drew herself up to her full height, which was not very high, and said, "It isn't anybody's first choice, dear." The taxi appeared around the corner and crept toward them.

"He's fine," Carl said. When the taxi pulled up he lowered Marguerite's fragile bones onto the ripped upholstery of the backseat. As the car pulled away he felt a flash of guilt and he called, ridiculously,

"Thanks for coming!" He could see the white blur of her tissue in the window as she waved good-bye.

Patient has been prescribed

Walter was awake and watching *Matlock*. He was drinking a cup of coffee which must by now have been quite cold.

"Faking, Uncle Walter?"

"If I pretend to fall asleep, she falls asleep, too," Walter said, and slurped.

"That's not very polite," Carl said.

"Well, Jesus. You know I think the world of Marguerite. But if I have to hear one more word about her grandchildren in Boca Raton I'll fall asleep and never wake up."

"She thinks you should go back into the convalescent home."

"Convalescent home, my ass," Walter said. His eyelids were heavy and he held his coffee cup loosely on the arm of his chair. "You keep convalescing, and then you're dead. What day is it, son?"

"Thursday."

"Thursday's bingo night in the home. I won once. Jar of cold cream."

"They gave you a jar of cold cream?"

"That was the prize," Walter said. He put the coffee cup down on the table, leaned back, and closed his eyes. "I gave it to Marguerite. That's how the two of us got started."

"Oh."

"Yeah," Walter said. "Don't worry. I'm fine."

History:

That night, Walter fell out of bed. What woke Carl up from a restless, dream-drenched sleep (since he never knew the people whose illnesses or accidents were described in the reports, and never saw the doctors who dictated them, his periodic nightmares were filled with faceless strangers undergoing unidentifiable medical procedures while Carl, helplessly, watched) must have been the thud of Walter's body hitting the floor. He sat up in bed, not knowing why he was awake, and heard a ragged, whispery gasp from the other side of the hall. When he got to the bedroom Walter was looking up expectantly from the floor.

"I fell out of bed!" he whispered.

"I can see that," Carl said.

"I feel okay though."

"We should probably go to the hospital."

"I said I feel all right."

"I heard what you said," Carl said. He kneeled down and put one arm under Walter's back and the other on his arm and pulled him to a sitting position. His uncle's back felt meaty and solid through his T-shirt. But he was unsteady on his feet, and in the car he closed his eyes and didn't seem to feel well enough to talk.

At the emergency room they put him under observation, but they could not decide what exactly had happened to him. Carl stood at the foot of the bed, facing the digital flickering of the medical instruments. He felt calm. It wasn't the first time they'd been to the ER and in all likelihood it would not be the last. He examined the screen and thought of all the tests he'd seen, the signals from inside Walter's body: the CAT scans, X rays, EKG. How many people ever saw inside somebody else, that deep, that far? He was proud of it somehow.

"Sometimes people just fall out of bed," the intern said to Carl.

"Is that your actual diagnosis?" Carl said. "I want to see the chart."

"I can't give you the chart."

"I want to see the chart," he said, and grabbed it from the intern's hand. Walter grinned from his bed and said to the intern, "He knows everything."

"You need to rest," the intern said.

Carl took the chart out to the hall and sat down with it. The jangling noise of the hospital, even though it was three o'clock in the morning, and the occasional spasmodic blinking of the fluorescent lights, and the bad-smelling, recirculated air were making him claustrophobic and irritable. He rubbed his eyes and looked at the chart, the scrawlings of medications and symptoms. Everything about his uncle was here, Walter on paper, his body reconstituted as a record of its processes and ills. He thought, this is a body of information, and there arose before him a brief image of Walter's naked body, made not of flesh and blood but of a shell of data like tattoos on air. In this image the body was fine and translucent as a moth, numbers running down the arms and separating into five fingers, diagrams banded across the chest: statistical, eternal.

"Mr. Mehussen?"

Carl looked up at a blond woman extending her hand.

"I'm Dr. Newman," she said. "I'd like to talk to you about your uncle. And I'd like to have his chart back, please."

Patient appears fragile but in good spirits. Is able to communicate symptoms and receive information.

Dr. Newman had straight, thin, slightly greasy blond hair which swung as she talked. Under her white coat she wore khakis and sensible brown shoes. She was in the middle of saying that falling out of bed, while a traumatic event, might not have meaningful consequences for Walter's condition, when he realized who she was. He glanced at her sharply.

"Do you have a question?"

"I just—you're Dr. Newman."

She ran a hand wearily through her hair and nodded.

"Dr. Amanda Newman."

"Yes, that's me."

"I do your tapes," he said.

"My tapes?"

"Transcription," he said. He watched her nod again, smile politely, and then recalibrate her manner to the one she used while dealing with people employed, however tangentially, in the medical profession. She took a deep breath, moved her shoulder closer to his, and became at once friendlier and more professional.

"You have excellent diction," he told her.

She raised her eyebrows. "Thanks," she said.

Walter spent the night under observation. Carl spent the night in the hallway, drinking bad coffee from a paper cup. They were running some tests. They were awaiting results. Dr. Newman was still on duty, and at times he could hear her cool, clear voice giving orders and asking questions, and the sound of it was oddly soothing to him, reminding him of his office and his work. He closed his eyes to focus on it. Other people waited near him, flipping through magazines, or whispering softly together. They were all quiet, dazed-seeming. A woman came through and began to search around all the seats, saying, "My bag. I know I left it around here somewhere." Then a man came and put his arms around her and led her away, glancing guiltily back over her shoulder, as if the bag were a shameful or deeply personal subject, not to be discussed. He heard one of the nurses say, "Dr. Newman!" and Dr. Newman say, "In a minute!"

Walter was asleep, wheezing rhythmically. The other patient in the room was groaning in pain, a distant, constant sound like traffic. It didn't seem to be keeping Walter up. Carl wasn't sleepy, but he slipped into a kind of a trance in the hallway, slouched in his seat. He didn't know what to do except sit and not sleep, sit and be vigilant. Whatever happened he would be awake and present for it. He thought about when his mother died, and someone—a teacher—came and said to him, "Your mother is dead," and it seemed like because it had happened off stage and out of his sight that it could not be real or true. He tried to feel sad about it but he couldn't. He kept trying to really grasp the fact of it, and he would sometimes repeat to himself, "My mother is dead," and the words would make him cry but he still did not entirely feel it. The fact was too big. It defeated him. The days around the funeral passed in a blur of dark mystery, adults wearing black, speaking in whispers. There was an association of being pressed in by crowds and of the smell of unfamiliar food cooking. Instead of grief he developed a sense of irritation and injustice, of being unfairly put upon. More than anything he wanted to find someone to complain to, maybe a teacher or someone else at school. He wanted to say that if only he had been given more information, more evidence, more time, then he would have been better prepared.

Procedure: patient will be informed as to the likely future developments in his condition.

Early in the morning the shifts changed and the new nurses came, pouring themselves cups of coffee and bustling around the station. He was looking down at the floor when he saw Dr. Newman's brown shoes. She sat down beside him.

"You should have gone home and slept," she said.

"Why?" he said.

She laughed shortly, on the exhale.

"Because you look tired."

"So do you," he said, and she did. The skin under her eyes had turned blueish and looked wrinkled and taut. She had pulled her hair back in an elastic, but a couple of strands had escaped it here and there. He noticed that she was carrying a chart, and he knew it must be Walter's. She cocked her head in the direction of Walter's room.

"Let's go talk to your uncle." She took a step but he did not follow and she paused and looked at him, waiting.

"Please," he said. Meaning please be a good doctor, meaning help him. Dr. Amanda Newman stepped back and put her hand briefly on his arm, and the touch of it was shocking to him (though not as shocking as it would be in the days to come, when she began to say his name at the beginning of her tapes: "Hello, Carl. This is a preliminary report on," and he would listen, fascinated, to this part, the intimacy of these four letters, *his name,* spoken by her clear voice, replaying it for minutes at a time, before he could move on).

"Let's go," she said.

He followed her to Walter's room, and she went inside, and Walter looked first to her and then to Carl, who saw his uncle's worried eyes ease, go tranquil, because Carl was there.

"Hi, Walter," he said.

" 'Lo," Walter said, and coughed with the effort. He lay stolid and unmoving, his arms exposed above the sheet. The skin there was blotched and veiny. The other patient thrashed uncomfortably in his bed while his visitor, a younger woman, tried in vain to quiet him. Dr. Newman began to explain that Walter could go home, that there would be observation, that there would be additional medication.

As she spoke Carl saw the cool black letters of her report unfurling in his mind.

Assessment: the heart labors.

He stood still with the revealed truth of it—that in the end, the real end, Walter was not going to be fine—and a pain bloomed hotly in his chest as if his body were offering Walter's body sympathy of its own kind. The tape in his head clicked and rewound, whirred all the way back to childhood. What he heard then was Walter's voice, smoke-tinged and hearty; what he smelled was Aqua Velva and tobacco and sweat. They were standing in the doorway of the living room, looking in at it, Walter behind him. He felt Walter's big hands pressing a bit too hard on his shoulders, the weight of them forcing him to slouch, and he was eleven and his heart flew up when Walter said, "From now on, son, this will be your home."

SALVATORE SCIBONA

Fine Arts Work Center in Provincetown

THE PLATFORM

She never meant to betray her captors, only to defy them. In town, quartered in the half-destroyed ducal palace, was a unit of soldiers from up and down the country, a week shy of receiving discharge papers, with not enough to do. The local boys had challenged them to a tournament of footraces. Was it too much to ask for one hour to go down to the square and watch? Her mother and her grandmother went onto the terrace to confer and came back to say they would not allow it. Men in the military were separated from their families and so reduced to savagery. No no no, her mother said. This was Lazio in 1878. She was seventeen. She would be their prisoner forever unless she did something about it.

By the time she got to the races all the boys from town had been eliminated. The soldiers were running one-on-one heats from the steps of the palace to the fountain in front of the church. They were in their undershirts, charging with their heads back and their chests pushed forward and their arms flapping madly, and at the end they dunked their heads in the fountain. Most of the town was in attendance. Her mother and her grandmother would get word of her transgression and she didn't care. In the championship race were two officers, brothers from Bologna named Marini. She had a deck of playing cards in her skirt pocket. She resolved that after the race she would wait for the crowd to disperse and then she would approach whichever of them had won and proffer the cards as a prize. But it didn't turn out that way. The winner was carried off on the shoulders of his comrades, so instead she gave them to his brother.

From the backseat of Vincent's Buick, Mrs. Marini watched the woods passing. In the half-light of early morning, they were only a smudge in the picture frame of the window. And then the woods gave way to empty fields. As it grew lighter, she could make out individual trees and busted cornstalks littering the fields, and puddles in the muddy low places, glimmering. She was both riding in a car and was outside the city, two events that had never before coincided.

Mrs. Marini had mixed feelings about cars. There were people in Eleventh Hill, her part of the city, who could hardly afford spare buttons but they scrimped to buy a car and then threw away the rest of their money on gasoline. Bennie Scarlatti drove a car, and he came to the church for soup with his little girls on Tuesdays and Saturdays, which she knew because she washed the bowls. Look at the streetcar. What was that for? Look at the booth on the corner of 11th Avenue and 16th Street where you could wait for the streetcar and then it would come and take you to whatever part of Cleveland you wanted. Mrs. Marini had a theory. The theory was that people watched too many Western movies, which fooled with their heads and made them think the ideal was not that you got married and bought a dining room set and planted a garden behind the house and the kids weeded this garden and picked the beans and the escarole and dug up the potatoes and you stayed in the neighborhood for a long time and you played cards with your friends and when you died people got all worked up because you'd been known to them. No. The ideal was you bought this car. And you pretended like someday you were going to escape and drive out West, but if you ever did when you got there you would have to eat sand and you would have no company (because you wanted to be free from people, remember, you wanted a new life) and eventually you would get shot in an argument over a horse.

It was true Vincent and Lina had a car. They weren't any relation to her, but they'd asked her advice before they bought it. It was unclear why. They must have known what she would say. She would say, "No, don't do it." And they asked her anyway. And she said, "No, don't do it." And still they bought the car. Knowing them as long as she had, and after years and years of her instruction—how you double tie a shoe so it doesn't come off on your way to school, how you sew a hem on a pair of trousers so even you can't see it, then later, how you keep your books so you don't end up in line for soup at the church like Bennie—after all that she'd thought some judgment had sunk in. She told them, she said, "I thought maybe something had sunk in." Then dear, sweet, cross-eyed Vincent pointed out the pretty tires and grinned like an idiot. Still with them maybe, maybe, it was reasonable. Vincent had had work straight through the thirties, at times when everybody else on his block was unemployed. He'd become the guy you asked to put in a word for you at the bricklayers' union. Also Lina had her job at the overcoat shop. Also they had no children still. And if they didn't have a car Lina would never be able to see her parents on the farm.

Lina said, "Come take a drive with us. We're going to see Mama." This was about once a month for four years.

Mrs. Marini said, "Please torture me in a jumping box going up and down and side to side for twenty hours. No. I think I can live without."

"But it's nice out there. Mama would like to see you."

"No. No no."

Then on a Wednesday, Lina said, "Mama called. She says she wants you to come."

"Oh good, I'll look at the cow."

"She says she *really* wants you to come."

So Mrs. Marini was riding in a car, outside the city, looking out the window. Mrs. Marini was outside the city for the first time since her husband, now long dead, had dragged her onto a train thirty-two years ago for a weekend at the lake, in Sandusky, in 1906.

She propped her eyeglasses at an angle to her face, the stems resting on her temples, because it made the image sharper. She found herself noticing again and again the way the woods crowded to a neat, straight line on the edges of every open place, like there was a barricade holding them back from the orchards and the cornfields. The squareness, the man-made shape of every clearing, the way the trees clung to the hill slopes, and protruded almost horizontally along the steepest parts. And it was clear, as it was not clear in the city, where people coddled apple and plum trees planted in rows on their back lawns, that Ohio had once been a single, dense forest, open only where the rivers divided it. They were living in a barely domesticated country. With her handkerchief she rubbed some steam from the window to see better.

She leaned her head against the glass and did not move for a long time.

"I think she's sleeping," Lina said from the front of the car.

"What do you mean, sleeping? I'm looking out the window."

"You haven't said anything since twenty-five minutes," Vincent said.

"You know this because you're keeping track."

"You haven't moved either," Lina said. "I was watching in the mirror."

"What are you watching me for? I'm an animal in a cage that you're doing some experiment."

"It's okay to sleep. People sleep in cars."

"My eyes were open, Mrs. Scientist, Mrs. Watching My Every Motion. Who sleeps in a car?"

"People sleep in cars," Vincent said. "It's a long drive."

"I am looking out the window. I am looking out the window."

"Okay, you're awake," Lina said.

"I'm awake and I was awake before."

"You were awake before."

"Who sleeps in a car?"

Mrs. Marini had seen Lina's mother, Patrizia, only twice in the four years since Patrizia and Lina's father, Umberto, had moved out to the farm. One funeral and one wedding. Mrs. Marini had never believed they would go. Nobody did. But they left before the house was sold, three months before Lina married Vincent. (Lina refused to go with them; she stayed at Mrs. Marini's house until the night before the wedding.) For as long as Lina's family had lived in Eleventh Hill, Umberto had been carrying on, making his Plan known, making people mad at him because there was the suggestion in this that 18th Street wasn't enough, that Eleventh Hill wasn't enough, or Cleveland. That they all ought to be embarrassed if they were happy there.

In the early evenings, when she was younger, Lina sat at Mrs. Marini's dining room table, copying out the articles from the morning *Press* to practice her penmanship, waiting for Umberto to come get her after he finished work at the tool and die shop. Then like an invading barbarian he charged, without knocking, through Mrs.

Marini's side door, the girl squealing, running, as he chased her out the kitchen, through the front room, up the stairs, until he lurched back into the dining room where Mrs. Marini was already mopping up the slop from his shoes. The red-faced yapping girl was clamped under his arm like a battering ram, and her long black hair came loose from its pins and veiled her face. Then he asked her in a voice so mumbled and grumbly Mrs. Marini could hardly make out what he was saying, in dialect that softened all the consonants and left out most of the vowels at the ends of words altogether, the way Sicilians talked to each other when there was a Northerner in the room and they didn't care if she understood. He shook her until she waved her arms and said, "Carmelina, are you ready to go?" And she howled back at him in this foreign language, like she hadn't spent all day speaking the King's English at school, and crisp, court Italian to Mrs. Marini at the supper table as she copied the English newspaper, she said, "Where, where are we going, Papa? Where is it? Will we have rabbits and goats? Where are we going?" And he said, "Are you ready to go?" And she was in a frenzy, screeching and yelling, "Where, Papa, where, where?" And he said, "Wyoming."

Wyoming Mrs. Marini had figured out was their family code for this Plan of his, the place where he would take them. In Wyoming, Umberto had once informed her, the land was absolutely free, as much as you wanted, as much as a city.

"You send a letter to the government, and they send you the paper and tell you where to go," he said. "Easy."

"Who told you this?"

"Guy at work told me. A serious guy. His brother was there."

"I have to tell you something, Berto."

"I don't want to hear."

"That was fifty years ago."

"Look how big it is. You ever look at a map? And nobody lives there. A big place." He spread his arms wide. "And you can live like a real American."

"Not for fifty years, and the Indians would kill you anyway."

"You can have cows, as many as you can count. And you take your family there and you can see forever. It's nothing like here—absolutely no garbage."

"Please, don't tell me anymore."

"And the water is clean."

"Why don't you go there—right now?"

"Patrizia says it's too cold. I don't know who told her this. She won't go. Also, the guy told me you can't grow anything because it doesn't rain so much."

"So what do you eat, cowboy, in this place that you can't even have a garden?"

"Beef."

Patrizia wouldn't go, so they settled on Ashtabula County, Ohio, because it wasn't much colder than Cleveland and you could grow grapes there.

Mrs. Marini didn't believe they would ever move away, or even that Patrizia believed it. Then the drapes were gone from the kitchen windows. Saplings grew out of the gutters.

Patrizia said they almost never got decent, sharp cheese anymore, like the cheese Lina and Vincent had brought from the city today. "Nobody comes to see us," she said, hanging the rabbit from a hook on the back porch, its blood dripping into a bowl on the floorboards. She sighed. There was, in this sigh, in this dropping her hands to her hips with a soft noise like sheets flapping on a clothesline, an unmistakable accusation: You were the closest friend I had in the world— this was what Patrizia meant to tell her with that sigh but didn't have the nerve to say aloud—and my husband dragged me out to this godforsaken place where we don't even have a toilet inside, where you knew I never wanted to come. I liked baseball, I liked canasta on Thursday nights as much as you. And it's been four years. I have a telephone. You could have gotten a telephone, too, and we could have talked. You could have said, "Vincent, let's drive out to see Patrizia. She must be lonely." But you didn't come.

"It's nice here," Mrs. Marini said. "You must be able to see a million stars."

"We can hear cars coming"—Patrizia tore the hide off one of the rabbit's paws—"from a mile away."

And there's never an excuse to dress properly even on Sunday—said the rip of the skin from the flesh. I can't go to church. Let me repeat, no baseball. I have to listen to Berto and his idiot plans, his raving over and over about the eggs that are two hours out of the hen and the yolks that are red like they're supposed to be. What difference does it make? Eggs all taste the same. Think of what I have for conversation here. Think of the talking we used to do. The strolls with my arm in your arm up the hill to see your husband's grave and plant flowers. How Lina and me, the day after you buried him, we came over and the door was locked and we looked in the window and you were lying on the linoleum in the kitchen under an afghan. And we washed your face and took you home with us, because you didn't know how to boil water anymore, you were out of your mind. How I listened to you for nights on nights that he was gone and what were you supposed to do?

"The vineyards look beautiful," Mrs. Marini said stupidly. She turned on the spigot at the side of the house to wash the dandelion greens.

"They pay you by the sugar content. If there's no sun, the grapes are tart, you get nothing. Last year, we let them rot on the vine. Probably Lina told you."

Look at this house, Patrizia silently beseeched, look at the paint coming off because we can't afford paint, we don't have time to paint. See the barn? See how it's leaning to one side? A stiff breeze could knock it to a heap of boards on the ground. And I wish it would. I pray for that. You thought we were poor before. And you left me here without even a little talking now and then, just a stop to bring me some cheese and have a cup of coffee. You didn't have to go trim the grapes with the others. You could have stayed inside and I could have stayed in like today and we could have talked.

Patrizia unhooked the rabbit and brought it inside. Mrs. Marini carried in the dandelion greens and laid them on a towel in the kitchen to dry. Patrizia dropped the rabbit in a roasting pan with some onions and carrot. She went outside and honked the horn on Umberto's truck to let them all know to come in for supper.

Mrs. Marini had to sit down. It was cold. Her hip was bothering her. She pulled the morning crossword out of her purse, unfolded it, and flattened it out on the table. Through the window, she could see Patrizia slam the door of the truck and trudge in her work boots through the mud toward the back porch again, her body rocking from side to side like a man carrying pails of water in both hands— just like a man walks, except for her breasts hanging against her stomach. She wasn't wearing a brassiere. Mrs. Marini thought, I have committed a crime.

Now the sun fell into the kitchen window frame. The vineyard leaves outside were inky blue and still. Had it been a little warmer, and had the vineyards climbed a few hills instead of lying flat like this, over a plain, it might have been Lazio. She might have been ten years old, looking out her grandmother's kitchen door. The sun illuminated all the specks of dust and splashes of dirt on the window glass and illuminated the supper table and the crossword.

Patrizia came in and slipped on her house shoes. There was the sound of pots clattering, plates, a knife against a cutting board.

Minutes passed and they said nothing. Mrs. Marini was unable to do anything with the across clues. She put down her pencil, wondering why they weren't talking, opened and closed her hands to stretch her fingers. The rows of vines led straight and shimmering from the house into the distance, as even and neat as typescript, and seemed to meet at a far-off place under the sun.

At the train station in 1879, with one suitcase, with one bottle of water, waiting for the train, looking at the vast country, the terraced hills, the vineyards. If she told anybody they would have stopped her, they would have locked her in a room. Running away to marry a man she'd talked to exactly three times, the loser of a footrace. I will never see them again. I will never see this place, ever again. She'd been unable to find Ohio on a map and thought maybe he meant Iowa, Iowa is right here in the middle. Never having looked at the hills with anything but boredom, angry boredom, until today. Never to see her mother or father again.

The silence had lasted too long to have been just a busy pause. It wasn't, Don't say anything for a minute I'm trying to remember where I put the good napkins. Had they been strangers, Mrs. Marini lost on a road and come in to ask directions, there would have been no silence, no disconcerting minutes thinking of what you might say to ease the moment back into familiarity, into the land of canasta partners from way back carrying on about whatever, about nothing really, just enjoying each other. Strangers can talk and talk and at least there's no silence, and also there's the pop and surprise of hearing in a few minutes another person's life condensed to its most basic phrases— born in Siracusa, one child, used to sew corsets at Higbee's downtown, haven't had a glass of water in thirty years, drink only coffee and wine—that kind of story. With friends you know all that and the only things that remain to be said are the dull day to day—woke up, washed my face, went to feed the rabbits, one of them gone missing—that and the secrets of feeling you could never tell a stranger.

Waiting at the train station to be a stranger to everyone. Waiting for the train to come and looking at the hills and even stepping off the platform, back into the weeds. Maybe she could get back without anyone noticing that she'd left. Time to linger on her mother's terrace, recording each detail of the view, the shadows cast by the chestnut trees, the missing roof tiles. Time to consider. Time to keep the promise she'd made to cut her sister's hair. The weeds around the platform bending against her legs. What if this man beat her? Who could she go to in a country where there was no one who understood her language? From inside the station, the eyes of the man who'd sold her the ticket peeking out. A man she didn't know, who was wondering, maybe, why this girl was standing so still in the weeds around the platform. The expanse of sky. Her sisters would inherit her things. The light sparkling on the slag between the train tracks. With one suitcase.

Maybe Patrizia likes it here. Maybe it reminds her of home.

She and Patrizia used to be able to tell each other secrets without saying a word. They used to move from the back porch to the kitchen silently and suggest whole stories. Patrizia could identify what Mrs. Marini had eaten for lunch by the way she held her cards, how far from her face, how often she reorganized her hand. And now they were deaf and dumb to each other. Mrs. Marini could only guess what Patrizia was thinking. She had no idea what this loud chopping at the onions, this banging of the pots might mean.

Then Patrizia was staring into the bottom of a saucepan.

Mrs. Marini stood up to set the table. She opened the cupboard. She said, "I forget. Which glasses do you use?"

Eventually to forget the names of the streets. Leaving now meant never coming back. Wanting to keep in her brain every word her grandmother had ever said to her. Wanting to have the shrillness, the insistence of the woman's voice in her head and not to forget it. One bottle of water. Phrasing the telegram she would send from New York to the man who'd said that he would wait for her, a man she would never have met if his brother hadn't been lifted up and carried away. Stepping on and then back off the platform. Then turning and seeing that nobody else was checking a watch, waiting there for the train. To her right, the opening in the trees from where the train would come, to her left the opening where it would go away without her. To leave now meant this was the last picture she would have of the place in her mind, that she would always think of it as looking just the way it did that afternoon, and her family looking just the way they had at lunch that day. In this way none of these people would ever die. They would be fixed, in Lazio, in time. She would send no address. She would receive no news. Leaving now meant she would have them always. Stepping back onto the platform.

"Umberto wants to go home," Patrizia said.

"Oh, thank the Lord," Mrs. Marini said and meant it. "We'll make a party. I'll get all the best things. You can stay with me until you get a house."

Patrizia gripped the handles of the pan. "I mean he wants to go back," she said. "His brother died and there are no children. He left the house to Berto."

"Which house? In Siracusa? What are you saying?"

"And he says if I won't go that's fine, but he's going."

"It's not our affair," Vincent said. "It's not our thing to decide."

"It's not— Excuse me," Lina said, "it's not his to decide either."

Umberto cut a leg off the rabbit and passed it to Lina.

Vincent said, "We cannot—"

"You're a married man who, therefore—what a burden—can't just act like he's eighteen and go buy a car because he *feels* like it or go to another country because he *feels* like it," Lina said. "Because— what a *weight* what a *pity*—he has a wife and a family and a house."

Mrs. Marini said, "Twenty-four years."

"Because," Lina said, "excuse me, but there is a person at this table who never wanted to come to this country in the first place. But *you* said she was coming, so she came. And who never— Mama never wanted to move to this paradise of donkey labor in the first place, but you said she was going. And she went and not a word of complaint. Not a groan. Nothing."

Vincent stood up and started to spoon the pasta into the bowls.

"Why don't you say something, Mama?"

"Mrs. Marini, do you want more sauce?" Vincent said.

"Don't raise your voice to your father," Patrizia said.

Mrs. Marini put her thumb and forefinger together, said, "A bit, thank you."

Umberto said, "Where's that cheese?"

"Look at your wife five years ago," Lina said.

Vincent brought the cheese on a plate with a little knife and set it on the table in front of Umberto. "Things happen between married people that you don't understand them from the outside," Vincent said. "You know this."

"Twenty-four years, Berto," Mrs. Marini said.

Patrizia was chewing very slowly. Her hands were still. She seemed to be looking into the empty space over the corner of the table.

"Look at Mama five years ago," Lina said, "and look at her now."

Outside, Mrs. Marini could see the sun had gone down. The vineyard was dim. There was a stripe of pink light left in the sky.

"My wife did not say why she's not coming," Umberto said. "She's welcome to come. Tell them why, Patrizia, go ahead."

"*Welcome*," Mrs. Marini said, "is a word you use for strangers who want to come in your house."

"Tell them, speak."

"Will you pass that cheese?" Patrizia said.

"*Answer me*," Umberto said.

"I don't want you to go."

"That's it. No other...thinking. No 'I like this here,' 'I prefer that here.' Just 'I don't want you to go.'"

"This rabbit came out nice if I say it myself," Patrizia said.

"Is that it? You like rabbits?" Umberto said. "You like rabbits, we'll get rabbits then."

"If you prefer for us not to talk about this," Vincent said, "if it's a private thing."

Patrizia finished chewing, "It's a little stringy, but this one was older."

"If you want me to drop it, Mama, I will," Lina said. "I don't want to, but I will."

"There is room in my house for both of us and rabbits and visitors," Umberto said.

Mrs. Marini said, "*My* is what you call your house when you are an unmarried person or your spouse has died."

"No, go ahead, talk," Patrizia said. "This cheese is beautiful, or I'm just deprived and we don't have it so much."

"You see? You see what she does?" Umberto said. "It's good cheese, Vincenzo, thank you."

Vincent stood up and put his napkin on the table.

"Why should she have to give reasons?" Lina said.

Vincent picked up his leg of rabbit and headed toward the door to the back porch.

Umberto addressed his plate, "This is my own child who raises her voice to her father."

Vincent stopped in the doorway.

"And who's going to wash your floor," Lina said, "and cook your supper and shave your face?"

Umberto took the heavy copper serving spoon from the pasta dish and tapped it against the table. He closed his eyes.

Vincent went back to the table and sat down.

"It's a natural thing that when a man is old he wants to go back to his home." Umberto tapped the spoon on the edge of Lina's plate.

Patrizia had her eyes fixed on Umberto, and Mrs. Marini could see, for the first time, something icy, something like anger in her face.

Lina put her hands under the table and pushed her body into the back of the chair, slowly. She ran her tongue carefully over her upper lip.

"You'll see." The tap tapping of the spoon against Lina's plate. "Vincenzo will want to go back, too, give him some years. He wants the sea, the la-de-la," the taptaptap of the spoon, "the songs, his father's house."

Vincent was watching Umberto and his lips became thin. He looked tall, seemed to be looming over the side of the table. His right eye strayed off to the side. It gave her the impression that he was watching all sides of the room at once.

"Your mother's dead, Berto, and your father, and your brother," Mrs. Marini said, "and your sister. And all your friends are over here."

He adjusted his grip on the spoon.

Vincent's left eye seemed to be looking at her, and the right one concentrated on some spot down the hallway.

There was something bare and restrained in the way Patrizia was watching her husband.

Lina didn't move.

Vincent picked up the pasta dish. "We should soak this." He walked to Umberto's side of the table. "Here, let me soak that spoon." Tap tap. "Papa, I want to soak that spoon."

Umberto looked at the window. "I wish," he said. The spoon fell out of his hand, onto Lina's plate. "There should be a reason that she gives me."

Vincent picked up the spoon and went to the sink. "I didn't want to interrupt," he said. "Go ahead."

Patrizia spread her hands on the table, pushing on it, like she was keeping it from floating into the air. She opened her mouth, stared at her husband. But then she turned her face and said nothing.

It was dark outside. The window had flipped images and projected a picture of the four of them, at the table, waiting.

Waiting for the train, looking behind her. One suitcase and one bottle of water. Stepping off the platform. Thinking that in this way everything here would remain as it was on that afternoon, that they would always be here—but knowing this was a lie. Knowing it was an illusion and that someday she would admit to it. That she had left her family, that she had allowed them to die, or killed them. Then looking at the chestnut trees down the track and around. And, God forgive her, stepping back onto the platform. Then a puff of steam over the trees, the sound of the train. The train swerving into view.

And later—in her kitchen on 18th Street, in the house she'd shared for thirty-five years with this man who was her consolation, her right arm, her pearl of great price—the timer went off and she opened the oven door. She called to her husband in the front room. She said, "Nico, come in and carve the roast." Waiting a minute and him not answering. Not turning to go into the front room (but knowing he was in there, lying on the sofa), just standing in front of the oven, saying it louder, saying his name, louder, and waiting. The door to the oven still open and the heat rising to her face.

Mrs. Marini lifted her plate in both hands and stood up. At first, she wasn't sure if Patrizia could see what she was about to do. Patrizia with that look on her face like, What has it come to, the hands struggling to hold down the table. Mrs. Marini lifted the plate higher. And then Patrizia with her eyes—the eyelids twitching. Do it.

So, Mrs. Marini threw her plate at the floor. And the bones of the rabbit skittering under the chair. And the smash. And the dish a bloom of splinters, like the crown of a thistle that's come open.

She reached for her glass.

NATHAN ROBERTS

University of Virginia

THIS IS NOT SKIN

There are 1,811 miles between Independence, Missouri, and Oregon City, Oregon: the famous Oregon Trail. We did it backward. And we did it from Portland to St. Louis—our route slightly out of focus, like a movie you've been watching too long before realizing it's the projectionist's fault and not the filmmaker's, the story line marred by the fact that the characters never quite looked clear. That's Audrey and me. She was like a drug I no longer enjoyed, to which I'd nevertheless grown addicted. A recurring theme in my life, but more on that later.

Even the drag queens seemed to see that I was making some sort of mistake. The day we left, they fluttered around me like winged creatures, whispering warnings in my ear. My boss, Chocolate Jones—a black post-op transsexual who passed so believably as a biological woman that she once held down a day job in the children's section of a department store—took me by the wrist and pulled me close. "You have to be careful of that child, Pure One," Chocolate said. "She's got itches she don't know how to scratch yet." Chocolate called me Pure One because, for the two years I'd tended at LaBar, I was celibate. The other bartenders, the cocktail waiters in cutoff jeans and designer tank tops, the performers who looked stunning in drag and the ones who looked desperate: all of them spent nights tricking for sex and change, while I wore long-sleeved thermals and construction worker pants and avoided human contact like someone allergic to his own skin. Chocolate held onto my wrist. The U-Haul truck was only a few feet away from us, daylight exposing its small dents, the scratches on the airbrushed mural of "Paul Revere's Ride." It was unpleasant for me to feel Chocolate's hand around my arm, but she thought she was doing me a favor by pulling me physically into her world.

Several yards away Audrey stood surrounded by a small crowd of female performers, women with slick pompadours, dark ties, and huge dildos stuffed down their trousers. At night all cats are gray, sure, but in the sun you can see not only their colors, but the startled expressions on their faces as they slink away in a sort of instinctive panic. Audrey was more girlish than her drag-king buddies; there was a gracefulness in the way she put her hip forward while she stood, a coquettishness conveyed by the bend in her wrist when she let one of them light her cigarette, a stylishness to her clothes despite the fact that they were covered in paint. I watched Audrey try to laugh mannishly. The girls loved her, swooned over her jokes and her paintings. "Why do you have to leave?" they must've been asking her. "I'm going to graduate school," Audrey would have said, not sure whether to punch someone's arm or kiss a cheek. She'd just finished her joint BA/BFA at Reed College and the Pacific Northwest College of Art, a five-year program which Audrey, the little genius, managed to complete in only six years. Audrey had become a friend out of default soon after I moved back to Portland: She was a regular at LaBar, and she went to college with my housemates. Her studio was near the cabaret, and she used to come in after midnight, splattered with acrylics from the thick self-portraits she painted on glass panes and mirrors bought at second-hand stores. She never went home with any of the women—not as far as I knew.

"That girl's nothing but a LUG," one of the drag queens said. They were always calling her that, a lesbian until graduation; I never considered that it might be true because the same people said crueler things about me. "I hear he's got a tiny dick," a performer would occasionally stage whisper to a regular. A customer once approached me and said, "I'll give you twenty bucks if you let me see your penis." When I declined he offered me fifty; when I declined that, he turned to a table of laughing friends. "It's not small, it's disfigured." "Erectile dysfunction" was another popular theory. "Get that boy some Viagra." Or, "Don't bother, he's straight." Sometimes people would ask me if I was queer, and occasionally I said yes. Often people asked me to go to bed with them, and I always said no. Customers loved me twice as much because I wouldn't sleep with them, and I took home more tips than anyone else.

As I watched Audrey say good-bye to her friends, Chocolate knelt beside my duffel bag and zipped it up all the way, then put the bag in the truck for me. Although I didn't know it at the time, she was leaving me a going-away present. I waved to Chocolate and the other queens, climbed into the passenger seat of the U-Haul. A moment later Audrey was sitting beside me, in the driver's side. She winked and said, "You're a good friend." She wasn't being sentimental, she was quoting *Thelma and Louise,* the scene right before they drive into the Grand Canyon. It was my job to say the next line, "You, too, sweetie, the best." We talked that way.

Then, as Audrey turned the ignition, Chocolate Jones stepped up to the truck and I rolled the window down. I wanted to say something about how everyone was acting as though I wasn't coming back. To explain that I was only along for the ride, chosen to be

Audrey's driving partner because, as she put it, I was the only other person she knew who led a life of leisure. (Audrey never quite understood that I *worked* at LaBar; she assumed I was there on a want-to-be basis, like her.) I would be returning by plane in a week. I was going to remind Chocolate of all this, but I never got the chance. She grabbed my ear, pulled me toward her, and whispered, "I forgive you."

All this by way of prelude; the title-sequence, if you will. The bit of narrative that takes place while the actors' names appear on the screen. As the story proper begins, a big moving truck pulls away from a crowd of dykes dressed as boys and drag queens dressed as flamingos. It's daytime, and the performers are assembled not to bid the travelers farewell, but because this day is Peacock in the Park, a midsummer cross-gender extravaganza. The bartender has abandoned his coworkers and boss on perhaps the most important day of the year. The players: Audrey and me. Supporting cast: a dog named Montana, a flask and a Thermos of bourbon, a cooler full of cookies in plastic bags, and a book, the importance of which will be revealed shortly.

We rolled into Spokane after seven hours of terrain that, once past the Cascade Mountains, was flat and numbing and foreshadowed the vast flatness ahead. Facing forward, looking out at the darkening horizon, we felt like we should be losing ourselves in the storyline of a film. Audrey pulled the truck into a parking lot. I said, "Let's keep driving."

"We're taking a *leisurely* pace," she said.

We dined that night in the first of many family restaurants; as we progressed through the country, the restaurants became more family-oriented, and Audrey and I looked less and less like we belonged. But that first night, in Spokane, we still didn't know what to expect.

Audrey squinted at her pale green salad and said, "We have officially entered the land of iceberg lettuce." After dinner we found a saloon and drank. It was Audrey who insisted on calling all the different bars we visited *saloons.* "We're in the untamed West," she said, "and cowboys drink in saloons. They smoke unfiltered cigarettes and have shots of whiskey. They replace conversation with ass scratching."

It was in the motel in Spokane that I discovered my mistake. The old, hardbound volume of short stories I'd intended to bring was missing. I had grabbed, instead, an artifact I hadn't thought about in years, left to me by my dead friend Susan: *Studies in the Psychology of Sex* by Havelock Ellis. I first saw the book in my bedroom in Seattle: the police were downstairs, a coroner pronouncing my housemate dead, and there it was on my pillow. I read the title, stroked the cover. I even smelled it. But I never opened it, not until Spokane.

Audrey was sitting in her own bed, next to mine, thumbing back issues of *Art in America,* nuzzling her dog, and drinking from the flask. Not drunk enough to pass out, I opened the book. The title page bore the imprint of Susan's college; the copyright date was one-hundred years old. It began, "Throughout the vegetable and animal worlds the sexual functions are periodic. From the usually annual period of flowering in plants, with its play of sperm-cell and germ-cell and consequent seed production, through the varying sexual energies of animals, up to the monthly effervescence of the generative organism in women, seeking not without the shedding of blood for the gratification of its reproductive function, from first to last we find unfailing evidence of the periodicity of sex."

What did it all mean?

For the record, I'm a sadomasochist, S/M for short. I can say that more easily than "I'm gay" or "I'm an addict" because the label is at once more evasive and more precise, and the indoctrination rituals are more mysterious but more carefully plotted. It's not S *and* M, people get that wrong. The *and* makes it sound like they're two separate things; the slash is supposed to show how they're intertwined. After I graduated from Reed—a full decade before my housemates and Audrey—I moved to Seattle's Capitol Hill neighborhood, like so many eager graduates before me. To write a screenplay. That was where I first started tending bar. When I first moved to Seattle, it was getting all this attention from journalists in bigger, glitzier cities, and though it didn't live up to the hype, it was better than most places. There was even a downtown bar that catered to filmmakers: It had several bookshelves stacked with nothing but screenplays, from big Hollywood epics to independent films to unproduced local crap left there by people just like me. An aspiring auteur could hang out for hours, reading other people's work or editing his own. I would sit alone and correct misspellings in sophomoric scripts, draw large question marks with a black Sharpie around problematic passages, write "brilliant" or "pathetic" on the title page.

My life in Seattle had everything to do with *night*life. If I were narrating it as a movie, my flashbacks would be dark, with the rough, jerky quality of a handheld camera. Aside from the place where I worked, and the screenplay bar, you might've found me at one of a handful of seedy, underground clubs. Some of them were the back rooms of lowlife bars, while others were private concerns in abandoned warehouses or people's basements. I saw some cartoonish things at the drag bar in Portland, but while living in Seattle I saw human behavior that was beyond that: like *Fantasia* compared to *Heavy Metal*. I saw flesh, and I saw defiance of flesh. I got my eyebrow pierced with a friend, and the guy who did it told us, "Don't let anyone shit on your face for at least six weeks." I thought it was a joke—I laughed, thinking, How hard could it be not to get shit on your face?—but when I saw my friend two weeks later his forehead was swollen and discolored, the surgical-steel piercing encrusted with pus. "I tried to wait," he told me. "I just couldn't."

Havelock Ellis said, "The sexual invert may be roughly compared to the congenital idiot, to the instinctive criminal, to the man of genius or the color-blind; and such a comparison is reasonable." One night when I was still new to the scene, and to the drugs I was beginning to use, I walked into a businessman's rec room and was assaulted by the smell of crap and amyl nitrite and bleach. "Just as the ordinary color-blind person is congenitally insensitive to those red-green rays which are precisely the most impressive to the normal eye, and gives an extended value to other colors—finding that blood is the same color as grass, and a florid complexion blue as the sky—so the invert fails to see emotional values patent to normal persons, transferring those values to emotional associations which, for the rest of the world, are utterly distinct." The first thing I saw, entering that rec room, was a fifty-year-old woman getting her nipple rings ripped from their sockets, and in the anemic yellow and blue light, the blood seemed more orange than red, like some kind of twisted mother's milk.

Disgusting, sure. But also exhilarating. Not that the surge of excitement was sexual, exactly. I can't say any longer what, exactly, sex is. That's what S/M taught me: the forbearance of sex in favor of other pains and pleasures/movement outside the body, or into the body, so deep it doesn't matter/it isn't about *who* you like to fuck, but *how*/the abolition of gender, that passé vestige of binary thinking. I might've spent entire weekends getting fucked, or fucking, then spent a month of Sundays being whipped, or whipping, without skin so much as touching skin. The "periodicity" of sex, the confusion therein: alternating between physical desire and the need to hurt.

I went with friends to check out a bondage night and ended up participating in an "Amateur Hour." Up on stage in a silly leather outfit, I looked into a crowd of people dressed exactly as I was, and before I knew it they were volunteering to be spanked. Women and men approached me afterward, offering to *train* me. I didn't get it. I thought, You want to teach me how to spank you better? Soon people started to know me—secret glances at cafes, even at the screenplay bar—and I developed a reputation for being an excellent young Dom, even though I still thought of myself as a wallflower—shy and voyeuristic—and really, when it came down to it, I preferred submitting to others.

My screenplay drew upon all this. The film was meant to be a smart, sci-fi thriller, part autobiographical fantasy. It was about a kid who has this involuntary ability to enter people's dreams. He can't control it, so it's torture for him—because hell is other people, you see—and when he's awake he's exhausted, and when he's asleep he experiences the innermost fears and desires of others, so of course he takes lots of heroin. And he has sacred images from other cultures tattooed all over his skin, up and down, dream talismans, hoping that—written in the flesh—the language of at least one religion will spell something true.

Over the course of the film he develops friendships, and he falls in love. But he's privy to his friends' dreams, and he's shocked. Not by the darkness of human nature, but by its unvarying banality. As you might expect, there are gangster types—or government types, it's unclear—who want to exploit his ability. During moments of respite, he and his friends talk pop culture and philosophy. At one point the protagonist says, "With great power comes great responsibility," and one of his friends asks, "What is that, Hegel?" and he says, "No, Spiderman."

When we got to Montana, Audrey asked me to drive. "Fasten your seatbelts, it's going to be a bumpy ride." I climbed into the seat and tried to start the truck, which lurched and stalled. Looking down, I discovered a five-speed stick. I told Audrey the problem, explained to her that I didn't know how to drive a standard transmission. She was mystified that I could've spent a whole day on the road without noticing her shifting. "I thought you were fidgeting," I said. "I didn't realize there were gears involved."

"Why the hell did I bring you?" she asked. She got out of the cab, climbed on the hood and lit a cigarette. Smoking became a thing for us on this trip: what we did with our mouths when we were sick of talking, what we examined when we grew bored of observing each other. The way, for example, a cigarette burns differently in different parts of the country: the dark, choking smoke it emits in humidity; the bright orange cone shape it takes when it's hanging out the window of a truck going seventy. I got up on the hood and smoked with her. When we were done, Audrey flicked her butt into the street and said, "I'll teach you."

So in Missoula, in a truck the size of a suburban house, I learned how to drive a stick shift.

"No, you bitch. Let up the clutch."

"You bitch."

"Fuck you."

"Well."

I was amazed that it didn't take more than an hour to figure it out, even with the dog behind me, in the extended cab, yelping every time I made a mistake. What wasn't easy was having to learn something from Audrey. I was the one who had taught her to smoke like Bogart and steal a scene from the background like Steve McQueen; I'd taught her to see a film like a painting, to read it like a story; told her that Fellini hadn't been heavy-handed when he named a photographer Paparazzo, but that the word *paparazzi* had entered the world though Fellini's film. But soon I was jolting and lurching through

Missoula, grinding the clutch—hey, it wasn't our truck—stalling at intersections and steering back onto I90, where I could upshift a few times and not worry about it again for a hundred miles or so.

Ah, Montana, what's it for? Eighteen-wheelers passed, cows chewed cud, sounds rattled from the cargo area behind us. We had believed it would be beautiful. Audrey had named her dog for an expectation of beauty. We weren't prepared for the mediocrity of the landscape once past the Rockies. "It's kind of flat," we noted. "Boring." The eastern part of the state looked very much like South Dakota, which makes sense, because geography doesn't necessarily observe state lines. In Butte we stopped for supplies, and the dog, weary of the cab, got away from us and began to terrorize the neighborhood with affection. We chased it through depressing streets, yelling, "Montana! Oop! Montana!" Like we were overzealous pioneers.

Once the dog was tethered, we stopped into a saloon. We told ourselves we were experiencing local culture, but one bar looks like any other when you're on an interstate. When you stop at a bar every three or four hours, they begin to blend together. In Butte we were kicked out after Audrey told a local woman, "I think you're real handsome."

The woman got up from her barstool. "You *do* know I'm a girl, don't you?"

Three men at the other end of the bar had been watching us, nudging each other every time Audrey bought a round of drinks. When I saw them stand up, I moved my bar stool between Audrey and them, to keep her from causing a scene. They came over and crowded against me. Audrey stood up. One of them elbowed my beer into my lap; another took hold of my hair and pulled my head back, brought his other hand around and clasped my throat with his thumb and forefinger, pushing in. "You've got greasy hair," he said. The third man moved toward Audrey and she, doing her best to be scrappy, stepped back and spit in his face. The man who held me said, "Stop smiling." He might've been a lover, telling me not to top from the bottom. His grip loosened and he said to his friend, "The dude's fucking laughing."

I had enough air now to say, "Don't stop on my account." I expected that to make him angrier, but instead it surprised him long enough for the bartender to intervene.

On our way out, Audrey said, "They were going to kill you."

"To know life is to fuck death in the liver," I said.

She laughed. Then she said, "A good woman is hard to find."

How to describe the conversations we had? In the limited space of the cab, with dog and smell of dog, cookie and cracker crumbs all about us on the seat, rotten fruit and melted ice at our feet, Audrey's voice bounced from one door of the truck to the other. Our first entertainment was the recital of movie lines, from such disparate classics as *Dune* and *My Dinner With André* and *Sunset Boulevard* ("We didn't need dialogue, we had faces!"). When that grew tiresome, we began to irritate each other for entertainment. Audrey liked to point out things to me like the fact that I have "middle class teeth." She said, "You can tell you had braces: your teeth are *too* perfect." Apparently, people with real breeding are born with decent teeth. And she loved to say, "Aren't you hot?" She would pull at my long-sleeved thermals. I would flinch, and she would say, "For Christ's sake, take some clothes off." Then I would scoot away as far as I could get in the cab, rub the spot where she had touched my shirt as though a welt had risen there, and say, "I'm fine. I like it warm." But she had a point. After the air conditioner broke, the seats could get so hot they seemed to merge with my body, like the time when I was a kid and the bandage on my skinned elbow came off in my sleep and I woke up to find the fabric of my sheets fused with the scab. The only thing that cooled us was beer.

In Billings I went into a service station to buy a six-pack. Audrey let Montana out to take a piss in the grass. There were people everywhere inside the store, eating Subway sandwiches and Taco Bell. There was a tall, wiry woman—about Audrey's age—in the Taco Bell line who had her head bowed to one side, her dyed-black hair obscuring most of her face. Her hands were shaking. She stood in relief to the pastels of the crowd behind her. There was a tattoo, winding its way in a Magritte-style cursive around her biceps, that said, *This is not skin.* She saw me looking at her and her lower lip went into a terse little spasm; then she bit it, clearly trying not to cry. I looked away. When I got back outside, a young couple stood near our truck with their towheaded kid. They were staring at Audrey; Audrey was glaring back. I got into the passenger seat and sat there with the beer in my lap. Audrey got into the truck with me. The kid ran up to the truck and kicked our front tire.

Toward the end of the Montana stretch, she started telling me about Cranbrook. There were plenty of kids I knew at Reed who'd gone to fancy private schools, but they never talked about them with any enthusiasm. Audrey had actually liked her boarding school, with its separate art institute. I antagonized her by pretending I didn't know what Cranbrook was. "It's only the Exeter of the Midwest," she said, and I said, "What's Exeter?" In Northern California, where I had gone to high school, a place with a name like "Cranbrook" would be a reform school; respectable schools were named after presidents, county seats, or local heroes. Audrey looked at me like I was another piece of filth cluttering the truck, and said in the voice of a dilettante/debutante, "If it weren't for Cranbrook, I would never have become an artist." I showed her my middle class teeth and said, "I'm not a stripper, I'm a dancer!"

When the tape player broke, we had only the radio—which we kept on *seek.* While I drove, Audrey swiveled in her seat to dote on her fed-up dog. She would kiss Montana's leg, saying, "My lover! My lover!" Then the dog would squeeze between the seats and lift the other paw. While she drove, I read her interesting passages from *Studies in the Psychology of Sex.* The book had words like *tribadism, hyperesthesia, psychosexual hermaphrodism,* obscure words I didn't understand but which made a mysterious kind of rhythmic sense. Flipping through the pages, I found descriptions of both Audrey and myself, though I didn't dare say so. I wasn't sure whether the descriptions were accurate or anachronistic or just plain mean. It said, A sexual attraction for boys is, no doubt, that form of inversion which comes nearest to normal sexuality, for the subject of it usually approaches nearer to the average man in physical and mental disposition. The reason for this, it said, is obvious: boys resemble women, and therefore it requires a less profound organic twist to become attracted to them.

I came home to find Susan dead on the living room sofa. Or more accurately, her boyfriend found her and I found them, his arms gripping a body that had been pale and frail even in life. I'm aware that this sounds like some kind of Seattle cliché, but that's the thing: the way you can see yourself in narratives everywhere, so that everything in life is *expected,* but it never assuages the pain.

Susan left us things. One relatively prudish housemate found a dildo on her bed that evening, a Post-it note attached that said, "Frigidity." Another housemate got a guide to local volunteer programs and a note that said, "Selfishness." Over the next few days, reports came in from friends and acquaintances. Strange items had arrived by post, unsigned. One person received handcuffs with a note that said, "Timidity." Another had a box of condoms on which was written the word, "Disease." The boyfriend's gift was the last to arrive; it was a large, empty box with no note at all. Mine, of course, was the Havelock Ellis sex book. The attached Post-it read, "Denial."

The bondage clubs and the S/M dungeons, the parties and the raves carried on without us. My friends and I stopped attending, stopped calling each other; a few of us stopped giving in to some of our vices, the way I stopped having sex, stopped doing the semisexual things that replaced sex, stopped taking drugs. Looking back, I think we all misread the notes, glanced at them fearfully and gave up the wrong sins. The food addict stopped taking crystal meth, and got fat. The coke addict gave up pot, and wasted away to nothing. The alcoholic gave up heroin, which was really quite difficult to do, and he gave up intimacy, which he hardly missed at all. He moved back to Portland because it felt safer than his parents' home in California; he checked the Reed College housing board, found new roommates, took a job in another bar. He found friends who didn't use sex and drugs to define themselves—or, well, of course they did, but they were different kinds of sex, other drugs. He found a mothering transsexual, Chocolate Jones, who didn't punish him for sneaking drinks behind the bar, but laid the shots out for him. And he found Audrey, who also eschewed physical contact, and with whom he had other interests in common: bourbon, beer, movies.

In South Dakota no one can hear you scream.

Things between Audrey and me started to fall apart at Mount Rushmore. The day before we'd made a pilgrimage to Devil's Tower—the place to which Richard Dreyfus made his pilgrimage in *Close Encounters*—and Audrey had been told that her dog wasn't allowed on the trails. She assumed the same would be true at Rushmore, so to preempt any complaints she fashioned the leash like a harness and pretended Montana was her Seeing Eye dog. After we spotted other dogs on the trail, she continued to wander the park in sunglasses. I thought it was hilarious at first, but after an old man in golf shorts came up to her and said, "I want you to know you have a beautiful dog," it felt wrong. "Stop it," I said.

"Fuck off," she said. "I'm having fun."

I was holding her Thermos, so I sprinted ahead of her about twenty paces and left it on a bench. Then I stepped aside and watched her. "Where's my Thermos?" she said loudly. "Montana, good girl, find my Thermos." The dog tried to wander off the path. Audrey kicked Montana's head, then used her knees to steer her squarely in the direction of the bench. Once there, Audrey sat down and patted her surroundings in seeming obliviousness; then, suddenly, she clutched the Thermos. "Good girl," she said, patting the dog. The people around us stared at me, like I was the asshole.

After that, Audrey wouldn't speak to me for miles. Even the Corn Palace in Mitchell, South Dakota, and restaurants with five different kinds of mayonnaise couldn't break the silence. Finally, when we stopped for drinks in Sioux City, Iowa, Audrey said, "I never treated you like a prostitute." The game. I struggled against saying it—the next line from *Pretty Woman*—loath to reenter dialogue, and to hear her voice again. But I relented. "You just did," I said.

There was particularly heavy carousing in Des Moines. On our way back to the motel I stalled the truck several times, almost stranded us in an intersection; at the freeway on-ramp I hugged the shoulder closely then overcorrected. The weight of the truck heaved with a single, tremendous wag and nearly went over the railing on the opposite side. Audrey laughed, throwing her hands in the air like she was riding a roller coaster. I snorted and kept my head low, steered us back to the motel. In the parking lot, Audrey put her hand on my shoulder; I jerked away from her. She came up closer and tried to put her arm around my waist, but I stepped aside. All I wanted was to bury my face in used linens. "Autistic people don't like being touched, but they don't mind being squeezed really hard," she said. I told her to mind her own business. She said, "That's autistic, not *artistic*."

What happened in the room is something I remember differently each time I think about it. I might concentrate on the sound of the air conditioner, rattling like a smoker's cough, the stale air infused with the smell of ashtrays. Or I might think about the expression on Audrey's face as it moved from drunken to excited to repulsed. Right now I'm remembering the basic actions, the movement of the scene, how Audrey—stinking of the road and of saloons and of her dog—climbed on top of me as I lay in bed. She began by massaging my shoulders.

"Don't," I said.

She grabbed the book and opened it to one of the pages I had eared. "While there can be little doubt that some sexual inverts do possess unusual sexual energy," she read, "in others it is but apparent; the frequent repetition of seminal emissions, for example, may be the result of weakness as well as strength." Audrey tossed the book to the floor and said, "Ha!" Then she kissed my neck and forcibly rolled me over. She leaned close into my face as if to kiss my lips, but laughed instead, falling off of me and onto the mattress. I moved to the other bed and crawled under the sheets, assuming the fetal position. Audrey followed, again climbed on top of me, straightened me out, straddled me, held me by my wrists. I said, "Get your stinking paws off me you damn dirty ape." Then I felt my face flush and my eyes sting. She squinted, spit bubbling from her lower lip, and began to slap my face playfully. "She's my sister," she said with each blow, "she's my daughter. My sister, my daughter, she's my sister *and* my daughter!" With this last exclamation, Audrey struck me quite hard.

I remember one night—this was three, maybe four months earlier, I think—Audrey came into LaBar with a group of her artist friends. She was the youngest, and the others treated her with affection. Not just the pretentious cheek-kissing affection I would've imagined, but hand holding, arm touching, shoulder squeezing. It was a mixed group—men and women, queer and straight—but they all seemed to know how to relate with their bodies. I wondered if Audrey got something from their friendship that she couldn't get from mine. Then I made them a round of drinks.

We used to talk about it, my heroin-and-meth addled friends in Seattle, speculate as to what might have caused our psychosexual aberrations. Were we spanked too often or too seldom as children? Were our diapers not changed regularly? There's an underlined passage in the one-hundred-year-old sex book with a note in Susan's handwriting that says, "You." It offered this, echoing the passage Audrey read to me in the motel that night, that "the sexual impulse itself is usually weaker, even when, as often happens, its irritability assumes the fallacious appearance of strength." Oh, it made only too much sense. "The parched sexual instinct," the book said, "greedily drinks up and absorbs the force it obtains by applying abnormal stimuli to its emotional apparatus." Audrey slapped me again, this time lighter, more playfully. "It becomes largely, if not solely, dependent on the energy this secured." She brushed my cheek with the backs of her fingers; I could smell her breath. "The abnormal organism in this respect becomes as dependant on anger or fear," the book says, "just as in other respects it may become dependant on alcohol."

Then there were the words other people had used to characterize us: what Chocolate had meant by Audrey's unscratched itches; what Susan had meant by my denial; what the boy at the gas station had meant by kicking our tire. It was a moment when we might've seen ourselves in each other, realized that we were people with identity politics but no identities. Instead, I concentrated on Audrey's aggression. While she was arousing my fear and anger—using her wiry, half clenched hands to apply abnormal stimuli—I sobered a little, got excited a little, and struggled against her.

Audrey said, "When you're slapped you'll take it and like it."

"Harder!" I said.

"Take off your shirt," she said.

Well-trained, I complied. But clearly Audrey hadn't expected my tattoos; she paused, staring at them as if trying to translate the Chinese characters, unravel the Celtic knots, piece together a narrative made by the hieroglyphics. I don't know why Audrey thought I always kept my arms covered, but she hadn't anticipated those images, or the scars from removed piercings, or the tracks in my skin. I lay there exposed, read, like a betrayed writer whose juvenilia has been published without his permission. Only I wasn't a writer—no, not that—I was just a bartender with a mark in his flesh for every mistake he ever made.

The next morning the midwestern heat was out early. I got up first, and went to the motel lobby to fetch Styrofoam cups of coffee. The receptionist stared at me. When I got back to the room, Audrey was up. I approached her cautiously. Montana was stretched out across her lap; my duffel bag was next to her, open; Audrey was holding the flask. She looked haggard, like the hardened woman she'll one day be, like the women she so admired. I said, "Hair of the dog?" She passed the flask to me.

As I sipped, she tossed a photograph onto the mattress. "Who's this?" she asked.

I sat down and looked at the photo. It was of a young black man standing at the corner of Hollywood and Vine. He was delicate, almost pretty, and he was smiling, but his eyes looked like they were staring out at something a thousand miles behind whoever was taking the picture. On the back was written the name Joshua Carter. It took a moment for me to recognize Chocolate Jones. As a boy. Before she became a woman. Which, strangely enough, was before she became a drag queen. I said, "Where did you find this?"

"It was in the side pocket," Audrey said. "Who is it?"

"I don't know," I said.

"It was in *your* bag."

When I didn't say anything more, she got up and walked out to the U-Haul. Audrey took the first shift. After I climbed into the cab and she started the engine, I asked, "What were you looking for?" She didn't reply; she decided to crash the truck instead. I relate to the sentiment. At the on-ramp—where I had almost toppled us seven hours earlier—Audrey drifted to the shoulder. Gravel rattled the truck's underside, startling the dog, which yelped and jumped into the front seat. Audrey threw out her hand and lost control of the steering wheel, sending us over the guardrail, tipping the truck over, so that it slid sideways down the embankment. The truck was on its side when it stopped moving. I was pressed against the passenger door, which was flush against the earth, and Audrey was above me—held in by her seat belt. Montana was right in front of me, squeezed up against the dash and the door. I looked around, breathed, and counted my limbs and said, "We've had an accident." Audrey groaned, unbuckled her seat belt and fell against me. "But nobody's killed," I said.

"Do over, man," Audrey said. "Do over."

We climbed upward, out the driver's side door, and pulled the dog out by her front legs. Then we opened the door in back, revealing the truck's payload. It was the first time I saw what we'd been transporting for a thousand miles. There was one large reading chair, its wood splintered, and a dozen or so medium-sized boxes containing clothes, books, and artwork. The paintings were destroyed, of course, broken into thick pieces. The heavy paint had prevented them from shattering completely. Many of the paintings—carelessly packed—had probably been ruined well before the accident. She'd rented the largest truck to transport cargo that would've left room in a minivan. Audrey scooped up chunks of glass and pieces of twisted picture frames from the boxes and began throwing them into the grass. The dog slumped against Audrey's legs. The truck's rear wheel continued to spin slowly in midair. I took her and hugged her, and for a while she leaned against me and almost sobbed.

Then she took a deep breath, said, "Shit," and pushed me away from her. She lit a cigarette. I sat next to her on the grassy embankment, took her cigarette to light the tip of my own, then gave it back to her.

Later, the police arrived, reports were filed, money was wired through Western Union, and I was amazed to watch Audrey purchase a brand-new Saturn, something she had apparently planned to do anyway once we were in St. Louis.

There were injuries. I had a bruise on the right side of my face; Audrey had a black eye. My neck was sore and Audrey was stiff and uneasy walking. The dog didn't move except to whimper and huff. Once things were arranged with the local authorities, we got back on the road in the new car. I felt nauseated by the smell of dog, body odors, cigarette butts, and new car. I felt nauseated, too, by the shakeup, the abortive sex, and most of all by Audrey's quiet. She drove until we were in St. Louis, sometime past one in the morning. Mysterious, beautiful corn fields illuminated by moonlight; miniature golf courses becoming real golf courses; suburbs expanding until they grew into the first real city we'd seen since leaving Portland. Before finding her new apartment in St. Louis, we stopped into a bar— not a saloon, but a *bar*—and arrived just in time for last call. Audrey ordered as many shots as the bartender would give her at one time, paid for with the money from Western Union.

Her apartment was in the Central West End, an outrageously fancy neighborhood not far from Washington University. Audrey had trouble finding the place; she'd never been there before. She matched the address of a five-story condo-style building against an address on a slip of paper, shrugged her shoulders, and tried a key. Her apartment was on the third floor, and if you leaned out a little you could see a corner of Forrest Park from her terrace. The rooms were completely furnished: a bed, sofa, and matching chairs, a desk, kitchen utensils, even clothes in the closets that, because they were conservative, might've been picked out by Audrey's mother. The walls were covered, mostly with paintings, most of them Audrey's— self-portraits in thick paint on glass with decade-old frames, mock gilt flaking off.

"My dad is so sweet," she said, and there was nothing more to say, so we fell asleep side by side in her bed.

In the morning Audrey spent at least an hour in the bathroom. She cleaned herself off, applied more makeup than I'd ever seen her wear (to cover the bruises, I supposed), dressed herself in a rather sharp-looking shirt and blouse. I was reading when she finally emerged. Her hair was pulled back, her lips were red; her skirt was tight and her hips voluptuous, her breasts on prominent display. She was the ugly girl played by an attractive actress who gets a makeover and suddenly becomes popular. "How do I look?" Audrey said.

"Very good. I must say I'm amazed."

"You were darling to help," she said. "I couldn't have done it without you." Then she limped into the kitchen and made coffee. I followed her. The movements were simple. She merely opened a cupboard and retrieved a jar of beans, dumped some into the grinder next to the sink, opened another cupboard for the filters, and put it all into the coffeemaker on the far counter. What was striking was the way she seemed to know, by instinct, where everything was, as if she'd lived in the apartment forever. One of her paintings hung in the kitchen; in it Audrey's hair was shorter than I'd ever seen it, and her expression was sneering and tough. I touched it and it rattled against the wall. With just a little more pressure, I could've broken it with that one finger.

We had enough time before I had to be at the airport to visit the famous arch, the Gateway to the West. I never expected to be amazed. Against the humid, blue gray sky, it looked like it had been painted there. Then a plane flew by, and for a moment I thought it might pass through the arch. Audrey said, "It's beautiful, isn't it?" We both looked upward. She said, "It was designed by the guy who founded the Cranbrook Art Institute." It finally occurred to me to ask why, if Cranbrook had been so wonderful, she hadn't gone there for graduate school. She said, "I didn't get in."

When she dropped me off at the airport, Audrey's parting words were, "So, now you know how to drive a stick shift." Then she thought better of her hardness, hugged me and said, "Oh, Scarecrow, I think I'll miss you most of all."

There are 629 miles between Portland, Oregon, and Oakland, California. When I landed at PDX, I took a cab to my house, loaded my car, and pointed it south. I'd grown acclimated to driving, the way you can be sickened by the sway of a boat, but once you get your sea legs it's the ground that feels shaky. Packing again was easy because I'd never really unpacked.

I've heard from Audrey once. About a month ago a large envelope arrived with a yellow forwarding sticker from my address in Portland. Inside were three photographs of Audrey. She's gotten a tattoo. It's monotone and shapeless—*tribal,* they would've called it at the tattoo parlor—all form and design but no meaning. It begins from behind her left shoulder, runs its way around her biceps, and ends just past her elbow, barely encroaching onto her forearm. In the photos, the flesh around it is still pink where it's healing. Audrey is naked from the waist up in two of the pictures: one a front view and the other from the rear. In the third picture she's wearing a white tank top and smoking a cigarette.

She wrote a note on the back of a Mount Rushmore postcard. It said, "Thought you'd want to see the ink. I also thought you'd want to know Montana died from internal injuries. There's nobody here to play with." It was signed, Love Audrey. I threw out the two photos in which she's shirtless. The third picture I keep on my desk. I've never been someone who collects photographs, not until now. They're still images; I mean, they're not *motion* pictures. I miss Audrey and her dog, just as I miss Chocolate and the drag queens at her bar and my stupid friends from Seattle, especially the dead ones. They were flashes of Technicolor—a brief trip through Oz—hanging in the periphery of my inward-looking color blindness, only to reveal themselves to be as colorless as me, once I raised my eyes and saw them.

MARY STEWART ATWELL

Washington University

BLUE NIGHT, CLOVER LAKE

In the picture, we are five. Four blonds and a brunette, slouching against a white fence, trying to look bored. We are not bored. We are fourteen. If we are athletic we wear tennis skirts, tank tops designed to show the shape of our arms. If we are not athletic we try to look sexy and wear shorts cut to display the line where bone meets muscle. We are emulsified, moisturized, anointed. We shaved our legs this morning, balancing each ankle in turn on the lip of the porcelain sink, and in the picture we throw our hips to the side to unstick our thighs, which are tacky from scented cream. We are fourteen.

Behind us is a paddock, where horses, brown and roan, snuffle through the hot clover. Beyond the paddock are woods; beyond woods, a lake. Beyond the lake are more pastures, where, on certain nights, we lie on damp nylon, sniff the charred wood's ash, laugh until daybreak. Beyond the pastures is the world. We smile hard. We loop our arms over each other's shoulders.

These days we meet for lunch at a white-tablecloth restaurant, where the manager lets us scatter ashes over the linen and stay as long as we like. When we pass the picture, when we smooth the creases and study the vanished girls, we say *so young,* we say *we were so young.* The faces are grainy, out of focus. We are staring into the sun.

That summer we live in a cabin called Magnolia. In the mornings the boys we have always known stand under our bathroom window and sing *sugar magnolia, ringing that blue bell,* hopping around while we cover our mouths and laugh. Just last year they shunned us, darted like flushed birds, but now they walk us to the dining hall, flat palms insistent on our shoulders and backs. They sit behind us with their arms around our waists and tell us dirty jokes, slip their headphones over our ears; *isn't that great?* they say, *isn't that fucken awesome?* When they forget to think about sex, they disappear from us for days.

Because we are the oldest, we have been given the privilege of setting up the dining hall for meals, sweeping and mopping the floors after, *unless there's puke,* the boys say, *'cause there's no damn way we're mopping up puke.* There is never puke, and we don't mind the job. We line up at the kitchen door, take the basins of fried eggs and grits, sling them across the tables, and laugh if they slide off the other end. The most domestic-minded of us girls, who will tranquilize herself comatose for her own wedding, neatly sets down the chipped plates then retraces her step with fork knife spoon, fork knife spoon. All the silverware is warped, deformed into art by boys who stick the tines into table grooves and press down on the handles. When they are bored, our boys bend the knives to make us bracelets.

After breakfast we push the long-handled brooms slowly, slowly. Because we are the oldest it is our prerogative to show up late, to be wearied and surly. Bells ring across the pastures and the little kids are building model rockets, lining up for go-carts, currying and tacking the horses while sweat and yellow strings of pee spool down their jeans. All us girls gave up on horses last year and claim not to miss them, but every once in a while someone will break from the pack and drape herself over the fence, calling, in a flush of regret, *come here, sweetie, you've got a burr in your mane, let me get it out, please?* We ignore these breaches of etiquette as we ignore each others' back zits, weltering and obvious above the straps of our bikinis. We will spend the rest of the morning at the lake, laid out on beach towels like corpses on biers. It is our official position that we are bored beyond succor.

We have showed the old picture to our current boyfriends. We have watched as their eyes caught on the girl in the middle, the tallest, the blondest. They recognize everyone else—the one with the glasses, the one with the freckles, the moody brunette—but who is the beauty, who looks just past the camera, gnawing on the corner of her lovely full lips? They don't ask; they are afraid of hurting our feelings, but we roll our eyes and snatch the picture away. We are used to evaluating ourselves in relation, could tell them in a second who has the nicest breasts, the firmest ass, could tell them—though they'd never ask—where she got them. The personal trainer, the boob job bankrolled by a dead great-aunt.

But *our* bodies are not the subject at hand.

Rosie, we say. *We don't have the first idea what happened to her.*

There are other boys besides the boys we have always known. They are older, working at Clover Lake for the summer. One of them is Dutch and has a yin-yang tattoo, but he teaches canoeing and we don't like to get our hair wet. Another, Scottish, bums us cigarettes from the pack he smokes behind the camp store. The one we like best grew up south of Richmond and has, to our ears, the most dangerous accent.

He stands with his head thrown back, lip curled like a rock star, and scratches the line of hair that runs down from his navel.

After lunch, we check the staff board at the back of the dining hall. We follow him to the archery range and sit on a green table that scrapes the backs of our thighs. He glues tricolored feathers on the arrows and tells us about his girls, laying them down in the fields on his granddaddy's tobacco farm, a felt blanket under their shoulders and yellow leaves brushing his face. The birches behind him are sun-bleached and shadeless. We have taught ourselves not to blush.

One of us, the runner, who will bust her ankle all to hell in the Boston Marathon, finds him passed out at dawn in a clearing beside the lake. She skids, stops, pats her face dry with the hem of her shirt. Says his name. There's a bottle of Jack between his legs, one arm flung up over his eyes, and he's smiling a smile she'll look for on men's faces the rest of her life. She stares at the patch of bare skin above his loosened belt. Cicadas whirring, the sun lemon-hot even this early, air knifed with the scent of hay that has been drying all summer on the hills beyond the lake. She checks her pulse, runs on, tells no one. She can barely look at him for days.

He is the one our mothers would have warned us off if they'd thought of it. He's a sophomore in college, drives a loud black Jeep, can keep a soccer ball in the air for a minute and forty-five seconds. One of us claims that he made out with her cousin Irene last summer at the Tastee-Freez, but we don't believe it because we know Irene, who is fat and easy and pouches her lips when she smiles. In our dreams, which we invent separately, staring up at the hot pale clouds as we lie beside the lake, he pulls up at our door with cigarettes and wine coolers and whisks us off into a night flared by heat lightning. He spreads a blanket among the red-dirt furrows. We lie like princesses and wait for whatever is supposed to happen next.

These days, we know he is only the worst thing our mothers failed to warn us off. We're all polka-dotted with moles, which may turn malignant while we sleep.

We see that Rosie is the favorite when the director lets her drive his truck. For seven summers the director has met us at the gate in his fetchingly rumpled khakis; he flirts with our mothers and jokes with our fathers and introduces us, again and again, to his lovely blond family, lined up on the steps of their cottage like a secular choir. He is a tall, good-looking man with a fox-colored beard, and several of us, the daughters of the drunkest and most brutally tanned of the country-club mothers, are tempted to imagine ourselves into this family, where no one would ever slap us across the mouth for putting the shrimp fork where the dessert spoon is supposed to go.

Because he likes us girls—*his girls,* he says—he gives us rides to the lake in his ancient Dodge pickup, which has a mangled right fender and sounds like a blender set to crush. Three of us climb in the bed, jockey for the spots on the wheel wells; the others squeeze into the cab and deejay the radio, though we know the only station we can get is Top 40 country out of Eden, North Carolina. The director loves George Strait and Garth Brooks, music our parents call white trash. At home we'd pretend to agree, but we are secretly partial to the all-girl bands, forever peeling out of a no-good's driveway while he hollers into the dust their wheels kick up. We belt the words to "My Mama Done Told Me" and "Maybe Jesus Loves You (But I Know What You're About)" and want nothing more than to be those girls, trailing glittering insults behind us like a broken string of add-a-pearls. One of us, the only one with a decent voice, will drop out of a freshmen sociology class called *Fancy, Don't Let Me Down: The Evolution of Women in Country Music.* A paper on Patsy Cline's cultural relevance will bait her to tears.

We sit by the tetherball pole talking about how much we want a cigarette, though we've only just started stealing our mothers' ultra-light menthols and have yet to form a habit. The director walks up from the tennis courts; we fall silent looking at his red knees, which we find not beautiful but interesting: the mysterious anatomy of a grown man. He is burned and peeling and smiles like a bright day. *I don't have time to drive y'all around,* he says, tossing Rosie his keys. *Sugar, you know your way around a stick?*

We look at Rosie, but she looks down, at the curl of silver in her hand. We feel, just as when the boys tease us, our individual appalling imperfections, and we know for the first time that she is beautiful in a way that makes all the difference. We say nothing. We smile at the director, and wait until he is out of earshot to fall on each other and chart our illicit day. We'll tear around the back pastures, gulp the scent of unmown grass and standing lake water, savor the cigarettes we've hidden in the bottom of tampon cases. We'll sing about cheatin' cowboys and new moons. We'll watch Rosie, her long tan fingers keeping the beat, out of the corners of our eyes.

We know something now that we did not know this morning—that to be born beautiful is to be born singular, and lucky. We suck in our tummies, straighten our spines, but we know now that we are the backup singers, waiting for the spotlight to embrace us with its radiance, convinced against all hope and wishful thinking that it never, ever will.

On the morning Rosie wears a halter top to breakfast, we leave the dining hall while she's in the bathroom and walk to archery without her. We spread out on the green equipment table and read each other the questions to a sex quiz. *How sensitive are your breasts? Extremely, moderately, or not at all?* None of us, to date, have done anything more than kiss, but we would like to catch the attention of the boy with the rock star lips, who is priming wooden bows a few yards away. Before long it's clear that he's not listening. She strolls up the baked hill, arms poised at her sides.

We want him more than ever, now that we see she can have him for the asking. We look at the flat plane of his belly above the sag of his basketball shorts, the white points of his hipbones, and we start to squirm, convinced low-down in our stomachs that nothing else will content us. *What if I hit that one?* Rosie says, pointing at a flat pink balloon sandwiched between two hay bales. *Are you giving out prizes today?* He throws his head back, grins at the horses wading through the heat-warped air. He fixes his eyes on the smudged charcoal line where the field shades into trees.

The top is secured by a bow at the back of the neck. When he pulls the string Rosie gasps, and we surround her. We scream in outrage, trying not to think about her breasts, which—we've been reading the romance novel excerpts at the back of the sex-quiz magazines—we liken silently to globes, to fruit. Nearly crying, she needs us, and we feel better than we have in days. We frown at the culprit, but he's looking away again, contemplating the scraps of cloud lisping over a green yellow sun.

We are crazy in love. Those bold hands. Anything he's touched is prize enough.

It storms every Friday, the night of the dance. Blow dryers fry the fuses and we stand in the dark, pressing our noses to the screen door, watching lightning fork and fizzle over the lake. Rain hammers designs on the green pool. The girls in the next cabin have a battery radio; we mouth the words and twitch our hips, eyes glazed. Then somebody kicks the door open and we holler into the middling dark, forgetting that we've just taken showers, that we were waiting for the lights to click on so we could fluff our hair and smear on lip gloss, jockeying for position at the big mirror over the sinks. We forget, for the length of the storm, the most important thing our mothers taught us: *always behave as if someone were watching.*

Out there, we have been fooled into thinking Rosie is still one of us. She sits on the end of her bunk and reads the last questions from the sex quiz while we comb out our tangles, smooth lotion over our goose-bumped legs. *How often do you experience orgasm in the missionary position? Always, occasionally, or never?* But when we realize she doesn't care how she looks, flipping her wet hair out of her face, we disown her again. We invent reasons, pass them between the bathroom stalls. *I think Rosie ran out of deodorant. Does she even... shave, or Nair...* you *know?* For the spoor of almost invisible blond hairs poofing out the leg of her panties, we have nicknamed her Sasquatch.

She sits in a circle of light, cheek pillowed on her hand.

We pretend not to know, but we know.

The cloud-bank sunset fades, the air saturated with the blue shadow of spent rain. They have wrapped the deejay booth in a daisy chain of red and green lights, and cardboard palm trees, salvaged from some nightmare prom, are propped against the pushed-back tables. On their benches, children twitch. We move, the four of us, to stand beside the window.

Years later, when we stand by the keg at fraternity parties, someone will always say *remember when we hung out by the water coolers at Clover Lake, waiting for a good song to come on.* And one of us, the one everybody else thinks has a drinking problem, will stare into her flat beer and say *I'm still waiting for that good song.* And the rest of us will sigh, because we don't want to admit that the songs we loved then, whose lyrics we held in our mouths like charms, are all on mix CDs you can order off cable, stacked in warehouses on made-up streets called Heartland Avenue and American Way. No one knows what happened to the morose guitarists, the sneering and unaccountably sexy frontmen, but they have cluttered our heads with all manner of detritus, so when she says what she says about the good songs we've lost, someone else, perhaps the one who remembered the water coolers with such fondness, will roll her eyes and say *well, cry me a goddamn river.*

This is how we recover from nostalgia. Before long, someone will remind us that dancing was never the point. We wore each others' clothes, which were the same as our own but unfamiliar enough to seem interesting. We liked pretending to be someone else, even if it was only the next girl over, and we liked tugging at our necklaces as we waited for our boys, who looked slicked-down and uncomfortable, to slouch across the room and tell us jokes. The windows were pushed up all the way and we would have sat in them but for the screens, studded with the black specks of dead flies.

We have, by a process we could not explain, determined who is going to make out with who when the slow songs dim the lights. Who will sneak into the juniper bushes with her hand in whose pocket, who will let who with the hand here and the tongue where. Tomorrow, when our parents park their Volvos and Beamers in the circular driveway in front of the director's cottage, they will find us glued into couples, sitting on this lap or that one, wiping tears—we must have tears—from the boys' freckled cheeks while they shift around praying we don't notice their erections. This is how we've imagined the summer's conclusion, but we cannot imagine what we will do to Rosie. Who is so much taller than the rest of us that she couldn't trade clothes with anyone. Tinted green by the strobe lights, she leans on the deejay booth drinking punch from a Dixie cup. We hope her teeth turn pink.

The slow songs come sooner than they should. We feel the sweat on our skin under the boys' hands, and we wouldn't presume to wonder what comes after the teeth on the neck, the tongue in the ear; we are in love with the symptoms of lust, adrenaline-shocked knees and the flavor of copper, and we only want more. The boys grab the backs of our dresses and stammer times, meeting places. Over their shoulders, we smile deeply into each other's eyes.

Rosie is dancing with the boy from the archery range. He wears khakis and a blue button-down, daringly untucked, with a smile that looks ready to slide off the corner of his mouth. Our boys, who miss Rosie but know better than to say so, watch them from the water cooler. Even the director knows, leaning against the wall in the door-way's shadow. Even the children, those snotty and asthmatic versions of ourselves, are pointing, singing the kissing song. *First comes love, then comes marriage.* Outside, the bullfrogs reiterate their disapproval.

We know the feeling—that carnivorous longing—that presses them together, but we don't know how it feels to have it satisfied, and it occurs to us, watching now, that we may never find out. How to glitter as they do, hear nothing but the arrow thrumming, exactly where you wanted it to strike.

When we pass the picture at our three-drink lunches, it takes us a while to remember who snapped the shutter. Of course: it was the tennis instructor who lived with us, who was only three years older, who we spent most of the summer ignoring. The daughter of the director's golf buddy, she told us the first day that he guaranteed we would take to her, make her our older sister. She repeated this as if the fact that we did not love her—thought her, truth to tell, square and silly and not a little dumb—was a failure for which we owed re-dress. After the dance, she lies on her bed and flips pages of a ro-mance novel while we get ready for bed. She untacks the picture of herself and her boyfriend under a hoop of gardenias, kisses his flat shiny face again and again.

And we were right about her, the tennis instructor. In later years, when we are seated at her table at weddings and sorority functions, she never fails to look horrified. She will be the first on the scene, when we pin Rosie down under the clothesline. But we don't hold grudges. We hear she's living in the Oklahoma panhandle with an Air Force husband, and we'd like to say for the record that we wish her all the best.

We crowd into the two shower stalls and sluice the sour indoor sweat from our chests and armpits. We spritz our skin with orange-freesia-peach-petunia body spray, pull on slips and cotton shorts. We line our running shoes up under the bed.

Rosie has showered alone, brushed her teeth alone, and now lies in bed with her reading lamp tuned on a book of crossword puzzles. We ask her if she'd like to go down to the pool with us and look at the stars, then quirk our eyebrows when she says no, she's sleepy, she's going to bed. We tell ourselves, and each other, that we don't give a good goddamn. We use phrases we've only heard from our brothers, like *flying fuck*. Our estrangement, self-willed as it was, makes us feel helpless. The plastic mattress sounds like applause when she rolls.

We have done this before, not to make out but for cow-tipping, snipe hunts. Two of us blah blah, not loud, on the pool deck, while the others follow the paddock fence to the stables, where the boys they have chosen or been chosen by are waiting in the smell of manure so ancient it has almost become earth. The two who are left put the petals of our namesake magnolias over their eyes like compresses. A twenty-minute shift and it is their turn, to the stables and up in the hayloft, where the floors are slick with counselors' condom wrappers. The horses ramble past us in the darkness. We feel their presence like changes in the weather.

One of us thinks she has fallen in love.

One of us knows better.

One of us, kissing a boy whose mouth tastes like old shoes, feels sick and wonders if she might be a lesbian.

One of us almost does it, but changes her mind at the last minute. She will discuss this in such detail that we'll begin to feel as if we, too, almost did it. We'll agree that blue balls is just something guys invented to make us feel bad.

Easing the screen door open, under the cover of the tennis instructor's ratcheting snores, we see Rosie wiggle out of the bathroom window. The sight—long white legs and the slim kick of her body— stuns us to silence.

We sneak into the cabin and fill a makeup bag with sunscreen, razors, old tubes of lipstick. We crouch under the clothesline. We wait.

This is what we forfeit, when we crouch under the clothesline and wait for Rosie to return so we can jump her, scribble her face bronze with lipstick, cut four times on the pale skin of her belly, drip nail polish remover into the places where the blood wells, push hard on that empty vodka bottle—care package relic from somebody's sister—until we pry apart her thighs: the chance to sit on our new boyfriends' laps while our parents sign forms and pay balances. The chance to come back next summer; the chance to come back, in those first college years when we say we'd rather pull out our fingernails than waitress and get paid to do nothing. Spend the weekdays yawning by the pool or the rifle range, the weekends riding to and from Richmond in the back of somebody's Jeep, sipping gas-station wine from narrow paper bags and feeling the wind blow up our dresses. Clouds of bees over the oil barrel trash cans, the moon full as a grape over the black water. And that smile, laced with hazard, that he must have practiced in the mirror till he got it just right.

We give up the chance to send our daughters here, which is why our mothers, those climbers, picked this place to begin with. They wanted to point at our bridesmaids and say, *They went to Clover Lake together. Since they were seven. I know, isn't it sweet?* On a sticky blue

night when the bullfrogs rumbled and the horseflies buzzed a des-
cant, we waited under the clothesline, and we fucked it all up.

In the car we play mix tapes titled *Summer Memories.* Certain
songs contain interludes of nonsense, slow syllables warped to burbling
by a decade on the dashboard.

On the way home from lunch, the one with the picture tucked in her
Kate Spade will sideswipe a nephrologist's Mercedes at the corner of
Boulevard and Monument. The glass in her hand, one last wine
spritzer for the road, shatters on the dashboard. When the nephrologist, who once took our old friend Rosie to a winter formal, runs up,
he finds her examining her bloody hands, murmuring the words to
what she claims is a Rodgers and Hart number, but which the rest of
us would recognize as a campfire song. Something about friendships
true, by a lake so blue. We'd sing it, but damn if we haven't forgotten
the verses.

In the rearview there is blood on her mouth, blood in stripes
down her cheeks. We have contacts; we have lawyers; we have friends
at the district attorney's. The rules are in our favor. She stares at the
spider web windshield, the splintered afternoon.

She tells him the mistake could not be hers.

DEVIKA MEHRA

Southwest Texas State University

THE GARDEN

When Pia walks into his flat in Bombay, she thinks it's a joke. She looks up at Adil, the man she has agreed to marry, waiting for him to ask the rightful occupant of this miniature box to step out of his hiding place.

"So what do you think?" he asks, mistaking her smile for approval.

Her instinct is to pick up her bags, say No thanks—this was supposed to be romantic—and return home to Delhi. But Adil looks so proud.

"I like the windows," she says.

"Really?"

She unzips her bag and takes out a fresh T-shirt. He offers her a hanger. Pia wonders if she should move to her girlfriend's house, which, in any case, is where her father thinks she's spending the weekend.

It isn't just the room's tiny size or squalor. It's the impermanence of the furnishings, essentials thrown together with no design. The largest object is a metal cot clothed with mismatched linen and shriveled pillows. A curry-stained stove rests on a counter along the wall, its umbilical cord connected to a gas cylinder. No telephone, no air conditioner. The only features are the waist-to-ceiling windows on two of the four walls. Half-open, they draw in the saltiness of the Arabian Sea, the smell of fish and damp gutters.

Pia asks for the key to the toilet, more to compose herself in private than out of physical necessity. She moves down the hallway, unlocks the door, and squats over a simple hole in the ground. The stink of human waste hangs in the air. Her thigh muscles twitch; she steadies herself. Pia can't help but think of Adil's room. Had he noticed her hesitant step that could neither go forward nor turn back? Crossing the threshold meant giving up a way of living, all those high standards she had been schooled in since childhood. Good breeding, her father called it.

Yet the ugliness of his place has already begun to seduce her. Its illegitimacy is a sort of comfort, like the time she crept into the servant quarters at the back of her house and lay curled up for hours on a thin, soiled mattress.

Pia met Adil six months ago when he was in Delhi modeling for a condom advertisement and she was studying journalism. He pressed his fingertips against her many books, marveled aloud at the knowledge encoded in her brain. Before he knew her, Adil confessed, he'd done cocaine, freeloaded on women, posed nude for money—now his ass was hanging in black-and-white in some rich faggot's dining room.

Then, during a hiking trip to Ladakh, she agreed to marry Adil. A week later, she informed her family.

"What does he do for a living?" her father asked.

"Adil's an actor. And he isn't rich or anything."

"Oh," her father said, too self-conscious to take on the role of a Hindi-movie parent. "Well, it's up to you. At twenty-three, you're mature enough to know who you want to spend your life with."

Some part of her was disappointed by his tempered reaction.

Now, Pia wonders if she is being foolish. There is a loud thud on the toilet door. "Arre hurry up, or I'll su-su in your Kelvinator." The knob wriggles like a netted fish.

The neighbor, Mackrand, she guesses. Adil has told her about him.

"Stop playing with yourself bhainchod, save something for your rich girlfriend."

Pia pulls up her panties. She can hear Adil's voice in the hall, then the neighbor's. "So who's in there? Some slut?"

Pia stands with her hand curled around the knob. She doesn't want Adil to witness her embarrassment. She collects herself and, a moment later, steps out. A stocky man with a towel around his bare shoulders faces her.

Mackrand smiles, his round cheeks making dimples, then he turns and glances up as Adil approaches. "Aaay give me an intro to her, yaar."

Pia avoids Adil's eyes and wipes her hands on her jeans. "I'd better go back." She motions to his room.

"Man, she's much taller than her photo. She looks like a cross be-tween Kareena Kapur and Preity Zinta. Fair and innocent. Sexy, too."

Pia shuts the door. The baby blue Kelvinator stands in the corner like a spectator; fruit flies hover around its sticky frame. Adil has un-packed, folded her clothes away in his closet. He comes in as the kettle on the stove steams.

"Tea?" He turns off the heat.

"Why didn't you say something to him?" She already knows: It's because Mack has set him up with some big-shot director.

Adil looks at his feet, a sulky droop to his lips. "Mack's like a brother to me. What could I do?"

"Anything. You could have said anything." Pia realizes this could become an excuse to move to her friend Maya's house. "You just stood there like a chicken," she says.

"Look, I'm sorry. It won't happen again."

She allows Adil to put his arms around her and rock her gently. His spontaneous affection surprises her, like a sudden rain, and she soaks in it. By comparison her parents' kisses are dry, careless brushes against her cheek.

Adil goes to the counter, picks up a tall steel glass of tea, and holds it out to her. It is cupped in his palms like an offering.

"Sit," he says and pulls a chair toward her.

She takes a seat. The tube light makes her feel like they're in an examination hall. "I need to call home."

"I'll take you downstairs. We can go to the beach after that. But tell me what you want for dinner, I can cook some fish."

"I'm not hungry."

"Eat something, no?" Adil selects a coconut from a stack. He slices the crown off with a butcher's knife and empties the liquid in a glass. She sips slowly and watches him. He is beautiful—tall with narrow hips. His lean body is almost hairless; tight muscles define his shoulders and legs. His face is oval, widest at the cheekbones, tapering down to a square jaw. He has dark eyes and a protruding, wet mouth, like a fruit.

Adil carves the milky flesh from the shell in bite-size pieces and feeds it to her with his fingers.

"Shush," says Adil, when they reach the landing where the landlord lives. "Uncle doesn't allow women to stay overnight." Pia smiles and puts a finger on her lips. Invisibility is new to her. She takes exaggerated steps, hums the Pink Panther tune in her head. When they reach the ground floor, Adil introduces her to a third paying guest: an up-and-coming veejay who calls herself Fleur.

"Adil talks about you all the time. Everything is always Pia-says-this and Pia-does-that." Fleur speaks in a birdlike voice. She wears pink hipsters that show off her pierced belly button.

"I've heard about you as well," Pia says, though she hasn't. Adil rarely talks about his female friends.

"Really, like what?" Fleur turns to Adil and ruffles his hair. Her gun metal eye shadow accentuates her light eyes.

"Only your finer qualities, don't worry," he says. "Pia needs to call Delhi. She'll pay for it."

"All yours," says Fleur.

Pia dials the number on the ancient phone. She watches Fleur, the way she jokes with Adil. Her body sways into his—one bump for every sentence.

Adil and Fleur talk about the film industry: no work these days, bullshit money. Arre did you see that new Venus flick? Big hoo-ha and now it's flopped. Producer gave Twinkle the role 'cause she's Dimple's daughter. Big name, influence and all, so what do you expect? And who the fuck lip-synched for her, just horrible, yaar.

On the phone, Pia's father picks up. "Where are you?" he says. "Your cell phone is out of range."

"At Maya's house." Pia cups the receiver to block the noise.

"Uncle's been looking for you," Fleur says. "He wants rent."

"I'll deal with it," Adil says quickly. Mack walks into the room. "Janeman," he whispers into Pia's ear, and presses a hand to his heart.

She tries to concentrate on her father's voice. "Our filly runs on Sunday in Bombay. Hope you're going to be there."

"Adil, you're on for the screen test Saturday," Mack says. "Better show up."

Fleur cocks her head to one side and sticks her finger at Adil. "You're the man! Isn't he, Mack?"

Mack scrapes his ear with a hairpin. "The chutiya's not a man, he's superman. "

"Is your friend Adil joining us?" Her father will be coming to Bombay the day after tomorrow for the annual derby. He'll stay at the Oberoi Hotel, two hours from Adil's flat in Lokhanwalla.

"Yes," she says. "We'll both come."

Adil laughs. "Fleur, you have the MTV act nailed."

"Yo!" Fleur jumps in the air. Her breasts jiggle and then settle in her tank top.

"I'll send a car for you," her father says. "You know that Adil needs to be properly dressed. What's that racket in the background?"

"The television. I'll call you later." Pia puts down the receiver and turns to Adil. "My father is sending the car to pick us up on Sunday."

"A Porsche or a striped Jaguar?" Fleur says, sucking the tip of her thumb.

Adil tries to hide a smile.

"Neither, actually." Next to Fleur, Pia feels dowdy in her tailored pantsuit. "Adil, we should leave. I want to get to the beach before dark."

"Don't mind her. She's not potty trained," Mack says, pinning Fleur's arms behind her. "Stop by when you come home."

Home? The word rattles in her head.

Juhu Chowpatti is nothing like a beach. The sand is filthy. Jagged seashells poke out like warnings. The only people in the water are squatters shitting or washing their laundry against salt-bitten rocks. Adil and Pia sit on plastic bags, shelling roasted peanuts, inventing ways to describe the sea.

"The waves roll toward us," Pia says, "like huge fists. Your turn."

"Erm ... the waves roll toward us like a forming thought."

"Nice." She thinks of how they'd watched the blue waters of Pong Yong Lake in Ladakh turn a mysterious emerald at noon. Adil had asked her to recline on the shore to pose for his camera, but the photographs mostly showed her long fingers interlacing across her face. Now, she turns toward Adil and surprises herself by kissing him.

"There's Kareena Kapur," an impish beggar boy screams. "Aay-haay, Kareena is giving Akshay Kumar a chummi." A group of pot-bellied boys form a circle around them, tittering like thin-legged chicks. Adil lifts his arm and chases after them.

"Let's go." He looks impatient.

They walk against the wind. Lame ponies pulling carriages trot at their heels, the drivers begging them to take rides. On the slope above, overlooking the sea, the homes are minifortresses surrounded by barbed wire and guards. They remind Pia of her own house.

"When I get famous," Adil says, "we can move into one of those."

"And in the meanwhile?" she says. Adil likes to talk about his future.

"You can redecorate."

"I can't live like this. In these sort of conditions, I mean."

He doesn't reply at first, just looks out at the horizon. "Okay, I'll join Daud's gang as a hit man and buy you an eight-bedroom apartment. Happy?"

She grins. "Only if all the rooms are sea-facing."

"How about if I build you a houseboat? Great view even when you take a shit."

"How about if I say get famous first?"

"Pia, you ever taken the ferry? Come on."

She and Adil squeeze into a rickety wooden boat, squashed among mothers and children in synthetic clothes, half-asleep cows, sweaty workmen, and motorcycles. Adil looks at her and laughs. "What?" Pia yells over the drone of the engine.

"Remember when I met you at that pool party?" he says. "I was dripping wet, and you stood there, this graceful woman I hardly knew, listening to my crazy ideas."

"You're lying." Pia strokes a sleepy cow on its neck.

At night, Adil drags the mattress to the floor so they can lie side by side. The table fan doesn't keep the mosquitoes away—they're like a net around her. Adil faces her, the blanket bunched around his heels. His skin is tanned and glossy, except for the birthmark on the rise of his hipbone. The mosquitoes don't touch him. Familiarity maybe.

Pia keeps her cotton nightdress on. Sleeping naked, she has been taught, is inappropriate. Having sex isn't appropriate either. Sex is the mysterious blackout in Hindi movies, the missing frames after rain-swept song-and-dance sequences, the lovers' clothes wet with longing.

But lying here with Adil, she feels comfortable enough without Wonderbras or blow-dried hair. As a kind of game, he shows her how to tear open condoms with one's teeth. Pia pokes her thumb into the condom's sticky mouth, laughs, shakes her head, and watches Adil demonstrate different sexual positions. "For posterity," he says. He rolls on his back and pulls her on top of him. Pia giggles. She bounces up and down. She can feel him beneath her, sense his desire, but of course it is only make-believe. Pia knows how to control herself. "It's not right," she says. "I feel dirty." She is a decent girl, a virgin, the type men want to marry.

Pia returns Adil's overtures timidly at first: stroking his chest. When it feels safe, her tongue traces a slow line to the bottom of his stomach, pausing where the dangerous dark hair emerges. "But what will you think of me?" she says when Adil asks for more.

"I'll think you're a whore, so what? I'll say it right now, you'll be a whore, a slut, a cheap rundi..."

"Stop it," she says.

"Your father's not watching," he tells her, placing his hand be-tween her legs. "No one cares over here."

The morning sun floods the room like a searchlight. The sound of the sea, the water's tug-of-war with land, is unfamiliar. Heat sinks into her. Adil has left without waking her. She lies between the clut-ter of clothes and bedding and last night's dirty dishes. The shadow of a palm tree flickers across her body like a reptile. If a man, say Mack, should come in and drag her by the hair to the toilet, rape her, and throw her into the opaque sea, no one would know.

The streets below are narrow and wounded, teeming with beggars and stray dogs eating litter. Shacks sprout behind hoardings painted with busty starlets clinging to bare-chested, mustached heroes. Lokhanwalla smells like a ghetto. But the advertisements still accu-mulate like obstinate desires, attached to street lamps and dilapidated houses. It's the neighborhood of strugglers: kids who were condi-tioned to be engineers and doctors, but flocked to Bombay deter-mined to reinvent themselves into Shah Rukh Khan, or disco kings like Govinda. Adil's no different. His father was clubbed to death in a worker's strike when Adil was thirteen. But he doesn't like to talk about the past. "That part of me," he has told her, "is dead."

Pia pictures her own father in his black satin pajamas and embroi-dered slippers. He laughs over her mother's latest antics—her foolish fear of cats, her failing memory. He and Pia are the intelligent ones: a team. Then she thinks of Adil. When he meets her father, Adil wants to ask ridiculous questions about his beginnings, his struggles, his business strategies, the road to riches. She tries to remember what Adil knows about thoroughbred racing. Nothing.

The mattress she slept on feels hollow. Even so, she wants to lie here forever, to vanish into the dirt and clutter all around her—lose herself. She looks out the window and sees a hijra lurking on the neighboring terrace. The hermaphrodite walks with one hand on her torso, swaying her thick hips. Her hair hangs in thin spikes over her brightly painted, manly face as she hides beneath the clothesline and chews her betel leaves. If the hijra gets caught in a decent home, she will be beaten. She spots Pia staring and spits juice at her. The shiny red saliva spatters against the window. The hijra lifts her sari, threatening to display her double sexuality, then disappears behind the drying clothes.

A moment later, Adil comes in, holding paper plates. He wears tight Levi's and rubber Bata slippers. He puts the food down and throws himself on her, kissing her palms. Her skin feels damp under his lips. "You're still here," he says.

"Where did you expect me to be?" says Pia. "On the moon?"

"Yes, on the moon, but you're still here." He wraps one arm around her neck, nibbles the tip of her nose.

How easily she surrenders to his affection, sinking into his lap, cradled, whispering nonsense—baby talk. She can't help herself, and it scares her. Pia strikes out at him. He ducks her blows, eyes half-closed, amused, still holding her firmly and planting kisses in between the violent gestures.

Adil pushes her to the ground and pulls down his jeans. She removes his penis from his underwear and squeezes, feeling its pulse as her thumb reaches its smooth tip. She inhales his smell, the curious essence. "Fuck," Pia says in a throaty voice she doesn't recognize. He tries to free his dick from her hand, but she will not let go. She watches him wince as he pries open her fingers, stubborn tentacles, one by one.

Adil lies between her legs and encircles her wrists, placing her arms on either side of her head. He hesitates as he looks down at her.

"Don't think," she says, and pulls him inside her.

Her body yields to Adil's weight, the shock of his immersion. She feels him rise and fall inside her. Behind him there are half-open windows and unknown streets, and beyond that acres of deep sea. Nothing seems impossible. She feels the suck and swell of water, tastes its salt on her tongue as she bites his skin.

"Ouch," he says.

The plain sound of Adil's voice makes her wholly aware of lying here pierced and naked. Adil's face comes closer. It seems twisted, as if in pain. He is so close his black pupils smear into a single gaping eye. "You look creepy," she whispers.

He stops, still inside her.

"What?"

"Talk to me. I need to hear something. Tell me what makes you sad or happy. Just tell me things."

"You already know about me, you mad woman." Adil places his hands under her hips and lifts her toward him. "So I'm creepy?"

"I didn't mean it like that. Just your eyes. Can we go on?"

Adil raises himself on his arms and begins to move quickly. She hardly recognizes him as he punches into her.

In the afternoon, Adil takes Pia to watch a platform skit at Prithvi Theatre. He stands behind her, his arms fitted comfortably around her waist, and she leans back against his body. After the performance, they sit in the café. Fleur smokes a joint and talks to Adil. "I gave a blow job, the works, and the chutiya still said no. That's what a loser I am."

"I think you're a great veejay," Adil says, and squeezes Fleur's hand. "Right, Pia?"

Pia tries to compose a clever reply, something that will make her belong. "You can do better. Fuck him."

Fleur sneers and stubs out her cigarette. "Yeah, right. What the hell would you know? Adil, want to watch *Zadugar* tomorrow? It's free." She waves two tickets at him.

"Can't. I have my screen test." He practices a fight move: a left jab. "Just watch, Natraj is going to launch me. I feel it in here." He thumps his heart.

"Do the test first, then—" Pia begins.

"Wowie!" Fleur says, cutting her off. "My Aby-baby's going to be a superstar."

"When I get famous," Adil tells her, "I'll make you queen of veejays."

Fleur claps her hands and then hugs Adil. "I love you, you fucker, you know that?" She wipes her eyes dry with her fist.

Unsure of what to do, Pia looks away.

On Saturday evening, Pia goes with Adil to Film City. Mack waits for them outside Natraj Studios. "You're late," says Mack. He spits his gum and opens the door for her. "Welcome to our funtastic abode."

The rumbling sound from the industrial generators makes the sweltering space seem alive, as though they were inside some huge ravenous beast. Thick black tubes snake around the walls. Stage lights stud the ceiling. A shapely, baby-faced actress bedecked in a shimmering sarong reads a Bollywood magazine. Beside her, a pudgy man wearing a lime green suit sits surrounded by his sidekicks. Adil and Mack join the circle. Spot boys weave through, serving glasses of tea.

Pia listens to Adil talk to the man. "It would be a great honor, Natrajji, if you could give me a small chance to work under you." His voice is sweet and hopeful.

"What about her?" Natraj points his tiny cell phone toward Pia. "Would she like a small chance, too?" He sputters into laughter.

"Oh no, sir. Pia is my fiancée." Adil gives her a little push. She steps forward.

"Nice choice," Natraj says.

Pia has the urge to slap his baboon face—inform him exactly who and what her father is. For Adil's sake, she stays silent.

Natraj shifts his weight. "Okay, the story is boy loves girl, parents create a big hungama, couple elopes, then some bukwas, let's see, few songs, dances, and a happy ending." He pats the actress on her bum. "Shilpa, go do a sequence with our hero. Let's get some action."

Shilpa stretches her arms languidly. The magazine on her lap slips to the floor. KAREENA DUMPED! the cover reads. "Where's Tiny?" she says.

A midget carrying a makeup kit follows the actress into her dressing room.

Adil removes his watch, gives it to Pia, and steps onto a junglelike set. A backdrop of snowy mountains and trees flickers on the wall. The dance tutor hops in a circle, demonstrating the steps. Adil faces the camera and stares ahead at some distant spot that is secret and urgent. For a brief moment, Pia sees him detached from the ordinary, like a painting, exquisitely framed and held up to the light. When Adil stumbles over a word, she feels responsible. When he delivers a line with ease, it's as if he has spoken only to her.

A technician asks Pia to move. "Your shadow's in the way," he says, and makes her shift to a corner. She sits on an abandoned prop and glances around. Mack walks up beside her. Pia is grateful; she pinches his arm and grins.

The set thunders, the roof pours rain. A disco beat unfurls from the speakers. Fog machines cloud the stage, and Shilpa emerges from the smoke like a miracle. She closes her eyes, rotates her hips. Tiny jumps onto the director's chair, unbuttons his trousers, and mimics her movements. The crowd of extras hoot and shriek.

Maybe he *will* be a star, Pia thinks, watching Adil's lips slide over Shilpa's quivering, wet navel. And what will I be?

Adil slithers up Shilpa's body and lip-synchs to a love song.

The next day, her breakfast is placed on a turquoise dish embellished with white daisies. Adil has his eggs on a paper plate. He eats fast, doesn't daydream or shift his food around. The fork's trajectory is a straight route: into his mouth and out again to stab the eggs. Adil finishes, then lies down, his head propped by his elbow. They've had sex again, and now he gazes at her, as though nothing she can do will disappoint him.

"What?" Pia says. "I can't eat if you stare."

"Okay, I won't." He picks up her left foot and kneads the sole with his thumbs. "You eat like a bird."

There is a knock at the door, then a man yells, "Adil, are you there, beta?"

"Oh, shit," Adil whispers. "One minute, Uncle." He pulls on his shorts. Be quiet, he signals to her, and goes out to the corridor.

The landlord's voice is only slightly muffled by the closed door. "Last month's is overdue, Mister. I'm not a charity, you know."

"I'll pay by tomorrow latest, Uncle. I've even asked for those passes for you and Aunty to watch the shooting at Sun and Sand Hotel."

"I heard a girl's voice last night," the landlord says. "You know the rules. No hanky-panky in my house."

"There's no one here, Uncle, by god," he says. "Just my sister from Delhi."

A door slams in the hallway. "Adil shweety," Mack teases. "Why are you standing here in your phunky knickers? Yaar, put on a tie, there's a producer-looking guy asking for you. I told him to come upstairs."

Pia hears sharp, measured footsteps. Instantly, she recognizes them. Her heart clenches.

"Is Pia here?" asks a familiar voice.

"Mr. Burman, sir," Adil says. "Yes, but let me tell her you're here. She's resting."

Pia feels a sickness inside her as if she is falling from a great height. It can't possibly be him, she thinks.

"Sleeping till noon. What is she, ill?" says Uncle.

"May I go in?" says her father.

Adil opens the door and her father faces her. Pia tries to sit up, but her body doesn't respond and she lies stretched on the mattress, shirt inside out, no makeup, her hair disheveled. For a moment, her father looks uncertain, as though he wants Pia to be someone else, not his daughter, sprawled on the floor. She expects him to back out in horror. But he stays.

"I thought I'd stop on my way from the airport and pick you up myself," he says, averting his eyes almost casually and looking out the windows. "Your friend Maya said you asked for the car to be sent here."

"Yes, I came in the morning," Pia says in a choking murmur, and then sits up, holding the sheet tightly around her chest. She can smell his lime cologne. Its fragrance floats around Adil's room and turns it back into the tiny box she walked into when she arrived.

Her father straightens his silk tie as if to set everything in order: the damp heat, his half-naked daughter, Adil in his underwear, the gutter stench, and flies that litter the shoulders of his jacket.

Pia searches for something to say. Why did you come? she wants to ask. You have no right to be here, this is your fault. Instead, she reaches for her jeans and puts them on under the sheet. She tucks in her shirt and stands up. "What time is our race?"

"Four P.M." Her father glances at his watch, then places his hands in his pockets. "I want to get there early. Are you still interested in going?"

"Yes, I am." She wishes he would growl or scream, slap her, drag her out of here, do what he needs to do. But he will never be tempted into forgetting who he is.

A small, balding man with owl-eyed spectacles now stands in the doorway. "So this is your real sister?" he says, examining Pia as if she is a rotting fruit he'd cut open.

"Yes, Uncle," Adil says softly.

Pia looks at her father as he processes things. She tries to remain calm, but all she wants is to hide her face.

"I'm not listening to anymore 'Uncle please,'" the landlord tells Adil. "If you don't have rent, I'm throwing you out—sister and all."

"Uncle, give me till tomorrow."

Her father snaps open his briefcase with a solid click. "How much is it?" He takes out ten thousand rupees stapled together with a bank sticker. "Will this do?"

The money lies on the counter like a weapon. Uncle stares at it, his fingers pocketed deep in his trousers.

"It won't be fair to accept this, sir," says Adil.

"Well, this is hardly the time to be concerned about being fair. Just take it."

Adil takes a step forward and picks it up. "Sir, I'll definitely pay you back this evening." He wipes the bundle against his shorts. He takes a look at her father and then hands the money to his landlord.

Uncle counts the cash quickly. "It's good," he sniffs and slips out the room.

Adil closes the door. His eyes look shifty. "Pia, if you want to leave with your father now, it's fine."

"No, I'll wait for you," she says, because it seems the right thing to say. Pia slips on a sweater over her shirt and buttons it.

Her father studies his watch. "I'll go ahead then. Why don't you follow when you're properly dressed?"

"Mr. Burman, sir, I'm really sorry about all this. I'll return the loan."

"Forget about it. Just wear a suit or you can't enter the members' enclosure."

Her father picks up his briefcase. Wait, she wants to say. Pia tries to hold together something inside her: maybe a hope, an unmanageable emotion that topples under its own weight.

Kabhi Kabhi plays on the radio in Mack's room. Pia waits in the corridor for Adil to lock up. Mack's door is ajar. He lies on the floor, staring at the ceiling, arms and legs spread wide, as if he's on a crucifix. His large, watery eyes flick to the side. "Hey, Queenie," Mack whispers. Pia looks away and hurries downstairs.

She and Adil climb into a yellow and black rickshaw. "Mahalaxmi Racecourse chalo phatafat," he tells the driver. The open flaps allow the dust rising off the road to strike their faces—no tinted windows to buff out the glaring sun. A beggar boy chases after the rickshaw, his bare feet slapping against the hot Tarmac.

Pia wonders where she would be now if she had never met Adil. Gossiping with family at Sunday brunch? Playing golf with her father? Home, she thinks.

Adil places her hand on his thigh and rubs it. "You're not angry, are you? I'll pay your father back even if I have to turn into a horse myself and run the races."

She tries not to smile. "Stop acting silly."

"You're so sexy it makes me silly."

She pushes him away. "You saw what just happened. I mean, my father caught me undressed. Do you have any idea what that means?"

"It means you love me and no one can change that. Not even him."

"I've been humiliated in front of everyone. My father must think I'm a...I don't know what. And all you can do is play the fool."

"I told you I'd pay him back. I promise, okay?" He lifts both her legs and swings them over his knees. "You have the sweetest toes."

"You probably use the same lines to pataou all your girlfriends," Pia says, putting her legs back down. Despite his softness, she realizes Adil is tougher than she is. He knows how to move on.

Their rickshaw halts abruptly at a major intersection. Coca-Cola billboards tower over the fuming traffic like new gods. A cart stops alongside them. It has shutters on three sides and a barred peephole. School children sit silently in the dark. They stare out onto the street, their tiny fingers poking through the mesh wiring.

"Look at that," Pia says. "Like chickens being sent to a slaughter-house."

He glances at the children. "They look happy."

As happy as we look, she thinks.

The driver cranks up a hit tune. He shakes his head and hums along.

"You liked *Zadugar?*" Adil asks him.

"Wah! What a phlim," the man says. "Aamir Khan has double role, eleven songs, and tip-top dancing, but fighting was so-so. No daum in villain."

"Pia, let's go see it tonight," Adil says.

"Don't you understand? For God's sake, he caught us. He *knows.*"

"So?"

"What if it were your father? How would you feel?"

"My old man is dead." Adil stares at the moving white stripe on the road and starts singing along with the driver.

———

When they reach the racecourse, Pia joins her father in the owners' paddock and they watch his filly, Secret Treasure, trot by. The diamond shapes on her father's midnight blue tie match his gray flannel suit. Pia stands near him; her shoulder touches his arm. She is foolishly satisfied with her father's appearance. He is tall like Adil, but his features have a harder, authoritative look.

Secret Treasure waits to be mounted. She strikes a practiced pose: left leg forward, ears pricked, head held high, sun hitting her smack on her shiny coat. "Get a good jump, lie third or fourth," her father instructs the young jockey. "Make your run in the straight and don't try any tricks."

Pia smiles at his advice. Always practical. Do what you know and get home free.

Adil waits for them at the gate to the paddock. "You missed the fourth race," her father says. "Mystique won by four lengths. I had a big one on her."

"That's great, Mr. Burman." Adil shakes his hand. "Sir, who do you think will win the main event?"

"The bookies are pretty hot on my filly. Two to one favorite." He looks at the race book. "The colt Indictment could cause a few hiccups, but I'd say the field's fairly clear." Her father takes out his wallet. "Place your bet at the first enclosure—they give better odds. And here, put twenty thousand rupees on Win for me."

Adil takes the money and heads toward the bookmaker's ring where the serious punters in their old jeans and Terylene shirts stand.

"Pia, you look exhausted," her father says. "I hope you haven't caught something. You have to be careful of your health."

"I'm fine."

"You don't look fine to me." He turns up the collars of Pia's shirt, removes a stray thread stuck in her hair. "What you need is a warm bath, a nice clean bed, and some rest. No more vagabond nonsense. Now let's go to our box and order you a drink."

"What about Adil? They won't allow him in the member's enclosure without us."

She and her father stand in awkward silence. Pia stares at a pair of men walking past her. Kabir Oswal: twenty-four, single, chauvinist, heir to Oswal Steel. Jeh Mehta: twenty-seven, married, unfaithful, source of income uncertain. They blend together into a single stroke of crisp suits, monogrammed shirts, and veneered faces. Pia imagines Fleur in her pink hipsters and pierced belly button among this jeweled crowd. She envies her.

When Adil returns, her father leads the way to the long, white balconies on the second floor that perch over the track. "I borrowed four thousand rupees from Mack. I've put it all on your horse, number four." Adil tells her. "Damn thing better win."

Her father stops to greet friends before they sit down. "Pia, you sit in the middle," he says, placing her between Adil and himself.

The Topiwallas, an old Zoroastrian family, have the box in front of them. It is designated by a brass nameplate. They own the chestnut colt Indictment. The large family sits as though enthroned there by nature.

"Good luck," her father says to old Mrs. Topiwalla. "May the best horse win."

"May the best horse win," she repeats, flashing a smile. She wears the same canary yellow crepe de chine dress every time her horse runs. "I can't say exactly how my Indictment knows, but he always does his level best when I wear this lucky outfit," Pia has heard her say.

"You've met my daughter, Pia, haven't you?"

"Of course. And what a lovely girl she's become." Mrs. Topiwalla waves a finger toward Adil. "And this is your..." Her eyes scan the skinny knot of Adil's tie, the absence of cuff links on his sleeve, a coffee stain at the kneecap of his khaki pants, his bulky white socks. The valuation, Pia thinks.

"Oh, he's a friend who lives here in Bombay," her father says.

Mrs. Topiwalla pulls out a scented tissue from a tin and dabs her neck. "Well, good luck all."

Pia looks up at the suspended monitor and watches the horses move into the gates. Adil leans over and speaks to her father about the race. She shifts her right leg and nudges Adil's elbow from her thigh. He is talking too much. Nervous chatter. Her father sits back in his chair, his left foot tapping the floor, and listens. Pia tries to visualize what her father must think. How dramatic Adil is. How he speaks with his hands, his features vibrant, his voice too loud.

A shrill bell rings. Her father adjusts his binoculars and leans forward. The gates open. *Under starter's orders... they're off,* says the commentator. A storm of pounding hooves moves past the boxes, and the jockeys' colors flash kaleidoscopically in the sunlight. The horses bunch together, galloping along the mile-and-half track. Mrs. Topiwalla shuts her eyes. She keeps them closed during the race, says it's too much pressure. *As the field hits the straight it's the pacemaker Baywatch... followed by Arabian Rose... hotly pursued by Aerogramme and Indictment close behind on the rails.* The hurried tempo of the commentator's voice quickens the heartbeat. *But the favorite... found a gap...*

Adil stands up and yells, "Secret Treasure—move your butt!"

The Topiwallas glare at him. "For god's sake," Pia hisses.

"Sorry, sorry." He places a finger on his lips and sits down.

In the homestretch it's Indictment followed by Secret Treasure... quickly making ground...

The crowds in the first enclosure press themselves against the railings of the track and yell out the favorite's name.

Her father shouts, "Come on, Secret Treasure!"

Pia follows his lead and stands up. Mrs. Topiwalla mutters a cryptic prayer. She wonders if old Mrs. Topiwalla has ever played puppet with her thumb stuck up a condom. *It's Indictment and Secret Treasure running neck...* Pia wants to ask her: "Does your lover blush when you brush those huge teeth?" *Secret Treasure is pushing... she's giving it all she's got...*

"You can do it, baby!" Adil yells, throwing out his arm. Voices crescendo as the horses gallop past the boxes; dust from their hooves rises like a funeral fire. *It's Secret Treasure and Indictment still Secret Treasure and Indictment.* Pia wants to ask her, "Have you cleaned a window stained with a hijra's red spit?" Mrs. Topiwalla sticks her fingers into her ears. Tell me, old woman, have you ever tasted the sea? *Yes, oh yes... the hot favorite....* Pia watches Secret Treasure stick her head forward, just a nose ahead of Indictment as she races past the finishing post.

Her father slaps his hand against his knee. "We did it!"

Adil lets out a whoop and kisses Pia, then embraces her father. "It's quite all right, thank you," her father says. He smoothes his hair, excuses himself, and hurries down to lead his filly into the paddock. Photographers surround him. Acquaintances try to catch his eye. The crowds do a little jig, and throw rose petals on her father and his horse. "Wah! Wah! Burman sahib! Well done, Secret Treasure."

"Let's cash the booty," Adil says. He leads Pia downstairs to the bookmaker's ring. The bookies sit on high stools. Desperate punters clamor around their knees as though they were selling nonstop fares to heaven. Adil gives the man his slips.

The bookie glances down and hands them back. "Sorry, no good."

"What do you mean? My horse—number four won." Adil points to the chalked results on the long blackboard behind him.

"Mister, your number four hasn't even seen the track yet. Your bets are on the next race." The man sighs. "Odds are fifty to one. What are you? A fortune teller?"

Adil looks confused. He opens his mouth, then shuts it again.

"I can't believe this," Pia says. All the confusion she felt in his room is balled into a mean fist. "I've put up with your friends' snide remarks, watched you flirt with every woman in sight. I was ready to give up everything to be with you. And you can't place a simple bet. You can't even pay your own rent. How the hell do you expect me to marry you?"

Adil's eyes are empty.

She is going too far, but she wants to go even farther—get Adil to do what she can't—make him shake her by the shoulders and say, This won't work, I'm leaving.

"That was all Mack's money," he mumbles.

"What about my father?" she says, working herself up. "What's he going to think?"

"What about me?" says Adil. "How do you think I feel?" He tosses the slips in the air. "You people think you know it all, don't you? Money, horses, fucking suits and ties, but what about love? You know shit about that. Shit."

"Stop shouting. This isn't some stage set," she says, and turns to leave.

Pia joins her father behind the track at the stables. The filly stands sweating; a white residue stains her bay coat where the saddle was.

"You should write a little essay on the race for college," he says. "Yes, Papa."

Flies buzz around the horse's head. Her eyes are dilated and she breathes heavily. Pia puts her arms around Secret Treasure and buries her face in the animal's neck.

"I'm going home," Adil says, when he catches up with her after the prize ceremony. "What's your plan?"

"My father and I are having tea at the hospitality tent." She shifts the enormous silver trophy to her other arm. "I'm staying with him at the hotel tonight."

Adil's arms hang at his sides. "I'll call you."

Pia nods and watches him walk away. She thinks Adil might turn around, but he doesn't, and then he vanishes into the crowd. Left alone in the paddock, she listens to the amplified voice of the commentator declare the day's winners and losers.

Her father reads a novel: *The Other Side of Midnight.* He pushes his gold-rimmed glasses firmly against his nose. She'd like to speak to him about Adil, tell him how she feels so she can make sense of things.

Pia fiddles with the knobs on the console between the twin beds that control the piped-in hotel music.

"Turn down that noise, please," her father says.

Pia switches it off. "So, what did you think of Adil?" she says before he can resume his reading.

"Decent chap," he says, without looking up at her.

"Then you like him?"

"It's not a question of like or dislike. A man is known by his profession, his deeds, and a woman is judged by... by the dignity she keeps. At least that's how I've tried to bring you up. What I saw this morning, well, you could hardly call that place a garden."

"Adil loves me, doesn't that mean anything?"

He looks at her curiously, as if the notion of love is something she has invented. "Darling, if you think you can live happily ever after in a filthy box, then go ahead. The decision is yours." Her father reaches to turn off the light. "Good night," he says, his words harmonized with the click.

Pia turns to her side and hugs the pillow. The linen has a scratchy texture, as if no one has ever slept on it. If this were a movie, she'd climb out the window, desperate to join her banished lover who'd wait below singing some melancholy song. They'd dance like Laila and Majnu under the moonlight, make love in discreetly edited footage, and drink from silver cups of poison.

The hotel operator has put the line on DND. Pia wonders if Adil has tried calling. She misses rubbing her toe against his leg; she misses the weight of Adil's body behind hers, his hand cupped resolutely around her breast.

The air conditioning deadens the sound of traffic on Marine Drive, the main road that wraps around the shoreline. Adil says the city was once a group of small islands, but greedy developers pumped out the sea and dumped earth in its place until the land ate up the water. An unearthly green light from a neighboring skyscraper blinks at her. The windows are still wet from the evening rain.

Pia goes to the bathroom, sits on the toilet seat, and checks the messages with the operator. Nothing from Adil.

She looks at herself in the mirror and pulls a face. "How lovely I have become," she says, mimicking Mrs. Topiwalla's British accent. The fat hotel towels look tempting. She runs a bath. Do what you know and get home free, she sings to a made-up tune, as the water splashes into the tub.

Her cell phone rings in the silent, dark bedroom. Pia runs to get it. She looks at the flashing number. It's Adil.

"Why is your line on Do Not Disturb?"

"My father's sleeping," she says, walking back to the bathroom.

"I was going to mail this letter I wrote but Mack says I should read it to you. It's not elegant or anything. It's about me, how I feel, okay? So no sarcasm."

"Just read it."

"Okay, here goes: *It has stopped raining and the sun from behind the clouds is making everything in my room look yellow. I can hear crickets outside, and I want to tell you about this small village in Assam, where I lived with my family."*

I don't want to know, Pia thinks. It's too late.

"It rained ten months in the year, and there was always this diffused light, which makes me remember all this in black and white. There was never any electricity, and our home was lit by kerosene lamps. They have a thoughtful flame that made everything look graceful, and during my bath, I'd love to watch the water shimmer down my skin."

Sentimental, but she knows what he means. Soft towels lie at her feet.

"In the evening, the drives on my father's scooter felt like victory laps. I was nine years old and I rode in front with him, holding the handles. The roads were hilly and winding, lit dimly by the scooter's headlights. We could hear the hum of grasshoppers and crickets and fireflies, it was as if God (if there is one) had lined them up like an orchestra along the road to sing for us, and the darkness ahead made it seem like we could go on forever."

Pia digs her nails into her fingers, and curses him silently. Just when she has made up her mind, he talks about forever, about miracles.

Adil pauses. "There's more but you'd call it silly. I'll read it anyway. *I wonder what put me in this time capsule? Maybe the crickets outside my window. But now they are gone and there are too many mosquitoes.* That's all I want to say. Tell your father I'm sorry."

She can hear Mack's voice in the background. "Yaar, let me say hi to Queenie. Is she coming with us for the film?"

"I have to go," says Adil. He hangs up before she can say a word.

The hot water gathers in the shallow tub and the rising steam blurs the mirror she is looking into. "I am a lovely, lovely girl," Pia says to herself. She engraves her full name on the smoky mirror. Lovely fool, she thinks, watching her eyes emerge through the clear lines. She imagines herself with Adil, Fleur, and Mack with all his crazy talk, telling her to stop by. How successful Adil and his friends are, living alone, independent, and Pia is furious at herself for who she is.

She enters the bedroom, the numbing air-conditioned darkness. Her father's eyes are shut. He makes no sound. She walks to the windows and pushes the shutters open. A strong wind hits her face, whips through the thin fabric of her nightgown. Leaning over the sill, she watches the waves roll in, full of hope and vigor, only to break against the rocks and wash away again, taking bits of the shore as they retreat toward some invisible future. Tireless motions. If it were possible, she would set the sea free, release it from the pull of gravity, the dutiful opening and closing.

She turns around. Her father still sleeps. Stripped of consciousness, he looks faded. She sits beside him, nudges his shoulder. His head droops off the side of the pillow into his chest; a strand of spit worms out from the corner of his half-open mouth. For a second, she thinks she has somehow killed him. Her fingers tighten into an unbreakable grip, determined to wake him; and she shakes his body so hard that her whole world seems to shake with him.

COURTNEY JONES

Hollins University

IRREGULARITIES

My body stopped being able to tolerate onions around the time the baby inside me, who I sometimes forget about but who never forgets about me, stopped tolerating them. This was right after I had started trying New Things—onions were a New Thing for me. I was into trying New Things after I read an article about their positive effects in a woman's magazine that was in the waiting room of the cardiac care unit, where I am an administrative assistant. And just after I began to enjoy onions, my baby appeared and wholeheartedly disagreed.

He revealed himself to me in this way Easter Sunday when I ate my older sister's cornbread dressing with onions. I booted it right back up while my parents, sister, and brother-in-law were starting in on the 7UP cake I made for dessert. Immediately before all this, my sister had accused me of using a generic yellow cake mix as a base. According to my sister, who is married and the mother of 2.4 jet skis, real women make cakes from scratch, so I had gone one step further and made the pineapple topping, which she has been known to burn.

These dealings with my sister (the president of the Highland Country Club's Bridge and Pinochle Brigade) have certainly made me nauseated on other occasions, but this was different. I booted right through dessert, the Easter egg hunt my parents had for the neighborhood children, and a visit from my cousins. You should have heard me. My sister and her husband finally scooped me up and helped me to the back bathroom, so I wouldn't frighten the guests. "What is *wrong* with you?" my sister whined. I booted loud and rough, the way I've only heard a man do it. I booted like it was my job.

Since Easter, when I started to know about my baby and he started to know about me, eating has been touch and go. The kid loves carrots, but I detest them, so I know he didn't get that from me. He loves all vegetables, which I hate. I am now led blindly by his appetite to the freezer section of Food Lion, where he chooses broccoli, cauliflower, and large bags filled with more than one vegetable that he likes to eat together. Peas, carrots, and snap bean medley is his favorite.

In this magazine article, which I really did think would overhaul my life, there was a list of thirty New Things to try, so I ripped out the page, took it home, and stuck it on my freezer.

The first New Thing I did was color my hair with a seven dollar Frost and Tip kit from the Revco (did you *paint* your hair? screamed my sister, who only has her hair done at Aveda), then I sponge painted my guest bathroom using a handful of crumpled newspaper and pastel tones I mixed myself down at the lumber store. I used peach and light green and started a festive beach motif in there: I bought a seashell soap dish, a shower curtain with sailboats and lighthouses painted on, breezy green curtains for the window, and a shampoo that claimed it smelled like "a rainy May morning at the shore." Decorating was a New Thing I tried.

Then I went on to spicing up my meals because I read it would rev up a sluggish metabolism (though, honestly, mine wouldn't run if you set fire to it). First I experimented with curry and ginger root, bay leaves from the New Herb Garden I started after I decorated my bathroom, and a garlicky marinade for chicken that *Southern Living* (a New Magazine Subscription for me) highlighted a few months back. Then I decided to ask for the tiny shavings of red onion on my sandwich at the Turkey Gobbler and I found I quite enjoyed them— the extra bite of flavor, the mild crunch amid the soft turkey and cheese. This prompted me to try other toppings on my sandwich, too. I tried sprouts, which I couldn't taste or feel, tomato, which I found cold and slimy, and banana peppers, which were much too strong for my tastes.

Now I ask my baby: Why the onions? It was the only New Topping I liked! He's forcing me to take all kinds of other things, but if I send him a delicious, self-indulgent sliver of onion, he balks and sends it right back.

Pregnancy is looked down upon around here because we Administrative Assistants work for doctors who act as if they can't set their watches without our input. Six weeks of paid leave to nurse and wipe and cry is unacceptable to them. They even hint around at the interview, which is illegal of course, but I didn't mind because I had no plans to get pregnant. After what seemed like a million years of college, typing was something I could do. I really needed the job. These doctors need us to run them like vacuum cleaners, plug them in at the beginning of the day and shove them around to all their various appointments and surgeries. I push mine to his meetings, his case studies, and all over the world to medicate.

My boss, James Soleander, M.D., doesn't even know yet about the baby inside me, though I believe he ought to. He's the one who put it there. But he's always forgetting where he put his pen when it's tucked behind his ear or where he has laid his beeper though it is usually clipped to the belt holding up his slacks. So I can see how it happened. And I haven't told him. I'm waiting to see if he can just sense conception the way that I did, if he can feel that a part of him has taken off on its own to form another the way the people of the First Baptist Church around here have been known to do when they disagree on something. But he's shown no signs. I read in another women's magazine in our office that some men will get sick right along with you, but he looks fine: his face and neck browned from afternoons on the back nine, his eyes sparkly from the eight hours of sleep he gets every night if he isn't on call.

This morning around eleven, I go to the Turkey Gobbler and ask the man behind the counter to make my "special" (turkey, provolone, spicy mustard, red onions, Kaiser roll) without onions. He forgets. I can see why. He appears to be shrinking. His body seems to be folding into itself with every step down the counter, his arms disappearing into his blue button-down shirt as he pushes my Kaiser roll down the extra-long white cutting board.

He is having a bad day, which is something that I try to think about. I am one of those people who, on the bus to work, likes to offer her seat to people who look like they need it more than I do. I have always been sympathetic to people in this way, which is why I like my job. Talking on the phone is another thing I can do, and if your child has a hole in his heart and his cardiologist never remembers to return your calls, you might want to talk about it. I take the extra time with patients so James Soleander doesn't have to. And I must have been thinking of this—how I would offer this man my seat on a bus and then how in just a few months I will be one of these people getting *offered* a seat and then if my baby has a hole in his heart...—because I don't notice it when he reaches down into the onion bin and sprinkles them on my revised special sandwich. I don't even check the sandwich until I get to my office, sit in my ergonomically correct rolling chair in front of my ergonomically correct keyboard (both gifts from James Soleander), and unwrap the wax paper from my special sandwich.

It assaults me, and my baby, immediately. When I lift the top of my roll, the curly ribbons of purple onion are stuck in the spicy mustard. They sneer at me. I pull them off with my fingers, and fling them in the trash can on the opposite side of the room. The smell is on my fingers after that, and even though I scrub and scald them in the Ladies' Room, every time I go to scratch my nose or touch my face I can smell the onion I never wanted in the first place and this *baby* inside me has the most awful fits.

My day settles down a few hours after the onion business. Though the odor of a red onion wouldn't leave a room if you threatened it, my baby and I get used to the smell and forget it is even there. I call the airline and book a flight for Dr. Soleander and his wife, Donna, to go to a medical conference in Hilton Head. I fill out a purchase order for the tickets, seal it in an interoffice envelope, and hand-deliver it to Patrick, our business manager. He has my favorite peanut butter candies in a jar on his desk, but when I go to reach for one, my baby says *No.* I rub him through the waist of my favorite silk pants that soon will not fit. *C'mon!* I silently whine. Still he says *No.* It's like he's the parent now. He's confused our roles, and I'm hoping this isn't going to become a pattern. I already see how it's starting. He won't let me stay out late. I am under no circumstances to have a cold beer after work with the other Administrative Assistants or we will both be in big trouble. And the smoking habit I cultivated in my parents' garage when I was fifteen is now *definitely* out of the picture, thanks to a warning from the Surgeon General. Who knows what he might do under these influences: grow an extra arm, come out faceless, voiceless?

James Soleander, M.D., notices the onion immediately when he comes in to check his messages, though he has not yet, apparently, noticed our baby. He is wearing a royal blue cashmere sweater that I assume is new because I've never seen him wear it before. I don't own any cashmere and had never really come in contact with it until I started working for him. Even my older sister doesn't own any that I know of (I would have lifted it for my own) and she has *everything*.

Sometimes when Dr. Soleander is out for the afternoon, I do my work on his office computer just to touch the cashmere coat he leaves hanging on the back of the chair. Sometimes I drape it over my shoulders and wear it all day like a cape, complaining to the other Assistants that my air conditioner is out of control, my office is too chilly.

"What's that smell?" Dr. Soleander asks, taking a few steps back. I look down at his shoes. He also has nice shoes. I stop my Dictaphone with the pedal below my desk and remove my earphones. I am writing a cover letter for an article he is sending to the *American Journal of Cardiology*. His voice was soft and slow in the earphones and I had just gotten to "studying the role of low-density lipoprotein cholesterol, period, new paragraph," when he walked in.

"What?"

"What's that smell?" he asks again, looking around. "The onion smell."

"It's an onion," I say. I wink.

"Go figure." He sits on my desk and slaps the red folder he is holding on his thigh. "Know something? Onions are my favorite vegetable."

Are you flirting? I want to ask. Am I your girlfriend? I want to ask.

"Are they a vegetable?" I ask. I have never really thought about it that way.

"Well, what else would they be?"

"You've got a point."

"They're certainly not a fruit!"

"I hear you."

"Though I could eat one like a fruit, I really could. I could pick one up and bite straight into it like a pear." He slaps the folder on his leg one more time and hands it to me. Inside is a jumble of white paper, his mottled handwriting scratched on it from top to bottom. "Think you can make sense of this?"

"Is this an article?"

"Yeah, it just needs to be typed. I knew you could understand it." As he walks out, he lingers in my doorway and looks me over. I think maybe he can see right through me to the tiny kernel of a baby, our baby, but he just winks and walks back down the hall to an office which is furnished better than my apartment, to his closet full of cashmere.

My affair with James Soleander, M.D., did not start in the way many interoffice affairs do. And I would not exactly call it a regular thing— when the mood hits, we just *do*. I have been known to be whimsical (frosted hair and beachy bathrooms, for instance), so this is not entirely out of my character. Ours is not the typical boss/secretary— ahem, Administrative Assistant—affair you might see on a soap opera. There was no standing behind me and breathing on my neck or looking down my blouse as he dictated a letter, no inappropriate rear end touching by the coffee machine, and, as far as I know, there was nothing missing in his life that he suddenly saw in my life late one evening while arranging slides for a presentation about hypoplastic left heart syndrome. His wife is beautiful and sweet, well groomed, charming at parties. She's an anesthesiologist and comes down to our floor every once in a while to ask him what he wants for dinner or to leave a flower on his desk, and as she passes by she always gives me a little wave. She and my older sister have the same wave—all fingers, no palm or wrist, like she's tickling the air.

Dr. Soleander is attracted to my heart. He's become addicted to my irregular heartbeat, the strange *thmp, thmp, THMP-THMP, thum, thmp, THMP-THMP* that I told him about right after my general practitioner noticed it at a routine physical. No doctor had ever picked up on it before, and when I expressed my concern, James Soleander had me sit on his desk so he could listen for himself. He blew on the stethoscope to warm it up before reaching up my sweater and placing it on the bare skin right above my bra. He listened for a good ten minutes and drummed out the beat with his left hand on the desk right beside my thigh. *Thmp, thmp, THMP-THMP, thum, thmp, THMP-THMP.* He closed his eyes prayerfully.

Neither of us said anything and a strange tingle crawled up my legs and arms, like he was sprinkling me with glitter. I was suddenly, desperately, attracted to this man, my married boss. To break the silence I asked, "So, I'll be okay, right?" my voice cracking.

He nodded over and over. I could smell his aftershave. "There's art in imperfection," he said, finally, parting his lips and breathing in slowly. "True beauty lies in nature's mistakes."

He sat back in the chair and rubbed the side of his face with his hand. I could see his eyes were glassy, as if he had a fever. He looked at me dead on, and though my breathing stopped, I could hear my funny heartbeat loud and clear.

Dr. Soleander took my chin in his hand. "You have the most beautiful heartbeat I've ever heard," he said, and then leaned forward and kissed me on the mouth. Then he kissed me where his stethoscope had been. Right over my irregular heart.

No one had ever been interested in me for something that was wrong with me and so we did it—*it*—right there on his desk, his ear cocked down toward my heart the entire time. When we were through, he laid his head on my chest and listened to my irregularity some more, and I stroked his hair the way I now figure I might stroke the hair of our baby when I prop him against my chest. After some time, Dr. Soleander's beeper beeped. I pulled up my panty hose, retied his tie, and shuffled him off to a meeting. Then I stood in his closet. I opened my arms and fell forward into the cashmere and it held me there until five after five, when the day was done.

As it turns out, James Soleander's wife cannot go to the medical conference in Hilton Head because of a Girl Scout cookie convention that she is involved with, so he asks me to go with him instead. He blushes and my heart pumps its erratic beat up in my ears. "I really need someone there to help me keep my schedule," he tells me, not looking at me, but winding his watch over and over. Our latest encounters have been spontaneous and strange—his car or my car, outside on the smoking porch, the elevator. I've suggested my apartment—some wine, a movie—but he doesn't like things to be planned. When surprised or nervous, my heart beats loudly, and this is what he likes to hear.

So when he invites me on the trip, I have a small inkling that my boss is more than that, that he is my *boyfriend,* and though I've been fighting off this feeling, I give in a little to the idea. I put my hand over my lips and silently tell my baby to be good for just one week. I don't want him to ruin things before they even really begin.

We got to Hilton Head. Dr. Soleander and I bring with us on the plane about five or so boxes of those cookies Donna sells and we eat about five boxes or so. He gets drunk on vodka and lime juice and laughs at me the whole time, spewing chewed Thin Mints on his tray.

"What an appetite you have," he says. "I've never seen someone your size eat like this!" I reach above my chest and feel the beats. They go wild. "Seriously," he says, shaking his head. "You're something else."

"Oh, please," I say, embarrassment covering my face like a hot blanket.

"No, really. Donna's not like you." He swirls the vodka around in the glass, staring in. "She's not this loose, this free. You're free."

"She's really great, though." I say, trying not to get my hopes up about my doctor boss and our nonrelationship. "She's so nice. And I hear she's funny."

"She's nothing like you." He turns to me and puts a hand on my cheek. "You and your quirks, your youth, your onions that you suddenly like and then suddenly don't, your heartbeat. You're genuine. The way you come in my office when I'm gone and wear my sweater and jackets."

"How did you know about that?"

"Your perfume." He smiles. "I like you because you're *special.* You're *strange.*"

"You're drunk," I say, dismissing him.

"And why aren't you?" he says, pushing his drink over to me. "Have some. I've seen you drink before at the office cocktails. I thought you went out on Wednesday nights with the other Assistants?"

"I stopped drinking about a month ago," I say, looking straight at him, hoping he'll suddenly sense why. *I'm carrying your child!* I silently scream.

"See, this is what I'm talking about. You and your quirks. All or nothing."

His words make me shiver. "I'm cold," I say. "Can I wear your jacket?" He wiggles out of it and I pull it around my shoulders, run my hands over the cuff. I wonder if I can carry our child home in cashmere.

We keep our separate rooms at the hotel for receipt purposes, but I mostly stay in his room watching television and paging him when it is time to change appointments or lecture rooms. I order room service all day, never minding the bill. I steal all the towels, and a robe. I go down to the beach and eat frozen lemonade and funnel cakes from the nearby stands while he is presenting cases on myocardial infarctions in African American men with Jewish fathers, or something comparable. There's always a variable. He loves variables. I spend some time thinking about my tiny baby and watching cooking shows, and for the first time I see myself as a mother, maybe with aprons and cookbooks and playpens. I imagine a big white wedding that my sister can coordinate and finally be happy about! I think maybe I will tell Dr. Soleander about the baby when we get back, as I'm nearly three months along. At night he listens to my heart, and my baby listens to my heart, and we all fall asleep by it and wake up to the distant roar of the Atlantic Ocean.

As it turns out, my baby is not the spitting image of his father— something that I'd hoped to hear at a baptism, baseball games, and neighborhood picnics.

As much as James Soleander, M.D., adores my irregularities, he does not pass this love on to my baby, who (like so many boys before him) bails out on me after a mere three months in my life. He leaves the day after we get back from Hilton Head. I can understand why, I suppose. I mean, all my Administrative Assistant friends insist that I've been no fun at all since I've quit going out. I've become *old*, they say. And I was so difficult about feeding him the things he liked. And as much as I've read in these various women's magazines about pleasing a man, I couldn't seem to please him, the one that really mattered. I can see his logic.

And as it turns out, my heart is not the only part of my body that is irregular. My gynecologist says my body might not be able to hold onto a baby. My reproductive system, he says, "may very well be *malfunctioning*."

Though I never told James Soleander, who has been clinging to Donna since we got back from our trip, that we once shared a sack of cells in my malfunctioning belly, I do tell him about this glitch in my reproductive system.

I knock on his office door and he seems a little annoyed that I'm there. He, after coming back from our sunny vacation that held so much promise for us, has apparently bailed on me, too. "Hi," he says, too cheerful, waving me into his office. "Sit down." He points to the chair on the other side of his desk and sits down in his. "What's up? Are you feeling better? Personnel said you were sick."

"Just a little flu."

"It's that plane air."

"Sure. Want to hear something strange? I might not be able to have a baby," I say quickly, picking at the seams of the chair. He stares at me and then frowns. I look away. He says he is sorry. He is oh so sorry.

"Had you planned on settling down, having children?" he asks. I sit there, trying to gather up the breath to speak. I wait for him to lay me down on his desk, fold over the waist of my skirt and listen to the spurt and putter of my Malfunctioning Ovaries with his warmed stethoscope. I wait for him to decide he loves them as much as my Malfunctioning Heart, but he just takes the pen from behind his ear and scratches his head with it.

"No one really knows why this stuff happens," he says. He leans back and crosses his arms over his chest. "Nature is a mischievous being."

———

Even though now I can go back to doing all the fun things I did before my short-lived relationship with this baby, smoking cigarettes
and drinking beer and ordering my food any which way I can stand
it, I don't do it. I don't even eat at the Turkey Gobbler anymore,
where I assume the man is still shrinking into his button-down. I
haven't got it in me.

What I've got is heartburn. Heartburn all the time.

Suddenly heartburn has taken over my body day and night, and
breathing and eating and sleeping are all suspect activities. I stay up
at night and read my crumpled list of New Things to try. I'm interested in Taking Swimming Lessons (No. 8), Learning How To
Change My Oil Filter (No. 19), and Making Better Friends with My
Sister (No. 30). I inspect fruits and vegetables with her on a trip to
the New Natural Food Store and she gives me sidelong glances. I
think of quitting my job and start researching schools so I can go
back to school and be an English professor, talk about split infinitives
or protagonist/antagonist all day. I wish for a life less medical.

When Dr. Soleander sees me grimacing and clutching my chest,
he calls me into his office and seems concerned. I tell him about my
heartburn. He asks me, "What side do you sleep on at night?"

"What do you mean?"

"Well, it matters what side you sleep on because of acid reflux."
He taps each side of his chest with a pen.

"I don't know which side I sleep on. I'm asleep."

"Switch sides and see how you feel," he says, stuffing his planner
in his jacket and checking his belt for his beeper. He has a meeting
that I have somehow forgotten. We have not had one single en-
counter since my uterus died, and he has been taking home his jacket
at night. I mean, it was never a regular thing, anyway.

"But you're a heart doctor! Can't you do something about this?" I plead, holding my chest.

He shakes his head and rushes out the door, smiling. "You know, you slay me sometimes, you really do. Heartburn has nothing to do with your heart at all. It's a gastrointestinal matter, really." And with this he is gone, shaking his head and laughing, turning around every few steps to look back at me and laugh, and then disappearing down the staircase.

MICHELLE HOOVER

Bread Loaf Writers' Conference

THE QUICKENING

Frank wouldn't lift his head as he worked. He kept his arms high in front of him, the path of the knife under his hand neat, unstopping. What he cut fell in a mess at his feet. He didn't watch what he worked at and breathed only through his open mouth, breathing and singing a little against the smell.

It was just a few years before the first war. Everything important could be touched or tasted, weighed in our hands. We were to butcher eight hogs that day and sell the meat of four of them, worth more after butchering than hogs brought in on foot. Frank swung about, his arms greasy to his elbows, the front of his shirt hung with grease and hair and waste. He spoke of sausages, of real meat for supper. How I would have to prepare them in a skillet with a molasses gravy. The gravy boiled up black in front of us while he talked, the sausage skins puckering in the pan above the heat. We started work in the morning, before we could quite see. The walls of our barn and washhouse colored and the sun rose. The scraps of fat the knife cut away slipped from under our feet.

I had raised a fire first and started a large barrel of water for scalding. It would be some time before the water was right—hot enough to clean the hogs, but never so hot it cooked the meat. Nothing gets them so clean. This is how you do it. You dip your finger in three times. You count out slow one, two... and on three, if the water is ready, you will feel it burn when you take your finger out. Frank shot the hogs in the dark. The noise of the gun broke against us. It seemed too early in the season to begin this work, the ground still muddy from summer, the cold unsettled, but I had started the water and we were hungry.

Our neighbor Jack Morrow shared the butchering with us and he would share the meat. He pulled the hogs up with the block and tackle and stuck them so they bled from the throat. Frank squatted below him, keeping his head turned to the side, and held the buckets that would catch the blood. He watched the water as it warmed beneath my hands.

"They bleed better in a warm fall," Morrow began. We answered him by dropping our heads. The sun was rising and would soon grow bright.

"It would be better with sons, I think." Morrow looked at me with this. The ground at my feet was warmed by the fire but damp with wet. My arms ached as he spoke. I remembered the small stone marker that stood beside our house. It was well out of sight. "To help us I mean," he went on. He always went on. "A shame to do all this work and have no one see the way it's done."

"Sons would be more..." I started to answer, but left it. Sons would be more to feed, I had thought.

"With boys you have to start when they're young, before they get other curiosities. You have to set them right. Raise them to know the work." Morrow grew quiet. His arms settled to his sides. He stared at the stomach of the hog before him while the hog bled out. "There isn't much pleasure this way."

Frank talked about supper from where he crouched, the steam in the kitchen, our table and his chair. His words fell back while Morrow watched the body of the hog twist about, spitting from its throat. The water turned to steam beneath my hands.

We tossed the hogs in one at a time, wetting the ground around the barrel as the water jumped. They floated on their backs and we fetched them out again. Our hands grew red and wrinkled. We cooled our fingertips in our mouths, and I could taste the hog and the mud it had lived in with the water on my tongue. Frank and I scraped the hides. The hair fell to the ground beneath us and salted it with its white, fine color. Frank swept the back of his hand under his nose.

It didn't make Frank sick, this work, only restless and singing to himself. He shook his head to remember the words of a song and to remember where the words were to rise and fall. He grinned at the rhymes he made. It was strange to see a man so wet with grease sing this way, strange how it lifted me from the work at my feet.

Morrow cut along the length of the stomach, letting the innards spill from the wound. We shared in scooping the rest of the innards out with our hands. We began at the head, running our hands deep into the body. The stench came out from under our fingers as we loosened the stomach, the intestines, the weak fat around the liver, until it all dropped out to fill the barrels at our feet.

Frank looked at the skins, the way they were emptied out, and he stopped his singing. It was high in the day by the time he stood looking on them, the sun sharp against the hides, making them pink, limp, the light behind glimpsing through. He looked at them and the grease from the work on his skin made him slick and transparent. He felt bloodless, he said, swinging on his feet. I saw this in him before he spoke, his face hollowed out by the end of the summertime. He said he was hungry. He was all done out. It had been two long seasons since he tasted the like.

We had raised this meat, seen it birthed, give birth, seen it eat our food and whine when it was hungry. Had watched it walk, fatten, warm itself in filth. We had raised it to be used. We took it to the feeding tray and forced it to eat, forced the mother to feed her young as they lined up against her stomach. They sucked at her while she slept.

We spoke always of eating when we butchered, listing the foods that came to us with the seasons. We could remember the flavors of every meal, the last time we had known a pear, apples, or jelly. The changing texture of our gravies. We whispered about these meals to one another, speaking all at once... *Fried potatoes, sausages, hot noodles, corn bread and eggs. Greens beans cooked in onion, laid beneath a slab of bacon, creamed corn and peas my mother made, served high up on a plate. Warmed in the pot all day so you couldn't see what it was. Run together in a stew, in a juice, sauces and all of it dripping. It tasted like the only food you should ever want to have. My mother, too, it's a wonder. It's a wonder what some women know.*

At the end of the day, Frank's skin was red with scrubbing the grease from him. He walked into the kitchen smelling of soap and waited in the middle of the room with his back sloped, head down. The kitchen was full with me and my work to feed him. My hands felt swollen and heavy, my figure large in that place now that the night had come in. The fire in the stove and a single lantern on the table gave the only light. I darkened whole walls of the room just by stepping from side to side. Frank kept his eyes on the frying pan. The grease popped and licked at the sausages. The heat and the warm spicy smell rose from the pan to the air above it, turning through the room until it touched us. The smell would be inside our clothes for days. Frank drew a chair from the table and took his seat. I stood over the pan and felt I could fall into it, where everything had flavor, and the sausages warmed inside the juice that covered them and wouldn't let them burn. Frank hardly moved. When I turned from the pan, he looked through me, hungry for the smoke that traced my stomach, my arms, the sweat on my forehead. Hungry for the fat, untender meat.

I placed three large sausages on each of our plates and spooned gravy along their lengths. We sat in front of the food for a time with our heads lowered, the smoke warm on our faces. To his breast Frank whispered, "Amen."

We ate quickly then. Our jaws sore, our mouths open, licking the grease from our lips. We sat across from each other, bowed to our plates, with few words between us. The meal slowed as we tired. I looked up at Frank and found his shoulders had hardened, grown wide, somehow stronger, the skin of his arms and face wet with the labor of his eating, younger seeming. I sat straight and felt full again, softened by the heat of the room. My arms muscled and lazy after the day's work, myself open, easy in tasting the meat. Frank began to tremble. He stood to help himself to more from the skillet and started on these before he sat, intent on his chewing. He stared at the table ahead of him as his fork struck the plate, slipped into his mouth, and struck again. Shutting his eyes, he continued this, striking down, his hand tight in holding the fork and trembling still. He scraped up the last of the grease.

"Finished?" I asked. It had darkened outside. The windows looked solid with it, and I felt I knew nothing beyond that door and never would. The weather that came over us came from another place. You couldn't expect any good from it. The good man across from me, he seemed not of this room and too difficult to learn. We lived together with our belongings in separate corners and tried to forget how strange we were to one another. I looked at Frank and he rested with his eyes only half-open, his cheeks slack, his palms spread wide and flat against the table, holding on.

He stood and walked to the bed and stretched himself out. I sunk in beside him and listened. His arms shook as he slept. I knew the look of him, at least, after all those years. Knew his smell. I rested and felt my fingers turn against my stomach, working still at the sausages with my empty hands. I had worked for hours at them that afternoon, while Frank and Morrow delivered the meat to the butcher in the next town. Bent over near the smokehouse, I sat on a small stool and lifted my eyes only once to see the quiet of our house. I stared for a time at the way the house had settled against the ground. The gray fields spread out from either side of it, fallen and unplanted, and I could see the trees far off that broke the level of the fields. It would rain soon, I had thought, and the rain might turn to snow. The house sat in between the fields and the coming weather, the walls weak seeming, the rooms between them empty, the building distant from me and far, far from the living. Birds circled the sky above where I worked and they begged for the meat. I couldn't see the families who lived nearest to us. Their houses were miles down the road.

I worked at the sausages as I began to sleep, and I heard the rainstorm set in. My hands stretched the entrails again, tied one end of each length and held the skin open. How clear and frail the skins seemed as they stuck to my fingernails. I pushed the ground meat through and worked to make a stout sausage link, tied swiftly at the end and put aside. Another empty skin, the mound of spiced meat lessening, my arms tired as they held the delicate work up close to see. Pieces of meat fell to my lap and where they fell they stained me. My fingers worked as I tried to sleep, the smell of the meat still strong. I could taste the meat and taste the grease of our supper between my teeth. My hands, when they finally grew quiet, fell to my stomach and I felt a fullness there. A quickening to accompany me.

BRADY JOHNSON

University of Minnesota

MICHIGANDERS, 1979

To the deputy, who feels now more than ever that he is not such a young man, it all seems to move much too slowly. There should be a sense of urgency to all of this, a sense of secrecy and discretion and quiet. It should be a cloudy night with no moon and they should all shut off their lights right before pulling into the driveway of the house. It is instead a bright, warm day, with a strong, kicking wind.

Holding the steering wheel with two fingers of one hand, he lights a cigarette with the other and holds the first pull inside his lungs until it burns. He coughs, then coughs again; he feels it throughout his chest and thinks that even though he is not such a young man he is not old enough to feel pain like this. He rolls down the window and tosses the cigarette. He wonders if he is impatient because he is scared. He has never done anything like this before. But he is required to be here. New legislation has been passed. He is not happy about it. And ahead of him, in three separate cars moving at exactly the speed limit, are three social workers who are also not happy about it.

The deputy taps the gas pedal, nudging the front of his car up closer to the rear of the car just ahead of him. The social worker keeps his speed and direction constant, but through the dust cloud the deputy can see him hunch over, tightening his grip on the wheel so that he can drive even more perfectly.

When they pull into the long gravel driveway, a cloud crosses the sun. The deputy swings himself out of the car and feels the wind pick up, smells the dust shrouding him. He watches the social workers in their cars. Each has opened a door but none have stepped out. One of the men checks the time. The other gathers his files. The woman begins to write, still sitting in the driver's seat. When they finally do step out, they stand for a moment and observe, and the men scribble vigorously on clipboards.

The deputy looks at the house, the yard, the thick woods extending past him to the road. The driveway is much longer than it seemed at first. The yard is sandy, its grass yellow and dry and limp. The house looks as though it's shedding; paint peels away from the frame, and most of the shingles have curled. The house was once green—or yellow. And now it is no color at all. There are no toys in the yard, no rusted tricycles or headless dolls. There is nothing odd about this windswept yard, and at first he thinks this is a good sign, but then wonders if maybe it isn't. There's no way to tell. He has never done anything like this before.

The social workers slam their car doors shut. The men run hands across foreheads, cinch up ties, and pull at shirt sleeves; the woman simply stands there, waiting. They all turn to look at the deputy, still standing in front of his car and beginning to feel his jacket heat up in the sun. The deputy stares back at them until he remembers that he is here to lead them into the house.

Together they walk to the front porch, the deputy ahead of the others, his hard-soled shoes making loud sounds on the wooden steps. He knocks three times on the screen door with its cracked storm window still installed. Though it rattles, and though they wait a full minute, the door does not open. He knocks again and when there is no answer, the social workers look at one another and one of the men heads for the side of the house. The deputy hesitates, thinking, we're not supposed to split up, legislation has been passed. But then he turns and follows the lone social worker anyway. He thinks about telling the other two to wait where they are, but looking back he sees that they will. The deputy, to be sure, says, we'll go around back.

They walk around the side of the house and the social worker peers into the windows quickly and says nothing. The deputy stays behind him, trying not to look at the house and its windows, trying not to notice anything at all out of the ordinary, trying to decide if finding a problem and fixing it and being sure would be better than not finding a problem at all and going home but not really being sure. The social worker walks quickly and glances into windows and out at the woods without slowing down, making it all seem easy and natural and normal, making it seem as if he has indeed done this a hundred times.

When they reach the back door, which looks strangely similar to the front door with the same wooden porch and storm window, they can hear the other two pounding on the front door. It's hard to tell if they can hear the sound as it comes through the house or from around the side. The deputy knocks loudly and waits, but the door does not open. The social worker looks at the deputy and nods. The deputy grabs the doorknob and turns. It isn't locked, which for a moment makes him feel a little better, because he will not have to break in, but then much worse, because if there are children inside, it shouldn't be this easy.

When he pushes on the door, it resists. There is something blocking it; it makes sense to him that not everyone uses a back door, that some people might push a table against it to look outside while they eat breakfast, or a dresser, just to get things out of the way. But the door is unlocked. Whatever is on the other side of the door is not meant to be there.

The deputy pushes harder against the door. Something heavy slides across the floor, something that makes a scratching metal sound. He has to lean into the thing with all of his strength and when the door finally opens wide enough for him to slip inside there is dust in the air and a stale, musty smell. He holds his breath as he squeezes around the door, then lets it out slowly and lightly and sniffs at the air. There is a bad smell, but nowhere near as bad as what he feared. He stands in what must be the kitchen; it is dark, but he can hear the gurgle and hum of a refrigerator. A table butts up against the door and he can see the scratch marks it made in the linoleum when he pushed it aside. The tabletop is broken in a pointless way, its plastic surface punched through in short, sharp slashes.

The deputy pulls the table by its legs, away from the door. From the front of the house he hears the other social workers knocking on the door, and the sound is deep, echoing urgently, as though it were very important that they get in immediately. The deputy rushes through the kitchen, not stopping to look around, feeling his foot kick something, which goes skittering across the floor. Behind him he hears the social worker walk into the kitchen and stop.

The front door is unlocked and when he opens it, the other male social worker stands there with his fist raised to knock again. The deputy half smiles at him, thinking it's a little odd that he didn't try the knob at all and then realizing that he, the deputy, needed to let them in. He holds the door open and the social workers step inside, the man giving him an odd look. And, of course, both of them start writing.

The deputy isn't sure what to do. He stands there in the tiny foyer, his arms folded across his chest, hands gripping his elbows. The air is dusty and humid; he can smell it and feel it on his fingertips as he rubs the fabric of his jacket. This part of the house feels small and cramped and too dark. He looks around, his eyes adjusting now to the darkness, and sees a room to his right, a sitting room or living room of some sort, empty except for a single wooden chair in the corner facing the wall, a shaft of light filtering through a thick-curtained window. To his left looms a closed door. He walks to the door and grabs the knob. It refuses to turn and leaves flecks of rust on his palm. So he turns around again, facing the back of the house and the kitchen and the wide hallway leading to it. From here, looking down the hall, there seems something strange about the way this house is put together, something about the space he can't quite explain.

The social workers have drifted into the hallway, still writing, still flipping papers on their clipboards. That's all they do. They stand, leaning in close to one another, writing whatever it is they are writing, filling out whatever forms need filling out. Quiet now, except for the scratching of their pens, they still lack an appropriate sense of urgency; there is no worry on their faces. As they write he approaches, slowly, not sure if he'll say anything, not sure if he'll try to get them moving or tell them, okay, we're here, I got you in, do what you have to do.

He says nothing, moves past them, leaning back against the wall more than he needs to in order to get around them, and steps silently into the kitchen, aware of his shoes on the linoleum. The room seems brighter now, the sun coming in from the open back door and a half-curtained window. Cupboards and drawers cover one wall from floor to ceiling, except for where they box in a tiny gas stove. On the opposite wall is the sink, and a long, abnormally deep tile counter half covered with dirty plates and glasses and forks. The deputy walks over to the sink and turns the faucet. The tap sputters once, then stops. Looking down, he sees that the floor is crisscrossed with scrapes and nicks and cuts. Long black streaks lead from the wall to a refrigerator pushed into the far corner. On the floor before the refrigerator lies a pile of paper stars, cream-colored and clumsily cut. From beneath the refrigerator door pokes half of a star, the other half caught inside, as though the stars had tumbled out of the refrigerator.

He sidesteps to the counter, tattooed with red and purple stains. As he looks closer he sees that the counter is spotless from its front edge to a point halfway back to the wall, as though someone has just wiped it clean with a wet rag. He can even trace the rag's path, the tiny arcs separating clean from dirty, as though the job had been stopped halfway through. Then it makes sense: many weeks' worth of stains cleaned by a child unable to reach all the way back to the wall. And now he wonders if this is a good sign.

The cleaning job looks fresh, a day or two old, maybe. Sure, there's no way to tell that a child did this, he thinks, but it's hard for him to imagine an adult up and leaving two children alone in a house in the middle of cleaning the counter. The deputy spins around and looks at the walls. They, too, are half clean, wiped free of grime up to a point roughly even with his eyes. Above that point are splotches of brown and green and flecks of hardened grease, bits of lettuce wilted black. His eyes wander up the wall and he sees that the stains fade near the ceiling, where there are brown smudges in the corners, which he knows from his own walls are made by years of cigarette smoke. Then he leans back and sees, stuck to the ceiling in a perfect S shape, a single strand of what can only be dried spaghetti.

The social workers have entered the kitchen. The deputy glances at them and points a finger at the ceiling. The men nod in unison without looking up and one of them says, we should find those kids. The deputy takes a breath and hitches up his pants and looks around. There's still a part of him that expects them to take the lead, but they simply stand there in the doorway, pens pocketed, clipboards grasped comfortably before their waists. So he turns and walks past the refrigerator in the corner and into another long hall, this one much narrower, much darker.

He stops abruptly and one of the social workers bumps into him from behind. The hallway is very dark and very long, too long, it seems, for the house to be able to contain it. He takes another step forward, his eyes wandering over the floor and walls and ceiling, trying to take it in as fast as he can and then going back over it all once again, feeling that something is wrong with this hallway and at the same time feeling the stupidity of the idea. It is impossible to tell whether the hallway leads to the front of the house or off to one of the sides.

Behind him one of the two men clears his throat and the deputy turns around and says, go ahead, find the kids. The men look at one another for a moment, hesitating. The woman looks right at the deputy. He sees her shoulders fall just slightly, her head tilt a little to the side. The deputy thinks about taking it back, thinks about saying something like, okay, just hang on a sec here, maybe I got a little ahead of myself. But then the social workers squeeze past him, the woman included. The hallway is very narrow, and the deputy has to press against the wall to let them by. He lets them pass without saying anything, but watches them closely, thinking he should at least watch them. When they reach the end of the hallway, they turn right and disappear, as though they know exactly where to go. Maybe they're good at this, he thinks.

The deputy takes out his big flashlight, clicks it on, and shines it over the walls, dipping the beam down to the floor. Dust has settled near the intersection of floor and wall—thick gray dust that lightens in shade the farther from the wall it gets. His light crosses a dark, dustless stretch of floor, barely the width of his two feet put together, running down the center of the hall. He casts his light down this shiny stretch as far as it will carry, almost down to the end of the hall. It is as though whoever made this path has been very careful to walk only here, to avoid the walls.

Bringing the flashlight's beam back toward his feet, he sees that he is right. Next to him on the floor are the jumbled prints of the social workers' shoes, prints which run down the hall as far as he can see. But around them, under them, are the prints of children's bare feet—half a heel here, three toes there. And none of these tiny prints is anywhere near either wall, except for two, both of them made by a right foot, directly next to his right shoe. They are smeared toward the molding, but clear enough to identify. Moving the light up the wall, the deputy sees a handprint, small and dark and smudged. And now it's easy to see why he had been warned. These things are impossible, this dark hallway with its well-trod center, and these severed foot- and handprints. And it's easy to imagine what has happened here, easy to imagine a bearded man, six foot something, grabbing a child by the neck as she turns the corner to race down this hall away from him and then throttling her until her right foot hits the floor, twice. It's easy to imagine a squat, toothless mother tossing a plate or heavy rolling pin at a too-quick boy as he ducks and plants a hand on the wall for balance.

Whispering comes from down the hall. The deputy rushes forward, not bothering to watch his step, and when he reaches the end of the hall he turns right and finds himself standing in the doorway of a bedroom. The two men bend over a little girl—sleeping or dead. The deputy steps into the room and sees one of the men lifting and gently tugging at the girl's hair; the woman stands against the wall, looking away, her arms tightly crossed, one of her feet tapping furiously. The deputy starts to open his mouth to say something, to warn them and remind them of why he is here, to stop them from doing whatever they are doing, but one of the men puts a finger to his lips and whispers, quiet. The deputy shuts his mouth and leans back against the doorway, pretty sure he doesn't want any part of this.

The girl lies on her side, one hand thrown across her forehead, the other palm-up in front of her. She wears tiny white shorts and a thin blue shirt that has cinched itself around her waist and pulled up past her belly button. The deputy can see her ribs, but they don't stick out dangerously. Though there are scrapes on her knees, they are light pink and have scabbed over. She seems small, four years old, maybe five, but the deputy thinks for a moment that it's just the angle from which he's seeing her—or the position she's in. Her legs bend at the knee, parallel to one another, her feet bare, white on the top, and black on the bottom.

The deputy watches as one of the men backs away while the other takes a soft hold of a lock of the girl's hair. As her head moves, the deputy sees that beneath it, on the mattress, is something dark and shiny, and though he thinks at first that it is blood, he sees it can't be that—too thick. He is, after all, old enough to have seen a great deal of blood; he's not such a young man. The social worker holding the girl's hair whispers something the deputy can't hear and the other man glances around the room. The deputy signals to them with his hands, asking what they're looking for. The man closest to him makes a drinking motion. The deputy shakes his head; the kitchen sink isn't working. The man glances around again and then makes a scissoring motion. The deputy reaches down to his belt and pulls out his jackknife and passes it to him, and the moment the man takes it the deputy has a feeling he shouldn't have just handed it over without looking back at the silent woman first, without looking at her to see her face, to find out what, if anything, she thinks of all this.

But now that he's handed over the knife he doesn't look at the woman, it's too late, and he watches as the man slices the girl's hair free of the dark stain. He tugs a little, very, very gently, using only his fingertips, then kneels down and cuts another clump and another. The second man gently lifts the girl off the mattress. He then wraps her in his arms, brings her close to his chest, one arm beneath her knees, the other behind her back. She's awake, the deputy can tell, but very, very sleepy. Her eyes open and then close, then open and close again and stay closed. Her arms slide up around the social worker's neck and hold on tight, a movement that seems deliberate. She buries her face in his chest, but doesn't cry, doesn't make a sound, and at the moment the deputy sees her dark curls and one of her smudged cheeks and the mole just above her left eye, he thinks, no wonder she was left alone. No one could hurt such a beautiful thing.

The other man pulls out his clipboard and writes quickly. The deputy looks over at the woman, expecting an angry glare, expecting her to know that this is wrong, that this isn't good, expecting her to let him know with her eyes that by handing over his own knife he is part of it. But she doesn't look at him. She has her clipboard out and is writing, too, and probably has been writing since the deputy handed over the knife. That makes him feel better, but then worse; he has no idea what she's writing now, has no idea if she's reporting on this whole thing, the haircutting with the deputy's knife.

The man carrying the girl pushes slowly past the deputy and leans over close to the deputy's ear and whispers, grape jelly. He smiles then, and starts to walk out of the room, but the deputy puts a hand on his shoulder and says, wait. The other social workers stop writing suddenly and the tiny bedroom goes even more silent, as though even the draft in the air has been stilled. The deputy looks at the man with the little girl. The man straightens up and narrows his eyes in warning.

The deputy looks at the woman and says, maybe she should take her. The woman looks suddenly panicked. Then she looks at the deputy, who puts his hand up and says, just to be safe. The woman glances quickly around at the men, as though she's been accused of something, or is expecting to be at any moment, but then she pockets her pen, tucks her clipboard under her armpit, and extends her arms to the man holding the little girl.

The man with the girl glares at the deputy but then hands the girl over to the woman. She has trouble holding the girl at first, having to slide her arm up the little girl's back to get a solid grasp, pushing the girl's shirt up to her shoulders in the process. The clipboard drops out from under her arm and clatters to the floor and for a moment everyone holds very still. Finally, the woman gets an awkward but decent hold on the girl, tugs her shirt back down, and heaves her up onto her chest. Leaving the room, the little girl's head almost smacks into the door frame. But still the girl is quiet.

The two men look questioningly now at the deputy, as though confused by losing one of their group. The deputy says, there's another one, to which the men nod. The deputy steps out of the room and finds himself in the hallway again, feeling a little foolish and a little amazed that the social workers were able to stand over that little girl, cut her hair, pick her up, and carry her out of the house without her making a single sound. He's a little relieved, too, at the woman's leaving. There was no other choice. He's bothered by the woman's clumsiness with the girl, maybe because it never crossed his mind that a woman could be so awkward with a child.

Even so, there's something about it now that seems okay, something about it that makes him think, no, this little girl will not be one of those who will never speak again, she will not be one of those whose eyes have died, who will be unable to make friends, who will be afraid of the dark until she is fifty. She might demand clean sheets every day for the rest of her life. She might never eat grape jelly again. But she will not, he thinks, and for a moment almost believes, be one of those who will suddenly leave her own children when she has them. The deputy has never done this before but he's starting to feel that it's not so bad after all.

The deputy now asks the men where they should look next. There is one more child. They both shrug their shoulders. To the left, the long, dark hallway leads back to the kitchen. And to the right, the deputy now sees, is another hallway, adjacent to the bedroom. He starts walking. This leads to another, much shorter hallway which the deputy follows to another room whose door is closed. The deputy takes a breath, blinks once as hard as he can, and turns the knob.

The door opens halfway and then butts up against something. The deputy squeezes through and finds himself in what appears to be another bedroom. But it is impossible to tell. Unlike the little girl's room, empty enough that he noticed only the bed, this one overflows with wooden chairs piled atop one another, a two-legged table on its side, boxes, stacks of newspapers, a television missing its screen so that its innards are laid bare, a rusted-out coffee percolator, a box of chocolates still wrapped in yellowed plastic, plastic baby bottles, a stroller missing three wheels, and, he notices, a pile of stuffed animals, most of them either monkeys or giraffes.

The deputy is amazed. It is as if the house had been tipped on its side and most of its contents slid into this one room. It's impossible to tell how big the room is. Hidden behind what he's already seen are even more things. A mangled ironing board. A fish tank full of marbles. The deputy pushes forward but can just barely get his feet into the room. He wonders for a moment whether the other child might be in here somewhere, but he doesn't see how. He, or she, would have had to pick apart these stacks of useless broken things, crawl inside, then put the whole thing back together again—and, he sees, would have had to replace all the dust. If they can't find the other child he will come back and rummage through this stuff himself, but it will be easier to check the rest of the house first. As he backs out of the room, one of the social workers says, see anything? The deputy steps back and makes room for the man. The social worker takes one look and says, let's check the rest of the house first.

But there seems to be nowhere else to check. The men walk back through the short hallway to the little girl's room. They look under her bed, but find nothing. They walk slowly back down the long, dark hallway, into the kitchen. They open the refrigerator, search through all the cupboards and even the drawers. But there is no other child. And strangely, no bathroom. There is no hallway to the front of the house, save the one they first walked through. There seem to be no other rooms, but at the same time the deputy feels that the house is much larger.

They have not checked outside. They have not even considered looking in the woods, have not considered the possibility that the second child has taken off, headed for a neighbor's house for help. They have not considered the possibility that the second child has wandered off down the road and gotten lost. They have not considered the possibility that the second child is being held somewhere by someone. They have not considered that she might be dead. And perhaps there is no second child.

The deputy walks through the back door, feeling the social workers close behind him. They are of no use now; they are simply following the deputy. New legislation has been passed. The deputy has to be here. But what, after all, do the social workers themselves have to do? It is as if all three of them—one having no idea what he's doing, the others knowing exactly what they should be, but aren't, doing—just, plain, simply, only have to be here.

Stepping out into the big backyard, the deputy wonders now if the social workers aren't angry about the new legislation. He has done half the work here, more than half the work, and it's not okay anymore. He was warned rather than prepared. He feels suddenly impatient, more impatient now than when the whole mess started, and he's sick of the social workers dragging their feet behind him. He is required to be here, required to take the lead and make sure the social workers do no wrong. He stares out at the woods beyond the yard. They go on forever and then rise up a high hill whose top he can barely see. There's nothing more he can do.

Turning to the just-standing-there social workers, he asks, are we supposed to go into the woods? The social workers stand there and shake their heads and one of them says, only if there's a missing person. And you do that.

The deputy says, yeah, and looks back at the house. There is an entire second story they haven't searched, and he thinks about the locked door near the front of the house, the door whose knob turned his hand a rust color, the door he now knows leads to that second floor. He heads back into the house, not caring whether or not the social workers will follow. He rushes through the kitchen and into the long, dark hallway, hearing the echo of his footsteps against the walls and ceiling, glancing about for any other door they missed, something smaller than usual, since that is what he's come to expect in this house. But there is nothing, just dust and dark and cobwebs swaying from the ceiling.

He reaches the end of the hallway and realizes that he's come the wrong way. He turns and is startled by how close behind him the social workers are. They pull up short and flatten themselves against the walls, letting him pass, and he rushes back down the hallway, through the kitchen, and finally to the front entrance of the house, to the locked door. He grabs hold of the doorknob, desperately hoping that the second child isn't standing on the other side of the door, watching in absolute fear as the knob shakes, trying to decide whether to hold it tight with two little hands or run for some far-off room or closet.

But no matter how hard he tries, the knob simply won't turn. The deputy's hand slides and he can feel the rust flaking off, can almost hear it hitting the floor. He lets go and backs off a step, feeling his chest tighten from the effort. He says to the social worker who cut the little girl's hair, give me my knife. The social worker hands the knife to him and the deputy squats down in front of the knob. He opens the blade, wipes it quickly on his pants, and sticks the tip in through the keyhole next to the base of the knob. He has no idea if this will work. He has never done it before. He takes his flashlight from his belt, holds the knife still, and hits the butt of the knife as hard as he can. He grabs the knob and twists, but it still won't move.

The deputy swears under his breath and looks more closely at the doorknob. Wound around it, in the tiny space between the knob itself and the metal plate connecting it to the door, is a loop of rusted wire. The deputy pries at the wire with the knife until he can grab an end of it. Then he pulls it away, the wire unfurling and clicking against the knob.

When the last of it has come out, he stands up and puts away his knife and flashlight. A breath forces itself from his mouth, a hard breath that whistles a little in his chest, and he is suddenly very aware of his sweat, of its dripping down beneath his hot jacket. Feeling the social workers just behind him, he grabs the knob and turns it. It makes a rusty, grating sound. He pulls the door open, blinded by a bright shaft of sunlight in which a cloud of dust blooms. He shuts his eyes tight and in the afterimage on the insides of his eyelids he sees the scene again, all in fuzzy reds and blues: the lines of stairs leading up, a railing, a block of light. He opens his eyes and there she is, above him, six years old, with the longest hair he's ever seen on a child, her eyes enormous and red-rimmed, standing at the edge of a landing atop the steepest stairs he's ever seen, flanked by a curtainless window, her hands sheathed in yellow latex gloves and placed one atop the other in a tight grip on an ax handle, just below the head. He steps back and feels the social workers behind him, feels them step back also, and then watches as the girl's eyes dart from one man's face to the next, her head twitching from side to side just barely, her hair quivering with the motion. None of them move and the girl seems ready to turn and disappear up the stairs, and then finally the deputy walks up two of the stairs and makes his own face level with the girl's. He tries to get her to stop darting her eyes around, but she won't; she keeps looking from man to man, from face to face, gauging the danger, it seems, ready, it seems, to turn and scurry up the stairs into the darkness and maze of the second floor and disappear forever, never to be found, never to speak again in her life—a moment that the deputy feels is beautiful and horrible at the same time, as he reaches a hand halfway to the girl and says, okay.

The girl hesitates then, and though she doesn't look away her eyes hitch and sink slightly, and the deputy can see her shoulders relax, become soft and heavy, and the head of the ax tips forward. The deputy glances down and sees that the end of the ax handle rests on the floor of the landing. She couldn't hurt anyone with it; she wouldn't have time to raise it. She is completely helpless here and doesn't even know it. The deputy looks into her face again and stretches himself forward, his neck exposed, and wraps his hand gently around the ax, just below her hands, close enough that he can feel the roughness of her gloves, and takes it from her. She holds onto it as he pulls it gently away from her, but then she gives it up, her hands moving back to her chest automatically, like the movement of a plant. The deputy keeps his eyes on her and hands the ax to one of the social workers, who accepts it silently. Then the deputy takes another step forward and holds both arms out to the girl, waiting for her, and the look on her face makes him think that she knows what will happen if she does come to him, even though he himself has no idea. She looks at his shoulder, or a spot past his shoulder, and then steps forward and raises her arms, and he picks her up and stands, cradling her with one arm and placing his other hand on her stomach.

She is so light when he has her in his arms, so light for a six-year-old. They back slowly down the stairs, the deputy aware of the little girl's head, into the front hallway, the deputy watching her eyes, knowing where he's going now without having to watch his step. They move to the front door, the social workers shuffling around to hold the door open, the girl with that same distracted look, down and to the side and at something that might or might not exist. This is not a stare or a daze; something is going on inside this girl's mind, something the deputy will never know. And just when he thinks that what he sees is what he's been warned about—that stone-eyed, cold, dead look that means this little girl has been ruined—she looks him straight in the eye and stares and doesn't blink, and when she does he almost trips stepping through the front door. And he knows then that someone has ruined her. They step out of the house into the strong, kicking wind, and the girl takes a breath and squints and looks away from the deputy and sighs so softly he can only feel it.

LIZA WARD

University of Montana

DANCING LESSONS

In June of 1959, the day before Charles Starkweather was to be electrocuted, my mother went out and bought a Studebaker Golden Hawk. Teenagers were gathering around the Nebraska State Penitentiary, waiting for the lights to dim when 2,200 blue volts went slamming through the murderer's body. I'd been watching them strut up and down across the television screen from the safety of our parlor. They were defiantly hanging off the hoods of cars, slugging beer, their eyes fixed on the prison windows for some sign of Starkweather's passing.

When Lucille, our housekeeper, cried my name, I catapulted off the love seat. I charged through the foyer, fearing the execution had already happened. I found Lucille standing at the window in the bright green kitchen, wiping her dark hands on her apron as she watched a gold car pull up the drive. My mother was behind the wheel, honking and waving, her scarf billowing out behind her. Lucille placed

274

her warm palms on my shoulder. "Lord, Susan, what your momma got herself into this time?" She squeezed me and chuckled. "Daddy gonna have himself a fit." I pictured my father with a red face, pounding the desk that had once been his father's, or yanking at his tie. It was the only sort of fit I could imagine him having, in the safety of his study behind a closed door.

Then my mother charged into the kitchen through the garage door clutching the car keys in her fist. The kitchen was filled with the scent of mint cookies, my mother's favorite, but she did not seem to notice.

"Girls," she said, "come on." She reached for my forearm and then for Lucille's. She tugged us through the kitchen door and into the cool garage. The brand new car sat ticking in the empty spot beside the dusty Chevrolet we'd driven from Chicago to Lincoln the summer before, when my grandfather had died suddenly, leaving the steel company and the house to my father.

My mother opened the driver's side door of the Studebaker. "Meet the limited production 1957 Golden Hawk 400," she said. "Without even a scratch." The car was solid gold with cream-colored tail fins and white leather interior. My mother put her hand on the hood and looked at Lucille. "So what do you think?"

Lucille didn't say a word. She crossed her arms over her chest.

"Well," said my mother, "Do you love it?"

Lucille shook her head. "You don't wanna know what I think, Mrs. Hurst."

"I do so," said my mother. "I always want to know what you think, Lucille. It's very important to me." My mother was always saying these sorts of things. Whenever my mother bought new clothes from Miller and Paine on my father's credit, she pulled Lucille up the pink carpeted staircase. I'd watch my mother hold dresses with tags still attached up to Lucille, parading her proudly in front of the mirror, like a ringmaster who has tamed a lion. "Don't you look lovely," she would cry, or, "That color complements your dark complexion so well. I don't want it after all. You keep it!" Lucille never seemed to object to these displays of affection, but afterward, she would sit in my room and brush my hair while I cracked bubble gum and listened to *Gunsmoke.*

"Folks gonna talk," Lucille said cautiously, circling the Studebaker. "You don't do anything halfway, do you?"

"Of course I don't." My mother clenched her fists. "I saw it in the sun off the Cornhusker Highway. I had to have it right then. I've never felt this crazy before about anything."

"*I* love it, Mother," I offered. "I think it's beautiful."

My mother turned to me. She crossed her arms. Her elbows looked sharp beneath her silk shirt. "Get in then, Puggy," she said. "We're going for a ride."

I trotted around the front of the car and opened the passenger door. My mother climbed slowly inside, watching me, and then suddenly stuck her palm out, freezing me where I stood, my hand wrapped around the chrome door handle.

"Take off your shoes, Susan," she said. "God knows where you've been."

I frantically shed my saddle shoes by the wheel of the Chevrolet and climbed in beside her. The white leather was warm with the late June sun and smooth as the inside of a shell. My mother fixed her scarf in the rearview mirror, and pulled on her driving gloves. She turned the key in the ignition. The car rumbled to life, and she inched it out of the garage. A ray of sun caught the face of my mother's watch and splashed over the dash in a happy gold circle. My mother was small and neat with black hair and smooth tan skin. The turned up nose so unfortunate on my own face lent hers a sprightly charm. I hugged my arm around the flesh hanging over the waist of my skirt. I tried to suck it in. My mother jammed her foot on the accelerator and the car launched backward. I saw Lucille lift her hands to her face. I heard a honking horn. I turned around. My father was just then coming down the drive on his way home from Capital Steel, but my mother failed to see him, and the back of the Golden Hawk Studebaker coupe rammed right into the fender of my father's Packard.

My father got out, slamming the car door, and silently inspected a broken headlight. He approached my mother's window slowly, as if he were trapping a wild beast. Then he bent down and peered inside the car. "What's this about, pet?" He was trying to seem openminded. His blue eyes were wide and his brow was raised. It made me want to giggle. Beads of moisture clung to his temples.

"What does it look like. I bought a car," my mother said staring straight ahead.

My father shook his head in disbelief. He was leaning his elbows on the door. "Why would you do that?"

"I'm tired of being surrounded by your father's things," my mother sighed. "Dead this, dead that. I want my *own* things."

My father's face turned red. "I don't understand why you would do this without talking it over." He paused. "It's like you're sneaking around, Ann. Why would you do that?"

"This whole town's ready to pop." My mother shrugged her shoulders. "I got the itch."

"I can't believe this," said my father, mopping his brow with his handkerchief. "This whole thing would be amusing if you weren't my wife." He smacked the side of the car with his palm. "Do you think money grows on trees, Ann? Is that what you think?" My father leaned his head through the window. "Tell me how much this boat cost."

My mother was boiling up. I could see it in her hands. The knuckles were white from clutching the wheel. Her eyes were hot and wicked.

"Tell me how much." My father was exasperated. "It's not even a family car, for Christ's sake." His tie had dropped over the edge of the window.

My mother grabbed the tie in her fist and tugged hard. My father's head lurched forward. "You ruin everything," she snapped. "You're so ungrateful!"

A storm of shock passed over my father's face. Then his features went blank. He pulled back his head, straightened his tie, and went inside to pour himself a drink.

Before dinner, I heard my father speaking on the telephone to some-one about the execution. My mother lay on the living room floor, her bare feet propped on the arm of the couch, a glass of wine in her hand, her hair fanning out over the oriental rug. I was unsure who had won. Even at dinner, after Lucille had gone home, my parents didn't really speak to each other. They sat on the patio getting drunk in the uncomfortable silence that all Lincoln shared. Each household seemed to hold its breath and wait for the lights to dim—although my father assured us that would never happen. Starkweather still wasn't dead, but my father wouldn't let me turn on the newscasts. "It's nothing to get excited about," he said, coming through the French doors from the darkened living room with another drink in his hand. "I want you to understand that Susan. It's not some holi-day." My father patted me on the head. It was my favorite thing when he did this. I was his girl.

My father sat back down heavily in his chair. The candles were burning low on the slate table. The fireflies winked at me in little sparks from the dark bed of the rhododendrons. "It's a time to mourn the lives that were lost," my father said, swirling the ice around in his glass. He peered into the bottom of his drink and took a long sip. "It's time to applaud the efficiency of American justice."

I pictured blue electricity coursing through wires in the basement of the penitentiary.

My mother snorted and poured herself more wine. "You didn't even know the dead people," she said to my father. "Don't pretend to be involved." The bottle of wine was almost empty. Her eyes were wet and flashy, burning with life. The leaves rustled excitedly in the trees along Van Dorn Street.

My father would not let it rest. "We're all involved. These were people our friends knew, people my father knew," he said. "It was senseless killing." He looked down at his hands. They were folded around his glass. My mother's hair had come down over her shoulders. She shook it dangerously close to the flame, and looked at my father. He pulled the candle to him, out of her reach. I picked at a splatter of wax left in its wake.

"What sorts of things are you telling our daughter, Thatcher?" My mother slugged the rest of her wine. "They're your friends who knew the victims, not mine. Your country club friends. I didn't choose them and neither did Puggy." She stood up. My mother grabbed the edge of the table with one hand, and my shoulder with the other for support. I did not like her touching me this urgently. I was glad there was no one else to see it; her needing me to stand when I was the one who should be needing her. It was embarrassing. She was always embarrassing me here. She didn't cook. She didn't go to church. In Chicago, my mother had surrounded herself with a wild group of professors she called liberals. At her birthday party one year, a man had danced with another man, a woman in a fedora recited poetry until her knees gave out and she landed on the coffee table with her skirt hiked up to the edge of her stockings.

"Let's turn on all the lights in this spooky old house and just see what happens," my mother said. She clapped her hands. "Let's do something. I want to celebrate something." Her voice was heavy and thick. She started toward the French doors and stumbled over the ledge in the dark. My father was waiting. He caught her around the waist and held her. He picked her up and carried her into the living room. I stood by the bookcase, watching in the dark.

"Turn on the lights," said my mother. She swung her legs violently. Her heel caught one of the china frogs on the end table and knocked it off. It smashed to pieces against the bookcase. My father held her tight. She stopped struggling then. My mother's head hung limply over his arm. Her legs dangled. "I'm so sorry," she said, and started to cry.

"I never liked that thing much," my father whispered. He wasn't angry anymore. He kissed her on the ear.

"Turn on the lights, please, Thatchy," she sobbed.

"I *can't* turn on the lights," he said, "You're too heavy. I might drop you. Then you'd run away and I'd be all alone." My father cradled her head. He stepped over the china fragments scattered on the carpet. He carried her through the shadows, and up the stairs to bed.

Nobody told me when to go to sleep that night. Everything was quiet. I stared out the windows at the street lights on Van Dorn, sniffing the cork from my parents' bottle of wine. I walked around the house in the dark. I turned on the television to find only static. I stumbled over furniture and thought of my grandfather's ghost, of the way Lucille had found him on the living room love seat dead from a heart attack, the newspaper folded neatly over his knee, the ice not yet melted in his drink. His cigarette smoke still lingered in our heavy curtains. I buried my face in the folds and inhaled, hoping for some secret knowledge, a whisper perhaps, from one dead world to another.

I sat at the kitchen table the next morning, counting out the penny candy money Lucille had given me for helping with housework. I arranged coins in bright piles, adding up how much I would be able to buy. My mother stood at the counter with the *Lincoln Star Journal* open in front of her. Lucille was cleaning out the oven. My mother was reading the details of the execution out loud. Her back was to me. Charles Starkweather had been electrocuted at 12:04 A.M. Two graves were being dug, in the Wyuka cemetery, and another nearby: one for the murderer, and one for the doctor who had been scheduled to declare him dead. The doctor had died of a heart attack outside the execution chamber, and everyone was talking. Starkweather's power reached beyond the grave. "Imagine that!" my mother said. "Don't you find the world tied together by such strange ironies, Lucille?"

"I don't know about that." Lucille stuck her arm into the back of the oven and scrubbed. "What I do know is the *house* looks like it got zapped last night."

I giggled. I couldn't help it.

My mother turned to me. She eyed the change on the table suspiciously. "Lucille really shouldn't be giving you money. We pay her. Don't you think *that's* a little ironic?"

I shrugged my shoulders. "I didn't ask for it," I said.

My mother reached over the table and brushed the nickels and dimes into her palm. The silver clinked against the back of her rings. "It's summer," she said to me. "You can't hang around the house all day eating candy. You're twelve years old." My mother smacked down the money in front of Lucille and opened the classifieds. "You should learn how to do something, Puggy. And you're not taking lessons at that elitist club. You and I are not a part of that."

I thought of tanned limbs splashing in aqua water just down the street. Floral umbrellas blowing in the breeze, the sound of tennis balls crisply smacking rackets. My mother said, "Daddy won't admit it, but I think we're part Jew. You can tell by my coloring. You take that into consideration the next time you go to that country club,

Susan. If they knew who you were, they'd never let you through the door." My mother returned to the newspaper, and buried herself in the pages. That's when she found his ad in the classifieds: Len Silverman, private dancing instructor. "Perfect, Puggy!" My mother cried, clapping her hands. "You'll learn how to dance!" My hard-earned money sat in a pile untouched, burning a hole in the counter.

The following week, Mother pulled out of the driveway in the Golden Hawk 400, on our way to my first dancing lesson. She took the long way past Wyuka cemetery. People had come from miles away to stare at the freshly turned earth on Starkweather's grave. They paid money for autographs his father had collected. People turned and stared at my mother's car as if she were part of it all. She waved and honked. She didn't seem to care about the broken tail lights.

Len Silverman lived on the other side of town. This would be our secret adventure. My father knew nothing about it. My mother turned to me and smiled as we barreled down R Street. Then she rolled her eyes. "You're nervous," she said. "Why are you nervous? I can tell you're nervous. You're shredding your nails." My mother grabbed my hand and pulled it away from my mouth. "You're always chewing on something," she said.

We pulled up along the curb beside Len Silverman's house. It was a single story brown house with a Japanese rock garden in front. The air was hot. The drawn shades stared blankly, seeming to hide secrets beneath closed lids. I sat in the passenger seat, waiting for something to happen. "Don't just sit there with your hands on your knees. Go ring the bell," my mother said. She looked clean and neat, unaffected by the heat.

"You're not coming with me?" I asked.

"Don't be silly. You're a big girl," said my mother. She nudged my shoulder impatiently. "Go on, I'm getting my hair done and I'm already late."

I opened the door and stepped hesitantly out of the car. I wanted to crawl beneath a bush and stay there until my mother came back. I knew she wouldn't know the difference. But a tall, lean man with blond curly hair was already standing on the doorstep beckoning me down the path. My mother waved at Len, blew me a kiss, and drove away.

"I was hoping to meet her," said Len as the Studebaker melted into the horizon. He put his palm on my shoulder and guided me out of the sunlight, into the darkened house. "That's a beautiful set of wheels. Your mother's pretty nice, too." Len closed the door behind me and the rest of the sunny world slipped away. I looked around. All the shades in the living room were drawn. Len moved up close to me and put his hands on my shoulders. My stomach knotted. I knew my father would be angry. He would want to know how my mother could have been so careless, but that did not make me feel any better. I half understood that my father's concern had more to do with his love for my mother than anything else. It seemed my mother was always testing my father's affections and that his frustration excited her, as if she needed to be disapproved of in order to love.

I could feel Len's hand heavy on my shoulder, the smell of his cologne thick and intoxicating as his silk sleeve brushed my cheek. I tried to slip my shoulder out from under his fingers. Len appeared not to notice this. I wiggled away, but Len put his hand right back where it had been, and squeezed.

"What's it so dark for?" I said.

"Fred likes it that way." Len's voice sounded airy and far away. I could see an Asian screen folded against one wall. A bright fish tank bubbled from a corner of the darkened living room. One blue fish drifted in circles around a pink ceramic castle.

"That's Fred Astaire, the Siamese Fighting Fish," said Len, releas-ing my shoulder and approaching the tank. I followed him farther into the room because I did not know what else to do. "Fred is anti-social. He eats all other fish. He needs to be completely isolated. Swingin' single," said Len, kneeling beside the tank. "No Ginger Rogers for this guy." He grinned.

I touched my finger to the clear glass of the tank and pretended to study Fred carefully. I could see Len out of the corner of my eye, his face swimming in the shadows of a magnified aquatic plant. Fred's flippers hung limp in the water, swaying softly in an invisible current, like the billowy silk sleeve of Len's electric blue shirt. Len sprinkled some flakes into the tank. The fish drifted effortlessly upward, and lipped the surface of the water. Len brushed off his hands on his pants and stood up. "Well," he said, "Shall we start?"

I didn't say anything. I imagined Len whirling me over the rug in the dark living room as I stumbled on my own feet, falling into his chest with the weight of an anchor thudding to the bottom of the ocean floor.

"When is this over?" I asked.

"Relax, sweetie," said Len. "It hasn't even begun." He looked at me then in the dim light and flashed his teeth. It was something about his eyes. No one had ever noticed me like this before. "Don't worry," said Len. "You'll be just fine." I was reminded of a story about a little girl with white kid gloves who walked straight into the jaws of a tiger. My heart fluttered. I felt for the first time as if I were playing a role in something more dramatic than the Starkweather homicides. Little girl disappears in the Heartland. Last seen dancing her heart out.

I followed Len down the hall, as if I were being pulled by a string. I followed him out of the darkness, through the bright kitchen, and into the studio. In the sunlight I could see dark roots beneath Len's blond hair. His hair looked soft as the pink mat in my mother's bathroom I liked to lace my toes through. I couldn't tell how old he was.

Len put his hands on my shoulders. He held me away from him and drummed one shiny shoe to an imaginary beat. "Relax, Susan," he said. "You're all wound up. Have you ever had dancing lessons before?"

I shook my head. I felt clumsy and stupid. My hair hung stringy around my neck. I wanted his hands off me. At the same time, I wanted his hands on me so I could feel even worse. I wanted to give up. I wanted to disappear.

Len looked into my eyes. I turned my face down and stared at his pants. "It's so important to believe in yourself, Susan, not only in dancing, but in life," Len said. He took one hand off my shoulder and lifted my chin away from my chest. "Head up. That's the first step. You have grace inside of you. Believe in that. We all have a little piece of the Buddha in our step." Len stepped away from me and started toward the phonograph. Then he came back. "I needed one last look at you." He paused. "I'm used to teaching ladies with their best years behind them. Has anyone ever told you how lovely you are?"

Something about the way Len spoke these words led me to believe he might really think it. I didn't answer him. I had never thought of myself as lovely. I was pale and chubby with dishwater hair. I wasn't the sort of person anyone noticed.

Len placed the needle on the record. A breeze from the open picture window tickled my neck. *"You don't remember me, but I remember you,"* Little Anthony sang mournfully. *"T'was not so long ago, you broke my heart in two."* A chill rattled my spine. I folded my hands over my stomach. I could not figure out where else to put them. It didn't matter. Len had already forgotten me. He wiggled his shoulders and hugged his arms around himself as if his own body were a precious object. He lifted out his arms and swayed them like tentacles.

His feet kissed the floor like falling leaves. His black shoes twirled. I pictured Len at the Lincoln Country Club waltzing around the ballroom, pursing his lips like a fish at all the ladies. I started to laugh. I couldn't help it. Hysterical giggles bubbled up from my chest, and burst in my mouth. I tried to swallow, but my body shook with laughter. I clutched my stomach. I bent over, afraid I'd wet myself laughing so hard.

Len swayed over to the record player and turned down the music. "Why are you laughing, you silly?"

"You look like your fish!" I covered my mouth. I could not believe I had said this.

"Oh, you are funny." Len shook his head. "I know your game," he said, wagging his finger and swaying his hips. He swooped toward me and tried to grab my hand. I pulled it away. I could not imagine myself dancing or clowning around that way ever, yet I had witnessed how the world hummed around unexpected events. Starkweather was proof of this. My own mother was proof, so I knew I'd have to dance with Len. I clenched my jaw. I lifted my head.

"You're just too beautiful," Len sighed.

I wrinkled my nose at him. I asked, "Where's the bathroom?"

I stood in Len's green flowery bathroom and stared at myself in the full-length mirror. I studied my face for a sign of my mother, but I could not find her in me anywhere. When I turned sideways my nose looked almost cute, but it would never be graceful. I narrowed my eyes. I sucked in my cheeks. I held my blond hair up in a pile on top of my head. I looked older, more sophisticated that way. For an instant I could see why Len wanted to dance with me. I had promise. I rubbed a flake of mud off my saddle shoes and brushed it under Len's bath mat. I waved my arms like tentacles around my body. I winked at myself in the mirror.

On my way back to the studio I stopped at the icebox. Rows and rows of all different types of soda pop winked at me in the electric light. Half-finished bottles of wine lined the side shelves. It seemed Len didn't eat properly. Maybe he drank too much. I felt lucky. I had Lucille to make me desserts. I thought of the pocket money she had given me, and how my mother had taken it away because she didn't understand what good things I did to make it all run smoothly. It didn't make a bit of difference how hard I tried. It only made a difference when I didn't try at all. I thought of my mother floating through rooms like she didn't care about anything or anyone inside. I thought how strange it was that people loved her because she seemed not to need them. Perhaps it was that easy to be loved. Perhaps not caring was her secret. I gingerly lifted a bottle of wine from the side shelf and pulled out the cork. I winced at the popping sound. I listened. Little Anthony's voice drifted softly from the studio. I lifted the bottle to my lips and sipped cautiously. I had never tasted wine before. It was acidic, mysterious, sweet. I took a longer gulp and then another. My body felt warm and loose, my face was hot. I placed the uncorked bottle back in the icebox and tentatively wiggled my shoulders. I breathed deeply. I lifted out the bottle one more time and took one last drink, just to make sure.

Len was sifting through his record collection. I came up behind him. "Did you find everything okay, Susan?" he asked.

"I did," I said, giving him a secret look. I batted my eyelashes. "Did you know my parents call me Puggy because of my nose?" I wanted him to tell me something nice about my nose. No one ever had.

"Well, you're not so shy after all," said Len. "Want to learn the rumba?"

"How about the cha-cha?" I held my hands behind my back and looked at the floor. I felt dangerous, like a torpedo careening through the dark deep ocean, my body its own secret weapon.

Len put on some Latin music and moved his hips. He sidled toward me, and put his hands on my shoulders. "Fantastic nose," Len whispered. "So expressive. Nicknames are a sign of love, you know." He pressed my nose playfully with the tip of his finger. This made me giggle.

"The cha-cha has a two step and a wiggle, like this." Len stomped his feet to the beat and gyrated his hips. "It's a sultry Latino number. Popular with the ladies of Miami."

I followed Len's lead, at first stiffly. I stomped my feet. I watched the floor. I stepped on his toes, but he seemed not to notice. But then I let myself go. I lifted my chin. It wasn't so hard to do whatever he did. Before I knew it, the beat was in my blood. It made sense. Cha-cha-cha. It was easy. I felt wonderful. Cha-cha-cha. I wished I was wearing a red dress. I wanted a flower to hold in my teeth. I wanted to spin across our living room carpet while my parents watched, shocked into silence by my sudden transformation.

"You're a natural," Len cried. "One, two, cha-cha-cha." Len's feet guided me like strings. We cha-cha'd from one end of the studio to the other. The wine gurgled in my throat. One step blended into another until I was moving my feet to my own separate beat. I wiggled my hips and wagged my head. I thought my mother might be wrong about the Jewish thing. Maybe I was Mexican, a love child from Domingo, the man who clipped our hedges and taught my mother Spanish back in Chicago. We danced until the music stopped.

"You are what I call a natural, Susan," Len said.

"Well, I'm part South American," I giggled. "That's why."

Len raised one eyebrow.

"Or Jew," I said, "Like you."

"Oh, honey, I don't think so," Len laughed.

"Oh, yes, I am," I said. "Teach me the tango."

Len put on another record. "One day I'm going to be watching you on *American Bandstand*," he said. "Justine Corelli's history. You'll be dancing with Bob Clayton. I'm sure of it. I can't wait to tell your mother."

"Don't tell her," I whispered. "Don't tell my mother anything."

The needle fumbled over the vinyl. The music started. It was as if I already knew the steps. I pressed my cheek to Len's chest. I held my arm out straight. We strutted across the floor.

"Do I smell chardonnay?" Len sniffed the air. "Or is that pinot grigio?" He circled his nose over my head.

"You're silly," I taunted. I pressed myself closer and clamped my eyes shut. His silk shirt slipped against my face.

"Oh, honey, really," Len sighed. He pulled out a handkerchief with his free hand and pretended to mop his brow. "Not so close. You're going to make me do something I don't want to." He threw the handkerchief over his shoulder, and let it flutter to the floor.

I wanted to know what Len didn't want to do. I felt irresistible. I imagined him kidnapping me because he couldn't bear to let me leave. I imagined him holing me up in some abandoned house on the prairie, holding a gun to my head, and begging me to dance.

The music rumbled through my ears. I let go. I stood on my tip-toes. I threw my arms around Len's shoulders. I pressed my lips to his neck.

Len snatched himself away as if I had burned him. He held me at arm's length. He shook his head and looked into my eyes. "Baby, baby," he said. "Where are you headed with your childhood?"

My stomach lurched. The wine stung my throat. I wanted to run. I hid myself behind my hands. The tears streamed down my cheeks and I couldn't stop them. "When is my mother coming?" I cried.

"Oh, sweetie," Len said sadly. "Your mother doesn't have time to pick you up today. *I'm* driving you home."

In the car, Len patted my knee. He said, "Darling, don't be angry.

It's all my fault. I'm not used to working with children." But I didn't feel like a child any more. I huddled against the door, not saying a word. I tried to make myself small, but I couldn't. I wanted to erase what I'd done, but I couldn't. I stared out the windshield through my tears, tracing the painted line on the blinding asphalt until we reached the cool manicured lawns on the south side of town.

When my father came home from work, he found me hiding under the rhododendrons. I'd masked myself behind the dark green leaves for over an hour, feeling sick, wanting to die. My father dragged me out by my wrist. My cheeks were stained with tears. My skirt was matted with dirt. "What's going on, Susan?" He shook my shoulders.

"Len left me in the driveway," I said.

"Who's Len?"

I didn't answer.

"Where's Mother?"

I pointed toward the house.

"Does Mother know you're out here? Did something happen to you?" My father said.

I didn't answer. I wiped my nose on my sleeve. If I had still been little, my father would have picked me up and carried me inside to keep me from dragging my feet. But I was too big for that now. He marched me through the garage and into the kitchen.

"Look what I found," he said, as my mother came through the door from the hallway, holding a glass of iced tea in her hand.

I wished she would drop her glass. I wanted her to burst into tears or throw her arms around me. My mother didn't do any of these things. She just stood there with her nice new haircut curling around her ears. She took a sip of iced tea, then set her glass down carefully. "Where have you been, Puggy?" She placed her palms behind her and clutched the edge of the counter. She shifted her feet in her clean white pumps. "I was worried," she said. "You were supposed to be back already. Weren't you?" My mother looked at her watch.

"Back from where, Ann? And who's Len!" my father demanded.

"Oh, relax. He had an ad in the paper," said my mother rolling her eyes, "for dancing lessons."

"I demand to know where. At his house?" My father crossed his arms.

"Don't ever demand things of me, Thatcher," my mother snapped. "It's not civil." She turned to me. "Why are you crying, baby?"

"I don't feel well," I said.

"Are you sick?"

"I swear to god." My father shook his head. "If you left her with some stranger, Ann, with everything that's happened, I don't know what I'll do."

"Stop preaching!" My mother stomped her foot in her high-heeled shoe.

My father cleared his throat. "Well, I simply want to know what's gotten into you."

"Oh, Thatcher, listen to yourself," my mother scoffed. "We all want to know things. I can't listen to you anymore. I want so many goddamn things you've never given me!" Her voice was shaking. "I want to move away from this flat, flat place. I want something to happen. I want my own life." My mother started to cry.

My father turned me around and looked me in the face. "Did this Len touch you, Susan? Did he hug you too tight?"

I wiped my tears away with my sleeve. "No, Daddy," I said. "Why would anyone want to do that?"

My father didn't answer. He just stood there. My mother was sobbing into her glass of iced tea. She balled her fists. She kicked off her shoes. She picked one up, and threw it at my father. The shoe hit the table leg. "You're so ineffectual!" my mother screamed.

My father bent down and picked up the shoe. He held it out to my mother, but she wouldn't take it. She just stared at him.

I opened the cookie jar and took a cookie to see if anyone would notice, but my father just stood there frozen with the white pump in his outstretched hand. No one said a word. I slipped out of the room, and went upstairs chewing my first bite of cookie. I could hear my mother sobbing. I shed my dirty clothes in a pile. I threw myself down on the bed. I heard a door slam and a car start. I shut my eyes. I finished the cookie slowly, hoping to find some part of Lucille buried in the thick sweet batter. I tried to imagine myself a different person, with a different heart, and a different body entirely.

I woke up with a start, and the windows were dark and I was hungry. I lay there shivering, my throat dry. The sound of music drifted softly under my door. I had no idea what time it was, but it must have been late. Everything else was silent. For a moment, I wasn't sure if I'd been dreaming. I sat up and looked down at my hands. They were bloated like starfish, and stiff, not part of someone alive. I imagined my grandfather sitting in the beige love seat downstairs, listening to records. The smoke from his cigarette drifted up into halos around his large gray head, melting into ghostly fingers by the street lights on Van Dorn Street. A firefly flashed against the screen.

I got up. I put on my bathrobe and opened the door. The hallway was dark. The music swelled up the staircase, engulfing me in some private mystery. It was bold, a full orchestra, yet somehow the house felt asleep. Stepping tentatively over the threshold, I tried to breath as quietly as I could, and started toward the bathroom to get a glass of water. My parents' bedroom door was open. Their room spilled out at the end of the hall, dark, empty, and ominous. I paused at the stairs. My fingers gripped the banister. The waltz fluttering up through the darkness sounded familiar. I thought I knew which record it was—

the one with women in hoopskirts dancing over the ivory album jacket. I started down the soft carpeted stairs, sliding my hand along the banister. Then I paused. It occurred to me my parents might have killed each other, because nobody had woken me up for dinner. My heart flipped over at the thought. Crazier things had happened. My grandfather had died in the living room of a heart attack one April evening as he sat quietly reading the paper. Charles Starkweather and his child girlfriend had knocked on the door of a house three blocks away at 8:30 in the morning and demanded pancakes while law enforcement was setting up roadblocks at the other end of the state. In Chicago, eighty-seven children were trapped and died on the top floor of Our Lady of the Angels School, while Engine eighty-five was mistakenly dispatched to Our Lady of the Angels Church.

I dug my toes into the carpet and continued down the stairs, pulled by the music, my breath caught, my chest fluttering. Light from the living room spilled out over the oriental rug in the foyer. I stood on the edge of it for a moment, wondering what mystery I would find in its glow, what ghosts would be whispering, what secrets they could tell. Everything in the world seemed to have stopped breathing. I was alone, the only one still dreaming.

I quickly sucked in my breath, and peered around the living room doorway. My mother was wearing her white nightgown and my father was in his pajamas. Their hands were clasped, their bodies intertwined. The music came from the old phonograph. The record spun beneath the needle. My father was turning my mother around slowly. They passed lightly through the shadows in corners. They gracefully circled my grandfather's heavy furniture. They balanced on the balls of their feet as the music swelled around them. My father was looking down at my mother as if he had never seen anything so beautiful. Her cheek was pressed to his shoulder, her eyes closed as if lost in a dream.

I wondered what had awakened my parents, or if they had even gone to sleep. Had they sat up in bed in the middle of the night stricken with love or rocked by the violent urge to forgive? I couldn't imagine what had happened to make them feel this way. I stood in my bathrobe, watching from the darkness with my hand on the edge of the foyer wall. Bitter tears stung my eyes because I didn't understand. They had each other, and nothing had ever looked so sweet.

CONTRIBUTORS

MISHA ANGRIST received an MFA from the Bennington Writing Seminars and an Individual Artist Fellowship from the Ohio Arts Council. In 2002 he was a Tennessee Williams Scholar at the Sewanee Writers' Conference. His fiction and nonfiction have appeared in *Michigan Quarterly Review, Pif,* and *Tin House,* among other places. He lives in Cleveland Heights, Ohio.

MARY STEWART ATWELL grew up in the Blue Ridge Mountains of southwestern Virginia. She received her BA from Hollins University and her MFA from Washington University in St. Louis. Her short fiction has appeared in *Apostrophe.* She has finished her first novel and is at work on a second.

KIMBERLY ELKINS's work has appeared in *The Atlantic Monthly, The Village Voice,* and *Mudfish,* and she has had three plays produced in New York, one of which was a finalist for the ABC Playwright Award. She holds an MA from Florida State University—where she won the Outstanding Creative Writing Award—and a BA from Duke University. A Virginia native, she currently lives in New York City and is working on a collection of short stories.

MICHELLE HOOVER was born and raised in Ames, Iowa, and has published short fiction in *CutBank, The Cream City Review, The Massachusetts Review,* and *Prairie Schooner.* "The Quickening" is an excerpt from "The Swallow and the Nightingale," one of two novels-in-progress. She lives with her husband in Williamsburg, Massachusetts.

BRADY JOHNSON was born and raised in Wisconsin and is a graduate of the University of Minnesota's MFA program and the University of Wisconsin. "Michiganders, 1979," an excerpt from a novel of the same name, won an AWP Intro Journals award and has been published, in slightly different form, in *Quarterly West.* He has also published fiction in the online journal www.dislocate.org.

COURTNEY JONES grew up in Mocksville, North Carolina, and graduated from the University of North Carolina at Chapel Hill, where she was a Truman Capote

Fellow. She received her master's degree and the Melanie Rice Hook Award in Creative Writing from Hollins University and continues to live and write in the South.

MATTHEW LOVE is an attending physician at Jacobi Hospital in the Bronx. Currently he is at work on a novel ("The Artificial Heart," set in the near future during the second Cheney administration) and a collection of short stories about doctors, patients, and illness.

PEYTON MARSHALL, a recent graduate of the Iowa Writer's Workshop, is a recipient of a Maytag fellowship and the Richard Yates award for short fiction. She lives in Iowa City and is currently working on a novel in which no animals are harmed.

DEVIKA MEHRA was born and raised in New Delhi, India. After graduating from Vassar College, she was the recipient of the Morgan and Lou Claire Rose Fellowship at Southwest Texas State University's MFA program. "The Garden" is excerpted from the novel she is currently working on. Her fiction has also appeared in *Ploughshares*.

ALIX OHLIN teaches creative writing at Portsmouth Abbey School in Rhode Island. Her first novel is forthcoming from Knopf.

MARY OTIS has had stories published in *Tin House, Santa Monica Review*, and the *Berkeley Literary Journal*. She recently finished a collection of short stories and is at work on her first novel. Originally from the Boston area, she now lives in Los Angeles.

NATHAN ROBERTS holds degrees from the University of California, Berkeley, Reed College, and the University of Virginia, where he was a Henry Hoyns Fellow in fiction and served as editor of the literary journal *Meridian*. He has written a novel titled "Peculiar," as well as a collection, of which "This Is Not Skin" is the title story. He currently lives in Philadelphia.

SALVATORE SCIBONA, a graduate of the Iowa Writers' Workshop and a former Fulbright Scholar, was twice a Fellow at the Fine Arts Work Center in Provincetown. He has received the James Michener/Copernicus Society of America Fellowship and a Pushcart Prize. His work appeared most recently in the *The Pushcart Book of Short Stories*. "The Platform" first appeared in *The Threepenny Review*.

SHANTHI SEKARAN was born and raised in Sacramento, California. She received her BA and MA from the University of California, Berkeley. She then studied fiction at Johns Hopkins University, under the generous guidance of the Writing Seminars faculty. Currently she is completing a novel that follows the lives of the characters from "Stalin."

RENÉ L. TODD received her MFA in 2002 from the University of Virginia, where she was a Henry Hoyns Fellow. She is a graduate of the University of Michigan Law School and practiced law in Washington, DC, and San Francisco before turning to fiction writing. She lives in Bethesda, Maryland, where she is at work on a novel.

LIZA WARD is a graduate of the University of Montana MFA program in fiction. Her short stories have appeared in *The Atlantic Monthly* and *The Antioch Review.* She is currently at work on a novel.

MICHELLE WILDGEN is an assistant editor with *Tin House* magazine. Her work has appeared in *TriQuarterly, Prairie Schooner, Tin House, Rosebud, The Madison Review,* and other publications. She received her MFA from Sarah Lawrence College and is now at work on a novel.

PARTICIPANTS

United States

American University
MFA Program in Creative Writing—
Department of Literature
4400 Massachusetts Ave., NW
Washington, DC 20016
202/885-2973

Bennington College
Program in Writing and Literature
Bennington, VT 05201-9993
802/442-5401, Ext. 4452

Binghamton University
Creative Writing Program
Department of English, General
Literature, and Rhetoric
P.O. Box 6000
Binghamton, NY 13902-6000
607/777-2168

Boston University
Creative Writing Program
236 Bay State Road
Boston, MA 02215
617/353-2510

Bowling Green State University
Department of English
Creative Writing Program
Bowling Green, OH 43403-0215
419/372-8370

The Bread Loaf Writers' Conference
Middlebury College
Middlebury, VT 05753
802/443-5286

California State University, Fresno
Department of English
5245 N. Backer Avenue
M/S 98
Fresno, CA 93740-8001
559/278-2553

California State University,
Long Beach
Department of English
1250 Bellflower Boulevard
Long Beach, CA 90840
562/985-4225

The City College of New York
Graduate Program in English
New York, NY 10031
212/650-6694

Colorado State University
MFA Creative Writing Program
English Department, 359 Eddy Hall
Fort Collins, CO 80523-1773
970/491-6428

Columbia University
Division of Writing,
School of the Arts
2960 Broadway, Rm. 15 Dodge
New York, NY 10027
212/854-4392

Cornell University
English Department
Ithaca, NY 14853
607/255-6800

DePaul University
English Department—
Creative Writing
802 W. Belden Avenue
Chicago, IL 60614
773/325-7485

Emerson College
Writing, Literature, and Publishing
120 Boylston Street
Boston, MA 02116
617/824-8500

Fine Arts Work Center
in Provincetown
24 Pearl Street
Provincetown, MA 02657
508/487-9960

Florida International University
Department of English
Biscayne Bay Campus—
3000 NE 151st Street
North Miami, FL 33181
305/919-5857

Florida State University
Creative Writing Program
Department of English
Tallahassee, FL 32306-1580
850/644-4230

George Mason University
Creative Writing Program
MS 3E4—English Department
Fairfax, VA 22030
703/993-1185

Georgia State University
Department of English
University Plaza
Atlanta, GA 30303-3083
404/651-2900

Hollins University
Department of English
P.O. Box 9677
Roanoke, VA 24020
540/362-6317

Indiana University
Department of English
Ballantine Hall 442
1020 E. Kirkwood Avenue
Bloomington, IN 47405-7103
812/855-8224

Johns Hopkins University
The Writing Seminars
3400 N. Charles Street
Baltimore, MD 21218
410/516-6286

Johns Hopkins Writing Program—
Washington
1717 Massachusetts Avenue, NW
Suite 104
Washington, DC 20036
202/452-1123

Kansas State University
Department of English
106 Denison Hall
Manhattan, KS 66506-0701
785/532-6716

The Loft Literary Center
Mentor Series Program
Suite 200, Open Book
1011 Washington Avenue South
Minneapolis, MN 55415
612/215-2575

Louisiana State University
MFA Program
Department of English
Allen Hall
Baton Rouge, LA 70803-5001
225/578-2236

McNeese State University
Department of Languages
P.O. Box 92655
Lake Charles, LA 70609-2655
337/475-5000

Miami University
Creative Writing Program
Bachelor Hall
Oxford, OH 45056-3414
513/529-5221

Michener Center for Writers
University of Texas
J. Frank Dobie House
702 E. Dean Keeton Street
Austin, TX 78705
512/471-1601

Mills College
Creative Writing Program
Mills Hall 311
5000 MacArthur Boulevard
Oakland, CA 94613
510/430-3309

Minnesota State University, Mankato
English Department
AH230
Mankato, MN 56001
507/389-2117

Mississippi State University
Department of English
Drawer E
Mississippi State, MS 39762
662/325-3644

The Napa Valley Writers' Conference
Napa Valley College
1088 College Avenue
St. Helena, CA 94574
707/967-2900

Naropa University
Program in Writing and Poetics
2130 Arapahoe Avenue
Boulder, CO 80302
303/546-3540

New York University
Graduate Program in Creative
Writing
19 University Place, Rm. 219
New York, NY 10003
212/998-8816

Northeastern University
Department of English
406 Homes Hall
Boston, MA 02115-5000
617/373-2512

Ohio State University
English Department
421 Denney Hall
164 W. 17th Avenue
Columbus, OH 43210-1370
614/292-2242

PEN Prison Writing Committee
PEN American Center
568 Broadway
New York, NY 10012
212/334-1660

Pennsylvania State University
Department of English
117 Burrowes Building
University Park, PA 16802-6200
814/863-3069

Rutgers University
Department of English
360 Dr. Martin Luther King
Boulevard
Newark, NJ 07102-1801
973/353-5279

Saint Mary's College of California
MFA Program in Creative Writing
P.O. Box 4686
Moraga, CA 94575-4686
925/631-4762

San Francisco State University
Creative Writing Department,
College of Humanities
1600 Holloway Avenue
San Francisco, CA 94132-4162
415/338-1891

Sarah Lawrence College
Graduate Writing Program
1 Meade Way
Slonim House
Bronxville, NY 10708-5999
914/395-2371

Sewanee Writers' Conference
310R St. Luke's Hall
735 University Avenue
Sewanee, TN 37383-1000
931/598-1141

Sonoma State University
Department of English
1801 E. Cotati Avenue
Rohnert Park, CA 94928-3609
707/664-2140

Southwest Texas State University
MFA Program in Creative Writing
Department of English
601 University Drive
San Marcos, TX 78666
512/245-2163

Stanford University
Creative Writing Program
Department of English
Stanford, CA 94305-2087
650/725-2087

Syracuse University
Program in Creative Writing
Department of English
College of Arts & Sciences
Syracuse, NY 13244-1170
315/443-2174

Temple University
Creative Writing Program
Anderson Hall, 10th Floor
Philadelphia, PA 19122
215/204-1796

Texas A&M University
Creative Writing Program
English Department
College Station, TX 77843-4227
409/845-9936

University of Alabama
Program in Creative Writing
Department of English
P.O. Box 870244
Tuscaloosa, AL 35487-0244
205/348-0766

University of Alaska, Anchorage
Department of Creative Writing &
Literary Arts
3211 Providence Drive
Anchorage, AK 99508-8348
907/786-4330

University at Albany, SUNY
Graduate Program in English Studies
Department of English
Humanities Building
Albany, NY 12222
518/442-4055

University of Arizona
Creative Writing Program
Department of English
Modern Languages Bldg. #67
Tucson, AZ 85721-0067
520/621-3880

University of Arkansas
Program in Creative Writing
Department of English
333 Kimpel Hall
Fayetteville, AR 72701
501/575-7355

University of California, Davis
Graduate Creative Writing Program
Department of English
Davis, CA 95616
530/752-1658

University of California, Irvine
MFA Program in Writing
Department of English &
Comparative Literature
435 Humanities Instructional Bldg.
Irvine, CA 92697-2650
714/824-6718

University of Central Florida
Graduate Program in Creative
Writing
Department of English
P.O. Box 161346
Orlando, FL 32816-1346
407/823-2212

University of Central Oklahoma
Department of Creative Studies
College of Liberal Arts
Edmond, OK 73034-0184
405/974-5668

University of Cincinnati
Creative Writing Program
Department of English &
Comparative Literature
ML 69
Cincinnati, OH 45221-0069
513/556-3946

University of Denver
Creative Writing Program
Department of English
2140 S. Race Street
Denver, CO 80210
303/871-2266

University of Florida
Creative Writing Program
Department of English
P.O. Box 11730
Gainesville, FL 32611-7310
352/392-6650

University of Houston
Creative Writing Program
Department of English
Houston, TX 77204-3012
713/743-3015

University of Idaho
MFA Program in Creative Writing
Department of English
Box 1102
Moscow, ID 83844-1102
208/885-6823

University of Illinois at Chicago
Program for Writers
Department of English MC/162
601 S. Morgan Street
Chicago, IL 60607-7120
312/413-2229

University of Iowa
Program in Creative Writing
102 Dey House
507 N. Clinton Street
Iowa City, IA 52242
319/335-0416

University of Louisiana at Lafayette
Creative Writing Concentration
Department of English
P.O. Box 44691
Lafayette, LA 70504-4691
337/482-5478

University of Maine
Master's in English Program
5752 Neville Hall
Orono, ME 04469-5752
207/581-3822

University of Maryland
Creative Writing Program
Department of English
3119F Susquehanna Hall
College Park, MD 20742
301/405-3820

University of Massachusetts, Amherst
MFA Program in English
Bartlett Hall
Box 30515
Amherst, MA 01003-0515
413/545-0643

University of Memphis
MFA Creative Writing Program
Department of English
College of Arts & Sciences
Memphis, TN 38152
901/678-2651

University of Michigan
MFA Program in Creative Writing
Department of English
3187 Angell Hall
Ann Arbor, MI 48109-1003
734/763-4139

University of Minnesota
MFA Program in Creative Writing
Department of English
207 Church Street, SE
Minneapolis, MN 55455
612/625-6366

University of Missouri—Columbia
Creative Writing Program
Department of English
107 Tate Hall
Columbia, MO 65211
573/884-7773

University of Missouri—St. Louis
MFA in Creative Writing Program
Department of English
8001 Natural Bridge Road
St. Louis, MO 63121
314/516-5517

University of Montana
Creative Writing Program
Department of English
Missoula, MT 59812-1013
406/243-5231

University of Nebraska, Lincoln
Creative Writing Program
Department of English
343 Andrews Hall
Lincoln, NE 68588-0333
402/472-3191

University of Nevada, Las Vegas
MFA in Creative Writing
Department of English
4505 Maryland Parkway
Las Vegas, NV 89154-5011
702/895-3533

University of New Hampshire
Creative Writing Program
Department of English
Hamilton Smith Hall
Durham, NH 03824-3574
603/862-3963

University of New Mexico
Graduate Program in
Creative Writing
Department of English Language
and Literature
Humanities Bldg. 217
Albuquerque, NM 87131
505/277-6347

University of New Orleans
Creative Writing Workshop
College of Liberal Arts
Lakefront
New Orleans, LA 70148
504/280-7454

University of North Carolina,
Greensboro
MFA Writing Program
P.O. Box 26170
Greensboro, NC 27402-6170
336/334-5459

University of North Carolina,
Wilmington
MFA in Writing Program
Department of Creative Writing
601 S. College Avenue
Wilmington, NC 28403
910/962-7063

University of North Texas
Creative Writing Division
Department of English
P.O. Box 133307
Denton, TX 76203-1307
940/565-2050

University of Notre Dame
Creative Writing Program
355 O'Shaughnessy Hall
Notre Dame, IN 46556-0368
219/631-5639

University of San Francisco
MFA in Writing Program
Program Office, Lone Mountain 340
2130 Fulton Street
San Francisco, CA 94117-1080
415/422-2382

University of South Carolina
MFA Program
Department of English
Columbia, SC 29208
803/777-4204

University of Southern Mississippi
Center for Writers
Box 5144 USM
Hattiesburg, MS 39406-5144
601/266-4321

University of Texas at Austin
Creative Writing Program in English
Calhoun Hall 210
Austin, TX 78712-1164
512/475-6356

University of Texas at El Paso
MFA Program with a
Bilingual Option
English Department
Hudspeth Hall, Rm. 113
El Paso, TX 79968-0526
915/747-5731

University of Utah
Creative Writing Program
255 S. Central Campus Drive,
Rm. 3500
Salt Lake City, UT 84112
801/581-7131

University of Virginia
Creative Writing Program
Department of English
P.O. Box 400121
Charlottesville, VA 22904-4121
804/924-6675

University of Washington
Creative Writing Program
Box 354330
Seattle, WA 98195
206/543-9865

University of Wisconsin—Milwaukee
Creative Writing Program
Department of English
Box 413
Milwaukee, WI 53201
414/229-4243

University of Wyoming
Writing Program
Department of English
P.O. Box 3353
Laramie, WY 82071
307/766-6452

Unterberg Poetry Center
Writing Program
92nd Street Y
1395 Lexington Avenue
New York, NY 10128
212/415-5754

Vermont College of Union
Institute & University
Program in Writing
Montpelier, VT 05602
802/828-8840

Virginia Commonwealth University
MFA in Creative Writing Program
Department of English
P.O. Box 842005
Richmond, VA 23284-2005
804/828-1329

Warren Wilson College
MFA Program for Writers
P.O. Box 9000
Asheville, NC 28815-9000
828/298-3325

Washington University
The Writing Program
Campus Box 1122
St. Louis, MO 63130-4899
314/935-5190

Wayne State University
Creative Writing Program
English Department
Detroit, MI 48202
313/577-2450

The Wesleyan Writers Conference
Wesleyan University
Middletown, CT 06459
860/685-3604

West Virginia University
Creative Writing Program
Department of English
P.O. Box 6269
Morgantown, WV 26506-6269
304/293-3107

Western Illinois University
Department of English
and Journalism
Macomb, IL 61455-1390
309/298-1103

Western Michigan University
Graduate Program
in Creative Writing
Department of English
Kalamazoo, MI 49008-5092
269/387-2562

Wisconsin Institute
for Creative Writing
Department of English
Helen C. White Hall
University of Wisconsin—Madison
Madison, WI 53706
608/263-3800

The Writer's Voice
of the West Side YMCA
5 W. 63rd Street
New York, NY 10023
212/875-4124

Canada

The Banff Centre for the Arts
Writing & Publishing
Box 1020—34
107 Tunnel Mountain Drive
Banff, AB T0L 0C0
403/762-6278

Concordia University
1455 de Maisonneuve Boulevard West
Department of English
Montreal, PQ H3G 1M8
514/848-2340

Sage Hill Writing Experience
Box 1731
Saskatoon, SK S7K 3S1
306/652-7395

University of British Columbia
Creative Writing Program
Buchanan E462—1866 Main Mall
Vancouver, BC V6T 1Z1
604/822-0699

University of Victoria
Department of Writing
P.O. Box 1700, STN CSC
Victoria, BC V8W 2Y2
250/721-7306